anachronauts

the first age

by stefan gagne

copyright 2010

special thanks to
my online readers,
supporting web fiction.
you made this possible.

for more stories, visit
http://pixelscapes.com/anachronauts

anachronism - [uh-nak-ruh-niz-uhm]
-noun
1. something or someone that is not in its correct
historical or chronological context.

The steady clip-clop of hooves echoed along the roadway. They'd been outfitted with uniquely designed shoes, alloys tuned to minimize the impact from trotting along the hardened black surface rather than a more natural dirt path -- and the steady puttering of an iron box underneath the cargo hauling carriage was reassurance that their heavy load wouldn't be too burdensome on the upward climbs, either. A standard arrangement, all told, for industrial hauling in this day and age.

The non-standard part would be the driver. She wore a simple brown cloak, suitable for weathering the elements, but even under its concealing cloth it was clear this wasn't the heavyset, well armed sort of burlyman hauler that usually rolled along this route. A head and a half too short and a hundred pounds and change too light, to say the least.

Not that this deterred the bandits any. In fact, it encouraged them -- their leader stepping right out of the tree line, waving for his comrades to join him. Why bother ambushing? A simple human roadblock would be enough for a mere slip of a girl.

(It wasn't the biggest blunder that these generic thugs could've made, but it certainly was one of the classics. Right up there with "He's just one man! We can take him easily!" and "Surrender? To the likes of you?!".)

"Hold where you are!" the bandit leader demanded, raising his nocked arrow, pulling back the bowstring. "'twould be unfortunate if I had to end the life of one so young, would it not?"

On cue, the carriage rolled to a halt, the driver tugging back on the horse reins. The clip-clop clipped slightly, clopped once, then stopped.

"You would be the Crimson Arrow Gang, then?" the girl asked -- face partially obscured by the hood, but not her moving mouth, tinged with an unusually blue shade of lipstick.

"You've heard of us, then? Of our total control over these wildlands, of how nobody gets through here without paying a toll? Excellent! That will make the task simpler. It seems our reputation has indeed grown," he asserted, swelling with pride. "Now, then! There'll be no woodcutting today, missy. We'll also take any valuables you have, and your horses. As I am a gentleman, we'll leave one for you to ride off on -- don't worry your pretty little head about that. Although... if I may suggest, you might enjoy riding with us onward towards adventure and riches! Far more enjoyable than returning to that pathetic little village..."

The girl tugged back her hood, to get a better look at them; revealing an unusually silvery-white hairdo, short and well kept. She studied the man, head to toe, evaluating him before making her query.

"Please correct me if I'm wrong, sir, but isn't a bow and arrow a bit of a primitive weapon for your people?" she asked. "I'm not certain why I should feel it's a threat. Certainly the projectile would be quick, but with some skill, avoidable--"

The other, less pompous bandits promptly raised semiautomatic assault rifles, backing up their leader's preferred huntsman's bow. Clicks and clacks of weapons being primed to fire and safeties released punctuated their reply.

"I see. That's more in keeping, then," she said. "Still, I'm afraid I'm not very concerned about simple kinetic metal pellets. I'd like to point this out because there's still time for you to lay down your weapons and surrender before you have to discover why I'm unconcerned."

"Surrender?" the leader asked, trying to hold back the laughter. "To the likes of you?!"

And THEN the silvery energy blaster was produced.

Ah, she thought. *That's indeed more threatening.* Before further unpleasantries could be conveyed, she threw off the cloak, and became a brief silvery blur, landing neatly in front of the horses... and crossing her shiny metal forearm bracers in front of herself.

When the weapons opened fire (a surprise reaction to her sudden movement, she hoped, rather than some true desire to maliciously do her harm) one arrow, sixteen rounds of armor piercing lead, and a beam of pure white light as wide as a man's fist were directed her way. And all of them deflected easily by the pair of domed force fields thrown up by her crossed forearms.

"What are you doing, Una?! Shoot these idiots!" another girl's voice called out from within the cargo hauler's covered passenger cabin. The irritated voice had to shout to be heard over the weapons fire.

"Emily, if I drop my shields, they could harm the horses!" the white-haired girl, hereby named Una, replied. She was holding her ground, despite the numerous impacts against her defensive shields, but unable to act beyond that.

"Oh, of all the... fine! Plan B! əɹɐɯ!uɐ, əɹɐɯ!uɐ, əɹɐɯ!uɐ...!"

The strange word, twisted back onto itself into a language that was no language at all, echoed with a more resounding force and volume than should have been possible within the cabin enclosure. But that sound was then droned out quickly by the snarling, growling noise of strange creatures waking from slumber, with deadly intent on their non-minds...

Specifically, a swarm of chainsaws now levitating out of the cabin windows, given magical life, which poured forth from both sides of the carriage and honed in on the bandits.

The "Crimson Arrow Gang" had faced down farmers, armed mercenaries hired by farmers, and even some of the more deadly varieties of enchanted beast the wildlands could have thrown at them. But when a fleet of airborne saws capable of easily slicing through the age-old wood of trees start menacingly floating your way in full defiance of the laws of physics, it's usually time to use the pants lavatory.

The panic fire redirected immediately, as the pack of animate lumberjacking tools surrounded them -- this time aimed at the metal implements of destruction.

Not that this had any noticeable effect on reducing the overall lethality of their situation. Bullet impacts simply caused the saws to spin in air a little before resuming their menacing. A reflective metal surface parried the energy weapon's blast, before whirling in a sharp arc to cleave the metal raygun in twain. A shower of sparks burst from the bandit's hands, the two halves of his stolen gun falling uselessly to the ground.

Oddly, the circle of woodsmanly doom had left a gap -- one that led down the road, away from the carriage. Seeing an opportunity, the bandits took the better part of valor and ran for their lives, slipping through that crack in the defenses and fleeing.

All save the leader, who tried to make a run for it, and faced the saws again for his effort. They'd *let* the others run. The bowman wasn't going to be so lucky.

"I know it doesn't look this way," Una tried to reason, while lowering her shields. "But honestly, we mean you no harm. All we want is information. I would like to reiterate my suggestion that you surrender; it would make this much easier for everybody involved--"

"I surrender! Oh god, I surrender!!" the bandit king screamed, falling to his knees and covering his head with his arms, defensively.

Airborne saws wobbled a bit, before collapsing to the ground, enchantment fading... but when the leader opened his eyes and peeked out from under one arm, he now found himself staring at the business end of a surprisingly similar energy weapon to the one his cronies had found... although this one was in the hands of the girl in the metallic dress-like garment.

"Who put you to this task, sir?" Una asked, her voice not the slightest bit fierce, despite this technically being an armed interrogation. "We looked into the history of your 'Crimson Arrow Gang'. You're petty criminals, survival oriented, simply stealing to keep your people fed and moderately wealthy. You have no reason to hassle the lumberjacks on their way into the deep forests, there's not nearly enough profit in it. Therefore, our guess is that you were hired. Are we correct?"

"You are correct."

That reply hadn't come from the bandit, however.

Further down the road, where it was narrowest between the two sides of the forest... the trees themselves creaked and groaned, leaning inward. Their branches crossed, forming a natural seat. Perched there upon the branches was a figure, wreathed in summer and autumn, colors of green and auburn. Her leafy feet did not touch the cracked asphalt road; she simply dangled there, idly swinging one leg, her glowing eyes bearing down on the girl.

Barken lips parted. "You are a long way from home, little animal," she spoke. "You have no true stake here. You were no doubt hired to stop my animals, just as I hired mine to stop the ones who harm these forests. Money... such a silly human thing..."

"Ah.... I'm.. not familiar with your species, miss--"

"Dryad."

"Miss Dryad," Una said, assuming it was a formal name. "But if I am interpreting correctly, then... yes. We were hired to clear the route so the lumberjacks could resume. The wood is needed to build communities down the road. Shelters, homes for those suffering in the elements."

"It's not my fault the animals are ill equipped to the rigors of the seasons," the Dryad said, with a shrug. "That doesn't give them justification to murder the trees. It does, however, give me justification to murder the animals. I have declined to, so far, simply turning them away... but now I see you wielding those murdering tools against my pack. I see the time for mercy is at an end. The weeds must be pruned."

She held two fingers to her lips, and whistled in the way wind slips between the branches on a breezy day. The trees began to move, parting the way... for figures like her, thin and mobile and leafy. Dozens of them. Already surrounding the carriage.

The girl took a step back, for the first time that day. "W-wait, wait, please, Miss Dryad..! We can come to a compromise--"

"No. No, we cannot. Slaughter the animals, children."

Moving quickly, Una grasped the dial on the back of her blaster. One twist to the right, and it could have the lethal force needed to... what? Burn down a few of them? Not enough. Her shields were directional, they couldn't stop an surrounding ambush like this. And her friend Emily in the carriage, even with her strange powers, would likely not be enough either--

A walking tree took one step onto the road. And then was swiftly jerked back into the depths of the forest, as if a snare had pulled it backwards with incredible force. Because that's precisely what happened.

Metallic twangs sang through the air, more snares firing, logs swinging, trees groaning under weight and howling in rage as the entire forest was rearranging itself. A figure blurred between the shadows between the trees, pulling a wire here, setting off a trap there, making a quick improvised loop over a branch there. An ambush to ambush the ambush was firing off, and being adjusted on the fly to compensate for the heavier, non-human foes that had wandered into it.

When the majority of the mobile forest army was pulled to the ground or up into the branches, the figure finally emerged from the shadows of the Dryad's tree arch, appearing behind her, a metal pistol held to her head.

"Incendiary ammo," the boy spoke, his voice calm, emotionless. "If you don't know what that means, it means fire. Human shape means a brain here I can burn. If not, it'll at least hurt. Friends'll be out of the snares soon, I think. Doesn't matter. Call them off or burn."

The Dryad's hiss was like crackling leaves, crunching underfoot. "This is merely an inconvenience, animal. You cannot kill me any more than you can kill the forest--"

The boy's other arm curled around her neck, hand raised to reveal a red pushbutton detonator in one hand, thumb on the trigger.

"I push this, I kill the forest," he said, again with no more feeling one way or another. No rage. Simply a series of facts, being presented in logical order. "Everything burns. This entire place, everything. Doesn't matter. None of it. Decide now."

"This is-- this-- agh! Wait, everybody, stop, WAIT!!"

THAT voice was loaded with considerably more emotion. Emily the Witch, a young woman no older than her companions, awkwardly stepped from her hiding place within the hauler's passenger cabin. She waved her arms wildly, trying to get attention -- almost knocking the pointy black hat from her head on the low cabin doorframe as she scrambled to get out.

"This is so... so stupid!" she declared. "Everybody, listen to me! Scout -- hands off the trigger! Nobody needs to get shot or blown up today. Now. ...as... a wanderer, one familiar with accorded bonds of wild forests, one respectful of nature's innate power and with respect due in turn, I hereby request peaceful parlay until the sun falls behind the branches! --dammit, I DEMAND peaceful parlay!"

And in that moment... the ambushes, the bandit (currently on his knees in a growing yellow puddle), the bombs, the blasters... none of it mattered to the Dryad. She focused her attention on the one in the familiarly shaped hat instead.

"I know the smell of you," the lady of trees said, a note of curious surprise in her words. "A sapling of Lilith... and yet I don't sense her influence about you. You are indeed a strange one. However, you know of the accorded bonds, it seems, and are due respect in turn for your station. Very well. What do you offer?"

Exhaling in relief, the witch pushed some of her irritability aside, trying to keep calm. "Look, not ALL of these trees are yours, okay? I know how Dryads work. You have a protectorate forest. You can't possibly claim to be defending the entire wildland in this area."

"...I suppose not, no," the Dryad admitted.

"So you've got no right to stop the.. animals from logging outside your haven. As much as I know you probably hate it, you're overstepping your jurisdiction and this crap has got to end! ...uh... I mean.. respectfully, ma'am."

"A defiant sprout, within this one," the Dryad said, smirking, if it was possible to do so with lips made of leaves. "Very well. Keep the animals out of my protectorate. They will never be considered for respect as your kind are, witchling, but I will leave them be. You have my word. ...I trust you will make your friend disarm those animal fire-devices?"

"Yes. Yes, of course. Fine. ...let her go, Scout."

The boy hesitated. No trembling. Just considered the situation for a few more moments, rather than blindly obeying... and slipped down out of the trees, landing easily on his feet. The gun and the detonator were held aloft, in a peaceful gesture, then set down.

The Dryad remained in the branches, watching the trio curiously. "You keep strange company, sapling. An outsider, with outsider spark... and this one. I would watch this one, if I were you. His shadow may hunt for you now, but the wild hunt in him is not something you can leash. ...keep the animals out of my forest and you'll never see me again. Farewell."

With business here finished, the forest guardian merged into the wood of the trees themselves, her arch splitting, trees seeming to visibly shrink back into the tree line. In moments, there was nothing unusual about the forest, leaving behind only tall oaks and empty snares.

Scout gathered up his weapons, before returning to his companions. And ignoring the suspicious glare he was getting from the girl in the pointy hat.

"You never said you were going to plant firebombs in the forest," Emily said. "Just the snares, for Plan C, in case the bandits fled back into the trees."

"Plan D," the boy said, with a shrug. "Made sense to me."

"I really, really, really, REALLY don't like it when people get all secretive and make these kinds of plans behind my back. I thought we were in this together," she said, crossing her arms and tapping her foot, obvious body language that the boy paid absolutely no attention to. "And what'd she mean, about 'the wild hunt' in you?"

"What did she mean, about being a sapling of Lilith?" Scout countered.

"...anyway," Emily said, changing the subject in the clunkiest manner possible, "We'll just redirect the loggers away from the Dryad's realm. Now that I know there's one out here, I can find a ritual spell in my book that'll clearly mark the borders. Guess we're done here, and about freaking time. That paycheck had better be waiting for us when we get back to the village, or we're not eating tonight. Let's get outta here."

"Not yet."

The hunter and the witch turned to the silver girl. Who still had her energy blaster aimed at the bandit leader, whose mouth remained agape in shock.

"Sir, now that you have surrendered, I have a question which is outside the scope of this particular task but of much personal importance to me," Una spoke, trying to sound as reassuring as someone with a gun to your head can be. "I would greatly appreciate your cooperation in this inquiry, and promise it will not detain you for--"

"What? Huh? What?" the bandit babbled, having trouble with the big words.

The boy spoke up for her. He knew what she was going to ask. It was the question that would be dragging them all over the wilds, after all. He knelt down, and looked into the bandit's eyes... his own empty, passionless, but somehow conveying vast importance. And vast dangers beyond the scope of a simple forest road altercation.

"Where," he asked, "Did you find an Orbital's energy blaster?"

a01 anachronisms

One week previous, there was no unlikely trinity of powers, no journey to undertake, no story worth telling. Not yet, at least.

Stories had a habit of happening around Edgar Wellbrooks, proprietor of the Olney Inn. Stories didn't happen TO Edgar, understand, simply... around. It was a common side effect of living on the Fringe, the contested area between two world powers, where all manner of odd characters wandered in and out. If the story didn't happen in his immediate vicinity, he'd at least hear about it, and pass it along. Stories of the mysterious wildlands of deep forest and weird creatures to the west, stories of the tall and powerful cities of metal to the east. Tales enough to keep folks buying beer, which kept him paid, kept him fed, and this the circle of life complete. In as much as it kept him alive.

The Olney Inn (located conveniently in the heart of the Olney Settlement, "The Breadbasket of the Tri-State Area") served well as a rest stop between worlds. It was on the road to the Washington Memorial, for instance. Not that the D.C. path got many tourists anymore, but the ones who were willing to brave the trip and see what was left of that great city usually were adventuresome sorts, willing to tell and/or make up stories for the local barkeep. To the west were the wildlands, where hunters and salvage teams would delve into Deep Virginia. Some of them even got as far as West Virginia, which was quite a feat. Those ones would always come back with something interesting, either salvage from a dead city, a mysterious Fae artifact, or at least a tale of barely getting out alive.

So, when a group of travelers of Mysterious Origin showed up at the Olney Tavern, wearing Mysterious Cloaks, hunkered down and trying not to look important (serving only to give them a Mysterious Aura), Edgar knew he had his work cut out for him and the rewards will be great indeed. If he could tease a story out of them, he could talk of the Mysterious Travelers to others and boost his business's reputation as a place where interesting things happened.

He waved away the busty barmaid (hired specifically for her bustiness, as she tended to drop drinks as often as she served them). Edgar would handle this crowd himself. He pulled a fresh order pad, tossed a towel over a shoulder, tried to look every inch the barkeep he could, then approached.

"Welcome to Olney," he said, while setting out a bowl of pretzels. "You folks just passing through, or are you here to see the sights?"

The tallest of the three figures, an old man with one of those droopy white moustaches you normally only see on wizened old kung fu masters in ancient movies, looked up from fiddling with a silvery salt shaker.

"Ahh... we are here to purchase items," he said. "That is all. There is nothing the least bit interesting or unusual about us. --what sort of metal is this? It's quite fascinating! Very light, yet well sculpted and aesthetically pleasing!"

"It's.. uh. It's just chrome. You spray the stuff on, and it gets shiny. I think. ...do you guys want to order anything?" Edgar asked, trying to steer the conversation back to normality. "I have some.. very uninteresting drinks, if you prefer..."

"Excellent! We will have your three least interesting drinks."

"Right. Two on tap brews. And what'll the kid have?"

The smallest of the figures looked up, regarding the barkeeper in confusion. (Edgar latched onto the unusual color of her hair, a silvery white, cut loose and short and straight.) "Kid? I am nineteen years old," she said. "Generally, that age range is identified as 'young woman'. --ah, wait, I understand! Is that number of years insufficient for this 'on-tap-brews' you refer to?"

"Uh... we generally go by Eastusa law, and no, they say you gotta be twenty one," the bartender noted. "Where are you folks from, anyway...? Some independent settlement?"

"That is where we are from exactly, thank you," the third figure, wider and distinctly more grumpy than the others, stated in angry tones. "Please obtain these on-tap-brews and one of whatever you feel is appropriate for the kid and that is all that needs to transpire. You may go now."

Shaking his head, Edgar returned to the counter to fetch two beers and a soda pop from the fountain. These folks would be a tough nut to crack, but nothing he couldn't handle.

The tavern doors swung open, tiny brass bell above them jingling away, like the laughter of the men who entered. Now, this crowd Edgar knew well... the Olney Frontliners.

Things had improved considerably around Olney since Eastusa's bureaucrats finally accepted their application for sponsorship. That meant Frontliner security, and that meant people would be more likely to hang around rather than do their business and scramble, for fear that the place would collapse under an attack from the woods. The Frontliners weren't just there to whack the big bad wolf, either, they represented a bond between this little farming community and one of the world powers. They had a big brother, and big brother had a bigger father looming out east. With them on your side, folks knew you were the real thing.

These specific Frontliners themselves, though, that lot Edgar could do without. Brash and arrogant young men, giant-killers who had no giants to kill, since Olney hadn't seen a raid in months. Their Officer could only keep these soldiers training and drilling and staying focused for so long, before they started simply blustering about town, occupying space and attention in an effort to waste away the hours.

They'd show up midday, as they had now, and drink all the way to closing. They'd laugh, and tell stories of various sexual conquests both real and fictional -- stories of little use to Edgar. He'd already heard all their tales of action against the Faerie Court, so there was no more coin to mine there. They were loud, annoying, and ran up tabs like no one else could. And if they spooked off his far more interesting patrons, he'd have words with their Officer, no doubt about that.

"...I'm not kidding, man, SWORDS," one of them, who Edgar recognized as a bulky guy with nine fingers named Demolitionist Gunther, was telling. He knew this story already, of course. "That's all they had. Pointy ears and swords, and they come charging at us! All war whoops and Fae blather. I mean, they HAD to know they had no chance, right? Nobody even got a shot off. Claymores took the whole group out."

"And that's my point, that they charged and died," Rifleman Johnson said, all grins. "Bam bam bam, kaboom, gone. They could've run for the hills instead of facing us and getting fragged. I don't get that, why do they even bother? Just get out of the way, or roll over and die, already. Nobody screws with America when America wants your turf."

"Hey, be fair, they could have screwed plenty if they had a caster. I've seen Fae mages and the like. Nasty bastards. You gotta put 'em down fast and hard before they can get a word in edgewise."

"Okay, a caster could've caused SOME trouble. But even the casters go down when you put a dozen Frontliner units on their asses. Command even tried to be civil, to send a Scout ahead with a truce offer, bail and forfeit your land and we won't kill you all. They stayed and fought, even knowing they didn't have a caster, didn't have anything that could stop us. That's just stupid. Just like the Grimms, buncha kiddie tale rejects--"

"They were defending what was theirs," a voice from the corner shadows of the tavern quietly replied.

This got everyone's attention. Except for the Mysterious Travelers, who were doing their best to look uninteresting. (The self declared young woman got a nudge by the heavyset traveler when she tried to take an interest.)

Edgar hadn't spotted the customer before. If he had, he would've served a drink. And would've raised an eyebrow, possibly even two, because the figure in question wore a Frontliner's uniform unlike any he'd seen before.

The boy couldn't have been a hair over twenty. He slumped in the corner booth, idly nudging around a pretzel from one of the many free bowls lying around the tavern. His uniform was disheveled, seams starting to fray in a several places. It had stains from mud and blood and more, halfheartedly cleaned out but still leaving telltale darkened patches here and there. The same careless attitude applied to his personal appearance; stringy black hair, generally uncombed, falling down to the nape of his neck wherever it wasn't sticking up.

"Who the hell are you?" Demolitionist Gunther asked, because he was the sort of person to ask that sort of question. His eyes flicked over the stylized icon of a crosshairs on the boy's shoulder. "New recruit? Officer didn't say nothin' about some rookie joining us, much less a Scout. We already got a Scout."

"They were defending what was theirs," the boy repeated from before, ignoring the questions. "That's what you were wondering. Why they'd fight to the death, knowing they were fighting to the death. Just defending. That's all."

The other Frontliners got up, chairs scraping in unison as they slowly moved to surround the boy's booth. Edgar swore under his breath; this could only go one direction, the one that led to losing a few tables and chairs in a wild brawl. Hopefully the Officer would offer to pay repairs again...

"Boy, I was askin' you a question," Gunther said. "What's your name? Looks like your patch got ripped up. What unit are you with?"

"Odds are, they had nowhere else to go," the boy continued, still ignoring him. "The wilds are sometimes just as dangerous to them. You fight with your back to a wall, you fight, period. Fight until you die. Can't show weakness. Can't be easy prey. They decided to go down standing up."

"Ohhh, I'm gettin' it now," Gunther said, a wide smile spreading over his lips. "Boys, we got us here an AWOL hippie sissy treehugging Section 8 punk fairy-boy grass smoking Grimm wannabe. ...I leave anything out?"

"Figure you got in every insult you could there, man," Rifleman Johnson confirmed. "I guess we could call him gay, too, but I think fairy-boy covers it. We can cut right to the part where we kick his ass now, right?"

(Motion peeked in from the corner of Edgar's eye, as the young woman stood up -- and then was forcibly sat back down by her companions. *Don't get involved,* the barkeep figured they were whispering to her. *Not our problem.* A common reaction when things went south in Olney.)

A light crunch sounded, as the boy chewed on a pretzel. "I just want something to eat. That's all," he said. "I'll leave now. Can leave through you, if that's really what you want. I don't care. It doesn't matter. None of it."

"Alright, enough of this talkity talk. Whaddya say, Frontliners? He's just one man! We can take him easi--"

A more exact evaluation of the potential difficulty of battle was not forthcoming from Gunther, as the boy moved with frightening speed, shifting from sitting in recline to pouncing the man in less than a second.

Panic took hold at first -- the boy landed several sharp, edge of the hand blows to the man's throat. A man without Gunther's bulk would probably have died right there and then; as is, he was only horribly incapacitated.

Then the real fight began. The Frontliners weren't slouches; they were trained for close quarters combat, for unarmed fighting, as some of the Fae were remarkably bullet resistant and keen to engage you up close and personal. The unspoken members of the unit, five strong in all, all went after the rogue Scout at the same time. There'd be no one-at-a-time attacks, black ninja style; it was a dogpile.

Edgar wasn't much of a martial artist. He liked movies about them, the few he'd been able to see; he had media recordings, expensive ones that had to be bought from traveling salvage merchants. But in the end, it was always just a blur of fists, feet, parries, blocks, throws, dodges. He couldn't recognize any of the moves, just the ballet of them.

This wasn't ballet. This was brutality. The young man moved from Frontliner to Frontliner, punching them, kicking at them, in some cases BITING them if need be to put each one down. When they grabbed him, he'd hurl his entire body weight around to throw the weight, or would ram one into the other by unbalancing them. Blood was flying within moments, bruises forming, even a few teeth soaring through the air.

The last one standing, Johnson, looked like he was ready to throw in the towel. He took several shaky steps backwards, hands up defensively... and the boy didn't seem to care, advancing on him, like some sort of horrible hunting dog. He was actually GROWLING... and in one final, sick lunge--

He rebounded off thin air. The young woman had interspersed herself in between the two men, throwing up one hand, with a flash of silvery metal like the top of a salt shaker -- and the boy simply bounced off nothing that was actually there. The distraction was enough to confuse him, to snap him out of whatever trance had him-- and the resounding impact of metal on wood was enough to bring him completely back to his senses.

That would be Officer Griffin's iron war mace, pounding against the doorframe. Once, twice, splintering wood.

"That's ENOUGH," he declared, in a voice would not be denied. "Enough. Stand, soldier."

The boy stood upright sharply... before slouching again, in the same apathetic, half-eyed stare he had before everything went to hell. He looked around the young woman, who was already slinking back to her table, doing her best not to be noticed -- and succeeding, as those still standing had bigger concerns at the moment.

"Name and unit, son," Officer Griffin said, his voice still firm... but non-threatening.

"...I'm a Scout," the unnamed Scout declared. "Frontliners unit Bravo Six, Austin. Sir."

"Austin? Austin, Texas?"

"Yes, sir."

"Son, nothing got out of Austin alive."

"Correct, sir. Nothing alive."

The Officer holstered his rune-scribed war mace, and scratched his chin. He idly cast his gaze to his soldiers, who were groaning and peeling themselves off the floor, then back to the Scout.

"I won't call you dishonest, son, but consider my position," he suggested. "It's highly improbable you're from one of the worst brush fire conflicts with the Fae in modern history. If you're lying, you're a disturbed young man indeed. If you're telling the truth, I'm guessing you're still a disturbed young man, to have survived what command deemed a situation with no survivors. ...finally, you've cleaned the clocks of my entire unit. You're aware of the regulations against enlisted infighting, and the penalties?"

"Yes, sir."

"I'll have to take you into custody until a military hearing can be convened. Until we can figure out who and what you are, at least, and hopefully get you the help you need. Are you going to come quietly, son?"

Edgar found himself actually leaning over the bar, straining to listen in on the story developing around him, waiting for the climax to come...

--when another figure burst on the scene, pushing roughly past the Officer.

"This entire village is about to get pounded flat!!" she declared, waving her arms wildly. "Everybody out! Out, out! Run for the hills!"

Not even the strange young Scout knew what to make of this. Confused silence was the beverage on tap as the third young person to enter the tavern today continued her hysterics, trying to rouse as much attention as she could.

"What're you doing lying around?! You've got to evacuate these people!" she told the unconscious Demolitionist Gunther. "Up, up! C'mon! Get a move on! We've--"

"Miss."

She spun on one heel to face Officer Griffin, so fast her ragged old pointy hat nearly wobbled off her head. It was adjusted back in place, as she obeyed the same "atten-SHUN" aura the Scout had.

"Miss, would you kindly explain what you're talking about?" he asked. "Quickly, now."

"O-Ogres," she explained, quickly now. "A legion of them are headed this way! If you don't get these villagers out of here by nightfall, they'll--"

"Ma'am, we've dealt with ogres before," Griffin patiently explained. "Granted, my entire squad isn't usually groaning and bleeding on the floor before engaging with them, but the village defenses alone should be enough. They're an unorganized lot and scatter easily."

"Not these. You didn't SEE these, okay? I did. Not you, me," she explained. "I got a real good look at them from above. They were marching in a perfect grid formation! Ogres don't DO that!"

"And how'd you see them from above, then?"

"I was flying, okay?! Do I have to explain each and every..."

The mistake was realized one moment too late. She suddenly felt quite conscious of the weighty old enchanted broomstick slung across her back. And the battered but still very pointy hat on her head. And the rune-inscribed book of magic in a hip holster slung from her waist...

"Under the Eastern States of America's articles of allied village sponsorship, persons of magical professions are to be arrested and executed. Soldier?"

"W-wait, y--"

Surprise took her, in the form of the nameless Scout clamping one hand over her mouth, and using the other to bind an arm behind her back. No way to read a spell aloud, no way to access a book to read from. Despite being marginally feral, he had plenty of strength to restrain a witch of equal years to him.

For his part... Officer Griffin simply sighed, and rubbed at his temples. "This is going to be a long day. Johnson? Quit staring. Go and get Scout Rowans, and dispatch him to find the ogres. I want to know if they're actually somehow organizing against Olney or if this is a deceptive load of magical hooey. Scout... whoever you are. Will you surrender to custody for the time being, until I can at least sort out what to do with you?"

"Sir," the Scout agreed, able to keep his eyes on the commander while still restraining the struggling, muffled-but-cursing witch.

"Good. Bring her. Keep that anti-caster hold in place. I'll get you a cell in the bunker. We're going to sort this mess out, one way or another."

From the bar, Edgar let out a long exhale. He probably wouldn't get to see the end of the story. He'd have to make something up, for when he told it to the next passer-by.

Rough stone, hewn and piled and mortared together. Roughly cut iron bars on the windows. Torchlight as the only true source of illumination, while the setting sun went out over the trees. Olney's jailhouse as every inch the primitive, medieval torture dungeon, save for the lack of actual torture equipment -- it was one of the first things built, before proper Eastusa sponsorship, before proper building materials could be traded for. Normally it only held drunks sleeping it off, or the occasional con man who thought they could make a quick swindle on the village and hightail it to the north.

It did not normally hold malicious, corrupted spellcasting witches who employed Fae powers to dominate and destroy all man hath wrought. Technically speaking it wasn't holding one now, but the law was the law, and all casters (human or Fae) were forbidden from Eastusa territory. Frontliners were taking no chances, using standard handcuffs behind the back, and a cloth gag with wound ball to keep her from speaking a single arcane syllable.

The same restrictions were not used on her cellmate, despite the fact that he was the only one who had actually assaulted anyone tonight. For his part, he didn't seem to need them; he was content to sit on the bench across from her in the same cell, one leg propped against it, holding his knee and stretching the muscle a bit. If you looked in his eyes, you'd see boredom, apathy... and perhaps something pacing in tight little circles while it watched you. If you knew what to look for.

Rifleman Johnson didn't know what to look for. So, he concluded they were both completely insane. He thumbed through the witch's confiscated spellbook, from the other side of the bars. Despite the elegant leather covers, a modern stainless steel three ring binding kept the removable pages locked into the book.

"Funny word art things," he concluded, unable to make much sense of the scrambled letters and fonts, each tightly packed within a square border, one per physical page. "This some kind of Fae porno rag? Or an honest to goodness weapon of mass arcane destruction?"

"She can't reply," the caged Scout noted, stating fact.

"Allow me my little entertainments, nutjob," Johnson said, setting the book aside. He'd gotten some steel back in his spine after nearly begging to surrender, back during the bar fight. Or at least he thought he had his steel back. "You're both dogmeat, anyway. Nothing I say will matter. Eastusa's decided it wants no truck with Fae powers, 'specially not human traitors trained to use Fae powers... and the Frontliners don't take kindly to AWOL crazies."

The lone Scout decided to ignore the Rifleman after that, focusing his gaze on the young witch. Who tried to avoid that gaze. And avoid Johnson. This meant she was pretty much limited to staring at the floor... and waiting.

"Y'hear me in there, Fairy Godmother? Thou shalt not suffer a witch to live, you know," Johnson taunted. "I wonder how they're gonna do it? Transport you over to Baltimore, hold a trial, lethal injection? Or maybe just burn you at the stake in town square, like the good old days? Serves you right for turning your back on humanity, throwing in with the Faerie Court--"

"Johnson."

The Rifleman got his feet fast, the standard reaction to one of Officer Griffin's entrances.

Griffin appraised him, nodding once. He was fighting fit enough. "You've got more important things to do than prove your ignorance to the prisoners," he said. "I want you on the line with everybody else still standing. We may have ogres incoming."

"Sir, you don't believe this skank, do you? She's tricking us. There's either nothing coming, or she's just trying to spook--"

"Soldier, I don't recall asking for your tactical assessment of the situation," Griffin reminded him. "Given the only clever thing you've done today is back off from this boy before he could kill you, you're ahead of your peers, but not by THAT much. Now. We may or may not have incoming. Won't know until *our* Scout relays back with his recon. I intend not to be taken by surprise, if things are exactly as the girl predicted. And that means you and Betsy need to be sharp and present. Can you do that for me?"

The Rifleman's mouth split into a wicked grin. He picked up his heavy assault rifle, throwing a switch to load up an iron shot core, Anti-Fae flesh piercing. "Ready, sir. Always ready. You know that."

"Then let's get to the line, soldier."

"Right. ...uh. Sir? The prisoners?"

Griffin considered the quietly glowering girl, staring at him with frustrated malice. He considered the unreadable young man with the tattered uniform.

"I can't spare anyone to watch them, so one of them will have to watch the other," he decided. "Son, she's not to leave without my say so, spellcraft or not. Same goes for you. Understood?"

The rogue Scout gave a brief nod. It was enough. The Officer signaled a deploy, and marched his way out, a slightly hesitant Rifleman following behind.

And then there were two.

The witch weighed her options. Schemed, planned. She knew that the boy knew that she was scheming and planning... a simple enough Insight, not one that required much effort, but Insight nonetheless. Could she act quickly enough? Could she get out before he could stop her...?

There was always the possibility of waiting. An opening would make itself known, eventually. Maybe during prisoner relocation, maybe even during the execution itself. Maybe the Officer would simply let her go... he seemed to be brighter than the rest of these jarheads, even if he had to follow his own little book of rules. ...or maybe one of his minions would get a little itchy and put two in her head before she could be funneled through proper channels.

So. Escape. Because the alternative was just too risky. She took a deep breath... and triple-tapped her fingers against her palm sharply, a familiar pattern.

The ordinary beaded bracelet on her wrist shifted shape, responding to the signals sent up the nerves in her skin, and reformed into an enchanted lockpick. It sought the handcuffs on magical instinct, without needing any external spellwork. The lock popped in moments, the gag yanked down by her freed hands immediately after. She had her sleeve pulled away, revealing one remaining square-bound spell of letterwork in tattoo ink, next to two pink scars bearing identical designs...

...a spell that would take a second to read aloud. Possibly two. Plenty of time for a boy with the Scout's speed to stop her. And just by hesitating long enough to consider that possibility it became an eventuality. He was watching her intently.

It was called a "mexican standoff," not that she really knew why. She'd never learned what mexican meant. Presumably it was an adjective meaning tense and prone to sudden, terrible violence when it all goes horribly wrong. Violence she'd very much want to avoid.

"If I read this spell, I'll be out of here," she explained. "Gone. It won't hurt you, and I won't hurt you. I swear. Just... let me go. Okay?"

The boy shook his head. Not very hard... just a tiny shuffle, left to right, eyes never leaving hers. "I'm under orders, ma'am."

"You don't work for him," the witch noted. "I can tell. I've got Insight, sometimes. I got it when I briefly saw the aftermath of that little tavern party. You're as much an outsider here as me, and you've offended them and their laws just as much as I have. I could get you out of here, too!"

"Orders."

"But you--"

"I take them from the uniform, not the man. It's... something I still do, despite," he said, without specifying what it was in fact despite of.

"They could kill you. I mean, they WANT to kill me, because... well, frankly, because they're ignorant back country bigots," she said, with a snort... letting her arms drop. No point casting her Escape now, anyway. "But after they're done with me, you're next. Armies never do things small. It's all bluster and shouting and murder."

"They could kill me," he agreed.

"Aaand... you're okay with that, then?"

His eyes finally drifted away from hers. Not far, just enough to gaze past her.

"It might be for the best," he decided. "For all of us."

This guy IS a nutjob, she thought bitterly. *Serves me right.*

"Serves me right," the young witch muttered, because she felt like chastising herself in a voice louder than a mental whisper.

He cocked his head, at that. "What serves you right?" the boy asked.

"Trying to do the right thing," she explained, slumping down on her prison bench, rubbing at her sore wrists. "It never ends well. I see trouble, I've got two options. I can poke my pointy little hat in the ring and try to help, and then everything goes sideways. Or I can keep my pointy little hat down, ignore it, and then everything goes sideways again."

No reply to that. So, eager to fill the space with her words of wisdom, as was her wont, she continued.

"I try to help a pixie glade from being bulldozed by a human settlement, and all that happens is the Animate bulldozers go out of control and level everything in sight. I try to whip up some potions to tidy up a contaminated well at an independent village, and it works great... until I accidentally unmask a conspiracy by a rival village to wipe those poor farmers out and take their land. Triggers a hot war out of a cold one, and I'm lucky to get out alive. And now, I spot something that should not be possible, an organized army of ogres bearing down on an Eastusa settlement... and in thanks for warning them of the dire peril, I'm going to be burned at the stake.

Hence. Trying to do the right thing never ends well."

That at least merited a shrug from her cellmate. A fountain of delightful conversation, this one. Time to take it to the offensive.

"That's me, Emily the Ever-Failing, Arguably Good Witch of the West. And what's your name? Or should I just call you 'Scout'?"

"I guess. Sure."

"...seriously? You just want me to call you by your, what is it, rank?"

"Role. Scout. Stealth, recon, sniper," he explained, reciting the book in his mind. "Observe and report. At times, surgical elimination of targets. Lethal, precision force. Key targets eliminated for maximum effect and minimum risk. Find an opening, take it. ...hunt. Hunt the prey and kill them. Always make the kill."

"Be all you can be, eh."

Another nod.

"And no name, then?" Emily asked. "Did your mommy and daddy just hate you that much? I could just call you 'Bob' but it doesn't fit. Or John, or Scott, or Tim, or Jack. Oooh, how about Ezekiel?"

"Scout. What I am is more important than who I am."

"And are you as insane as they think you are?"

He had to consider this one, before responding. "Don't think so," he decided. "Just incredibly dangerous to everything around me. What Court are you?"

That tossed her momentarily. "Err...?"

"The Faerie Court," he clarified. "The courts of Lady Summer and Lady Winter. Seelie, Unseelie. The Fair Wind and the Chill Gale. Queen-of-Life and Queen-of-Death. One of them had to train you in magic. Which one are you? What are you?"

Glaring, she gritted her teeth. "Neither, thank you very much, Mr. Scout. ...just because my original teacher was with the Summer Court doesn't mean I owe them anything. Nothing. I owe them NOTHING. I'm a witch, pure and simple. My magic is mine, now; I do what I want to do and I do it on my own terms."

"Like failing to save human settlements."

"...yes, things like that, thank you, good sir."

"All the other witches and warlocks I've met are predators. You're not one," he said, not bothering to phrase it as a question. It was just how it was. "All of them. Every one. You're different. And they're going to kill you anyway."

Before Emily could say something acidically witty or bitter or snotty or sarcastic, the heavy oaken door swung open.

In a flash, she had her mouth gag back in place, and her hands held behind her back. She couldn't redo the cuffs, but if she twisted her body to look at the doorway, they wouldn't know. It could be an opening. It could be what she needed...

The tall figure of Officer Griffin, his runic war mace ready to draw from its hip holster, stood there.

"We're leaving the village grounds," he declared. "Boy, caster hold on the witch. Odds are she's popped her cuffs by now."

And like that, he had her hands held there, another hand over the gagged mouth. Just in case. No feeling to it, no judgment, just following orders. No shot, no opening she could've exploited in time... no way to access the Escape spell tattooed to her arm. If this was truly the end of the road, then it was inescapable...

Griffin fetched the witch's broomstick, hat, and spellbook. He also fetched a burning torch from the wall.

"Are we bringing her away from the public grounds for the execution?" Scout asked, watching the Officer carefully as he made the inquiry.

"Are you going to follow your orders and bring her where I tell you to, son?"

"Yes, sir."

"Then we're leaving."

The trio departed the silent village without another word. Around them, war preparations were being made, tasks to attend to. Nobody spotted the death march, or simply didn't care enough to pay attention.

Although a window on the third floor of the Olney Inn opened with a tiny *creak*, and a white light flashed briefly, streaking into the sky to follow.

Emily wanted to scream, but the hand firmly held over her mouth prevented that from happening.

She wanted to scream at her captor -- to call the old man an idiot, a fool for ignoring her warnings. Scream at his masters -- for being blind to the reality of the world, for sticking to what they knew even if it got them killed. Scream at the world in general -- for allowing things like this to happen when they could have been avoided. And, honestly, to scream at herself -- for getting involved in the first place, or rather, for not allowing herself to not get involved. There was a distinction, there.

None of her screams would've been for mercy, or to plead for her life. That she was sure of. True, there was fear, the same fear she always had behind her eyes when she was stuck in situations like this, but she'd never let them see. Don't let them see weakness, don't let them smell blood, or they'll kick you and keep on kicking. She'd learned that one long ago.

They were a distance away from the village now, into the darkness around this tiny pinpoint of humanity... and she could feel the light rumble through the ground. The steady march of the ogres, coming from all sides, seemingly. A march in perfect sync, which should have been impossible...

Officer Griffin raised his hand, a signal to stop. The Scout paused in his hustling along of the struggling witch, as the commanding officer (or perhaps just the commanding uniform) unholstered his runic war mace.

"This was a gift," he spoke, answering an unheard question. "I'd heard not to accept gifts from them. Those gifts always came with a price. Still, it felt rude not to accept it. If I hadn't come along when I did, I don't like to think what those brigands would've done to her... low men, men of no character, who prey on the confusion along the Fringe. I only did what had to be done, what any honest man should have done. What I saw of her didn't make a difference to me, you understand."

"Sir?" Scout asked or prompted.

"The ears, see," he explained. "Pointy. Elven. She was a Fae, and I protected her from humans. Oh, I got a reprimand from command up in Philly for that one, but I accepted the reprimand without a word or thought. See, which one was my kin and which one wasn't, none of that made a difference. All I saw was a wrong that needed righting. She thanked me with a gift of this mace, and I understand a gift of iron from a Fae is a rare thing indeed. Said that so long as I never spilled innocent blood with it, as long as I used it to defend as I had done that day, that strength would never fade from these old bones no matter how weary and battle worn I grew. You can release the caster hold now."

Without hesitation, Scout's grip released, and Emily pulled herself free immediately. Her arm went to slide her sleeve up, to reveal her tattoos... but while he didn't pause to release her, she did pause before fleeing.

"You have my apologies," Officer Griffin said, setting down her broomstick, hat, and spellbook. He didn't look back at her, though... he was looking outward, towards the source of that pounding rumble, the approaching horde. "I don't write the laws, miss. But if I don't at least appear to uphold them, the town would lose hope. It's not a matter of losing face or losing respect -- it's a matter of hope. They need the rule of law to show that they can stand up to the darkness. Even when they don't fully understand that darkness. But I do, and I knew sure as sundown that you were right. My own Scout reported back minutes ago. The ogres are organized... and flanking around the settlement. There's not enough room to evacuate through. We can't defend all the borders at once for long, but we'll do what we can. You've got my thanks, ma'am. You can go on your way."

Yes, fine, whatever, an officer and a gentleman, so very doomed, time to leave, Emily's mind mumbled to herself. *You warned them, and that's all you have to do.*

She fetched her personal effects. Put on her beloved and tattered old hat, slid the spellbook into its holster with practiced ease. Propped the broomstick against one shoulder. Made no effort to mount it and fly away.

Flying away is not what an honest woman should do.

"If I came to help you, that means I came to help you," she explained. "Since telling you off wasn't enough, clearly I have to fight to keep you pistol packing city folk alive. It's your fault I have to get mixed up in this, you know. Jerk."

...and the old man chuckled. "Guess it is, at that. I won't say I wasn't hoping to hear it, though. I had a feeling. So. Tell me. How do we survive this?"

Right, then. To solve the problem, like a proper witch should do. Because nobody ELSE would have the brains to solve it without a witch around.

"There's no way an ogre has the brainpower to do this. They have a leader, someone organizing them," she reasoned. "You probably figured that out already. Ogre minds are weak, though, they can't simply be shouted at and expected to perform like trained soldiers. Flanking is not in their playbook and they couldn't read a playbook if you jammed it in front of their faces. That means you've got magic fuddling up their minds... or more like de-fuddling. I'm thinking it's a particularly warlike Faerie, maybe even a Winter Courter imported from the north, tasked to crushing humans on the edge of Fae territory. If the leader's dealt with, if the spell is broken, the ogres will snap out of it. They'll probably be so confused that your men can run them off easily, assuming they don't break and run on their own."

"So, a surgical strike, then."

"Yes sir, mister soldier man sir, ten hut," she agreed, with a mock salute.

"Good thing he's with you, then."

It was easy to forget the lone Scout's presence. Emily had to think for a moment before realizing what Officer Griffin meant... because behind her, the Scout was already loading a gun, and checking his equipment. ...where had he gotten equipment? Wasn't he in prison just minutes ago?

"I'm ready, sir," he said.

"Right, then. We'll hold the front line," Officer Griffin said, turning to leave. "We'll buy you as much time as we can to break their ranks from behind. Good hunting, soldier."

The veteran got a short distance away, before the boy made up his mind to speak up.

"...sir?"

"Hm? Yes, son?"

"If you'd ordered me to execute her, I would have killed you," he said, quietly. Almost too quietly to be heard.

Griffin considered this.

"Good thing for me I had more sense than that, then," he decided, and continued along on his way.

The pair crept through the edges of the forest, keeping the shadowy, rumbling figures of the ogres to their left. Never directly in front. Flanking a flanking force would have been difficult, if not for two factors.

One, stealth -- the boy's uncanny ability to avoid stepping on any stray twigs, to keep his feet moving despite uneven ground and fallen logs and low hanging branches. He slipped in and around and under and through any difficulties in his path. It was a bit unsettling to Emily, honestly; he was moving as if he knew the forest inside and out. Perhaps he did. Perhaps he didn't. If he didn't, and still was able to slip through the trees with this much ease, that said something she didn't want to consider.

Emily herself had given up walking. She couldn't keep up with his progress, not on foot, not in her traditional long-hanging gray skirts. Instead, she hovered a foot away from the ground on her broomstick, letting him find the best way through, weaving along behind him. There was nothing quite like impossible flight on a cleaning implement for soundless travel.

The other major factor working in their favor was the ogres themselves.

They were close enough to touch the beasts, fifteen foot tall walking piles of muscle and fat. They flattened trees as they marched, not even by swinging their massive clubs, simply by ... treading over them, snapping thick forest wood like dried out sticks. They marched in perfect formation, right leg left leg, timed and flawless, causing the earth to pulse. Meaty feet, pounding ground...

But the eyes. The glassy, half-sleepy stares. She was right about magical control, had to be; the silver circlets each one wore, hardly standard ogre war accoutrements, those were probably the link. If pried away from their heads, it'd break the spell... but breaking away only one or a few of them wouldn't stop the march, only confuse it a little. They had to find the one who wore the master circlet, the one headband to control them all. It was a guess, sure, but one she felt confident in.

She opened her mouth to explain this, wanting to relate this witchy knowledge to her silent partner -- and he pressed a finger to her lips quickly. *Shhhh.* At first she felt alarmed and annoyed by this intrusion in her personal space. (*Never lay your hands on a witch without permission, boy!* her mind screamed.) ...then she realized he had a damn good point, and killed any thought of speaking. It beat having thoughts killed by ogre clubs, after all.

Despite realizing the need for silence, she couldn't keep out a choked-back little cry of shock when they found the body.

They'd sent someone to confirm, someone to see if she was speaking the truth. He'd reported back what he saw on his radio. And then, the ogres had mutilated Scout Rowans.

He couldn't have been much older than the nameless Scout. They wore similar uniforms... they even looked sort of similar... except Rowans was in two pieces while her companion remained whole.

The ogres hard torn him in half. Torn in half, tossed the body parts aside, and continued the march. Uncaring. Killing and moving on.

We're going to die out here, her panic-thoughts whimpered. *I'm in over my head. I'm no combat mage. I have a spellbook, I know some tricks, but it's all utility magic. I never wanted to learn how to kill. A full blooded Fae spellcaster could easily burn me to a crisp, pull my limbs apart, torture me endlessly for weeks just because they could and I couldn't stop them. I shouldn't BE out here. I just wanted to warn them and then run for my life...*

"Won't let that happen to you."

Her thoughts broke off like one of the trees the Ogres were casually pushing aside, hearing that tiny edge of a whisper from the living Scout at her side.

He said no more, motioning for her to follow. *Leave that behind and come along,* he didn't say. *There's too much to do. Think about it later.*

Her broomstick drifted along behind in silence.

They found the target soon after.

She knew it on sight and wished she hadn't; the commander was riding in a pumpkin carriage, an enchanted gourd on wheels with no windows, only a single magically padlocked door. It moved under its own power, following behind the marching army, no doubt containing the spellcaster within. And, given pumpkins were only used by those of great power or nobility within the Faerie Court, whoever was in there probably could kill them both with a single word. Assuming it wasn't in fact Lady Winter or Lady Summer...

...wait, no. The pumpkins were from Summer's side of the court. Why would Summer be marching to battle? Sure, they had plenty of dust-ups with humans, but rarely on THIS scale. Not these days, at least, when the conflict was a cold war rather than a hot war. If it was a snow-sled following the ogres, that she could accept -- it'd be out of place this south of the Canadian border, but...

"...think we're out of their earshot," Scout said. "Whispering's okay. How do we get into the vehicle?"

"W-we don't," Emily admitted. "The lock... it's magical. I don't have any spells strong enough to work on that. I don't think ANY magic will, not even the pick I keep up my sleeve. Little short of an Archmagus would be strong enough..."

The Scout considered his options. He slipped a hand into a utility pocket at his belt, pulling out a small metal gadget of some sort. "They're looking forward, we're behind. They won't see this. Shield your eyes, it'll be bright when I start cutting..."

A tiny *fwmph* sounded, as the pocket torch fired up.

...a technological means of cutting? That could do it, Emily thought. The Fae were usually too focused on counterspells to consider what bullets and explosives and raw physics might do to their toys...

The Scout crept along the ground, sidling on up to the carriage. He crab-walked alongside it, and started to cut. It took a careful hand to apply the white-hot flame to a consistent spot on the lock. He could have hopped up on the footstep runners along the carriage, but the additional weight might have alerted the rider that something was wrong. Still... once that lock fell and the door opened, there'd be no going back. No time to hesitate.

Emily hopped off her small broom, holstering it to the loops she'd sewn onto her backpack just for that purpose, and crept up behind him, wishing she had his uncanny ability at moving over rough terrain. She nearly twisted an ankle on a loose rock, and the grass stains would be quite nasty to get out of her skirt later...

No time to complain, no time even to think. The lock sliced open quickly. Scout had a gun out already, a silencer screwed onto the barrel. He was in through the door, the oddly wobbling light from within swallowing him whole. Throwing caution to the wind, hoping for the best, and ultimately wishing she'd warned him that she was hardly a "You Shall Not Pass" sort of wizard, Emily jumped in after him.

The surprise of what she saw was nearly enough to freeze her in place.

The spell did the rest.

"ɘɿɘ५ʇdoʇs!" a voice shouted, sadly faster on the draw than the two young would-be heroes were. Not much faster, though -- Scout was already halfway across the room and taking aim with his pistol when the spell hit. It left him frozen in a mid-leaping dash, every muscle locked, gravity ignoring him for the duration. Emily was frozen too, but had barely gotten both feet into the room, much less being in any sort of combat stance. She cursed herself for not having a book drawn before entering. Hindsight can be a painful thing...

But hindsight was dashed completely by foresight, rather, the sight before her.

It was a FaePlace, a special room-within-a-room, far larger than the external pumpkin would allow for. A familiar spell, and one she'd used herself at times. Each one reflected the character of the caster... in this case, it was somewhere between an opulent throne room, and an armory. Glittering crossed spears and swords, jewels embedded in their hilts, each before a shield bearing insignias from the Summer Court. The owner loved weapons and loved opulence, and even if it was all useless Faerie dreamstuff that'd evaporate outside this Place, it mattered enough to serve as decoration.

The caster herself was not Fae, however. She stood by an ever bright candle of green flame, the main source of illumination in the room, casting dark shadows behind the frozen pair. But even in the strangely bright-yet-dim lighting, Emily recognized her.

"Hello again, runt," her former friend greeted her with. "This is a surprise. I was figuring the normals would have burned you at the stake by now."

"J-Jesse?!" Emily exclaimed, unable to believe her eyes -- and received a sharp slap across the face for her cordiality. It hurt even more when her body was locked in position by the spell.

"That's Lady Runeblade, thank you very much, weakling," the other witch hissed. She smoothed out her sparkly battle dress, all gleaming chainmail and lace and other bizarre fashionable elements, and stepped back, her candle-shadow casting over Emily. "I left Jesse behind. Lady Runeblade is far more fitting for one of my power. One who actually can cast spells without books, unlike the runt of the litter, the one we left behind along with my old name..."

"Wait, wait, look-- Je-- Lady Runeblade," Emily corrected. "Listen to me, alright? Please. I get this, okay? You're going to battle, prove your chops to the higher ups. But Olney's no threat to the Summer Court. I don't know who told you it was, but they're just... just a bunch of pissant little farmers! There's nothing there worth fighting over!"

The 'elder' witch, despite being no older than Emily, chuckled. "You're right," she spoke. "It's a worthless little town, and far enough from the Court to not matter one bit. Summer doesn't actively seek open war, it's not her way. But tell me, runt... what better place to test my new power than a meaningless village nobody will ever miss?"

Runeblade tapped the silver circlet on her head, matching the ones the ogres wore. The one headband to rule them all.

"Things are changing, Emily. We have power. New power -- new and strange, but power nonetheless," Runeblade explained, as she began to pace within her FaePlace, shadow shifting along as she went. "Those chosen by the Lady Summer, lifted up from humble human upbringing, will do well. Rising stars like me. But not you. You... once my slaves prove this power in battle, you I'll deliver to Lilith. She'll want--"

Her shadow passed over Scout.

It was easy to forget about him. He blended in, became a part of the surroundings, became a non-issue. He didn't speak up much. He didn't posture. He didn't act until he was ready to act. When two witches, one haughty and one terrified, were busy exchanging the expected words, he could become nearly invisible. But that didn't mean he wasn't there. He was simply lying in wait.

The shadow passed away as she continued to move, but Scout was no longer there.

She must have sensed a change in the surroundings, because she turned to look around -- and nearly got her head taken off by the pouncing warrior, who emerged from the other side of the room, wreathed in shadow until he passed through the light.

Her reflexes were sharp. Always the physically fit one, Emily bemoaned internally, as she rolled to the side and avoided the lunge. Her attacker landed in shadow again, and... somehow emerged from the other side of the room. Crisscrossing as he made his attacks, now armed with a combat knife rather than the pistol.

Slash marks appeared, many of them carving up pieces of her ridiculous battle dress, one appearing along an arm... and finally, one across her left check, as Scout landed in front of her, pausing to get ready for a final lunge.

If fire could have filled her eyes, if her voice could have shattered mountains, they would be dead where they stood and/or were frozen in place, in Emily's case. But her voice did resound with another deadly force, the power of the magic burned into her mind.

"uoꞁʇɔnɹʇsəᗡ!!!" she screamed, and the world went white.

On the plus side, Emily was no longer frozen by a spell.

Now she was frozen by fear. Probably not an improvement.

The pumpkin carriage was a smoking wreck, the FaePlace spell destroyed by the point-blank explosion of raw willpower. The three had emerged back in the real world, in the dark and ruined forest behind the ogre march, among the tree stumps and flattened grasses.

Scout had been knocked thirty feet away, and somehow landed on his feet in a perfect three point stance, knife behind him, ready to make another go of it. Emily simply landed on her rear. Painfully.

The one she knew before as Jesse was livid. Her battle dress was in tatters, smoke wisping from her hair -- but the circlet remained in place. Her look was one of absolute, rabid, quite murderous rage. No haughtiness, no superiority, just raw brutality. It was a look Emily remembered well, from their last encounter...

A jeweled saber was drawn from her back. This was personal, now. There'd be no spells, just blades. And it seemed Scout wouldn't have it any other way, either.

The Summer Court witch was not a mere back-row spellcaster, a human mortar cannon. She'd always been one for fitness and exercise... and for fencing. Always a keen interest in fencing. And when the two began to dance together, Scout's blade flashing against her blade, it was an equal battle of speed and strength and brutality.

That last part was the most frightening one. Emily hadn't seen Scout in actual combat, not yet... but she didn't like what she saw. The passive, expressionless boy, the quiet one, was meeting Jesse the Runeblade's rage and ferocity at every level. She didn't think the boy was *capable* of snarling, and yet there he was, like an uncaged animal finally given free reign to be what he was at the core...

Are you as insane as they think you are?

I don't think so. I'm just incredibly dangerous to everything around me.

It was the kind of animalistic frenzy a man could get lost within, maybe never to emerge again. The same very specific, very deadly madness that took all of Emily's friends, once upon a time, and turned them into things like Lady Runeblade. A long odds guess, conjecture, but Emily had firsthand experience on her side of what was likely to happen here. That's when she decided that something had to be done to stop the fight.

She drew her quick-access spellbook from the holster at her hip, flipping straight to the page she wanted. No searching, no checking a table of contents. She knew this book inside and out, having written it entirely by hand. She couldn't, she *wouldn't* cast spells from memory alone like Jesse had been doing for years -- but from paper, she couldn't be equaled.

Bending low, she scooped up a handful of loose rocks from the ruined forest floor, and scanned her eyes over the page, reassembling the right word, the right tones from the mapped out squared spell printed there. "Ϡɔoᴙs," she whispered, feeling the word become power become stored energy within the rocks, ignoring the wispy scent of ash from the printed page... and took very careful aim.

It's like a snowball fight. It's all timing, it's all aim. You wound up your arm and you hucked a load of balled up snow at your friend. In this case, replace friend with enemy and balled up snow with charged rocks, but otherwise the same concepts applied.

The window was small -- she had to hit Runeblade and not Scout, despite their frenzy of attack and counterattack, dancing around the forest floor. But she found her mark.

A bunch of pebbles should've simply bounced off that armored battle dress, harmlessly scattering. Instead, electrical current was discharged from the impact, funneling through the metal strips and buckles and right into her flesh.

One scream of painful surprise was enough of an opening for the fight to end.

Scout slipped around her, knife pressed to Jesse's throat, ready to swipe it side to side and lay open her arteries.

"NO!" Emily screamed, running forward, nearly tripping over the crushed branches. "Scout, no! You don't have to kill her! --SOLDIER! Caster hold now, that's an order!!"

It was like a transition from one segment of film to another after a jarring break. Where there was the face of the big bad wolf, there was the passive features of the silent Scout. Where a knife was at her throat, now a hand was clamped over her mouth, the other wrenching arms behind Jesse's back. The blade had been discarded, sticking out of the ground, handle up.

Without the ability to speak, she couldn't cast magic. Without being able to move her hands, she couldn't use any magical items, couldn't pull a spellbook (not that her kind bothered with them). Even as strong as she was, even as she struggled against the hold, this was a technique developed for years and drilled into every Frontliner fit enough to draw breath. All to keep her kind from being a problem. Jesse had been neutralized.

"No voice, no commands, no way to order your pet ogres around," Emily summarized, marching forward to be face to face with the enemy, staring down Jesse's hate-filled eyes. "Surrender. This stupid play-war of yours is done. We'll send you packing back to Summer and that'll be... that..."

Ogres shouldn't be *allowed* to move silently. It wasn't fair. Or maybe they'd just been so busy dealing with the crazed witch that they didn't notice her rallying the troops. But she didn't say a word! Spells needed a voice! How could she have...?

The enthralled beasts were surrounding them. They'd doubled back, flanked, circled, and were now ready to defend their mistress. Lady Jesse Runeblade looked... smug.

The club was already in motion. Precise, too. It'd smash into her side, fling her maybe a hundred feet away, kill her on impact without even grazing their commander. No time to dodge. No time to cast a spell. No time--

A silver blur snapped into focus in front of her, and her vision was blocked by a powerful blue light. A dome of energy had flared into being to her side -- and when the club smashed against it, the shield-bearer skidded sideways a few inches, but held fast.

White hair twirled as the newcomer looked over her shoulder. "Rub your thumb left to right along the Neural Band!" she shouted. "Then pull, hard!"

Emily had to fight down the urge to ask stupid, time-consuming questions like "Who the hell are you?" and "How did you block that club?". Fortunately Scout didn't even have the slightest inkling of a thought of a notion to ask any such questions. He simply released Jesse's mouth and swiped a finger along the band, before grasping, and pulling it back and over her head.

The witch's scream was ear piercing, as silvery wires slid out of her flesh, networked cables and links of metal tearing away from skin, pulling through her skull itself. The pain must have been blinding... but in the end, the silver band came off, trailing red-dipped leads and connectors with it.

If that scream was loud, the scream of the ogres was far louder. Their connection was gone, the organizing force that was making them move as one unit. A confused, terrified, and extremely violent ogre armed with a battle club could be a force of nature unto itself. Have a few dozen around you and it was murder on wheels.

They started hitting things. Hitting the trees, hitting each other, hitting themselves if they had to; they wanted to lash out and export the agony they felt deep within their brains on anything available. The silver girl had to parry several more club blows, weaving in and around the only humans standing to do it.

"We need to enact a rapid departure!" she declared. "I'll take the thief, you take the boy! GO!"

Oh, right, Emily thought. *I have a broomstick.*

And it looks like I'm going to live, too.

Eventually the ogres got tired of hitting things. Some collapsed on the spot. Others wandered away, bewildered. The army that never should have been simply wasn't any more, and nature sorted out the rest.

Of all the places Emily wanted to be right now, Olney was not at the top of the list.

It was quiet, at least... the battle had never reached the town. The Frontliners had set up extra defenses, Griffin had rallied the troops, but despite some odd noises in the distance, nothing had turned up to knock the town flat. Jokes were made, soldiers breaking the tension of the evening with horsing around, and life went on as usual without a care for the doom that nearly befell them.

...that would likely change when someone asked "Hey, where'd Scout Rowans go?" and they noticed the massive forest destruction and likely several ogre corpses lying around. But for today, life went on as usual.

Una (for that was her name, Una, she made a very polite and cheerful introduction of it despite hurtling through the air at high speed away from a war zone) had led them back to the upper floor of the Olney Inn, into the open window she had snuck out of originally. They could depart when night fell again, she reasoned, and depart by air. Nobody needed to know that Emily the Wicked Witch was back in town.

The other wicked witch was a different story.

She'd been laid out on the rough and uncomfortable inn bed. Sweats had broken out across her forehead, being tended to by Emily, trying to keep the bandages on Jesse's puncture wounds from being soaked through. The fallen witch was moving her mouth, as if to talk, but no sounds were coming out. The unfocused look in her eyes was worrying. Odds were, Una sadly noted, they may never focus again.

"Neural Bands weren't designed to be removed so suddenly, not while in operation... but... I couldn't think of what else to do," she said, while supplying Emily with fresh washcloths as need be, the three young conspirators gathered at their enemy's bedside. "I drained my shield's mass capacitor trying to keep the kinetic transfer of those impacts from sending me into orbit. We couldn't stay any longer..."

Emily set the cloth aside, and picked up her open spellbook again. "Ɛu!Puɘɯ," Emily she cast, the page vaporizing as she read the spell from it. An identical copy of the spell was on the next page, and the page after that. "Ɛu!Puɘɯ. Ɛu!Puɘɯ. ...I don't honestly know if this will work, it generally can't do much on serious wounds, but... it's better than nothing. Ɛu!Puɘɯ."

Scout leaned against the wall, by the headboard of the cheap bed. "This is dangerous," he noted. "She tried to kill us. Tried to destroy the village. She'll try again if she wakes."

"Yes, well, not all problems can be solved by killing people," Emily spoke, dismissing the boy with a sharp tone. "If she comes about maybe she'll have a chance to figure that one out. ...but you are right that we should be careful. We'll stabilize her and then bring her to the wildlands. I know a friendly colony of pixies, Summer Court, who will take her in. Then she's their problem. After that, I'm done with this mess, and all the better for it--"

The door slammed open. Scout looked ready to spring into action again-- but stopped, as the cloaked figures stood in the doorway, agape in horror and surprise.

"...what.. what madness is this!?" the wider of the two figures exclaimed. "Una! Explain yourself! You're out of your cloak and... and you brought these sub-Orbital surface dwellers in our rented domicile?!

Una quickly got to her feet, smoothing out her silvery one-piece dress, bowing sharply. "Tertiary Pragmatist Councilmember Lar, I welcome your return and--"

"Out with it, girl!"

"I had no choice," she said quickly. "If I didn't interfere, they would have died."

"Insufficient reasoning!"

"But--"

"Lar, please."

The other figure, more elderly with a well managed white beard, stepped around her companion and into the room. After a brief moment, considering the scene... he leaned down, and gave Una a warm hug.

"Daughter, it's good to see you," he said. "We were looking for you, scanning the skies and treetops. You did worry your paternal figure, you know."

"Sorry, father. I disobeyed and snuck out. I accept consequences," Una spoke.

"Now now, let's not speak so quickly of consequences. Reasoning is more critical, and even Lar will agree with that. I'm certain you had adequate reasoning, which if given a moment to explain, will come about in a satisfying manner."

"Right! You see, I was concerned about the fate of these two--"

"It's this," Scout said, holding up the Neural Band.

That chilled the room a good ten degrees. Lar stepped forward cautiously, taking the silvery headband from the boy, studying it... studying the wounded young woman in the bed. He could put the rest together himself.

"This technology doesn't belong planetside," he said. "It violates non-interference policy straight to the core. We certainly did not bring it with us today; how it got here is a mystery that requires resolution. The girl must have found out about this, and went to recover it herself and investigate the source, upholding the Orbital policy of noninterference. Although her decision to work alone is questionable, and this matter clearly is beyond her capabilities. Ono, we must return at once to consider this matter, after mindwiping the witnesses."

Tensions went up, temperatures dropped a bit more. Emily fingered at her blouse sleeve.

Una was first to speak.

"No," she said.

The taller figure, Ono, cleared his throat. "Daughter, please. He is right. We must not let our.. apparent mistakes cause harm to their culture. We will--"

"There has been enough damage to the minds of the surface dwellers done today -- and all of it our fault, one way or another, father. I won't be a party to any more. There is an alternative, which I have been evaluating quietly for several minutes contemplation. They can assist me in the investigation!"

"What?" Ono spoke, puzzled.

"What?!" Emily blurted.

"WHAT?!" Lar shouted.

"Hm," Scout considered.

Lar was first to react with more than one syllable, arms flailing in disapproval. "Primary Council Leader, this is unacceptable! An investigation must be carefully planned, must be assigned to citizens with appropriate talents and knowledge of surface culture--"

"My daughter has studied the culture of Eastusa all her lifespan. It is her primary hobby, if you recall," Ono said, the idea starting to take root behind his eyes.

"Oh, yes, I know all too well why the singular leader of our people just had to take a *dangerous* vacation with his doting daughter down to her beloved Earth for a 'New York Peace-Za'," Lar grumbled. "And how THAT little stopover turned into a trip to observe the floral growth at the Washington Memorial. I'm surprised we didn't end up visiting every one of these crude little villages along the way, for that matter!"

"She is of age, Lar. She has the talent and the knowledge. What's more, she is accompanied by a soldier of these lands, and... correct me if I'm wrong, miss, but you have the talent and knowledge of the Faerie race, yes?"

Emily, still a bit bewildered, mutely nodded.

"I can think of no better grouping," Ono decided. "She may require assistance in both sides of this country's struggles to find the source of this hypertech artifact. Even if we assigned citizens to help, I would want them involved, for my daughter's safety. That is... assuming they are interested...?"

Slowly, Emily raised her hand, feeling like a schoolgirl again.

"Question," she said. "...who ARE you people?"

Oddly, this set off a wave of embarrassment with the three outsiders. Una cleared her throat, and offered a bow.

"I'm Una point zero one, and this is my father, Ono, Primary Council Leader. That's Lar, a Councilman who works for my father," she explained. "We're aliens from outer space."

Emily gave up trying to understand after that point.

Most of the long-winded explanation using bizarre words with plenty of syllables was lost on her, but she picked up the basics, enough to convince her that she had hit her head earlier and was living out some bizarre mish-mash parody of the media she'd watched over the years.

They were Orbitals, Una explained. They lived in giant cities that hovered over the Earth without falling to the ground. They were from somewhere else entirely, and were simply here to watch us from afar, to learn about us, before they would move on to do the same to some other world. Her particular city hovered over Eastusa, tasked with studying it -- something Una took exceptional interest in. They had shiny silver technology that was fifty zillion years ahead of anything from Scout's world, and totally perpendicular to Fae magic. They were powerful, they were benevolent, they were quiet and distant, and they'd royally screwed up and dropped some of their tech on our world.

(For a moment, Emily wondered why she could accept metal machines that roared and hauled across great distances on wheelspokes while burning dead dinosaurs in their bellies, and could accept arcane powers of light and darkness that wove physics-bending willpower from nothingness, but shiny space people was too much for her to deal with. That was enough for her to accept that as crazy as this all was, it was real, and it was unfortunately happening to her.)

The Neural Band was a product of their civilization. Normally it was a learning tool, a way for teachers to communicate with classrooms of students, a rapid means of transferring thought. However, used on the weak-minded ogres, it became a weapon, a terrible thing that nearly destroyed an entire village of living, breathing people. This was why the Orbitals stayed out of our business, high and out of sight, even if they probably could solve a lot of this world's problems... they felt supreme responsibility for their power.

And for some damn fool reason (although "not having her memories scrambled" was top at the list) she numbly agreed to help little Miss Shiny Panties wander all over creation trying to figure out how a battle-crazed witch got her hands on their "hypertech."

Time slid by quicker, after that. There were arguments with Lar, who hated the idea to the core. There was tending to Jesse, who hadn't improved much at all. Renting of a wagon, to help them get her to the Summer Court, since flying this many people by broomstick and "jetpack," which is what Una called the strange small silver backpack she wore, was too awkward to suffice for long distance transport. Eventually, they snuck out of town, regrouped on the roadway beyond, the elder Orbitals left, and it was just the three of them plus one prisoner.

So.

"So," Emily said, feeling as if things had finally caught up to the here and now.

Una held up a hand, pausing her, as she watched her father and the grumpy politician float away, on their oddly broomstick-esque physics defying jetpacks. ("It doesn't really use jets," she'd explained, "It uses a quantum gravity coil powered by a mass capacitor to achieve a flight effect. But from watching your films, I assumed you'd understand 'jetpack' more.") Once the two were clearly out of earshot, she lowered her hand.

"I.. didn't want to tell them this, because I felt it was the only way father would agree," she said. "But I know you two never wanted to be dragged into our problems. You're just as much victims in this as your fellow Earthling is. So... you don't have to come with me, if you don't wish to. I will trust you to keep my secrets, without threatening your memories. Myself... I am willing to investigate these.. anachronisms, and do it alone."

Well! That's that, our work here is done, time to go, Emily thought.

"You realize you'll get eaten alive out there, right?" she said, instead. "I mean, frankly, you stick out like a sore thumb. You talk funny. You don't *really* know how things work. I've only known you for a day and I can tell already that you're gonna be chewed up and spat out by this planet."

"I'd like to think my years of study had--"

"You can't learn Earth from a book, or watching it through a telescope. Even one pointing down instead of up. ...I can't believe I'm about to say this," Emily forewarned, "But I *have* to come with you. I really, really don't want to. It's just another in a long line of instances where I mix myself up in doing the right-yet-stupid thing. But hey, why break tradition? ...fine. I'm in. I want to be the one to hand over Jesse to the Summer Court, anyway."

Una managed a weak, thankful smile. "Well, then... I welcome your assistance, Emily the Witch. ...and you, Scout fellow?"

He'd almost managed to slip into the background again. Una had an uncanny habit of spotting him, engaging him head on. She'd done it all night, and each time, some primal mindset in Emily had been surprised to see he was in fact still around.

But the boy shook his head.

"I can't," he said. Quiet. "I shouldn't."

Emily nibbled her lip. "I'm not afraid," she said, making a guess. "I don't think you're a danger to me--"

"You do. You just don't want to think that, and wish you couldn't," he corrected her. "I should go. Good luck."

Without a further word, he turned to his left, and walked straight into the roadside forest. He kept his ears trained, listening for the squeaky axles of the motor-assisted, horse-drawn cart, and waited for the girls to be long gone before he stopped walking.

It was for the best. He had his purpose. He had his eternal hunt. He wasn't one to work with anyone else, because he was supposed to be alone. They would understand that and would be fine without him. His walking resumed.

You will follow them.

His walking ceased.

"What?" he asked, aloud.

You will follow them.

"...they're not my enemies."

I never said they were.

"They're not my prey."

I never said they were.

"You want me to kill them?"

I never said I did.

"Then... what do you want?"

I want you to follow them.

"Why?"

You will find glorious hunting along their path, youngling. Is that not enough?

"If I'm with them, they'll just be in danger."

You will prove far more dangerous than the dangers they face.

"That's my point, actually."

You will follow them.

"If I refuse?"

The boy fell to the forest ground, a puppet with snipped strings. No heartbeat, no pulse. Not that he had any before, either.

An hour later, a stinging pain made him sit upright. He had to blink several times to clear his dry eyes, after they had been hanging open for so long.

Never forget you are dead. You are mine. Follow them. If I command you to hunt for them, you will. If I command you to herd them to their deaths, you will. The dead have no choices remaining to them. Go.

"...yes, Lady Winter."

Rising to his feet, the boy turned around, and resumed walking. He was out of the forest, down the road, and back with his new companions in short order.

end.a01

weapon [wep-uhn]
-noun
1. An instrument of war; an offensive or defensive
combat tool; anything used, or designed to be used, in
injuring, defeating, or destroying an enemy.

It's a good place, Emily thought.

This was partly what drew her to magic in the first place. They'd said the Fae were devious, cunning, evil-minded. You can't trust them, not ever. Universally horrible and wicked, and so on, and so forth. They'd talk and talk about the dark of the forest... but Nana hadn't much to say in response, except to say that men could be devious, cunning, and evil-minded. Didn't mean you couldn't trust them, not ever.

Pix was one Emily could trust. It wasn't that he was an innocent -- good and evil were concepts he had trouble with, complicated thoughts for a simple creature. But that was just it, they were just concepts. All that mattered to him was who he did right by and who didn't do right by him. Everything sorted itself out in the end.

When Emily first visited this glade a week ago, bringing with her a catatonic witch with severe hypertech induced brain damage, she didn't have a doubt in her mind about the decision. True, Pix was Summer Court through and through, a diminutive denizen of the dewdrops of ... Spring, since Emily couldn't find a proper word starting with D to complete that phrase. True, the Summer Court had been her blessing and her bane. But like the world of men, there'd always be someone to disprove the hard and fast rule of distrust.

It was hard to see Pix within his aura, the wellspring of green light that danced and flickered around him everywhere he fluttered. And he DID flutter, never quite holding still, darting in and around Emily, even if he generally tried to hover in front of her eyes. It was only polite.

"Can't say as such, afraid," he replied. "The Archmagus has her in custody. Don't think she was suppos'd to be attackin' that Human-Log. But that's Runeblade for ye, always itchin' fer approval, to show off her skill with some new toy. And a frightful toy it was!"

"Speaking of toys... anything more on that?" the young witch asked, trying to keep her eyes on her tiny friend. It was only polite, in return. "We're trying to track down the source of those... shiny silver toys." (Language she knew wouldn't confuse him.) "Where did Jess... where did Runeblade get her toy?"

"Ach, it's a thing as I'm not knowin'," Pix said, shaking his head sadly. "We're low in the court, Emily-Friend, low indeed. Scuttlebutt and whispers through the grasses, those we have, but I'm thinkin' the toy was mighty High-Knowing. Too high for this simple Log-Dweller."

Emily sighed, having a seat on said log. (She was the only human they'd allow to do that, without going into a frenzy of blinking lights and vicious swipes with near-microscopic daggers. Emily knew how to balance herself while sitting, to not disrupt the pixie's homestead.) "I was hoping it was just something she plucked off the ground. Stumbled across it, nice and simple. It still could be, in fact... or, it could be some vast secret within the court that accidentally saw light of day. Mighty High-Knowing..."

"Aye, aye," Pix agreed. "What with the eternal war-in-peace thing with her sister, to say the least of the troubles with yer kin, My High Lady Summer keeps her sneaky power plays pretty close to the chest. An' what a chest it is! Hoohah!"

The light flickered in what could be considered a bawdy gesture. Sort of the pixie equivalent of a sly wink. It made Emily smile... something she did so rarely, these days. The pixies could do that for her. Eternal optimists, to balance out her more realistic view that nothing quite goes the way you want. Funny thing.

"Funny thing," she said, turning her internal thought outward, as she tended to do.

"Eeer?"

"You guys. Low in the court. Pounded on and kicked around by both your own kind and the humans," she said. "Too small for anybody really to care about. But I haven't seen you unhappy, not once, not even when... y'know."

Pix fluttered and swooped, his cheer multiplying. "Aye, aye! Oh, a bedraggled lot we are, tiny things, aye. But the way of it is that gettin' nine kinds of snot pounded out of ye on a regular basis builds character, it does! Teaches you that ye can work through the worst of it. To be puttin' a case on a point, or a point in a case... I'm thinkin' the knowing of it that Runeblade'll be just fine, if not *better* from bein' shown she's not the top dog she thinks she is."

Emily snorted out a derisive laugh. "None of them were top dog, Pix. Lilith fed their egos, encouraged them to show their superiority over me... but she also took every chance to point out that they were still humans playing with Fae toys. Lilith was the *true* Fae, the only one that really counted. Head of that pecking order."

"An' yet Lilith's gotta answer to the Summer Lady, don't she? An' Summer answers to Winter and back and forth in turn in their peculiar sisterly way. Oh! Oh! And BOTH of them answer to the forces of the universe itself, an' I get the feelin' THAT'S gotta answer to somethin' in the end. Hah! That's High-Knowledge if it's anythin' but! Point is, nobody's safe from a good kickin', and that's as it should be!"

As if words weren't enough Pix kicked and kicked at the air, to the point where he twirled himself silly and had to pause a bit to recover his wits.

"Ahh... why, yer livin' proof of my theory!" he continued, clearly on a roll now. "No matter how many times Emily gets laughed at, bullied, arrested, or tossed into lake, she comes out okay in the end!"

"...yeah, thanks, I feel special now."

"Why, you could throw 'er to wild dogs and maul her to little bits, pull out an eye and chop off a leg, and she'll come up swingin'! You could set her to a burnin' pyre--"

"I. Get. The Point," she said, with additional hiss for emphasis.

"Happy to help!" Pix said, saluting and completely missing the anger. "So! Where're ye off to now?"

Emily the Witch rose from the log, smoothing out her skirt and brushing dirt from it. Wouldn't do to look TOO much like a road-worn country girl in front of her fancy new companions. "We're going to Baltimore," she explained. "Ah... the big Human-Log on the edge of the Crab-Sea. You know the place?"

"Oh, aye. Snuck in there a few times, just 'cause I could. Hah! Anti-Fae Spark-Eyeballs can't spot the likes of me!"

"Pix, no! Don't... don't *do* that, okay? Seriously. Listen to me here," she said, trying to emphasize. "That place is bad news for Fae. Humans hate you guys!"

"Yer human, you don't hate us."

"...yeah, well... humans hate you guys. And if they DO catch you in there, you're pretty easy to squish. ...and for god's sakes, if you see a big zappy blue light in a cage, don't investigate. Okay?"

"If'n it's a Horrible-Horrible, why're ye goin', then?"

"It's the blasted hypertech," Emily grumbled. "The.. shiny toys, like Runeblade had. Remember what I was saying earlier? About tracking them down? My companions?"

Pix fluttered in befuddlement. The hovering, glowing stream-of-consciousness philosopher Fae was bad at remembering the little details.

"We got a lead yesterday," she explained. "A Human-Thief. One of his goons had a shiny silver toy. He claimed he got it from some old soldier from Baltimore. We're going there to track him down, and see where he got his toys from. ...and yes, it's definitely a Horrible-Horrible, especially for a human like me, because I'm chummy with you. I'm going to need to stash my things before I go there, or they'll be on to me in a second."

"Yer-- ooh, I know this, I know this, wait... right. Witch-Hat! Witch-Book! Witch-Broomstick!" the pixie counted off. "Hidin' them, are ye? Well, nobody hides things like ole Pix. Except maybe Pix. Oh, and Pix! But not Pix, ole Pix is better than that codger."

(This was one of the problems with every single member of your race having the same name. Somehow they could tell one Pix apart from another, but Emily had to go by their colored lights and voice pitches. Names were useless once they filtered to English.)

"Pass me yer Witch-Things, and I'll watch over them proper," Pix offered. "Log-Safe. Give ye my Truth-Word on that. An' if yer ever needin' them, ye just give a whistle like I can hear it. Good-Deal?

Assuming they don't drift from his memory, Emily thought. But she knew where the log was, and after she left that stinking city, she could spend a few hours cajoling Pix's memory easily enough. She held out a thumb, which Pix latched on to as she shook it up and down. "Good-Deal," she agreed.

No hat. The hat had no power, but it was her hat, and she liked it. It was Nana's hat. No book... she'd be putting a few key spells on papers hidden under her clothes, and if the city folk wanted her to strip off her clothes, well, Pix HAD pointed out that nobody was safe from a good kickin'. And the broomstick... she preferred to fly, but surely taking conventional transport wouldn't be TOO rough...

She could endure. And then she'd be back, and have her things, and everything would be fine. No trouble at all.

a02 weapons

One foot here, a dirt road. One foot there, gleaming paved asphalt. Just like that, one ends, another begins...

They'd re-paved a ruined road, one that had long since broken up and given way to nature. It was still used, still a clear-cut through the wilds, but more than a century without proper repairs and it had given up the ghost. Only this one last leg had been saved, or rather buried and then a fresh road laid over its corpse. A tin sign proudly declared it to be the Theodore Roosevelt Highway... serving only to ferry people from this waystation on into the mighty city of Baltimore.

The money from taking on the Crimson Arrow Gang had paid for food and lodging, but there was enough left over to also buy bus tickets. Not very good ones, they had to hike down the country road to get to this terminal which was practically at Baltimore's territorial limits anyway, but Scout had suggested they'd look less suspicious rolling in through the bus line than they would flying in on broomsticks and jetpacks. The anti-aircraft guns at the top of the Freedom Walls would probably agree with him.

That meant an hour of bumping along on a manmade road in a manmade metal vehicle that belched smoke and puttered like an old man with whooping cough. Old media had predicted shiny flying cars in mankind's future, but post-post-apocalyptic mankind was content to let technology roll on without much improvement... Una's people had apparently ate their future for lunch instead.

Despite coming from a civilization that soared above the clouds in flawless cities of chrome, Una was way too thrilled with the trappings of "modern" society. The bus fascinated her. The rubbery grips on the floor down the aisle to keep you from slipping fascinated her. The hard faux-leather seating with its barely up to code seatbelts fascinated her. And above all, the power windows fascinated her.

She pushed a little button -- and the window went up. She pushed another little button -- and the window went down. Not very far, not enough to let in but a tiny wispy stream of air, but the mechanism itself was the point.

"Servos and motors! Clockwork gears meshing together, and probably belts and fans and sprockets and... oh, it's just so amazing!" she was trying to explain to a nonplussed Emily. "It's all so physical, so mechanical! I bet there's hardly any energy transfer in play beyond the raw kinetics needed to slide the plastic-glass. And you say they're called 'power windows'?"

"Mhmm," Scout replied, not paying more than the minimum amount of attention. He also was busy not paying attention to the outdated newspaper someone had left stuck to their bench-like seat with chewing gum.

"Truly, yours is a civilization of wonder. It's amazing you've survived this long using such primitive methodologies!" Una said in a manner that was actually not insulting in the slightest if you understood that she meant nothing unpleasant by it. "Of course, I've seen much of this in our observations of Eastusa, and the few recordings we've found. Roll up, roll up! Roll up for the mystery tour!"

Emily grumbled and tried to sink into the uncomfortable seat, which only made it more uncomfortable. "There's nothing mysterious about it. It's just bits of metal and things moving around. It's ugly, it smells, it hasn't changed in centuries, it's like a coffin on wheels. And the sooner we're off it, the better."

"This is a thing I cannot comprehend, Miss Emily the Witch--"

"IXNAY! Ixnay on the itchway!" Emily hissed.

"Ixnay? Who is this ixnay? I am simply stating that your society has endured, and that is wondrous. I have read the archives of other worlds visited by my people, and have read of worlds under less strain than yours that collapsed far sooner. So many succumb to conflict and self-annihilation! But even if you have not solved your problems, your world has persisted despite them. So amazing! So very *is that the city?!!*"

Even if the power windows weren't wide enough to let her crawl out, she gave a good try at it. Giving up, she simply pressed herself up close against the plexiglas, eyes wide in delight.

Baltimore was up ahead.

And it was ugly. It would be bad enough if the sky-high Freedom Walls were their usual faceless cliffs of gray stone, specially designed to resist even the strongest assault by the Faerie Court. Instead of being plain, however, a mural had been painted entirely around the length of the city's siege wall.

It was done in an ancient manner, bold lines and stylized people standing at odd angles. They were looking to the horizon, over the seas of Baltimore Harbor and its mighty kraken-resistant warships... towards a sunrise that was blue with white stars, radiant beams of red and white surrounding it.

That might have been inspiring if Emily had the slightest bit of patriotism, but not as much as the designers would have hoped, given the way the paint had peeled and cracked and weathered away in many places. The stalwart guardians of the American Way had melted slightly with years and years of neglect.

Did they ever consider they'd need to touch it up? Or had they just painted it and decided it would stand for a thousand years? she wondered, with some bitterness.

"A city. A real city, and from ground level," Una whispered. Almost reverent. "My father and I only saw New York from above, descending right into it under concealing shields. I saw the stone rings around cities from above. They were just... lines. Lines inscribing the communities within. From here, they are manmade wonders... truly, I shall feel safe behind those walls!"

"You'd be wrong to do so."

Both girls looked to their companion. He hadn't bothered looking up from the articles he wasn't reading.

"Lived in cities most of my life," he stated. "Eastusa thinks that the cities are how everything should be -- walled in and safe. It's an illusion. Even cities can fall. Walls just help them forget anything beyond exists. They're blinders and nothing more."

Emily paused a bit. Unsure if she should point this out, if she should break the magic spell.

"...Scout?"

"Yes?"

"That's the first time you've really talked about your past."

He gave a shrug, and folded the newspaper under one arm.

"You want more words, I can give them," he said. "You won't feel safe inside those walls, Una. People inside are just as dangerous as people outside. More than enough predators to fill two different forests. Adapted to their environment, they use buildings as underbrush, skyscrapers as the high leaves, but walk unaware and they'll take you all the same. Kill you, or worse. Still want more words?"

"...not especially, no," Emily decided. "Don't scare her like that, alright, Scout? Even if you're right -- even if people are basically scum and they'll use you at the drop of a hat -- there's no call to--"

"You're both wrong."

That got a funny look. But Jetpack Girl was all smiles, from within the hood of her cloak.

"Society is the act of gathering together for a common good. It's a pooling of resources, allocating towards both survival and satisfaction with life. By definition, cities are good, because they represent that hope for a safe and superior future. Laws exist to curb selfishness; the act of misdirecting resources and depriving people of what they require. As a result, on the whole, people will be kind, and will pull together. You'll see. --oh, the security checkpoint is ahead!"

While they were busy staring open jawed at their newcomer compatriot (well, Emily was, anyway) the bus had approached the Freedom Wall gate. *No more time for chitchat,* Emily decided, fidgeting in her seat, the smuggled spellbook pages around her waist starting to itch. Her gear was with the Pixies, Scout's weapons buried nearby as well -- but Una's was somehow "cloaked" from human perception as well as hidden beneath her actual cloak. (Lucky her.)

They would get through the checkpoint just fine. Had to. Then they just had to survive the big city.

For their sakes, Emily went against her expectations and hoped Una was right.

The money had gone to food, lodging, bus rides, and now city lodging and city food. Spreading it that thin meant you couldn't get the best food (not that Una was any less amazed) (not that Scout cared) (not that Emily didn't complain anyway). It also meant you couldn't get the best lodgings.

The Brickstone Inn was a recent addition to Baltimore. All the buildings generally had been razed in the first Faerie Wars following the Pandora Event... rebuilt rapidly, ignoring building codes, to pump some lifeblood back into the city... and then rebuilt again, this time for good, to show that Eastusa was back to normal. Most of the corporate brands were gone, including the big hotel chains, replaced by new ones. Even so, the Brickstone Inn wouldn't have rated more than two stars in any tourist's guidebook.

The elderly woman at the clerk's desk barely offered a grunt, swapping paper money for a metal key. There was no elevator; if someone was supposed to wander around town enforcing disability support building codes, they'd passed over this dive. Up three flights of stairs to a door which thankfully fit properly in its frame... if the inn had been THAT bad, the FaePlace might not have worked.

FaePlace was a complicated spell to read from its squared diagram, and one Emily had in short supply due to the difficulty in recopying it. But it proved utterly invaluable in the first nights they had spent together on the road...

On the evening after Olney, when they had first joined up on this little journey, the next settlement they stopped at only had two rooms available to rent. Obviously, they would have to divide by gender lines, Emily had announced -- Scout would get his own room to be all dark and broody in, and the girls would get the other one. She'd read by lamplight and copy her spells for the night, while Una turned in early. Simple, straightforward.

The first hint of problems was when upon entering their room, Una stripped naked.

Logically, Emily *shouldn't* care, she had thought. We're all girls here, ha ha, nothing we haven't seen before. Problem was, she grew up in a traditional farming village where the height of throbbing, glistening human eroticism was *exposing your ankles*. Anything more lurid than removing perhaps one layer of petticoats and leggings that would burn you up under the collar, and running around stark naked even in the privacy of your own home was only something you did very briefly when washing up.

While Emily engaged in a very admirable effort not to look at her, and not to say anything too alarming beyond the "GOOD GOD!" she exclaimed in the first place, she inquired as to why her road buddy had decided to get into bed in the buff.

"Is there a reason I am not supposed to?" Una had asked. "Perhaps some cultural difference? It is quite common back aboard the Arcologies, due to the way our beds work. Granted, there is also finer climate control... you appear to be uncomfortable with this, however. Hmm. Very well! I have designed a solution!"

"Yes?" Emily croaked.

"As the initial spatial allocations are resulting in your discomfort, I'll simply go sleep with Scout."

Now Emily couldn't avoid staring at her in abject horror. "WHAT!? You can't go trotting off to bed with Scout! What are you thinking? For decency's sake, you just MET him!"

"What does the length of our mutual knowledge have to do with resting quarter allocations?"

"A woman's got to have *standards*, okay?" Emily protested, feeling the urge to fold her arms in front of her chest, as if this might reduce the overall level of Yikes in the room. "I mean, come on! Just... If you just take off your drawers for every boy you meet--"

A light went off in her head like the reading lamp at her bedside.

"Wait. Resting quarter allocations?" Emily repeated. "You mean... you were going to sleep NEXT to him, not WITH him?"

"Well, of course. What else would-- ohhh! Yes, I see now!" Una said, a similar light going off in her head (but likely one powered by those strange 'mass capacitors' she was talking about). "It's a twist of the language, correct? That despite being the same core concept of proximity, one term involves sharing of comfort resources, and the other term implies sexual relations during a nocturnal period."

"...yes. Yes, that is what I meant," Emily said, praying she wasn't redder than her hair right now. "I'm.. not sure if the way you put it is horribly proper or horribly improper or both, but..."

"Well! If it is of concern to you, I have no strong interest at this time in heterosexual copulation with Scout," Una declared, holding up a hand of honesty and promise. "Given your reaction earlier, if I have interpreted its proper context correctly, rest assured I have no interest at this time in homosexual copulation with you, either. Although, if my understanding of the social guidance documents called 'teen date movies' are correct, then it would seem--"

Emily was busy looking up the FaePlace spell before Una could finish her theory about naked human interaction, and that had settled that.

The FaePlace was probably the most showy spell Emily kept in her library -- and the most useful. Enchant a doorway, preferably a wooden one in a strong frame, and you could link it to a magical pocket of space that wasn't quite entirely unlike the World of Faerie, yon legendary lost land of the Faerie Court. That meant it was like a waking dream... a place that shifted and molded itself to your thoughts. Sure, in a sense you were still physically in a rundown little inn room, but in another sense... you were home.

Whenever she cast the spell for herself, it would resolve to be a near perfect copy of her old bedroom back home. Cozy and warm, with a nice fireplace hearth, a soft bed of goose feather and plenty of books. If you tried reading them, they might be a bit sketchy or simply consist of a brief outline followed by plenty of blank pages -- this was a memory room, sculpted by desire and emotion, after all. And the things in here didn't really exist, so they couldn't be removed. Food would only nourish until you walked out the door. Bathing you could do, and handily enough, dry yourself the moment you stepped out. (Preferably clothed.)

Of course, that had been when the FaePlace was only reacting to her. From her research into the spell, Emily knew it would change based on designated occupants, growing new rooms to accommodate their needs -- giving Una all the private space she wanted to laze around without pants, if that's what Little Miss Rocket Girl so desired.

After the three of them had entered, the FaePlace reconfigured itself. A new common room had been added, for starters. It was, of course, cozy... but three kinds of cozy. It had a comfortable wooden rocking chair padded by an old quilt, next to an extensive bookshelf, this time full of tomes on magical theory. (She never had real magic books as a child.) But there were also strange silvery lumps of metal that couldn't possibly be comfortable to sit on... until you tried, and then felt like you never wanted to get up again. A simple, cleanly designed metal table would serve for dining, playing cards, or whatever you wanted to do. ...and there was shadows. Shadows in every corner, where the light didn't seem to want to reach.

The bedrooms, those were far more personalized.

Through a wooden doorway was Emily's old room... just as welcoming, just as delightful as she'd left it. Perhaps a bit more organized than it had been in childhood, more tidy, more functional. Trying to look its best for the visitors.

Una's room, now that that was something. Emily had her own imagined ideas of what their "Arcology" sky-ships were like, and they didn't go nearly far enough, it seemed. Everything in there... gleamed. It shone. The light faded in from nowhere, always so bright, always so clear. The bed was a metal slab, and yet, it was comfortable and warm and yielding to the touch. (Which almost, ALMOST made Emily see the appeal of lying starkers on it. ...almost.)

And... the view. The view of Earth. From above. There were no words to describe a sight nobody of her race had seen in hundreds of years, not like this. Even trying to put a description to it would be a disservice to the entire world. So, Emily had to pull her eyes away from it, to pretend to be aloof rather than be a slack-jawed country bumpkin in front of her super-perfect companion. But she swore she'd sneak in and get another look, another time.

...and then there was Scout's room.

It was probably not empty. There might be a cot in there. It was impossible to say, given it was completely dark, with no light sources whatsoever. The thick shadow refused any light in from the open doorway, refused any attempt to illuminate what lie within.

That would be terrifying enough by itself... but when she caught Scout's expression as he first laid eyes on his FaePlace home away from home... the *relief* on his face chilled her to the bone.

Arrive. Settle in. Food? Food could wait, Emily had decided. They were here for a purpose and the sooner they got their business done, the sooner they could leave. (The kicked puppy look on Una's face when she realized they wouldn't be staying to see the sights was kind of embarrassing, but Emily knew she had to keep pressure on to get the job over with. This wasn't happy vacation wacky fun time.)

Una was twice disappointed to learn that unlike the old "Sam Spade" movies she saw, whatever those were, they wouldn't be having shadowy conversations with stoolies and informants and hitting the pavement to explore the city, hunting down their lead. They were simply going to look him up in the "phone book".

"An acoustic communications device? Analog signals over copper wires? Oh, how very fascinating!" Una exclaimed, finding something to distract her from the business at hand, as always. Emily ignored her fawning over the ancient, battered telephone booth -- which someone had helpfully scrawled the names of various women who could offer a good time if you dialed their numbers. Of course, Una wanted to dial those numbers and enjoy these supposed good times, which is why she was outside the booth while Emily was inside, pawing through the yellowed pages.

"It's primitive," Scout described, thankfully heading off Future Girl for Emily's sake, so the witch could focus on pouring over the book. "We should have something better than this by now. Got the eastern pocket of the Internet back up, improved on it a little. But for intra-city, nobody bothered using anything other than what was already there. Years and years, all the same."

"That is the impression I have been getting in my studies," Una said, eager to engage the boy in chat. (Scout was quite talkative today, for a change. Ever since getting to the city. Hm.) "I have access to very limited media, only recordings brought back by anthropology teams. But even though the media is new, the content is hundreds of years old, and those city-images look very similar to modern cities..."

"Ain't broke, don't fix. If it works, don't change it. Don't think of anything new. Go with what you have. Simpler. Easier. Cheaper. War economy. Nostalgia. Desperation. Pretending everything's still fine, nothing's different," he said, in his usual clipped way of speaking. There was some bitterness to the quick phrases, though. "This city is dead, just stagnant water. Nobody notices. Nobody cares."

Emily leaned out of the booth, holding up a torn yellow page. "And on that cheerful note," she interrupted, "I've found our lead. He's in an apartment on the west side of the city."

Una clasped her hands together. "Excellent! So. As flying would draw attention from the authorities, how shall we travel? On foot? By bus, taxi, underground tram, gyroscopic vertical takeoff aircraft, zeppelin, or perhaps biplane?"

"...a taxi will be fine," Emily decided. She had a feeling she was going to be The Decider for this band of misfits, in the days ahead.

The topography of the city shifted rather dramatically, when they left Harbor Place.

Even the Brickstone Inn, as run-down as it was, at least had been built in the tourist-friendly section. The part of the city that had been polished up and made amicable, an ongoing reminder of the strength of Eastusa, the might of its coastal-locked naval power and its commercial interests. But go a few blocks away from Harbor Place, deeper into the city, and that tune changed considerably.

Here, buildings that were destroyed and rebuilt were never re-rebuilt. They were ramshackle arrangements of sub-code building materials, designed with an eye to hopefully not falling over and little else. Pavement cracked and sank into potholes, sidewalks split where weeds were growing, and steam from manholes delivered a pungent reminder that there was an entire underlayer of badly maintained urban support pipes down there.

Being a country girl at heart, Emily could only go by limited urban knowledge. She'd been to a few cities before, even this one... but only under duress, only when she had no other choice. Beyond that, she just assumed they were full of cutpurses and hoodlums and drug dealers and prostitutes and doomed homeless people. Odds were not EVERY person the taxi rolled on by was some sort of active urban sinner, but all the same, she was glad she was inside the cab and not walking the streets.

In what would clearly grate on her nerves in the days (weeks?) ahead, Una had precisely the opposite reaction. When she saw someone selling golden watches (stolen or replica, no doubt) from a portable tray, she commented on how wonderful it was to see citizens pitching in to assure a common temporal standard. When they passed those phone booth accessible good-time girls, she commented on how colorful and individualistic their costuming was, although she was puzzled as to how it could provide protection from the elements with so little fabric deployed. And so on, and so on.

Scout... well. Scout was quiet again. Emily focused on watching him, instead of analyzing the concrete blight. The city was making him moody, and considering over the past week his primary operating mood was "unreadable / lack of mood," that was quite a change.

"You hate cities, I take it?" Emily asked him quietly, while Una prattled on.

The boy rolled his head to the other side, towards her, away from the window. "I don't hate them. I don't love them. They're just... what they are. ...I'd rather be in the forests. Gotten to know the forests."

"But you said you grew up in a city."

"It died."

"Bad memories, huh...? You... y'know... wanna talk about that yet?"

A shrug. "Not really. No. See it this way -- you're not comfortable here. I'm not comfortable here. We're out of our elements. That's all there is to it. Think we've arrived."

Indeed, the taxi had stopped. Emily, who was keeping track of the money because it would likely vanish in Una's hands, counted off some of the few remaining bills for the driver, and they were promptly left to their own devices.

Una was craning her neck back, trying to stare directly up the face of the apartment building's seven stories. "Behind which of these outward glass viewing windows is Mr. Clay?" she asked.

"Welll... the phone book said apartment 45, so... probably fourth floor?" Emily guessed. She stepped up the tenement's stoop, pulled on the door -- and it was stuck. Defective? Rusted? She tugged again, and again, to no avail...

...while Scout smoothly stepped behind her, and pushed a small button with a label of "45 CLAY" on the call box. Oh, right.

There was a long pause, before a crackly electric speaker rattled off a curt greeting. "Yeah?" it offered. "Who's there?"

Emily cleared her throat, ready to lay out the fiction she'd composed in her head, the cover story that would get them the information they sought. "Hello, sir. I represent the--"

"I am Una, from Arcology #A076 of the Orbital cultural investigation order!" Una introduced herself, waving politely to the little audio speaker. "We are here to inquire about hypertech weaponry which you gave to a Mr. Teak of the colloquially named 'Crimson Arrow Gang.' Can you tell us where you obtained said item?"

A horrible silence followed. Emily's mouth worked up and down soundlessly, seventeen or eighteen different admonishments all bumrushing the gates of her speech center, jamming it up completely.

A buzz sounded over the door, the lock disengaging.

"You'd better come on up," Clay had decided.

His apartment was sparsely furnished. It was hardly up to the standards of a FaePlace; it was barely up to the standards of being a home, despite his claim that he was retired and mostly just sat around here all day. You'd think he would've wanted to sit around all day in finer surroundings.

The inside was just as shabby as the outside. Peeling wallpaper of unimpressive design, a pattern of dots and lines that existed only to say Hey, There Is A Pattern Here, Honest. The floor was bare concrete, with one simple oval rug covering the center. A kitchen off to the site... standard fridge, standard oven, standard cabinets, standard table. Living room had a television and a netbook casually shoved aside on a desk in the back. Clock on the wall to count the hours.

No pictures of family, no posters of old movies, no decorations of any kind... except a single star-shaped medal, hanging on a ribbon within a glass case.

"For valor against an incursion by the Faerie Court," Andrew Clay explained. "Back when I was with the Frontliners, before I quit. It was the pay, see. I had a family to raise, at the time, and the pay just wasn't good enough. Government work rarely is."

The old man continued to sip at a nondescript cup of coffee, coffee as dark as his aging skin, from a mug just as gray as his hair. He leaned back in his chair... lost in a thought for a few moments, before continuing.

"PMCs offer more money. Always have, always will; it's specialty work, more of a scalpel rather than a broadsword. You go to the Private Military Contractors when your job doesn't suit the government's Frontliners. Pay was better. Hours better; sure, I could be on extended assignment, but in my downtime I'd spend plenty of time with my boys. Quicksilver Security seemed too good to be true. Hah. You know what that means, right?"

"No, what is the meaning of it?" Una asked, genuinely wondering.

"You're not from 'round these parts, I take it," he said. "I'd always wondered where the metal came from. The others had theories, and I liked the space aliens one the best. Had some romance to it, some mystique... that one day we'd meet the little green men who made our toys. Hm. Does your entire race resemble young human girls? That'd be a hell of a thing. Bet they'dve flipped if they knew..."

"She's just a tourist," Emily broke in with. "And I'm sure she'd love to jump the next rocket to the moon, once we find where her technology is coming from."

Una blinked a few times. "Rocket? Huh? I've never been to the moon..."

"Your friend's right, miss alien. I'm an old man, now. Likely to ramble your ear off if you let me. I'll stick to what I know," Clay promised. "What I know about the hypertech. We figured out that's what it was called, but we just called it the metal, or the toys. It was.. safer. But we never found out where Graves got the stuff."

"Owner of the PMC," Scout supplied.

"Got it in one, son. Commander Leonard Graves, owner and leader of Quicksilver Security. Hell of a handshake on that man. When he clasped your shoulder, told you you were doing good work, you felt it right down to the core. He was the one who convinced me to jump ship, that I could do more good for America with QS, that the Frontliners were an old and tired pack of dogs. Sure, they innovated and got us out of hock at the start of the Pandora Event and the Faerie Wars... but now they were stagnant. Like the rest of Eastusa, always looking backward, relying on tech from the past..."

"While Quicksilver had tech from the future," Emily understood. "Or at least, seemed like it."

"The metal was something outta this world. Guess literally, now," Clay said, with a chuckle. "The power of those things... energy beams that could carve through rock like it was nothin'. Explosive blasts that could clear out a whole cluster of Fae beasts in one shot. Ordinary explosives do the same, of course, but these were... cleaner. Simpler. Point and kill. ...a lot of killing. Seemed that's all we did, just hunt and kill the Fae, some days. I was never put on guard duty, or assigned to install automated defenses like the Frontliners did. Quicksilver never installed any toys, never left any behind, it always came with us when the job was over."

Una considered this. As bubbleheaded as she might have been today, she could analyze with the best of them. "The technology resource was clearly limited; Mister Graves could not afford to lose what he had obtained. That means he had one set amount, and either very little was coming in, or he'd lost access to his source."

"That was my guess, miss. They had the metal stored at headquarters. I don't know where, exactly; I wasn't high enough in the company for that. But you had to sign for it, had to keep track of it, and if any was missing at the end of the day it came out of your pay. They hoarded those killing tools somethin' fierce. ...the killing.

Yes, I was talking about that. It's what led me to quit. What led my wife to leave me. All the killing..."

The soft spoken old man shuddered, once. Twice. He looked up to his Frontliners medal, apparently drawing confidence from it, enough to keep talking.

"Graves loved it, of course," he said, almost spitting the name out. "I suspect he turned down the more defensive contracts in favor of ones where they could really cut loose with the toys. Shock 'n awe. I killed ten times more Fae in my time with Quicksilver than I ever had as a Frontliner. ...and then we started taking the contracts on human settlements. Outside Eastusa jurisdiction, indie towns that had water disputes or other rivalries and needed hired muscle. I did one job like that, swore to myself I never would again, ended up doing a second job, and a third..."

Now Emily had the shudders. She was sitting in a room with a man who had killed... murdered at least three people. Assuming it was nice enough to be a simple one-person assassination, but if the Fae count was accurate...

"You can think badly of me," Clay suggested, as if reassuring Emily. "I don't mind. It's no less than I deserve, young one. Eventually I couldn't take it anymore. I don't remember exactly when I left... but I just dropped my gear, and walked away. Kept walkin'. Eventually I wandered back home to Baltimore, since I didn't know where else to go."

"That's... in accordance with what we were told," Emily said, trying to get her nerves under control. "That Teak had grabbed the stuff you dropped. He read your uniform name tag. Andrew Clay, Baltimore Division. That's how we knew to find you."

"So, someone's carryin' on with the killing with my metal," Clay said, not liking the sound of that... but giving into the idea, in short order. "Doesn't matter. It'd happen anyway, if I checked my gear back in with Quicksilver. Someone will always pick up a gun. ...miss. Why are your people, your Orbitals, so warlike? Why would you *make* those things?"

On the spot, all eyes turned to Una... who was clearly pinned under those gazes, unsure how to respond. "I... we... there is, I mean... --defense. That's all. We don't.. there actually are very few weapons in my society, and they are rarely needed. ...I don't know how Mister Graves got so many of them. If he had a representative sample of hypertech it should have been maybe five percent weaponry, at best..."

"Well. That's a question you can take up with him, because I don't know. All I know is we had a hell of a lot of shiny space guns, and we put 'em to a hell of a use," Clay said. "When I dumped my gear and came crawling back to the city like a yellow fool, Graves was livid. Fired me on the spot. I used what little money I had left from the divorce to settle here, and... just... be. That's all I do. I just be, children. And that's all I have to say. ...I'm tired. If you don't mind, I'd like to be left alone now."

"Ah... right. ...sorry," Emily said, although she had nothing specific to apologize for. She just.. wanted to apologize. "We'll be going now. Una, Scout--"

"If you don't mind, though, I'd like a minute with the boy," Clay requested.

"Er? ...well. Alright. We'll be out in the hallway. Una...?"

Emily led the slightly puzzled looking space explorer out of the apartment. No questions asked, just cleared out.

Clay sat back, studying the boy who sat back on his sofa. A mutual studying.

"Reckon you've seen the things I've seen in my years," Clay guessed. "You're young yet, but you've seen the things soldiers eventually see, nice and compressed."

"...yes, sir," Scout agreed.

"It hits everybody differently, and everybody the same. It's a funny thing. When all you've ever done, at least all you can remember, is killing... everything's killing. I'm a weapon without a holster. I could hit you over the head with my television, kill you. There's knives in my kitchen, I don't use them much for cooking, because they're also good for killing. There's crack dealers on the street, they could be killed. I've thought of ways to do it. I could go right on killing and never stop, especially if I found people who 'deserved' it. A little self chosen justification, to soothe the pain. Then maybe I'd eventually even kill ones who didn't deserve it. ...those're the kind of the eyes you're looking through too, huh."

"...yes, sir."

"And the girls? You worried about killing them?"

Scout had to pause, before responding. "...yes, sir."

"You can control it, son. Get the sense you know that, even if you've wandered from the idea. Take that killing power and focus it, redirect it, reshape it. You could stand guard over them, like a true Frontliner guards his community. It's harder than cutting loose, and many folks just end up eating their own bullet rather than walk that hard road. ...I'm stuck in the middle. I don't have what it takes to use it for anything else, so I just don't use it at all. I sit here. I'm waiting until I die, I guess. You're not, you're movin' around, so presumably you're gonna be facing the choice by virtue of that alone. To just carry on as a killer, or to become something else with it."

The clock ticked quietly.

"I don't want to kill them," Scout whispered, barely above the ticks of the ancient clock. "And they don't want me to kill. They aren't killers and I don't think they'd like me if I continue being one. ...don't know why I should care, but for some reason, I don't want them to hate me."

Clay nodded, softly. "A hard road, then."

"Yeah."

Luck was with their little quest -- hailing a cab to get out of the nasty side of town didn't take very long at all. This time around, Una was less prone to fiddling with the power windows or declaring the manifold joys and wonders of human society. In fact, all of them were less prone to fiddling, glancing around, or talking about anything at all.

Eventually the silence was broken by rumblings deep within the tummy of the space girl.

"Aliens get hungry too huh?" Emily said.

"I should have brought food pills with me," Una replied. "Plan ahead, be prepared. Pack twice the money and half the clothes. Stay in three star hotels for maximum ratio of comfort to price. Ah, that's from a tourism guidebook I found once in an anthropologist's lot of retrieved items."

"So, is Earth living up to your expectations? Knowing the sort of people that live here, now?"

Una started to reply. Paused. Considered. But came up smiling.

"Very much so," she said. "I.. realize I must seem quite strange to you, so entranced by things you find to be common. But what is common to me is rare to you, and 'viced versa'. So! Let's enjoy the afternoon by sampling the foodstuffs of your native people!"

"You may have to settle for fried greasy objects in a wax paper dish, with our budget," Emily warned. "C'mon. Let's get to the Food Court of Doom."

Historic Harbor Place had been kept the same for decades. Rebuilt, redesigned, but the original purpose of it -- to provide food and shopping to the few tourists that were visiting Baltimore -- that spirit remained even if the tourists themselves were uncommon. Sadly, along with that reincarnation of the facility came the Food Court of Doom.

That wasn't the official name, of course. Last time Emily was in Baltimore (not of her own volition, of course; she was dragged there by a particularly gung-ho human fanboy of an elf who wanted to 'see the sights' while in town) they had nicknamed this pit of burned meat and sloppy foodstuffs the Food Court of Doom based on the horrible gastrointestinal cramps experienced afterwards. Fortunately, this meant she knew what restaurants to avoid, and which ones were (hopefully) safe. In the end, plastic trays loaded with potato skins and bits of seafood coated slick in Chesapeake Bay Spice came to a rest at a distant table in the largely empty food court.

Emily left her food largely untouched; she was waiting to see if Una doubled over in agony and made a run for the restrooms after wolfing down the assorted crabmeats. Instead she focused on another stolen phone book page, this one for "Security Services".

"Security is only one of those services," Scout was explaining, having opened up again. (He seemed to do that when they talked about something up his alley, like cities or the military. But what else would he talk about, once they'd exhausted those topics...?) "PMCs are usually involved in dirty work. Black ops, wet ops. If you just want pure security, the Frontliners'll do it for you, especially if you have Eastusa ties."

"This is the aspect which confuses me," Una admitted. "From our data gathering, we have determined the 'Frontliners' are your government's military. Yet they seem to work for a sort of hire. Is that correct?"

Scout considered how to phrase it. "Yes and no. Different before, different now," he explained. "Frontliners were once a private industry think-tank, right after the Pandora Event, after the Fae arrivals. Military equipment makers and some PMCs getting together, trying to find new ways to fight an enemy that was already saturated across the country. They had good ideas. Good tools. NEW ideas. Frontliners supplied and trained the military in anti-Fae techniques, eventually beating the Fae back and reclaiming the coast, ports of call, the important roadways. Contained them in the middle of the country."

"So... Faerie Court in the middle, then fringes between, then Eastusa. And Frontliners guarding the border?"

"Not at first. No. They were still just a think-tank, grunts did the heavy lifting. But people trusted Frontliners, they were the heroes, the big name. The *brand* name," Scout emphasized. "Folks put trust behind a strong brand. So eventually 'the army' was rebranded, redesigned. They ate the old Frontliners company and became the new Frontliners military. Kept hope alive."

"A puzzling way to run an army, but... I suppose it's worked well so far," Una said. "Your people have survived longer than many other worlds in conflict that the Orbitals have observed from afar. So, why are there still these PCMs?"

"PMCs. And because, said before," the boy continued, bringing it around. "Dirty work. Black work. Frontliners won't do that. They guard, defend, sometimes strike to reclaim lost land, or to expand. But they won't attack human settlements, won't deliberately provoke the Courts. Won't work with anyone who doesn't pay taxes to

Eastusa. Need to hire your own miniature army for the hard stuff. PMCs. There. See?"

"And... one of these PMCs, one of extremely unpleasant leaning, is using my people's legacy to harm others."

"Mhm."

Scout took this break in conversation to eat some of his seafood, while Una considered the options.

"The proper course of action is to locate the technology and neutralize it," she stated. "I can accomplish a deactivation, but we do not know the specific location of the hypertech cache. Mr. Clay stated it was in Quicksilver's corporate headquarters--"

"--which is here in Baltimore," Emily said, tracing a circle around the tiny printed phone number. "Of course, they could have caches elsewhere too, but we have to start somewhere. I doubt they'll let us waltz in and trash the stuff, given they built their rep on the backs of the Orbitals."

Scout shrugged. "Broken into places before," he said. "Locked doors, alarmed windows, security systems, traps of any kind. ...armed guards. Doesn't matter. I can get in. I can remove any obstacle in my way."

"That's very badass of you, Soldier Boy, but you're forgetting a few things," Emily said, pocketing the page for now. "One, we have no idea where in the building the hypertech is being stored--"

"Search for it. Find it."

"It'd take too long. That's a lot of building to cover for just one guy. And that's the other problem -- if you want to play mister stealthy secret agent, we can't follow in behind you, and you need Una in order to deactivate any hypertech you find. *Maybe* you could sneak us in with you, but not if you have to search the whole facility room by room. And third, and finally... removing armed guards? How, exactly?"

"By killing them," Scout didn't say.

"..." he did say.

"Oh dear, and I almost forgot point number four," Emily said, sinking in her plastic seat. "The authorities. You know, the ones that will come poking around when all hell breaks loose, because there's no way to get us in there without drawing attention, because we'd be combing through the whole building, because Scout wants to play army fun time. The authorities who just LOVE tossing little witches into fires and dissecting aliens on network television. No. No, a thousand times no. We're going to have to approach this from another angle. We need to be *smart*. ...Una. Would you know the hypertech if you saw it?"

"Well, clearly yes--"

"This is me making a guess, but... would you know the hypertech if we were simply NEAR it, as opposed to staring right at it?" Emily asked. "Like... I don't know... scanners, sensors, tricorders, spinny laser radar dishes, fancy goggles--?"

"Goggles!" Una exclaimed, nearly knocking her tall lemonade over in surprise. "Yes, goggles! I can... yes. I can adapt my frequency-shift tracking system to project a visual display, and... hmm, I would require a pair of glasses, and some time to set up a connection between... yes. Yes, I think so. As long as I was within fifty feet of the hypertech, even through walls and floors, I would be able to spot it."

"Okay. Here's what we do," Emily said. "We don't bother sneaking in, or rather, we sneak in right under their noses. Pose as the cleaning crew or something, putz around through the building legitimately, find the stuff. THEN Scout can do his thing, since we'd have pinpointed the location and could be in and out in minutes. And then we get the hell out of Baltimore before anybody notices and starts warming up the stakes you tie witches to. Sound good?"

"Subterfuge!" Una exclaimed. "Sneaky plans and schemes! Just like a heist caper documentary film! We can be 'Una's Three'! Oh, this will be an activity that is most exciting in manner!"

"...right. Whatever disguise we make up? Una? You're not having a speaking role," Emily said. "So. We go, I dunno, mug some janitors, take their stuff, walk in. Make sense?"

"No."

Scout was the one doing the heavy thinking, now. Leaned back a bit, looking across the harbor.

"Passcards. Identification. Company association. Janitors need security clearance, and we can't get that," he said. "We need to be people who would not require clearance. ...or would be given clearance despite being total strangers. People a PMC would welcome... people promising them money for murder. Clients."

Emily nodded, slowly. Made a lot more sense, she had to admit. "That's great, except we don't have enough money to interest them," she said.

"Will this do?" Una asked, pulling out a two inch thick wad of one hundred dollar bills.

...Emily looked at the massive handheld fortune.

Then she looked at her $3.49 value crabcakes.

Then she thought about how she had to animate a bunch of chainsaws and fight off bandits and dryads just to get enough money to eat said $3.49 value crabcakes.

Maintaining as much control as possible, firmly pushing herself down in her seat to avoid leaping forth and throttling Little Miss Shiny Pants, she politely inquired, "Where.. did you.. get that much money, Una?"

"Oh, it's replicated from my Simple Matter Duplicator," Una said, showing off a tiny gadget from her pocket.

Her vision tinted slightly red. "Why.. did you NOT.. USE THAT BEFORE?!"

"Because duplicating local currency would lead to artificial inflation of your economy due to surplus monies being introduced without sufficient financial drains to accommodate the extraneous bills," Una explained, blissfully unaware of her impending death. "The Orbital rule of non-interference applies very strongly to the economic well being of your people. However, as we will no doubt not be actually paying this money to the Private Military Contractor, it is safe to use it as a prop in a subterfuge-- Emily, you appear to have broken your dining tray."

"Yes. Yes, I have," Emily said, her white-knuckled hands gripping two halves of a shattered tray. "Well. Okay, then. Let's go get Una's Three ready for battle. Before they end up as Emily's Two."

It took some cajoling to get Una to part with her ill-gotten gain.

The problem was in their chosen disguises. A cleaning crew could be simulated on the cheap... but they'd have more hurdles to jump to get access to the hypertech. Rich clients looking for a hired gun would be ushered in through the front door and shown the facilities... but they had to look rich. A girl in frumpy country clothing, another wearing a cloak over a Super Future Minidress, and someone wearing the world's worst Frontliner's uniform would probably not get the job done.

To be representatives of an indie settlement with a lot of green to throw around, they had to throw a lot of green. Una protested, wanting to minimize her interference in human culture, but eventually caved. It had to be done.

Of course, once she DID cave, "Getting Ready For Battle" turned into "Una's Super Ultra Exciting Earth-Style Shopping Adventure." Harbor Place had clothing outfitters aplenty, usually of the slogans-on-shirts variety, but a few upper crust boutiques existed to ensure visiting businessmen had somewhere to grab a new suit.

Scout was easy to outfit, even if he was reluctant to part with his, well, outfit.

"I wear my uniform," he had said.

"You can't look like a Frontliner," Emily had explained.

"I wear *my* uniform," he emphasized.

"You're not wearing your uniform. Now get in the changing room before I shove you in there."

In the end, he had given in, and was now wearing an Intimidating Black Suit. He was a bit too young to be properly scary beyond, well, his usual level of scary... but with the requisite dark sunglasses and a tiny wireless earpiece, he'd pass as a bodyguard for a visiting dignitary.

At first, of course, Una wanted to be the visiting dignitary.

"Absolutely not," Emily had denied. "Una, you talk like someone who ain't from 'round these parts. As in, several million light years away from these parts."

"Actually, Orbital Arcologies don't so much cross interstellar distances as they in fact--"

"You're going to play the part of my executive assistant, and that's final."

Fortunately, this role required Una to look pretty and stylish, and that seemed to placate her. It was her first non-shiny, non-ratty-cloak ensemble, and she took great care in putting it together. Finding exactly the right shades of white, gray and blue to go with her hair and makeup took longer than the other two outfits put together.

In the end, she went with a nice business jacket top, a skirt that was entirely too short for Emily's tastes, and pantyhose ("This material is quite unusual, in that--" and then Emily just tuned it out). She'd forgotten underwear the first time around, but Emily was VERY quick to point out that particular issue. Finally, a sensible pair of flats; Space Girl couldn't walk in heels and there was no time to teach her.

"Hmmm," Una evaluated, studying herself in the reflective mirrors of the boutique. "I am concerned that this assemblage of fashions have the negative side effect of distorting the overall body-shape of my posterior. Scout, what are your thoughts on this?"

"Eh," Scout mumbled, not really paying attention. Much to Una's mild disappointment.

As for Emily...

"...you look the same," Scout summarized.

"I do not," Emily protested. "See? New blouse. New skirt. Silk, see? Expensive. Trendy. Whatever. I'm fine. Let's go."

Setting up the meeting wasn't very hard. So many elements of this could have collapsed -- they may not have taken a Little Girl barely approaching twenty seriously. They may have turned them aside without an Eastusa-backed bank account to prove they had a line of credit. But fortunately, the cover story Emily had thought up proved to be a juicy enough bait for them to take the hook... no doubt they'd need more buttering up at the meeting the next day, but they could burn that casserole when they came to it. ...the cheapo crabcakes had obviously not filled Emily's stomach up enough to avoid excessive food metaphors, so once the shopping spree and nerve-wracking phone call to Quicksilver Security were through, takeout and a return to their FaePlace-assisted hotel room were in order.

Scout had declined additional chow, preferring to turn in early. Which meant walking into that abnormally-dark room of his, closing the door behind him. Una had insisted on changing into her 'relaxing casual sleepwear' on returning home, which now fortunately consisted of clothing -- provided the ridiculously fancy lingerie from her Executive Assistant disguise counted.

"...casual sleepwear? Seriously? And exactly what cultural artifact did you learn THAT from?"

"It appeared to be a travelogue about a cheerleader named Debbie, who--"

Emily sighed, and munched on her french fries. "Nevermind. Forget I asked. ...Una, seriously, we need to coach you on how this planet REALLY works. I'm just glad Scout seems to have a negative libido, considering all you've learned in your years in space is how to be a walking cliche of male sex fantasy..."

"It.. is not THAT bad, is it? In a manner of honest speaking, I do not wish to be making improper selections," Una insisted. "Although I do find the decorative aesthetics of these clothes appealing--"

"There's barely enough of it to be called 'clothes'!"

"Emily, please consider the alternative I have been utilizing for my lifespan. My people dress in very simple garments, hypertech-integrated, but hardly a fashion statement beyond 'shiny'. I am able to recognize this, now that I have your culture to compare it against. Such freedom you have, to personalize, individualize, express self through self-decoration!" she said, bouncing in her seat at the table (causing other things to bounce). "I cannot comprehend why you would not revel in such things. You did not even alter your mode of dress when we had ample opportunity."

"Why should I? Simple. Tasteful. Works. It's me. Doesn't get me much attention, and I like not being noticed, on account of how lately people who notice me usually end up trying to kill me."

"Such a negative view! You say I require an education about this world, but I would say you require an education about Optimism," Una suggested, being sure to capitalize the O.

Emily looked dubious. "I need to learn how to be cheery?"

"Well, I suppose, but I meant the philosophical standpoint," Una continued. "You see, with my people, two viewpoints prevail -- Pragmatism, and Optimism. Pragmatists see what *needs* to be done to endure and thrive, Optimists see what *should* be done to excel and exceed. Both have a role, one balancing the other. But *pessimism* has no place in either viewpoint; it pulls you backward. It says, 'this cannot be done' or 'this is how things always will be'. You assume that everybody desires your gruesome, horrible death, and thus it is so!"

"...Una, I don't think my attitude is bending time and space to change my destiny."

"No, but the attitude does mean that you cannot trust, cannot bond, and cannot achieve. Society is only as strong as the members willing to look to the future and shape it rather than be shaped by it!"

Emily groaned, setting her hamburger down. "HOW exactly did we get from 'You should put on some pants' to 'Emily's mindset is destroying civilization'?! I'll have you know that I... I mean... look, this isn't *about* me! We've got a BOY in here, you know! You need to have some self respect!"

"But I respect myself as much as is appropriate without pushing beyond the line of hubris," Una countered, puzzled at the suggestion.

"No, no, I mean... I... look, you're a girl, he's a boy, and if you keep this stupidity up you're gonna get him all hot and bothered, or... something..!"

"I have yet to detect any trace emotional responses of enticement from Scout. Are you concerned that he will force himself on me?"

"WHAT!?!"

"Please, I don't mean to offend! I'm genuinely confused as to where the problem lies!" Una protested. "I just want... I want to understand, Emily. ...I desire your friendship and for that there needs to be understanding, yes? Help me. Please."

Emily started to bark out a response, and stopped.

"Friendship?" she squeaked out, the word having tripped her up completely.

"Ahh... well... we are companions for the duration of this adventure... yes?" Una said, trying to find the right words, talking slowly. "I believe, as an Optimist, that we should have an understanding and mutual trust. A camaraderie, yes, that is what is needed! It will not only improve our performance at the task... but it will make the undertaking a pleasant one. ... but... I may be misinterpreting, and if so, I apologize... I am not certain that you... like me. Because I am misunderstanding things like casual sleepwear and the enticing of boys."

...slowly, Emily sat down. When had she gotten to her feet? When had she pushed her food aside, so she could lean across the table and shout angrily at the nervous looking girl? ...when had she started shouting?

"...y'know, I've always had this crazy idea," Emily said, swerving onto a tangent, intent to come around to the road again. Talking quietly, now. Seriously. "I thought... wouldn't it be great if Fae and humans understood each other? I wrote a book, once. It made its way to the internet. But it's not enough to fix the world's stupidity, and each time I tried to point out when people weren't bothering to even *try* to understand each other, they didn't even bother to try to understand that they weren't trying to understand. ...I gave up, after awhile. ...not a very Optimistic point of view, huh?"

"Ah.. no. No, that would not be," Una said, unsure. "This.. is a very personal description of your mentality and past activities. Are you comfortable telling a.. total stranger such things?"

"Oh, hell no. I don't spill my guts to strangers. ...guess I wouldn't mind telling a friend, though. And the point I'm trying to make is: if I want those two groups of whackos to sit down and understand each other... I need to practice what I preach and do my best to understand the crazy alien girl," Emily said... with a grin.

"I.. suppose so, yes," Una said, returning the smile -- with her own thankful, relieved one. "That would be appropriate."

"So. Let's back up a bit, and try again, this time without the yelling. ...no, I don't think Scout's going to, ah, force himself on you. ...frankly, I'm wondering if he's gay or something..."

"You are wondering if he is a colloquial internet insult against someone or something that is highly inadequate?"

"Let me put it this way," Emily said, trying again. "The reason humans take off their clothes around each other is usually to.. entice, as you put it. We'll turn this around, and ask -- are you *trying* to entice Scout?"

"Ah! That was not my intention, no..." Una said... pondering the idea.

"Right. Well, then. Acting in an enticing manner without intent confuses people, makes them uncomfortable. ...although Scout sure hasn't even noticed, much less acted uncomfortable, it's the principle of the thing. You should stick to REAL casual wear. And I'd be.. happy to help you find some, tomorrow. Deal?"

"Ah! Yes, this is a deal I am very much in approval of!"

Emily picked up her neglected burger, and took a big bite. Satisfying, and not just to her hunger. Una had a point... this whole madcap journey would be a lot easier if they weren't constantly getting on each other's nerves. If they could, to put it in sickeningly sugary and cliche terms, be Best Friends Forever. All she had to do was try to see things from Una's sky-high point of view, and have some patience. It'd be easy--

"What if I was in fact trying to entice Scout sexually?"

If the burger had gone down her windpipe by accident, odds are Una wouldn't know the Heimlich Maneuver, so some physical instinct managed to swallow it down sharply before her outburst burst outward.

"Whaaa?"

"To speak in hypothetical terms, of course," Una clarified. "You said that the problem lies in a visual message that conflicts with the underlying intent. But if the visual and the intent were synchronized, would that resolve the difficulty?"

"I... I..." Emily stammered, trying to think of what to say. Logic bubbled up first. "I.. guess...?"

"Oh, good! Then I have a complete understanding of the issue. Thank you for your assistance, friend!"

Cheerfully, Una began to finish off her supper.

Confusedly, Emily slowly worked her way through her own food. And wondered why she felt so alarmed just now. Had to just be a gut reaction of shock to Una's usual bluntness. That's all.

The next day was not one for comical misunderstandings, hamburgers, and lingerie. It was time to get to work.

Getting her game face on took longer than Emily thought it would. She'd talked so smoothly on the phone, to the anonymous secretary of Quicksilver Security. But holding that cover story up when face to face with whatever representative they sent to meet her, that would be another story. Her uneasy sleep that night didn't help matters much, either; she'd gone to bed well fed and spinning a bit in the head. Not good for keeping a sure footing the morning after.

The taxi ride to Quicksilver Security was uneventful, dropping them off in front of a squat three story structure. That was a relief; Una wouldn't be able to detect the hypertech cache that Mr. Clay had predicted would be here if the building was a skyscraper. The range was limited.

As they waited in the lobby to meet with a QS representative, with only a clerk tapping away to cut the silence, Emily paced a hole in the fine red carpeting. She'd made a mistake.

She wished she'd picked nicer clothes.

Una looked her part perfectly; she'd even added a clipboard to jot notes down on, and a pair of glasses with a thin hypertech coating that would let her identify the "frequency-shift" of alien technology, whatever that meant. (Emily made a note to ask Una to detail all the little gadgets and toys tucked away in her jetpack. It seemed to be a bottomless pit of tiny bits of hypertech, despite being far too small to store it all.)

Scout held his costume up well... he wasn't comfortable in his suit, which made him stand up stiff and straight. Good for a towering bodyguard type, the dark glasses and dark demeanor making him look a few years older than he actually was. You could believe he'd be the sort to come down on anyone who assaulted his 'boss' like the descent of man.

But Emily... well, she just looked like a slightly higher grade of prim 'n proper country girl. Nothing special. Nothing impressive beyond a silk blouse instead of a rougher backwoods fabric. She'd have to rely on oratory skills to get her part in this charade to work... and that worried her. Hopefully, whatever representative was going to meet them would be easily duped. Some stuffed shirt who handled potential contracts, and only cared about the numbers being waved in front of his face...

Ding went the elevator, and a muscular pile of a man stepped off, chewing on a cigar. His buzz cut would have buzzed audibly, that's how flawlessly army-minded it was. And a tag on his uniform shirt read *GRAVES*.

The easily duped representative was in fact Leonard Graves, CEO of Quicksilver Security, the bloodthirsty mercenary who personally led a number of ethnic cleansing purge missions.

They should beg off, find some excuse to go, and bail before they got one more foot into the building. But it was too late now. He was bearing down on them... all smiles. He'd grasped Emily's hand and was tearing her arm out at the socket -- no, wait. Just shaking her hand. It only FELT like dismemberment.

"Good to see you, good to see you!" Graves said, pouring the enthusiasm out like thick syrup. "Leonard Graves. You can't call me Lenny. Hah! I own this merry band of misfits, ma'am, and when I heard about your contract, when I was told you were waiting down here to talk to that stuffed shirt of a sales representative, I said to myself, 'No way, jose! This little lady deserves the star treatment!' So, how the hell are ya? How can we help you today?"

"Ghhk," Emily replied.

"Hah, don't know my own strength, sorry," Graves said, releasing her crushed appendage. "So. I hear the apple of my eye got hassled by ogres, is that right?"

"Apple? Eyes? What?"

"Olney, girl. Your hometown. MY hometown, too! I read the work order my executive assistant jotted down when you called last night. Any hometown girl deserves my direct attention. So, how'd it go down?"

He. Grew up. In Olney. Oh crap, Emily thought. She quickly gathered her wits together again, did the throat-clear, tried to grasp the situation again. Be the serious-minded, vengeful girl she'd invented last night...

"The Fae, sir. They drove ogres towards Olney last week," she explained. "Those filthy Grimms have always wanted to get their hands on our land. I TOLD the villagers, over and over, but nobody believed me! Well, I'd say the Fae proved their intentions, didn't they?"

Graves nodded, gravely. "I checked the headlines after reading your work request," he said. "Acres of forest mashed flat. One Frontliner dead. The army turned back, though..."

"We can thank our Scout for that," Emily said, half-truth being easier than a pure lie. "We don't know what the poor guy did, but whatever it was, sacrificing his life turned the tide. We were inches from being wiped off the face of the Earth by the... by the stinking tree-huggers of the Faerie Court!"

"That's the Fringe for you," Graves scoffed. "If the Fae had their way, we'd be pushed all the way into the Atlantic by now, eaten alive by the krakens! I say they're just lulling humanity into complacency by not aggressively moving on us... at least, not overtly. I wouldn't doubt the Olney incident was a dry run of some new war method of theirs. If we don't fight back, if we just sit around with the blanket over our head, we're doomed. The Frontliners are gonna lose the species for us by sitting back and defending instead of going on the offensive."

Emily forced a smile. "Looks like we're on the same page. You know my request.

I want vengeance. I want to strike back, and show them what happens when they even look at us funny. ...I understand you're the sort of person who can do that. You're right about the Frontliners; they sat on their asses and waited for the Fae to arrive. That Scout had the right idea, striking out at them. I want you to do the same. Punish them."

Perfect! The bait was even better than Emily thought it would be -- Graves had a personal stake in this. They wouldn't have to win his trust with money alone. A few more situations like this, and Emily might end up an Optimist, after all...

"You know what? Your money's no good here," Grave said, to add even more flawless victory on top of the victory the group already had pocketed. "You keep it. Olney's too poor to afford our fee -- I know you said you had plenty of green, but I'm not taking food from the mouths of babes. This one, this we do for free. You just say jump and we'll be on them like flies on a corpse. Nobody threatens my species, nobody threatens my HOME and lives."

"Ah... that's good, but I need to warn you," the not-actually-from-Olney witch said, trying to steer things back to the script. "Those ogres are bad news. If they've got more in the wings, you're going to need stronger ordinance than the Frontliners have. ...one of the selling points of Quicksilver Security is your... special hardware, correct? The ones you pose with in the ads? I've heard good things about it..."

Graves puffed out his chest, with pride. "Don't you worry. We bring enough gun to the fight."

"Even so... I'd like a demonstration," she said. The original plan was to be skeptical, to force them to prove their worth; she'd need a new tactic now. "Because... I don't want to throw you to the wolves, not an Olneyite. I want to make sure I'm not just making things worse. ...can you arrange that? I've just been *itching* with curiosity about your technology."

"Hrrmmmm..." Leonard Graves considered, chewing his cigar more, scratching chin stubble. "I can free up a few hours. Take you to the range, in subbasement two. Show you the works. Why not? Anything for a countryman. Phyllis?"

The secretary looked up from her typing. "Yes, sir?"

"Have Dennis meet us downstairs at the range, have him bring the samples from storage. We're gonna put on a show," he said, grinning. "Little lady, you know how the ole song goes, the rockets red glare...? Get ready to see those ole fireworks put to shame."

"Right! ...ah, my bodyguard and my assistant--"

"Hell, bring 'em along!" Graves said, waving a welcoming arm, gathering them towards the elevator. "More the merrier!"

Perfect. It's going perfect, Emily thought. *We're going to do this. Everything's going to work out fine.*

...why does part of me refuse to let go of the idea that it's all going to end up in tears and disaster, then?

A shooting range is a dangerous place. By definition, live firearms are being discharged there -- safety gear and proper procedure must be followed to avoid accidents. Even the most gung-ho kill-em-all mercenary type knows better than to disrespect the weapon in his hands by treating it like a toy.

Of course, most ranges are designed to withstand very small metal pellets being fired at high speed. Simple kinetic energy. This one had to deal with high yield energy weapons that were capable of melting sheet metal into white-hot slag... which was in fact the current demonstration.

Graves wasn't doing the shooting himself. Instead, his younger right hand man, identified only as "Dennis," had the large shiny silver rig strapped around himself, bracing the energy spraying nozzle against his forearm as it pumped a stream of destructive might bright enough to blind, if they hadn't been wearing eye protection. But even with goggles (thankfully large enough to go over Una's hypertech-scanning glasses) and hearing protection... the flash was intense, the roar hideous.

And Una's society built this horrible thing, Emily grimly thought.

In contrast, *Why are they using a mineral salvage drill as a weapon?* was crossing Una's thought. Her modified glasses showed a dull blue glow around the drilling unit, compared to the yellow glow around the other persons and technologies in the room. The blue roughly corresponded to the shift frequency she was looking for... as if the demonstration itself wasn't indication enough they had found powerful hypertech.

The all-clear bell rang after the metal target block began to cool. Headphones were removed.

"A beauty, isn't it?" Graves said. "We call it 'Big Bertha'. And that's not even the biggest bang you'll be getting for your buck. Honestly, we could dust an entire Faerie commune in one shot with the bigger toys... but what's the fun in that? And the practicality, for that matter. You want survivors. Otherwise, nobody's left to tell the tale and let the sparkly nature princesses know humanity's not to be screwed with."

"Oh, absolutely," Emily agreed, doing her damndest not to look completely horrified by the man's words. "Yeah. That's what I want. Absolutely."

"Hmph."

Given it was the first sound Scout had made since they entered the building, that merited all eyes turning to him. He leaned against the back wall, slouched, hands in pockets of his suit jacket. Not exactly the model of an at-attention guardsman. Seemed he was getting used to his clothes, now.

"Not impressed, boy?" Graves asked... but was still smiling. After all, this was an opportunity to show off. "Kids these days, nothing adults approve of lights their fire. You're a bit young to be in the security business. Get a few years under your belt, you'll come around."

"Didn't have to aim. Stand and spray. That's a fire hose, not a weapon."

"I'd say that's a selling point of this particular model," Graves said, watching as Dennis unstrapped the mining unit, returning it to the push-cart rack of various hypertech weapons. "Very little training needed. Even a complete meathead can do some serious damage with that thing to the enemy."

"Useless for close range. Useless for small targets. Useless for anything other than demolitions," Scout explained, coming quite close to Una's quiet objection in the process. "The ideal is precision. One shot, one kill. Even the strongest Fae can be stopped in a single blow if you know where to strike. Open the brainpan, the throat, plenty of spots will work. Quick and effective. Destroying everything in a two meter radius is sloppy."

"Being a bodyguard, no doubt you're keen on the fast takedowns. But we fight wars, boy, not muggers after your rich client's pretty little hide," Graves spoke, his smile slipping slightly. "Know what? Let's see your chops. There's an ordinary target board on the left side of the range. I wanna see this precision you're bragging about. Pick any toy you like from the mobile rack. Heh... Dennis'll show you where the trigger is, if you can't find it."

Clearing her throat, Emily tried to interject. "We.. we really don't have time to fool around," Emily said. "There's plenty left of your facility I'd love to get a look at.

For instance, these weapons; you have more than just this cart, right? Maybe if I brief you on the size of the commune, we can pick out--"

"I'll need a pistol," Scout said. "Standard reconfigurable sidearm, silencer modifier. It's my standard. All I need."

Without missing a beat, Graves selected a weapon from the locked display cases on the wall. "Normally we only give these to trainees," he noted. "They're not worth a damn in a real fight..."

Scout accepted the weapon, careful to keep it pointed away as he locked and unlocked the modular parts into a new configuration. It was a standard issue gun for military work -- one of the new models to come out of the original Frontliners think-tank. With a few tweaks it could be adapted for longer range work or for a faster rate of fire up close, depending on the situation.

"...a Frontliner Scout config?" Graves asked, curious as the last piece was secured into place. "Good for range and silence, but hardly any stopping power..."

"It has enough. Enough is all you should need. That's why it's called enough," Scout said, sliding his ear protection back on. The others followed in suit.

He stepped up to the line. Very relaxed. And
    crackcrackcrack
stepped back. Emily blinked a few times, not sure if she even saw him raise his gun...

After the all-clear, the paper target winched its way along the track, back to them. Scout ignored it, busy disassembling the weapon, to hand back to Graves.

"Looks like you missed twice, son," Graves said, smirking. "I only see one hole there. A well placed shot, but..."

...the hole was ever so slightly larger than a single bullet would have made. All three had gone through the board in the same exact place.

Graves took down the paper, verifying this, poking a finger through the hole. Nodding, slowly. "...fancy trick," he admitted. No smile, now; he was serious, as he looked up to the disinterested Scout, who had gone back to power-loitering. "Of course... doing that in the field, in the middle of a real life or death fight, that's different."

The boy shrugged, noncommittal.

"Tell me, boy," the merc leader ordered/asked, curious. "Could you really keep your cool and be Mr. Sharpshooter in the heat of battle? When the adrenaline kicks in, when the battle itself takes over...? Maybe you've seen some action. Got the feel of it. I bet you it's another story when your blood starts pumping..."

Another shrug would be the only reply offered.

I've SEEN him when his blood starts pumping, Emily thought, some Insight lightly poking at her through her nervousness. *When he was fighting Jesse, he was brutal, fierce. Only commanding him to stop broke him out of that rage before he went too far. But this... this is what he could be like if he's able to maintain self control. Which one is scarier, though...? A wild beast, or a precision murderer?*

...doesn't matter right now. We're wasting time, the witch thought-muttered to herself. *Una needs to scan more of the building, and these two getting into a swordfighting contest is--*

"Ah... pardon, sirs?" Una asked... meekly raising her hand. "I am vastly entertained by the war theories being presented, however... I would like to inquire as to the location of the.. privy?"

"--eh?" Graves asked, distracted from his slow, creeping evaluation of the 'bodyguard'.

"The smallest room?" Una tried. "The lavatory? The elimination chamber? The room of little girls?"

Emily groaned. "Bathroom. Where's your bathroom, Mr. Graves?"

"Ahhh. 'fraid we don't have a 'little girl's room'," he said, his smirk resuming. "Dennis? Escort the lovely lady to the little boy's room. It'll have to do, afraid. When you're done, bring her on up to the my office, then check the mobile rack back into the supply cache. So! I'd say it's high time we negotiate the contract. If that's alright with you, ma'am?"

Not optimal... they hadn't covered enough of the building. Hopefully, Una realized that, and was using this as a ruse to scan more of the subbasements. Without many other options... Emily nodded, agreeing. "Right. We'll sort this out so we can all get home before dark. No need to keep you after hours."

A solo mission! So exciting!

No, no. Not the right attitude to have. This was serious. Emily was performing admirably, holding up her false personality even under duress. Una owed it to her new friend to do the same -- to maintain her front. ...even if she wasn't quite sure what her character's motivation was, beyond looking at the walls to scan for hypertech behind them, and not drawing attention to herself. ...which she had done when she hit upon the idea to wander around and look, but... no! She was helping, she was doing the right thing. And at worst, she would simply visit the waste facility and return empty handed. No harm done.

Her temporary guardian, the young soldier named Dennis, was not talking. Talking was important, Una felt; it established rapport and understanding between two peoples.

"This certainly is an impressive facility you have!" Una said, looking at the featureless and completely uninteresting walls they walked by.

"If you say so, ma'am."

"And such, ah, fascinating weaponry! Quite unusual compared to what everybody else would have ownership for purposes of defense," she continued. "It's quite--"

"It's horrible stuff."

"--pardon?"

"That thing I was showing you? That's nothing compared to the stuff in the cache," Dennis said... his voice oddly grave. "Thirty seconds after we get to Olney our work'll probably be done. I can already tell what the boss wants to use, I've seen him use it before. ...hope you hate those Fae a lot. Hate them a LOT."

The tone was familiar. The sense of regret, of fear of the weapons...

Just like Andrew Clay.

"So, you... do not approve of the use of these technologies?" she tested.

"...you didn't hear this from me," Dennis said, pausing in their march. "But I'd rest a LOT easier at night if it all, I dunno, vanished. Gone. ...I've considered quitting, you know. After the things I've seen. But I've also seen how he feels about people leaving the company. I envy that old bastard who somehow got out with his skin, years ago..."

This is the opportunity! Una could see it, clear as day. Here was someone who felt as she did -- that the use of these devices, many of which were being horribly misused as murder tools, had to stop. Here was someone she could trust. She could find the cache with his help, maybe even neutralize it all right here, right now!

She dropped her voice to a whisper. "If I said I could make it all vanish... would you approve of this?"

"Pff. Right, lady. And maybe I'll grow wings and fly."

"I do not see spontaneous genetic mutation as a likely outcome, but I assure you of my sincerity," she said. "Please. I am just as disturbed by what we have seen today. I have the means to eradicate the hypertech your company has in holding. If you take me to it... I can solve your problem."

Dennis gave her a look... exploring, pondering. Wondering if this was for real.

"I can decompile the alloys they are made of. It's a simple procedure," she promised. "It would take moments. Please... help me. No one else has to die at the hands of Quicksilver Security. Together, we can win hope for the future!"

The younger technician bit his lip. "...third door. The third door, down that hallway," he said. "Access code 7734. I'll.. I'll buy you time. I'll run interference. But after that, you have to run, alright?"

"I shall run like the mighty sombrero wearing mouse, my friend," Una promised, offering the young man a bright smile. "Thank you. I knew that Earth had decent people, ones who could be trusted. Thank you so much."

With promised speed, she hurried down the hallway -- and there was the door, just as described. A numeric keypad would allow access, and behind that, the goal they had sought out. The legacy of her people, a wrong thing she would make right...

The door slid open effortlessly, the four digit number entered without issue. Sitting in the cavernous room was a large pile of gleaming, silver devices... glowing bright blue in the lenses of her modified glasses. The hypertech cache!

She took three steps and then collapsed in a shockwave of unbearable pain.

Vision blurred, neck muscles still jittering from where the hypertech device had been pressed directly between her shoulder blades, she tried to look at her attacker... but only saw Dennis, with a smiling expression. That could not be. Dennis was trustworthy. Why would he be holding some sort of weapon? Why would he be touching it to her skin again? And again? And--

Her mind gave up, collapsing on itself, falling straight into the dark of unconsciousness.

Paperwork should not be this hard to find.

"I'd forget my own head if it wasn't attached," Graves joked, still rifling through folders on his desk. "I asked Phyllis to leave a blank contract on my desk, but I swear, that woman clocks out sharp at quitting time whether or not she's got any tasks left. It's so hard getting good help like my main man Dennis these days..."

The office was tastefully decorated, cavernous, and with floor to ceiling windows overlooking the city below. The sun had already started going down... twenty minutes they'd been up here, while he rummaged, told little jokes, tried to keep them engaged...

Tried to keep them distracted. Notably, from the fact that Una hadn't returned yet.

"If this is a problem, we can just come back tomorrow," Emily quickly suggested. "There's no rush. Those.. stinking Fae will still be there a day from now. I'll just collect my personnel and be out of your way."

"Oh, don't worry about your Orbital friend," Graves said, never losing his friendly smile. "We'll be taking care of her. Unlike my secretary, I believe in getting things done. No loose ends at the close of the day. It's just good business, you know?

The paintings on the wall were hung crooked, Emily noticed. When did that happen? When did the room start to tilt, for that matter...?

Graves waggled a little silvery disk between his fingers, pulling it from a desk drawer. "Hypertech. Is there nothing it can't do?" he asked. "Take this little gadget, here. Good radius of effect, nearly irresistible. Destabilized the inner ear, throws off your balance, unless you're in physical contact with it. Even that big boy of yours can't make a move, can he?"

When did Scout get a combat knife? Emily had specifically told him not to bring any weapons..! Not that it mattered, as it clattered to the ground, the boy staggering forward. Trying to make it to the desk, trying to reach his enemy... his normally passive features peeling back to a snarl.

She recognized the snarl. The same one he had right before he nearly killed Jesse the witch. His control was slipping...

"Sooo," Graves continued, casually stepping away from the desk even as Scout crashed into it, bent over the surface, scrabbling to reach him. "You two, in league with the Orbitals. I knew I was right to secretly bug Clay's apartment. We used the same type of scanning tech that your little 'executive assistant' used... just in case ole Andy was fibbing when he said he dumped all his gear, years ago. Who knew it'd lead us to a living, breathing alien specimen?"

"Yyy.... yuuuuuh..." Emily tried to curse, fighting for air, fighting to stay on her feet...

"You two are nothing more than blood traitors to your species, your country, your *planet*," Leonard Graves accused, no longer smiling. "Here's what happens next. The alien, we'll hang onto her. But you two, you get the standard penalty for treason to the state."

Effortlessly, he drew a silver sidearm, and put a killing beam of energy directly through Scout's skull. Dead. Instantly dead.

He slumped against the desk, limp... with a hole in the back of his head that Emily could actually *see through*...

Only one option. He was aiming at her next. Her steps were lurching, wild, running as she did not towards the desk... but towards the window.

Throwing her arms in front of her face to protect her, Emily ran straight through the glass window, soaring five stories above the city, plummeting to certain death in the streets below.

Somehow, despite the wind whipping through her hair, despite the falling glass all around her, despite seeing her protector killed before her very eyes... she focused enough to whistle sharply.

It was sincerely the first time Una had screamed out in physical pain in her entire life.

If not for the nightmarishly intense pain, which left her little ability to think straight given it was being applied via nervous-system stimulation, she might have found the sensation curious and new and fascinating and terrible and something she never wanted to face again. As is, it was only the last two of the five properties that mattered to her now.

Dennis twirled the shock rod once in his hand, studying it. "I can't believe how great this thing has been," he explained. "I know, I know... raw torture doesn't get much in the way of results. So sayeth the Frontliner manual on interrogations. Good thing I'm not one of those weak sisters. I say it works great as a punitive measure... and it leaves no marks! Your culture really came up with some great stuff, 'alien'. My complements."

"it-it-it-iit..." Una chattered, trying to regain some control, to not see double and speak quadruple. She nearly was thankful for the primitive restraints that kept her in her chair, as they also kept her from collapsing to the floor. "It's not that's n-not what it is, it's for healing neural damage, it's on the wrong setting, you have to--"

"Wrong setting? I like this setting. It gets so much work done! But don't worry, we've had enough practice with this bit of metal to know how much can be applied and over what period of time without leaving permanent brain damage," Dennis assured her. "We need your shiny brain undamaged, at least in the short term. This is just encouragement, that's all."

"You said you wanted it destroyed!" Una shouted at him, not intending it to be so loud, but unable to stop. "You hated it, you wanted it gone, you said, I trusted, you said--"

"Hello? I *lied.* You HAVE heard of 'lying' in that chariot-of-the-gods space station of yours, right?" Dennis asked. "Or has your enlightened culture evolved beyond such petty things as lying, money, power, desire, and so on? I hadn't thought all those crappy old science fiction books about pansy-ass peaceful interplanetary beings were really true."

Because he felt like it, he applied the shock rod for more emphasis. Just a little, this time, just enough to make her jump.

"You... you do not have to continually hurt me," Una tried to suggest. "It serves no purpose. It has no function!"

"It's softening you up. You're going to be our new golden goose, teaching us all about the hypertech we've recovered but never figured out the user's manual for," Dennis explained, gesturing to the piles and piles of gleaming technology in the cache room with them. "There's plenty of it in here, as you see. We don't know what it all does. You do. And you'll tell us everything. Today we're just, you know, flexing the muscle a bit. Pointing out how this is going to work. We own you now. Soon you'll want to tell us everything."

Emphasis needed? Yes, very much. He applied it. ...then, straining to hear... nodded once, satisfied at the choked back sobbing he was hearing.

Listening in so closely did mean he jumped as if shocked himself when the video intercom clicked to life.

A grainy image of Leonard Graves flickered onto the screen. "Dennis. I take it the 'Guilty Good Guy' gambit worked?"

"Yeah, boss. We're already getting great data out of her, in fact... you won't believe the results of the biometric scan I took while she was out cold."

"Oh?"

"Our little wayward alien? She's human. Human anatomy, human genome. She's got the blue-tinted shift frequency of hypertech, but there's nothing alien to her. I wonder if she's told her friends...? I wonder if she even knows?"

"They're both dead now, so it doesn't really matter," Graves said. "You think she's ready to start talking about the unidentified metal?"

"Mrmm.. I've been going a LITTLE overboard on the persuasion," Dennis admitted. "Sorry, sir. I suggest we take five, then resume. This cupcake's not used to playing rough; I think she's probably done, but more couldn't hurt. Mind if I take a smoke break, meanwhile?"

"This is a non-smoking building, soldier. Take it outside. I'll be down in a few minutes to assist... just wrapping up with our other guest. Graves out."

The intercom flickered off as loudly as it had flickered on, with a crackle of an old, unreliable speaker.

Prick, Dennis thought, rolling his eyes. He glanced sideways at the girl, whose head was hung low indeed. "Don't go anywhere," he politely asked, before wandering out.

In the dark, Una was glad he'd left and couldn't hear her crying.

It's very hard to cast magic while you're crying. Pronounce the sounds wrong, any deviation from the twisted Fae-speak of the Way and the Word, and the spell will piffle out.

"...Ꝫu!Puꙫ... Ꝫu!Puꙫ... bughh-- dammit..."

Emily the Witch wiped her nose with the shredded tatters of her blouse sleeve, before resuming her work, trying to close up the few remaining major cuts and gashes with page after page of mending spells. Not that squatting in a damp city alley at night was a suitably sterile environment to work in... but she didn't dare leave. They might find her. They might find her and...

She was lucky to be alive. Luckier than Scout, who had been-- she was lucky to be alive.

It was the first chain of thoughts to come to mind, when she knew she was about to die. In trouble? Magic. Need magic? Call for it. Where was it? With Pix.

There was no way he should have been able to hear the tiny sound made by a human whistling out a tuneless tone. But he was a magical creature, no matter how minor, and loyalties ran deeper than distances. In an instant, she was on her broomstick, desperately trying to slow down her descent... and landing in a dumpster one block away from Quicksilver Security as a result. Again, very bad for numerous bleeding wounds on your arms...

So was crying into them, dammit. *Dammit. Dammit dammit...*

The unflappable cheer of Pix had been firmly flapped, when he circled down to join her. He stayed with her, quietly, while she patched herself up. Eventually, he dared to break the silence between them.

"Ye'll bounce back," he assured her, trying to assure her. "Ye always do--"

"So what? Who cares?!" Emily snapped back, glaring at him as she snapped her spellbook shut. (His light dimmed a bit, under that withering look.) "Hose her off and she's good as new, but so what? I screwed up. I always screw up! He's dead, and it's my fault!"

"Ach.. Emily, it can't be... look, yer intentions were noble! I know ye. You do the right thing..."

"Hooray for me, I do the right thing! I get involved, I do the right thing, and it never goes the way I'd planned. ...for crying out loud... Pix, I DESTROYED your colony, remember? The bulldozer?"

"Ach, that place?" Pix said, his smile returning, as he gave a dismissive wave. "Bah! Wasn't close enough to the water, got poor sunlight. Ye did us a favor bulldozin' it accidental-like. Found a MUCH nicer hollow log to call home."

"That's.. not.. the point. My friends are... were in there. I don't know what happened to Una. --and Scout's dead!" she repeated. "...he wasn't as bad as he thought he was. There was something wrong, something broken in him, but if he'd just TALK more about himself maybe I could've helped..."

"See? Seeee? You want to help. That's good, that is!"

"I'd probably have just broken him worse by trying. There was some sort of fight inside him... and he's been losing it, lately. I could tell..."

"Well, certainly wouldn't have gotten better if ye DIDN'T try. ...Emily. Look," Pix said, getting serious again, while Emily mumbled mending spells under her breath. "Yer tenacious. I keep tellin' ye that. We admire ye, me pixie kin. Ye move forward. The Fae, we stay put, we shuffle aboot, we run in circles, but yer always' movin' forward. ...don't think ye want to just sit here and keep licking wounds. Don't think ye want to just run back to the Fringe and read books all day. Do ye...?"

"...I can't rescue Una. I'm not a combat mage."

"Hah! See? Ye *want* to rescue the lass. Like I said, bloody TENACIOUS!"

"And HOW? How do I do it!?" she asked him. "No, really, tell me how someone like me can pull of that kind of stunt. I don't know anything! I have parlor tricks, that's all! Stupid little screwy tricks that don't do anybody any... good..."

She was a block away, hidden from view in the darkness. Far enough, secluded enough not to be seen... not that the figure stepping out of Quicksilver Security, in the distance, would've even bothered to search for her. He was too busy searching his pockets for a packet of cigarettes, and lighting up.

Dennis. The one who had taken Una away.

Shakily, Emily got to her feet-- no. No, shakily would not do. She *firmly* got to her feet.

"Pix. Am I still bloody anywhere?" she asked, not taking her eyes off the bastard.

"Ahhh... well, yes, yer hands--"

"Good."

She smeared the blood around, especially on her right hand. Then, for added effect, left some bloody trails on her face with her fingers... maybe like war paint? That'd be good. Made sure to adjust her proper and beloved witch's hat with the less bloody hand, though... the same one she then used to snap open her book of simple utility spells.

Simple utility spells, nothing of any major threat. Not that the tin soldiers would know that.

The light aura was a very ordinary spell -- a similar effect to the one pixies had around themselves by nature. Make an object, even some part of yourself, glow. Adjust the color and intensity with a thought... for instance, turn it into UN-light...

Dennis was lighting up when a walking spirit of bloody vengeance emerged from living shadow.

The nightmare approached slowly, so slowly that he wasn't sure if it was a trick of the poor lighting in this part of the city, his own lack of sleep, or what. When the shadows took on human shape, the darkness turning to a burning red light of anger focused in the woman's outstretched hand, instinct took over. Scary figure with doom in its eyes, therefore, shoot it--

Several mild shocks of electricity snapped across his body. His chest, his right hip, finally his right hand. Numb fingers dropped the pistol he had drawn, clattering to the concrete sidewalk. Before he could scrabble for it, the arm was within touching range.

It was the stupid little girl from earlier. Only it wasn't the stupid little girl from earlier. It was a woman wearing a witch's hat, covered in blood and rags, holding a spellbook and what looked like some kind of murderous malevolence boiling away in her hands.

"I am a witch of vast, unimaginable power," Emily the Witch quietly spoke. "I can turn your bones to jelly, your blood to acid, and your brains to paste before you can blink. I am the Faerie Court's Young Mistress of Pain, chosen prodigy of Archmagus Lilith, and you have wronged my friends."

The namedrop did its job. The Archmagus... the most powerful spellcaster of the Summer Court. Even Graves knew better than to tangle with the likes of her. It was told to be as fatal as insulting Lady Summer herself...

"The only hope you have to survive this night against the rage of the entire Summer Court is to lead me to the Orbital. Do you agree? Nod for yes, or shake your head and die where you stand for no."

"Y-Yes," Dennis agreed, before realizing the witch wanted a nod. He nodded hard enough to give himself a neckache.

With a twirl of a finger, Emily urged him to march right back inside the building, staying behind him with her oh-so-deadly light spell at the ready. ...when his back was turned, she allowed herself a shiver. If the earlier failed gamble was over the top, this one was so far over the top and down the other side she might not come back again from it.

Coming back from the dead to death-in-life was never enjoyable. It was one of the few times the one who now called himself Scout felt genuine physical pain.

It was akin to a lash across the back from a magically bound whip. There was no whip physically present, but that didn't matter. The pain was real. Nobody can sleep through that, even the sleep of the dead...

He snapped awake, jerking forward from the standard punishment for failing to live up to the standards set upon him-- and was jerked backwards, numerous chains holding him down to the medical examination table. Immediately he was straining against them, the cold iron staying firm, wrists and ankles but also additional loops and strands crisscrossing his bare chest.

Graves was taking no chances. He didn't even stand near the table, preferring to stay near the door, in case he had to bail out of the brightly lit medical chamber in a hurry. Not that he looked worried. He'd even taken time to fetch a fresh cigar for himself. (Being the owner meant you were the exception to every rule.)

"I should have believed the hype," Leonard Graves said, nearly apologetic. "I'd heard stories of an unkillable boy with Fae powers in a Frontliner's uniform. Someone given over to the Wild Hunt. A vicious bastard who's killed Fae and Human alike, a slaughtering madman. That sound familiar, boy?"

Scout bared his teeth, growling... then quickly worked himself down to normal. Apathy. Detachment. All the emotional controls he'd developed for himself. "You're incorrect," he said, his voice calm again, as if nothing of interest had happened. "I hunt those who hunt. Nothing more. I keep control."

"Uh-huh. I'd give you the whole 'we're more alike than unalike' thing, but obviously you'd disagree. Frankly? It doesn't matter what your reasoning is, or what mine is. You kill out of some weird sense of brutal justice, I kill for money and kicks, whatever, I'll concede the point. But I know your kind -- I've *fought* your kind. You're as much a killer as I am. Far too dangerous to let live. Which is a problem, given you already lack a pulse, from what the biometrics tell me. You're supposedly just as dead that redheaded twerp I blasted through my window. Bet she made a real nice splatter on the street below... "

...that managed to twitch through his emotional control. One hand made a fist.

"But with your kind, being dead doesn't seem to matter much, does it?" Graves asked. "The hole I melted through your head -- and my desk, you know, a damn good desk ruined -- it only *temporarily* killed you. The wound sealed up a minute later. After that, I knew what you really were: a miserable little hunting dog for the Winter Court. I've dealt with your kind before."

"...you know a lot about how to kill the Fae," Scout said. "But not how to kill me."

"Yet. *Yet*, boy. I've always wanted to find a way to put one of your lot down for good, and now I've got you to experiment on. So, you'll stay here, nice and secure while we work on you. But I don't want to learn your magically enhanced nature, your self-revival power, beyond learning a way to stop it. I don't trust Fae weapons, I trust science and human engineering. I'll get the power I want from the alien instead. Nighty night, boy."

His fingers reached for the light switch.

"You're about to make a serious mistake."

...Graves paused, smirking to him. "Oh? That so?"

"Yes. I hunt the hunters," Scout reminded him. "I leash the Wild Hunt, and usen it only to murder the murderers. You say you killed 'the redhead'? All you've done is kill yourself. But release Una, and I'll force myself to show you the mercy Emily would've wanted from me. ...do what you're about to do... and I'll do what I do. I won't bother trying to stop it."

"Those are iron chains, race traitor. You can't break them with Fae magic. I know a bluff when I see one."

"Choose now. Live or die?"

"...whatever."

Graves flicked the examination room lights out with the flip of a finger, and closed the door behind him.

The room plunged into shadow.

One minute later, the empty chains clattered to the surface of the examining table.

The two marched in near silence down the gray corridors of the building. Gray was a fine color, very properly military, except when only being lit by a glowing red fist of rage. Then it's the exact opposite of what you want, as it results in returning a sickly dull glow of menace.

So far, the witch hadn't blasted him to kingdom come. Dennis knew she'd have to speak in order to launch a spell, but he'd have no chance to silence her with a caster hold or anything of the like before she could turn him inside out... not if she was in with the Archmagii. Because he very much enjoyed breathing, compliance with her demands would have to do, until he could get the upper hand.

"You know... I'm glad you came here," he tried. "It's Graves. He's gone crazy... you know how many people he's had me kill with those horrible weapons? You don't have to threaten me; I'd be happy to help you get rid of--"

"I don't recall asking for crocodile tears," Emily spoke, continuing to trail behind him, spellbook at the ready. "I don't believe a word you say. You work for scum, you are scum. If you weren't you would've gotten out of the business like Clay did."

"You don't think I've tried?!" Dennis exclaimed, giving her a desperate look over his shoulder. "He'd kill me. He'd kill my family. My high school sweetheart, my baby boy..."

"Oh yeah? Where's your wedding ring?"

"...we're a modern couple. We don't believe in material--"

"I bet you pulled this act on her. You exploited her trusting nature," Emily glowered, Insight hitting her at a foul time. "You say one more word that's not in the subset of 'Here', 'is', or 'Una', and I tear you into component molecules, then I tear THOSE into atoms, then I tear THOSE into bits that will make physicists scratch their heads. Keep walking. And silently."

Dennis nodded once, and complied. Go along with it. Don't try the usual tricks, just roll, and wait for your opening. Then kill her. No, take her down, shock her, hurt her. This insolent race traitor was gonna get what she had coming... and he was going to enjoy it--

Drat. They had arrived.

"Here is Una. ...I'm just keying the number into the pad to open the door," he said, quietly. "That's all. Okay?"

"If gas vents open up or a turret pops out, my Death Curse will not be the end of you," Emily warned.

"...it won't?"

"No. You'll only spend rest of your life wishing it was. Now open the door."

He keyed the sequence in, gritting his teeth. "You are one scary bitch, you know that, right?" he grumbled to her.

"Not really, but I'm learning."

The door slid open... and Emily saw what the soldier had done to her friend.

I don't believe in killing, she reminded herself. So she contented herself with rearing one leg back, and swinging it forward with all the might she had in her body.

Her foot sank inches into his crotch, from behind. Dennis actually lifted off the ground several inches, his high pitched scream of agony cut off a moment after it began -- his brain simply gave up trying to process the pain and shut down. He slumped to the ground, unconsciously clutching between his legs, curling into a ball. Which made it a lot easier for Emily to roll him into the room and shut the door behind her.

She was kind enough to roll him on his stomach, so when he inevitably threw up, he wouldn't choke to death. She was a merciful witch, after all.

Emily holstered her spellbook and rushed into the room, producing the lockpick-charm from around her wrist. A familiar gesture, shaping it in her fingers, getting it primed and ready for an escape. She worked the handcuffs that held Una to her chair, trying to contain her anger long enough to get the job done. Remove the cuffs, help Una to her feet, use the cuffs to secure Dennis. Try to get Una together long enough to deactivate the hypertech. And then run, and run, and don't stop running until you're out of the concrete jungle and into the safety of the forests...

But Una wasn't in enough shape to stand properly, much less perform some mysterious scienc-y type ritual. Her legs were wobbly, shaking, muscles spasming like her nervous system was misfiring. "E.. em em em em..." she tried to say, in a jittering voice. "Hurt. He hurt he didn't have to but he..."

I DON'T believe in killing, Emily had to remind herself again, glaring at the crumpled form of Dennis. She put on her most compassionate face possible before turning back to Una. "I know. ...I'm sorry. But we've got to work. Can you deactivate the hypertech, Una? Just do that and I swear I'll get us out of here, and you can sleep for a week--"

"Here's another option -- sleep when you're dead."

Emily twisted her head around, staring down the business end of a long barreled energy weapon. Graves.

Escape? She had one copy of the Escape spell left, tattooed on her forearm... on the arm she was using to support Una. She could drop Una and bail. Not that she would, but she could. And she could... not do much else.

This time, Leonard Graves wasn't keen on taunting before shooting. ...at least, not any more than he had.

Exactly one second before he would have pulled the trigger, all power to the building went out, plunging the room into absolute darkness.

Cursing loudly, he fired anyway -- the cutting beam of light providing a flash-snapshot shot of the room, of Emily diving for the floor, pulling Una with her. The shot had missed wide.

Another shot, at where Emily would've hit the ground... but she'd already rolled out of the way.

The third shot went wide when he realized there was someone standing right in front of him, face to face.

"You were warned," Scout reminded him, in a voice no louder than a wolf's breath.

There was no light, only the sound of it, the meaty noise of fists pounding on flesh. Feet running, bodies hitting walls, then... the door sliding open. Graves had found the exit, and from the squeaking sound of Scout's fancy suit shoes on the floor, he would not be getting away unchallenged.

Emily pulled Una in close, but leaned up, trying to call out as loud as she could.

"Scout? SCOUT! Don't... you don't have to do this! You don't HAVE to kill him!!"

No response.

Next week, *next* week he would install more locking doors. All sorts of them, sealing doors, airtight doors, doors with combination locks. Riot barriers. Just the thing for cutting off pursuit. Just the thing he hadn't the foresight to include in his high tech underground military compound, of course.

By now, Leonard Graves had pulled on a pair of night vision goggles. He always kept them in his utility pack, always kept the utility pack on. A day at the office could very well explode into a firefight, and very well had. One thing that had gone right today, at least.

This meant he was no longer running into walls -- he was running for his life, cutting a path to salvation. The parking garage. Plenty of cover, plenty of space, just the spot for a fight. He knew the place well, and the whacko chasing him did not... he'd punch the Fae-fanboy's ticket in short order, chain him up again, and be home in time for a midnight snack. No problem. Right.

He burst into the garage, rolling behind a company car, firearm at the ready...

...and nothing came out of the open door behind him. The brat hadn't given up, no way, not that one. So where was--

"Behind you."

Graves turned on instinct and fired. It took a split second for his goggles to compensate for the flash from his energy weapon, which meant he couldn't see the fist that slammed into his rib cage. Feel it, sure, that was a given.

What he COULD see now, that was a horrible thing to see. It wasn't.. QUITE the Scout. It was a thing in his shape, but all tooth and claw, all *eyes*. Some hideous thing spawned of the darkness, stepping through shadow, emerging wherever it pleased...

He rolled with the hit, spinning out of the way and between two cars, evading again. The deformed thing appeared on the other side of the garage, then perched on top of a car, then gone again...

"Freak!!" Graves shouted, enraged at the sheer... unfairness of it. "Monster!"

"Yes. Freak. Monster. Both of us."

Center yourself, dammit, Graves thought. *You know his type, how they move. Shadow-step. It uses the darkness. That means...*

He changed hiding places. Instead of crouching next to the car, which would've provided cover in a firefight... he used his company key ring to remotely start up the car and unlock the doors. Waved the ring around madly, triggering every company car in range. The light sensors in the cars would detect night-like conditions, and automatically turn headlights on...

He timed it well, sliding his night goggles up just as the lights were coming on, casting one wall of the garage as broad daylight.

"Can't jump at me through the light, can you? You move in the dark," Graves pointed out, weapon drawn, lying in wait in the brightness. "You know, any second now the emergency generators will be on. This whole place will be like Christmas. I can wait you out--"

A hand grasped his ankle, reaching from the shadows beneath the nearest car.

Graves vanished from sight. His weapon went flying through the air, spinning end over end... clattering to a halt on the concrete near the door.

At Emily's feet.

"SCOUT! Listen to me!" she shouted into the garage, hoping it wasn't too late. (She had to help Una along, not wanting to leave her behind in the same room as that little bastard Dennis.) "If you kill him, we can't ask him where he got the hypertech! --if you kill him you'll just be what Lady Winter wants you to be!!"

...she hoped the lack of bloodcurdling screaming meant he was considering this, rather than tearing Graves limb from limb.

Two figures emerged from under the car... Scout, looking considerably less wild now, despite still being stripped to the waist and holding Graves in a vicious looking locking hold. "...you knew?" he asked, simply, as if engaging in a boring conversation.

"I.. I figured it out, yeah," Emily said. "The scars on your back. I saw them for a split second, back in the cargo room. Marks from the Queen's whip, whenever her Winterhounds displease her. ...jumping through shadows and surviving being shot in the head were also big hints."

"Then you know I have to kill him," Scout explained, as Graves's face started to turn blue. "He's my prey. If I don't hunt the hunters, if I don't focus on that, my control could slip and I could start stalking innocents. I could end up hurting you..."

"I'm... going to choose to believe you won't do that," Emily said. "I trust you. And you should trust yourself, for a change."

...Scout noticed Graves raising his hand politely, as if asking teacher if he could speak during class. He loosened the hold... not enough to let the man go, just enough to clear his airway.

The elder soldier spoke quickly. "I-If you let me live I'll tell you all about where I got the hypertech and I'll let you destroy what I have! ...there. There, you HAVE to let me live, like the lady says. You win, okay?! I lose! Hunt's over! ...please?"

There was one sickening pause... before Scout slammed him up against the nearest car.

"Talk," the boy ordered.

Una had just enough strength in her to deactivate the hypertech cache. All it took was a series of precision touches to their featureless controls... with that, the metal weapons and things-used-as-weapons went away, some crumbling to dust, some falling apart, others melting into slag.

Graves gave his testimony. Emily recorded it in her book. There was no more hostility, no more anger. All of them were tired and wanted this incident behind them as fast as possible. Scout helped Emily ease Una out of the building and into a taxi...

and soon, they were back in their FaePlace apartment. Risky, not leaving the city, but Emily refused to move Una any more than they had to.

They left the door to her room open, as the Orbital girl slept in her clothes, uncomfortable and still twitching occasionally with a muscle spasm. Emily spared a glance occasionally... making sure Una was there. And willingly feeling a twinge of guilt each time she did so.

...something about the FaePlace reflected Una's pain. Her room was still the super-amazing place of space wonder... but wasn't shining quite as brightly. The metal had been dulled. The overhead lights were dimmer. The place reflected the owner, sullen, hurt.

"I hope she'll be okay," Emily wished aloud

"She doesn't seem permanently damaged," Scout noted, shuffling one piece on the game board forward.

"That's not what I meant. Earth was... a big vacation, for her," Emily explained. "Play dress up, scheme little schemes, use her toys. Danger, sure, I don't but think she ever considered people would WANT to hurt her. Or would actually hurt her, for that matter."

"...getting hurt doesn't matter. We learn. We adapt. We endure and hunt again."

That could make the witch smile. "I'll agree to that one. ...ah... hm. I'll move my bishop... here. Your move."

Scout frowned at the arrangement of white to black pieces. (Naturally, he was fielding the black.) "I don't like games," he said for the third time that night, as he took a piece with his knight.

"No, but some part of you likes to compete and conquer. It's the whole reason you're afraid of yourself," she said. "So, we're going to funnel that constructively rather than fatally from now on. No more hiding from who you are, and no more hiding from us. I'm not turning my back on you."

"Because I could kill you?"

"No, I mean... I mean I'm not turning my back on your problems. Because -- and you may end up regretting being subjected to my personal idealism -- I want to do the right thing and help you. After all... you don't enjoy it, do you? Being a Winterhound."

"...I could enjoy it. She wants me to," Scout admitted, lowering his voice a bit, as he stared at the board. "But... you're right. I don't *want* to enjoy it. I get... lost, when I slip into the Wild Hunt. I need to constantly control myself, contain the instincts... "

"You know, Lady Winter doesn't usually turn humans into her hounds. Care to tell me how this happened to you?"

"...no. Not yet."

"I'll get you talking yet, boy. You cannot hide from my witchy ways," Emily warned, waggling a pawn at him. "Mark my words. Oh, and check. Hah! Get out of that one--"

"Checkmate," Scout replied, before he even swapped the final pieces. "I win."

"...what? No no, wait, hang on, you... that... oh. Damn."

As soon as one game had ended, he was setting up for another, lining up his pieces. "Guess I'll play again," he decided. "I think I'm learning, Emily. "

...she gave him a bright smile.

"Yeah. I think you are."

end.a02

mir-a-cle [mir-uh-kuhl]
-noun
1. an extraordinary event or effect that surpasses all
known human or natural powers and is often ascribed to a
supernatural cause.

Two jackets weren't enough. Three, now, three might've done it. Even with multiple layers, flying at night and so far to the north meant freezing your butt off. Not a good thing to do when your butt was riding a broomstick.

Transportation options had dried up completely. The trains out of Eastusa didn't run this far out, not one time zone over and so close to Canada. No major roads went where they were going, save for the ruined ones that had fallen into disrepair, connecting dead towns to other dead towns. Ground level was too dangerous to walk through, with numerous Fae settlements to deal with... Emily could probably negotiate safe passage, as the forests were primarily Summer Court, but after tangling with Jesse/Runeblade she didn't want to attract any major attention from the Fae.

So, flying it would have to be. She could tough it; she'd covered hundreds of miles on her own, before. At least this time she had Una to fly with. Una, who could wear her shiny dress with plenty of perfect, perfect skin exposed and oddly not feel the touch of cold darkness that came with northern nights. Hypertech, of course.

Note to self: Research a damn body warmth spell, Emily thought bitterly, not liking being shown up by Future Girl.

Still... it wasn't her showy friend or her own chill that was worrying her most. It was the third member of their party... the one somewhere below them, on foot.

Scout had assured the girls that he would be fine, that he could cover great distances "shadow stepping" between one patch of darkness and the next. He'd be able to match them for speed, and would meet them at the city limits by dawn... but that didn't keep Emily from worrying. Scout, alone in the deep woods, letting his Winterhound instinct carry him. Not a good formula.

"He'll meet us there," Emily muttered to herself. "It'll be fine. Quit worrying..."

"You are.. concerned for Scout?" Una replied, hearing her mumblings despite the rushing wind around them. "You care for him, yes?"

"He's just a hard luck case, that's all. I take hard luck cases. That's all," Emily repeated, waving a hand dismissively. (She'd long since mastered one handed broom flight. It made reading during long trips a lot easier.) "Plus I don't like him relying on the Winter's Gift to move around like this. It distances him from his humanity. ...y'know... I've been wanting to talk to you about this. I need your help with Scout -- we need to encourage him to accept his humanity. It's high time someone made an effort at humanizing him instead of treating him like a wild animal. You should engage him socially."

Una pondered this. "Social engagement...? A manner of which you mean...?"

"Y'know... interaction. Like he's a normal, healthy human boy," Emily replied. It was hard to put in words, especially words her outer space friend would understand. "Make him part of the group. Don't let him retreat into his little dark room, don't let him fade into the background. He needs to make an attachment to us. I think I've got a good rapport building already, but there's not much there yet with you two, right?"

"Yes... I see your meaning. ...and this is your suggestion, as his 'mentor'?"

"Uh, guess so. Yeah. I'm a professional human, I'd like to think I know a thing or two about being normal. Despite the pointy hat."

"You are simply his counselor, then?"

"...right. What do you mean, 'simply'--?"

"Very well!" Una decided, with instant cheer. "For the sake of our companion, I shall engage him on a healthy social level! I have been considering doing such, to achieve a similar emotional investment in him as I have in you. In fact, since we last discussed him, I have given the matter further thought. I have ideas I am eager to pursue which expand upon the concept, and may assist his ongoing development!"

The witch gave her companion a puzzled look. Which in itself was quite common; Una was often a puzzling person. "Uh. Yay? Una, you sure you get what I'm saying? See, what I mean is--"

"The city is ahead," Una said, pointing it out. "We should adjust speed and enact a safe landing at the designated meeting point. Let us rejoin Scout and resume our journey! Oh, I am excited about the days ahead!"

...that excitement was concerning. They were only a few days removed from one of the worst experiences of Una's life, after all -- tortured at the hands of a sadistic little army brat. She had awoken the next morning visibly shaken, nursing a cup of milk provided to her while repeating a mantra: "Optimism is to see hope in spite of counterexample."

At Emily's encouragement, she talked about what that meant, about the Optimistic philosophy of the Orbitals. It seemed to cheer Una up to explain how Optimists would let the light of hope guide them, no matter how dark the scenario before them. Specifically, that "One foul example of Earth's offerings should not cloud her judgment of the entire culture." If you gave up that hope, allowed prejudice and mistrust to bleed through, then that would lead you to see life in bleakest terms and relationships as risks. A good little Optimist apparently would sooner chew ground glass than stop looking on the bright side of life. (In Emily's interpretation, anyway.)

After that, it was smiles out of Una. Even her FaePlace room had been restored to its usual luster. Still, Emily had to wonder if the pain of that night was merely being masked, rather than dealt with.

...but that was the past. This was now. They had work to do.

Emily had to squint to see in the pre-dawn light. They had picked the spot out on a map (after Una had figured out how to find it on an Internet kiosk at the last train station) because it was out of the way, but by a landmark -- an ancient toll booth, no longer in service, near a stream. The tiny dot squatting next to the structure quickly resolved itself into Scout, much to her relief.

Much not to her relief, as she tugged back on the broomstick to bring it in for a slow landing, Scout was washing blood off of his hands.

As she came in for a landing, she must have been staring in horror, eyes wide. She didn't WANT to be looking at Scout like he was some sort of terrible thing to be feared, but human instincts had a nasty habit of overriding human desires...

"I was hungry," he explained. It was a prepared answer, one he'd no doubt been ready to present. "Just a deer. That's all. I didn't even notice it happen until it was done. But it was just a deer."

Not good. Not good at all. Both that he'd given in to his predatory nature so easily, so simply -- and that she was involuntarily treating him like an outsider. Right, then. Emily cleared her throat, composing herself, and reassured--

"There is nothing to be concerned about," Una said, moving to Scout's side. "It is a logical course of action for someone used to hunting for food, and there is nothing unacceptable or unusual about it. However, I suggest we settle your stomach with properly balanced breakfast foods after checking into the hotel. I know I myself am famished! Shall we proceed, Emily?"

"Uh.. yeah. That's what I was thinking," Emily said.

Dawn broke over the tall buildings of the Twin Cities, beckoning them onward.

a03 miracles

The Twin Cities sat on the ruins of what was once Minneapolis and St. Paul. The few buildings that were salvageable had been salvaged, and new ones had been built on top of the rubble of old, but plenty of hollow relics of those old townships remained. There simply wasn't enough money, time, or manpower to replace all the dead structures with new ones.

There was no good reason to resettle in this city, after the post-Pandora Event power structures shuffled the world map around. The Twin Cities were in a terrible location... surrounded by the magical forests of the Summer Court to the south, in middle America, and the barren lands of Canada to the north where the strange ones of the Winter Court played and preyed on anyone foolish enough to wander into their domain. They were too far from Eastusa to be of any value to them, and their independent status meant no government help in the form of Frontliners. They were alone, isolated, and surrounded by enemies.

Something in the citizens, though, refused to let go of the city. They rebuilt, steadfast and determined to make something of the rubble they lived in. Twin Cities had a fine industrial center now, not so good for the environment with cancerous pollutants, but very good for the economy as they produced everything from war vehicles to motor-assist carriages for horse drawn cargo hauling in the Fringe. Getting that cargo to buyers was difficult, given the collapsed infrastructure, but those who managed it reaped the rewards.

In later years, there was even a push for tourism -- the long abandoned but essentially intact structure known as the "Mall of America" being reborn as a center for trade and shopping. Since they were an independent settlement, there were no bans on Faerie visitors or Fae artifacts, which meant stores were as likely to sell talismans as they sold handbags or hand grenades. (Twin Cities citizens were a very survivalism-focused people.) None of the stores were owned by Fae, however. It was still a human town to the core.

Despite their successes, Twin Cities remained under siege. The pamphlets given to them by the security checkpoint / tourism officer explained in no soft words that they were to remain indoors after sundown, that the curfew would be enforced by roving teams of the citizen watch. Anybody outside during the dark would be escorted to the nearest safe location.

Winter crept down these streets at night, after all. And the Winter Court was very clever, very dangerous, and very alien.

What crept down these streets in morning was, in this case, a very grumbly witch and her two companions. Emily flicked irritably at the little tag, imprinted with the Twin Cities Watch logo and an identification number. It was dangling from her broomstick, whipping around whenever she took a step to smack her on the back of the head.

"At least they did not confiscate your Fae artifacts," Una suggested several times, trying to cast an Optimist's view on the harsh grilling they had given Emily at the checkpoint. "You can even wear your hat without fear! Truly, this city has a futurist's perspective on racial integration!"

"Oh, yes. I suspect next they'll be giving all witches little bar code tattoos on their arms and sending us off to camps," Emily muttered.

"I have read many fine tales of summer camp! I would very much enjoy canoeing and crafting macaroni art."

Ignoring her, Emily stepped up to their hotel room door, flipping her spellbook open to the chapter of FaePlace pages. (She had to clear the use of FaePlace with management. They charged extra for that, apparently, but it beat being kicked out when housekeeping tried to come in to change the sheets and stumbles across a magical homestead.) Speaking the Word with the Way, the door flickered briefly, and then settled down. Done.

"I'm too hungry and too annoyed to go rest my heels," Emily decided, holstering her spellbook. "I'm going to go find us something delicious to eat even if it kills me. Then I am coming back here, chowing down, and sleeping for hours. We'll find this mysterious 'Doctor Z' that Graves told us of later tonight and drop in on him tomorrow. You two settle in. Scout, crossword puzzles."

Scout nodded once. Since Baltimore, every day Emily had him do some 'homework', some sort of challenge to keep his instincts sharp without having to stalk anything living. It was a way to express his aggressive side in a controlled manner. Chess, checkers, sudoku, and recently, word puzzles. He didn't enjoy them very much... but usually found himself quite engaged in the activity shortly after starting.

"Please, take your time!" Una suggested. "We will be fine. Come along, Scout! I shall be your backup option if you require assistance with your crossing words."

Una grasped his hand, pulling him into the room. The door shut behind them.

Huh. Odd, Emily thought. But hunger jumped up and down in her stomach waving little flags, calling for attention, and she gave it no more thought.

Six across was the blood enemy of the Scout.

He frowned, tapping the page irritably with his pencil. It was just FaePlace stuff, a crossword from the magically-formed memories of Emily... part of her bookshelf by the fireplace he sat in front of. The fire wasn't real. The heat wasn't real, although it was welcome to his cold body. But the crossword... real or unreal, it was vexing.

"Hunting prey" was so easy to him. The art of stalking, of following, flanking, pouncing, making the kill... it was like breathing. He simply *did* it, and it satisfied him. Perhaps satisfied too much, too easily lost in the brutality. He had to make a conscious effort to dampen his less pleasant emotional surges, and focus his instincts on those who (by some ill-defined moral meterstick) deserved his special and very violent attention. But even with those self imposed limits, there was freedom in it, and the wonderful feeling of closure he felt when he conquered the enemy...

When the enemy was a series of white and black boxes on a page, taunting him, daring him to fill them in with letters... it wasn't as enjoyable. It was enjoyable to figure out the word, to fill it in and know that he had triumphed in some small measure -- but figuring out those words meant thinking in ways he didn't usually think. Which was the entire point of the exercise, of course; he was aware of Emily's goals in making him jump through these hoops. ...not that he had said much on the subject, but they were agreeable goals. But the *words*..!

"Aptitude."

"Hm?"

"Six across, aptitude," Una indicated, tapping the paper, box by box. "It intersects with Stimulus and Parry, as you see. ...ah. I apologize; this is your puzzle to solve, I should only be providing support upon request."

"It's fine," Scout said, jotting in the answer. There, yes, that did fit. That felt better, seeing that part of the puzzle locked down, regardless of who did the locking.

There was another puzzle here that was proving just as confusing to him, however -- specifically, Una's attire she had chosen, prior to sitting alongside him before the fire.

She explained that after flying all night, she needed to relax, and this was traditional attire for relaxing at home. It seemed a bit too... frilly and lacy and see-through and so on to be comfortable, but she wore it comfortably. With Una, Scout had decided, clothing was more about how aesthetically appealing it was and not about its social context. And clothing was something she had plenty of, having taken every opportunity to go shopping, on every stop they'd made since leaving Baltimore. Somehow, all of it fit within the storage compartment of her jetpack.

Perhaps it was what she said it was. It's not like Scout had much understanding of clothing. He preferred his uniform. It was the suit he died in, after all. It was... purpose.

So. Back to the fight.

"I don't like fighting words," he admitted aloud. "I don't have the right weapons."

"Pardon?"

"The words. Weapons. Haven't read a dictionary. Never did well in school..."

"That would put you at a disadvantage," Una agreed. "Perhaps you could study the lexicon of your language? I may be able to access the Orbital communications network. My reports to my father take some time to upload from this distance, true, but surely I can retrieve a study guide--"

Scout set the crossword aside, rubbing at his tired eyes. His tired mind. "This isn't me. Not what I do. Emily'll just have to find something else for me to try. ...I'm not able. I'm not like her."

"You are.. concerned your intellect does not measure up?"

"I leave the thinking to you two," he admitted. "You're better at it. Point me at the enemy, and I'll fight. It's all I'm good for, in the end--"

"Untruth!" Una accused -- poking him playfully in the nose. (...which made Scout go cross-eyed, momentarily.) "You have many admirable virtues, many talents beyond simply destructive ones. You are clever, as is expressed by the ways you fight. You use what is available to you to achieve your goal quickly, effectively. Decision making is indeed a strong suit for you, even if you have not had to apply it outside a battle context."

"Except when I lose control. Part of me wants to ignore all my training, and just... tear into the enemy."

"Ah, but training is something you have, yes?" Una asked. "You can have control, when you try. Like when you stopped Miss Runeblade, and that horrible Graves person -- or when you demonstrated at that shooting range. You can be very efficient in your tactics!"

"...tactics in war are not the same as tactics in life."

"But they are similar! I feel you will see this, in the days ahead. And aside from that, you are... adamant," Una said, selecting the word carefully. "You stand. You defend what you believe in... and who you believe in. ...when I was captured by that... by Dennis of Quicksilver Security, you were there. You saved me."

"I was hunting a killer. That's all."

"That was coincidental. I believe that you also sought to protect. That is a Frontliner, yes? Defense. Protection. Strength against the wrongs of the world, a beacon of hope! You have that strength, of character and of arms. ...a fine physique, a sharp mind, a strong personality. You are... highly admirable. I have taken note of these traits and find them very.. acceptable. Pleasing, even. ...and, if this is a subject you have ruminated upon... is your evaluation of my own traits acceptable as well? Pleasing?"

Slowly, Scout turned his eyes from the fire to the decoratively attired girl at his side. Something akin to the shape of a word, trying to fit itself into little white boxes, was dancing around his mind. What was this puzzle shaping into, now...?

"I don't understand," he said, honestly. "Una, what are you asking...?"

Una took a deep breath... came up smiling brightly, ready to explain. "I am engaging you socially via the standards of courtship, of course!" she confessed. "As noted, you are an attractive male with an outstanding number of qualities. I have found myself intrigued by your mysterious factors, as well! I would very much enjoy undertaking a romantic liaison with you, in hopes of forming a lasting emotional attachment."

"..." Scout replied. His mouth did indeed open without making a sound.

Una's cheeks tinted slightly red, before she could continue. "Provided you find me physically suitable for your needs, this may involve mutually enjoyable sexual coupling as well," she suggested. "I understand that my current attire is suitable for the purpose of enticement, provided that the intention is honest. The, ah, practice of such things, I have always been curious about experiencing firsthand. ...if that is a thing that interests you, of course! So. Are you accepting of my proposal of 'dating'? ...my dearest?"

Once, when Scout was stalking through the forest after a particularly cruel hearted Summer Court baron, he not been paying attention to his momentum as he flashed from tree-shadow to tree-shadow and slammed headfirst into a large boulder, stopping him cold. He didn't 'die', but the shock of it, the transition from something known and comfortable into a bewildering state of helplessness... it had stunned him. Stunned in the same way he was stunned now.

Una patiently waited, clinging to his arm. She might've been perfectly happy to wait like that for his reply all day, for all Scout knew.

".......I'm dead," Scout reminded her, because he had absolutely no idea what else to say.

"Yes, as you explained the day after we left Baltimore," Una said, recalling. "But your biological status does not seem to impede your lifestyle. In addition, I would be keenly interested in applying science towards finding you relief from this unfortunate condition--"

"No."

"While I am not a biologist, I do ultimately have the resources of Arcology #A076 at my disposal, which would--"

"No. ...I'm not yours," he said, pulling away from her, freeing his arm from her tender clutches. "I'm not anyone's except for one person."

"...would that be Emily?"

Boulder stun again. He evaded what that could mean, trying to stick to his original point.

"No. Lady Winter," he explained. "I am her pet. My existence belongs to her."

"I am not seeing how your current employer affects your ability to enjoy the company of the opposite sex. Provided that is in fact your preferred orientation--"

Even a predator knows when to retreat. Mind spinning, head having hit numerous rocks along the way, Scout quietly got his feet, and walked away without a word. Back to the comforting darkness the FaePlace offered him as his room.

Una was left sitting on the rug, blinking repeatedly, wondering what had just happened. ...she had approached this incorrectly, clearly. Her attempts to engage Scout socially, as Emily had suggested and as she had been pondering for some time, were unsuccessful. Some nuance, some subtle practice in Earth's socialization methods escaped her grasp. Perhaps she should explain what had happened to her friend Emily, and ask for suggestions on how to improve...

...no. She should not tell Emily. Una wasn't sure why, but she felt extremely nervous at the prospect. Una would simply have to figure out this puzzle on her own.

For now, she would retire to her room, to contemplate. Breakfast would arrive soon, and then the investigation into the hypertech source would continue. There would be time later. She could hold out hope.

Graves had a simple explanation for where he got his hypertech.

"Some little bastard up in Twin Cities. He goes by the name 'Doctor Z'," the cowed mercenary had claimed. "He sold me the weapons. Had a weird smuggler's route to get to his source... but when we got there, he doublecrossed me. We were lucky to get out alive with as much hypertech as we did after he sicced his freaks on us. You want to know where he's getting his fancy alien toys? You go ask the man up north."

There were the requisite number of back and forth threats -- i.e., if you're lying we're coming back here, I make it a habit not to lie to crazy bitches I'm sorry I meant witches, what was that I dare you to say that again, Emily this isn't helpful, etc, etc. ...in the end, with no other leads to follow, the group had decided to look into it.

Finding Doctor Z was both difficult and hard. It was a cheesy alias, like a mad scientist in an old movie, clearly not something you'd find in the phone directory. But any doctor using hypertech would stick out like a sore thumb, presumably, so a little inquiry into the medical community would work... call up a small clinic, say you're from out of town and have heard of some famous doctor, a Doctor Zed, or Doctor Zee, or something--

The very first clinic they called, the receptionist was quite... informative.

"That little witch doctor!?" she had said, with a scoffing snort. "You don't want to see him. I don't care WHAT his clinic promises they can do, there's never been any real scientific study into his methods. It's HIS clinic, you know. They just pretend it isn't. You're better off visiting us instead for your health needs blah blah blah blah..."

To verify, they'd called one other clinic and had a similar reaction. Go to the clinic at Twin Cities General. If you wanted something that was one step removed from circles of salt and headless chickens and dancing about, that is.

Given Graves's description and the low opinion held by every medical professional they had talked to, Emily was taking no chances. They flew up to the roof of the hospital late afternoon, on the shadowy side of the building. Once confirming the rooftop was clear (save for an empty helicopter landing pad and an unused basketball court) they armed up, got ready.

"It's real simple," Emily explained again, flipping through her spellbook, to get a Shock ready. "We sneak in, find the nearest unoccupied room. Una hacks the intercom system and requests Doctor Z report to the room. He grabs a Shocked doorknob, Scout pulls him in and restrains him. We interrogate him for the location of his cache, and--"

"I do not approve of this plan."

Emily groaned. "Una--"

"We are dealing with a biologist, yes? A man of compassion who apparently has been using hypertech to heal. A man of reason and sensibility!" she insisted. "There is no need for such aggressive maneuvers. If we are honest with him and forthright, I believe he will--"

"The last person you were honest with nearly tortured you to death!"

"Optimism is to see hope in spite of counterexample," Una recited, crossing her arms defiantly.

"Optimism is to fall into the same stupid trap over and over again," Emily countered. "And let's not forget how this guy uses smugglers, and tried to kill Graves!"

"I was under the impression you did not believe Graves's accounting of those events entirely...? And someone who opposes Leonard Graves' mindset is likely someone who would be right-thinking."

"Likely, LIKELY! You don't know Earth, okay? This world is brutal, the people in it are bastards, this entire city has been honed to a brutal, bastardy little point by a bunch of brutal bastards lying north AND south of here, and I don't trust this Doctor Z any farther than I could fly without a broomstick!"

"...uh..."

The three turned to face the white-haired young man who had just walked out the rooftop access door, a basketball tucked under one arm, balanced against the side of his white lab coat. One very confused looking young man, given he was looking at someone in silvery techno-dress complete with jetpack, a broomstick carrying witch, and a boy in a military uniform.

"Can.. I help you?" he asked. "The roof isn't really for patient access, you know..."

Before anyone else could react with shouting, violence, lies, schemes, or anything she disapproved of... Una stepped up and took charge of the situation. She didn't draw her energy weapon, didn't make any aggressive moves. She simply held up one hand, and repeated a traditional greeting, from deep memory.

"In the name of tranquility, may starlight brighten your path," she said, smiling tightly.

"...and the mysteries of space remain endless," the young man replied, too stunned to do anything but reply in the proper manner.

"Friends, let me introduce Doctor Z," Una said, turning around to face them. "Or, if I am correct, 'Doctor Zee', Z-E-E. Doctor, I am Una, of Arcology #A076."

The basketball bounced a few times, then rolled away.

"This... this isn't fair," Zee said, looking small and afraid, despite being as tall as Scout. "Not now. I've been here for *years* and only now do the Orbitals find me? ...I'm not leaving! You don't understand, I can help these people! I know it's against the rule of non-interference, but they're in such need of help, I can't sit idly by and--"

"Peace, friend! Peace," Una protested, trying to calm him. "Let us find a more comfortable surrounding to discuss. There is much information to share between us, which will clarify all matters at hand. We are curious about your use of hypertech, it is true, but... we will hear you out. I humbly request your trust on this matter--"

"Didn't we come here to destroy the stray hypertech?" Emily reminded her.

Una spoke quickly, disarmingly. "Father left this journey and its matters to my decision process and you will abide that," she commanded... nibbling her lip after saying it, as it was the first time she had outright commanded Emily to do anything. It may erode their friendship, but... it had to be said to put Zee at peace.

"I.. guess we better go to my office," Zee suggested. "I have some time before my next surgery. We'll discuss. And hopefully, you'll understand."

From birth, it was clear Zee would become a biologist. He was from a long patriarchal line of biologists, it was true, but even beyond that he had a fascination with the lifeforms catalogued within the Orbital data cores, creatures of a thousand worlds. Even the ordinary biology of an Orbital was fascinating to him, how it could be mended, adjusted, made whole after hardship. Granted, hardship was rare in the Arcologies, but accidents and disease were not unheard of. Zee's natural empathy combined with curiosity gave him a desire to know as much as he could about the healing sciences.

Even at a young age, he was acting as field medic when his family made an expedition to Earth. They were in the frozen wastes of Canada, tracking down the elusive Wendigo, a Winterfae of strange biology that his father had obsessed over ever since first seeing it through high powered sensory scopes from high orbit over the northern reaches. He wanted to study them in the wild, and if possible, capture one.

"Wendigoes?!" Emily exclaimed. "Are you cracked? You *voluntarily* were seeking people possessed and mutated by the Winterfae spirits of cannibalism?"

"They had a unique digestive biology that made my father curious," Zee had explained. "At the time we didn't give a thought to the dangers."

The Pragmatists of his home Arcology called the expedition foolish. They were, unfortunately, quite correct. Even straying off course considerably from their planned route, well beyond the eyes and ears above, they found nothing but ice, snow, and ruined cities buried in the magically enforced tundra. Father was about to give up, when in the ruins of Toronto, they encountered their prey... and found themselves the true prey.

"I don't recall much of that day, except the factual outcome of losing my entire family," Zee had said quietly. After a pause, he had continued.

Zee himself would have fallen to this ravenous spirit as well... he'd already taken several wounds, bleeding profusely. Death would have come swiftly, if not for slipping on a patch of black ice. Somehow, he fell THROUGH the ice... into a dark reflection of Toronto.

That was how he met Esrever.

"Ez-rever?" Una tried to pronounce.

"A Winter Court Faerie," Emily recognized. "Mirror-Lord, walker behind the glass, master of reflections, the one with no self image. Creepy."

Esrever came to him in the shape of a long-dead Canadian boy, near his age. He had been following them, curious about these people who bore technology like mirrors, silver and shining... and had decided to introduce himself before there were none of them left to introduce himself to. That might still have been the case, if he hadn't departed for a moment, returning with an Orbital dermal mender. Zee was able to save his own life with that device.

"He said it was from a secret place that only he knew of," Zee explained. "A place of mirrors, and mirror-devices like mine. Our typical visual aesthetic of polished metal apparently appealed to him, and he'd found a cache of hypertech somewhere in Canada. He never told me exactly where, though. Fae can be secretive, even to their friends."

Friends they had become, as Esrever brought him to a human settlement... the Twin Cities. There was no other option. Having gone so far off course, the Orbitals wouldn't be able to find him, and he couldn't get a message up to them. He was a young boy, lost in our world, with little chance to get home.

"I had to repeat to myself that Optimism is to see hope in spite of counterexample. This phase of my life, this terrible phase of loss and pain, would pass. There was hope ahead of me. I took strength in that, in knowing that as bleak and lonely as matters seemed, with strength I could build from there into something better."

A teenager in the Twin Cities, with only a vague working knowledge of the culture he had hung over all his life, had few prospects. He took shelter in abandoned buildings, found food where he could, and healed injuries of the other homeless drifters using his precious dermal mender.

That was where the idea came from.

"I could not just drift through my days. I could not weep for loss. I had to make something of myself. I was skirting non-interference already, by healing the sick who lived with me in those abandoned structures... and one day, I decided that non-interference was causing me an ongoing pain. I could not sit idly by with the knowledge of healing I had, in a city full of pollutants, full of cancers, full of industrial accidents. It went against everything I believed in to let people suffer when I could DO something."

He needed to establish a healing center. A hospital. A clinic.

But he had no money, no paperwork, none of the things he needed to pull himself out of non-person status. Investors would be required, from what little he knew of this world's economy. So, using the library's free Internet kiosks, he posted a request for investments in 'miracle injury healing methods'.

"It was a word that my fellow drifters used, regarding my methods. 'Miracle'. A dangerous word, I knew; all Orbitals were taught the risks of interference in a culture, in how hypertech could rapidly develop into a false godhead, making us seem like saviors. It was anathema. But I knew the word would serve well as bait. It would draw out the curious."

Curious people, like Leonard Graves of Quicksilver Security.

Immediately, he did not like the man. Clearly he only responded to the ad because he happened to be in town, and was curious as to what sort of miracle 'some dirty little hobo boy' could come up with. But a demonstration of the hypertech dermal mender snared Graves's interest right away. At first, he offered to buy the device, but Zee refused.

"I made the mistake of telling him I had access to more devices like it, and I only needed money to help me start my clinic," Zee said. "I should have just given him the mender. I baited the hook too well."

The problem was one of confirmation. Now Graves knew that Zee was an Orbital.

He knew of them, apparently. It was a hobby of his, following the conspiracy theory of the Orbitals from trace incidents when they had visited Earth. "Just a little investigative work to pass the time between jobs," he'd dismissed... but Zee could see through him as well as Graves saw through Zee. This wasn't about seeking the truth of a mystery, it wasn't about medical devices. Graves wanted whatever weaponry such an advanced civilization could have created.

Zee attempted to cut off the deal immediately. It didn't matter if Esrever could actually find hypertech weapons from the crashed ship; allowing Earthlings to access such things would be inexcusable.

Graves then politely informed the boy that there were a dozen soldiers in the room with him, he was armed with nothing but a glorified first aid kit, and this was not a request. Either Zee would provide access, or they could make him provide access, or he could simply die on the spot and be the subject of an alien autopsy.

With little choice left, Zee called to his closest friend in this world, Esrever, by a ritual means they had agreed to before. Seeing Graves keeping Zee hostage at gunpoint did not endear him to the Winterfae. However, not wanting the 'Child of the Mirror People' harmed, Esrever complied.

"The way through his strange reflection-world had been darkened, from the few times I had visited. The way to the hypertech source was slow, unlike the rapid travel I undertaken in Esrever's kingdom previously. He was planning something, delaying the travel. Despite wanting no violence, not even against these dangerous men, I dared not show Esrever's hand."

The group arrived at their destination, dimly lit, but definitely a large chamber filled with hypertech.

"Esrever told me he couldn't connect his realm to any of our Mirror-Cities in the sky, they were too far away... so I assumed this was a crashed exploration vessel, what little could be seen of it. He didn't have the right words, and guarded the secret too closely for me to make a more accurate guess."

On arrival, his comrade's gambit was revealed immediately.

Shadowy, crouched figures had been lying in wait. They were Fae, wearing tattered clothing and possessed of an animal cruelty, lips curled into snarls. Winterhounds all, hunting beasts of the Winter Court, and Esrever had bargained for them to deal with the men who would threaten his friend. This he explained after pulling Zee back through the mirror and away from the mercenaries, leaving them to their fate in that dark place.

"They survived, unfortunately," Emily noted.

"It both relieves me and saddens me to hear that," Zee admitted. "Relief that I had not led men to their deaths. Sadness to know they got what they wanted in the end... weaponry of my people. You say you destroyed their hypertech?"

"It will not trouble this world any longer. Do not blame yourself for this," Una insisted.

With the humans 'dealt with', Esrever and Zee made a deal. No investors, no outsiders, nobody the pair couldn't trust. Esrever would simply steal human money for him, using his ability to connect through any reflective surface to make the thefts simple. Zee didn't like the sound of that, but went along with it only if they could 'pay back' the money with interest, once his clinic was running and turning a profit. He kept accurate logs of every place across the country that Esrever had stolen from, and within a year, the money was paid back.

"...and that's where I am now," he said. "The clinic has been running for two years. We've helped dozens of terminal cases, preventing death, extending life. The money we make helps fund our free health care programs, so the homeless of the Twin Cities can get adequate medical attention. Optimism is to see hope in spite of counterexample -- to make something wonderful out of something terrible. This city still has its problems, and I cannot save everyone... but I cannot sit by and do nothing. I would like to think my father would be proud of my accomplishments. ...I would like to think that Orbital society could overlook this interference in Earth's culture. Will they...?"

Una absorbed the story, taking a half a minute to consider. Not much more than that.

"By law, by every standard we live by, this is abominable and must be stopped. True, you are healing rather than harming, but those lives should have ended and would have ended naturally without your interference. You have reshaped the course of this world's progress. There is no tolerance for that act allowed. ...which is why I am not seeing any reason why the Orbitals need to be informed of this data. If the report of your crimes is simply lost, then it is as if they never occurred, yes?"

Zee sank back into the chair behind his office desk, visible relief washing over his body. "...yes. I suppose that would be true. ...thank you, Una. I am glad you were the one to find me..."

But Emily shook her head, no relief present in her expression. "I'm sorry to break up the festival of hugs and back patting, but I feel a burning need to play devil's advocate here," she said. "If all of this is on the level, if this guy is some kind of walking saint trying to heal the sick out of pure goodness and shiny rainbows and sparkles and such, okay, fine. I'm okay with that. Rules are meant to be broken when they're damn stupid rules."

"Ah, Miss Emily, I assure you that I--"

"Not done talking," she interrupted. "I'd just like to remind my starry eyed companion that in the course of hunting down the source of this hypertech, we've been given completely plausible and heartfelt stories designed to endear us to the teller, which turned out to be a load of crap. How can we trust this guy? Oh, I know, he's part of your enlightened heavenly society, totally truthful, and so on. I'd *like* to buy that. But I want more proof than a long and winding tearjerker of a tale."

Una actually looked upset. A rarity, for her. "Emily! I--"

"No. She's right."

Doctor Zee rose from his chair, waving off Una's attempt to defend him.

"She's right, Una. One thing I've learned since coming here is that Optimism is hard to maintain when lies are one of the great lubricants of Earth society," he explained. "But I find truth to be a good counteragent to lies. I would be happy to show Emily how I am using the hypertechnology, to soothe her concerns. I have a surgery this afternoon which she can observe, if she desires. I won't hide anything from you and I won't take offense to your doubts. Agreed?"

"Agreed. Also... we need to get in touch with Esrever. The whole reason we came here was to trace down the source of the hypertech. As you've seen... men like Graves can and will exploit it, even if you're not being an evil little bastard. The source has to be eliminated or this planet's going to see interference the likes of which you can't imagine. THAT Una will agree to, right?"

Una nodded, slowly. "She's right. We can overlook this hospital... but we have to destroy the source. Will Esrever take us to it? Knowing how he seems to idolize our 'mirror society'?"

Zee considered. "I.. think we'd better ask him directly. If you don't mind going to the bathroom with me...?"

Crowding four people into the doctor's personal lavatory was tricky business. It was a very bare bones bathroom... but with a very large mirror, well beyond what would be needed just for washing up and making sure your tie was on straight. Clearly it had been designed for the purpose of maintaining the link between the good doctor and his Winter Court backer. It was a private bathroom, allowing him to converse without being spotted, and with a heavy sink you could step up onto if you need to... walk through the looking glass, really.

Not that they were doing that now. This was just a getting-to-know-you session.

Zee removed an ice-blue candle from his medicine cabinet, which sat alongside a dozen similar ones. He placed it on the lip of the sink, a spot normally used to hold a soap tray, but clearly intended for the candle. It lit itself, casting a cold glow around the room, not a warm one in any respect.

"Esrever, Esrever, Esrever," he chanted. "I would have words with thee. Please, hear your friend."

...minutes passed.

"...y'know, I haven't met any particularly friendly Winterfae," Emily noted. "Are you sure this guy is--"

The mirror clouded over with frost. Not completely; just a large oval patch. Soon, a 'finger' traced out words in the ice.

YOU ARE NOT ALONE, it noted.

"They're friends, Esrever. It's okay."

WINTERHOUND. SUMMERWITCH. AND

--the writing paused, as if the unseen eyes were gazing upon Una.

hello mirrorchild, it continued.

"Ah, hello, sir," Una replied, bowing politely. "I am Una, of the Orbitals. We come in friendship, although our request may seem unusual..."

The ice, which had started to evaporate, reformed. **I WILL ASSIST FRIENDS OF ZEE,** the mirror traced out, letters resuming their previous boldness. **WHAT IS YOUR REQUEST, UNA MIRRORCHILD?**

"It's the hypertech, sir. We need to visit the source, and destroy it. You realize how dangerous it is, having those items in your world."

"I agree with this," Zee added. "It's okay, Esrever. I have everything I need already from your secret place. The rest can and should be done away with. It'll also help keep me secret, keep me safe."

The mirror's frost faded away, leaving only the reflection of the four looking at themselves. The Fae was considering it. Eventually, the oval reformed.

THINGS HAVE CHANGED. FINDING A NEW PATH WILL BE DIFFICULT. IT WILL TAKE TIME.

He added, **A HEAVY PRICE MAY BE REQUIRED.**

"Well, there you go. That's the Faerie Court for you," Emily half-groaned. "I'm surprised he did as much as he did for free. Usually you're up to your neck in debt and favors before you get a crumb from them..."

Extra frost formed, for a longer reply. **IT IS NOT MY CHOOSING, SUMMERWITCH. IT IS SIMPLY HOW IT IS, NOW. I WILL DO WHAT I CAN. I WILL BE READY IN A DAY'S TIME. BE HERE. BE READY. O-K?**

"O-K. Thank you, friend," Zee replied. "Be well. ...hmm. It's for the best that we have some time to wait. I have a patient visit and surgery to prepare for, which Emily has taken a keen interest in. Ah... I can likely sneak her in as a visiting doctor from out of town, but I doubt I can pass that story off for all three of you in the same place..."

"Oh, that's quite fine!" Una said. "I have other interests. Doctor, do you have access to a bioscan unit? I recently underwent some neural trauma, and would like to perform a self examination, to be certain there were no long lasting effects."

"Well... yes, there's one in special examination room three. But I can't spare time to help with a scan..."

"I am not a biologist, but I have used such tools before during a seasonal apprenticeship. I will be fine for a simple task such as this! Come along, Scout, let us not take up the good doctor's time. We shall reconvene in the eatery on the ground floor, later today!"

...oh yeah, Scout's in the room, Emily thought. *I did it again. I let him fade to the*

background. Una didn't. I guess she's taking my request seriously to engage him more. ...I wish I hadn't ignored him ...wait, BRAIN scan?

"Scanning your brain is a simple task?" she asked, incredulous.

"I think you'll find, Miss Emily, that much you consider to be difficult is a trivial matter to an Orbital," Zee said, smiling. "So. Shall we see my patient, so I can demonstrate this fact to you?"

Zee had provided Una with a lab coat. It was enough of a disguise to get her around the hospital unimpeded, and given he trusted her not to cause mischief, she endeavored not to keep her curiosity about human medical centers from running wild. Just a quick inquiry about the location of 'special examination room three', followed by a brief journey there. While tugging Scout along.

He'd been quiet, far too quiet today. She wished he would speak, if only to hear his voice, but also to ensure his well being. Which indirectly played into her request. A little lie... or rather, only part of the truth.

The room was a fairly ordinary medical study chamber, human technology dominant... save for a simple silver disc on the floor in the corner, with a glass display screen nearby. It had been affixed to the wall by a metal arm, but Una knew that was a disguise. It would have floated there without issue if left alone.

"Excellent! I am familiar with this model," she said aloud, after closing the examination room door behind herself. "Its controls are simple, and I have some training in processing the output. Very well! We shall begin. Scout, would you please step upon the scanning unit?"

"...me?" he asked, puzzlement crossing his features. "You're the one with the neural damage."

"What, this little thing?" she asked, tapping the side of her head. "Honestly, I suspect no damage at all, and it would only take a moment to confirm that. A trifle I can attend to in time! First, I am curious as to your biology. Recall that I stated I was keen on assisting with your healing, yes?"

"There's nothing you can heal," he said. "Useless to try. I'm dead."

"Yes yes, so you say. If that is the matter, if it is so useless, then my attempt will be harmless, yes? So, up up, up you go!"

Scout found himself pushed along by the girl, who was actually muscling him over to the platform. Not that he was fighting back... he was too confused to really put up any sort of defense to it. He wobbled in place, before finding his footing on the small disc.

An ethereal series of tones sounded, as the unit began its scan. Silver light snaked up his body, a strange warmth that he hoped was indeed harmless (and useless). From his toes to the top of his head, it moved slowly... and then a warbly, broken clonking tone sounded as the display unit came to life.

"...well, clearly the Fae magic is confusing the display," Una said, trying to make sense of the strange symbols presented to her. "It seems to be telling me that there is both a massive system error and no error whatsoever. The pictographs are contradictory. Still, the basic scans are functioning! In my admittedly unskilled interpretation... your heart is not beating. You are indeed dead, in that regard."

"Told you," he reminded.

"But you are also alive!" she exclaimed, as if this was some huge revelation worthy of celebration. "Yes, your heart has been stopped, but somehow every other vital sign pulses with life. Your neural pathways are untroubled. Your digestive system is processing biomatter. Your reproductive system is healthy and functional."

"...what?"

"If I had to theorize... I would say you exist in a selective form of stasis," she decided. "Frozen a moment before true death, in a way that keeps you in a sort of... life-in-death."

Life-in-death. Just as Lady Winter had enjoyed calling his miserable state...

"You do not exhibit the biohazards of decomposing flesh. You are, for all intents and purposes, alive -- and despite your heart not beating, you are mobile and healthy. Much to your protest, I will declare you to be a living person; albeit one with magical maladies that are beyond my capabilities. Likely beyond Zee's, from what I know of our standard practice in case of terminal illness. Still... there is good news within the bad! ...does this not relieve you?"

"Doesn't really matter," he said, with a shrug. He stepped away from the machine, uncaring. "It is what it is. Alive, dead. I continue at the whim of Lady Winter. Science won't change that."

"That remains to be seen, Scout. I shall hold out hope!"

"Yeah. You tend to do that."

"Well, to unfortunately be callous, someone in our traveling troupe needs to do it," Una said, resting one hand on her hip, defiant. "Emily's mistrust and your despair require balance. I shall carry enough hope for all three of us!"

"...I'm not in despair," Scout mumbled. "You of all people can't know what--"

"You think I know nothing of pain and loss!?"

The sharp way she said that, without her bubbling upbeat tones, threw Scout for a moment. It was as if someone else was speaking. He considered replying, but had nothing of value to say in response.

Una glanced aside. "...apologies. I did not mean that to sound cruel. But... as much as I uphold the core of my belief, I think... sometimes you and Emily feel that I have nothing else but glee. This is not accurate. ...I have had unpleasant REM sleep cycles surrounding those events of Baltimore, as an example."

"Nightmares...?"

"Yes, that is the word. Intellectually I know that the event is over and done with... and I self-reinforce by putting the experience aside, in Optimist tradition," she said, meeting his eyes again. "But it may take some weeks for me to fully move through this. I have experienced pain and loss before. I recognize the patterns. They will make me stronger, in the end, if I allow despair to be a transitory state. ...I fear that you have decided the end of your process will be despair. That you will see nothing beyond it, Scout."

I think I'm learning, Emily.

Yeah. I think you are.

His body was not naturally very warm. Which made the warmth he felt quite strange. It couldn't exist, not truly, and had to be some sort of psychological effect. Nothing more. It would pass.

Scout found he didn't want it to pass.

A different warmth came as Una squeezed his hand. When had she held it? How long ago? Did he not notice?

"I will not despair for you, nor let you stay within despair if I can do anything about it," Una promised. "My dearest."

"...I think you should scan yourself now," Scout suggested. "We will want to catch up with Emily soon."

Una released his hand. She was looking away again.

"Yes... yes, I suppose that is true," she agreed. "It makes sense."

This must be what it's like to be Scout, Emily thought.

She was in the background. A figure that was accepted into the scene without question, but no attention paid to her. The white doctor's coat with the questionable status as a visiting physician it granted her was accepted by all those around her, by virtue of their completely ignoring her. No pointy hat to draw the eye. No bossy voice to command attention and respect. She was the wallflower, for a change.

For that matter, Doctor Zee was practically a wallflower as well. His "patient visit" was already in progress when he arrived at the comfortable hospital room. The child herself, chemotherapy having killed off her hair, was wearing a colorful knit cap to keep her head warm as she played with a stuffed giraffe.

But the doctor doing the consult was not Zee. From the badge, he was Doctor Stevens, a man in his fifties with salt and pepper hair and a serene disposition. Doctor Zee was, from the brief introduction Stevens offered, "an OR intern."

It was Stevens who explained that the therapy was not a guarantee, that they wouldn't know for sure if the cancer could be processed until the surgery was underway. Not that this mattered, the mother said in quiet tones, because there was no time and they were out of options. (She spelled the words, to obfuscate them, while her daughter played contently with Doctor Zee, who had brought a stuffed panda with him and kept the patient distracted in the mythical Background.) Nevertheless, it would be covered by the clinic's free treatment program, please sign these forms, initial here, and so on.

Emily followed the two doctors and various orderlies as the bed was wheeled down the hallway. Some faces grim, some with hope. The 'miracle' of the terminal case treatment center was always tempered with realism. Which seemed strange to her; surely this hypertech cure was infallible? Zee had said that what seemed difficult to a human would be trivial to an Orbital. Why the concern...?

In the background she remained, through elevators, through freshly renovated hallways. Deep into the building, past numerous other operation rooms where more routine surgery was taking place. Into a room with dim lighting... plenty of medical equipment around, but it was scattershot, almost like window dressing. The light had been focused on an egg-shaped bed, a silver egg. Hypertech.

After the anesthetized girl had been transferred into the egg, the orderlies left. And so did Doctor Stevens. The transition from background to foreground was practically tangible, when they were the only people left... aside from a set of six OR assistants, in full scrubs with concealing surgical masks and eye protection. They were the new background.

"I'm too young," Zee explained, once they had emerged from the fog of non-person. He was busy scrubbing up in the side room, illustrating to Emily how to do the same. "They'd never believe I was the one behind the core of this clinic's work. Stevens and a few others help me maintain the front. It's all camouflage."

"Otherwise it'd be like walking into an Eastusa city wearing a pointy hat," Emily realized.

"Exactly. People only put trust in what's familiar to them. It's strange... humans have lived alongside Fae for over two centuries now, but they don't turn to Fae magic when their health is failing. My science would likely be mistaken for magic, so I hide it behind mundane technology."

"People don't trust magic. There's no promise that a clever enough person could take magic apart and figure it all out," Emily explained, as she washed up. "It's bunk, of course. Magic has a science to it, maybe right even down to the, what's it called, subquartomic level or some such. But it's got a mystique around it, one the Fae gleefully enforce with all sorts of glamour and silly business. Keeps the yokels spooked."

Now properly sterilized, they entered the operating room.

Doctor Zee didn't have much to do, physically; the technicians handled the heavy work of making connections between the egg-bed and an identical one wheeled in from another room. They connected various 'mass capacitors', from the looks of them, much larger than the tiny thing that Una had once unplugged from her jetpack to show Emily. All Zee had to do was play orchestra conductor... fingers tapping at buttons on a glass control panel, making adjustments, preparing.

"In interest of being honest, I'm going to tell you the secret of my so-called 'miracle'," Zee said. "I can't cure cancer. Not a lick of it."

"...what?"

"Most Orbital healing technology is focused on two areas. One, remediating simple ailments and injuries. Two... full body biological replacement. Clone growth and consciousness transfer. When something like cancer or grievous injury occurs, we don't fix what's there, because often times we have no idea how. Why would we need to know, when we can simply dodge the issue...?"

"Wait, wait," Emily protested... even as her fears were confirmed, a pinkish mass starting to form in the second bed. One taking on human shape. "You... GROW a copy of someone, then dump their brains into it!? That's the trick?"

"No, no. ...let me be very precise, because I realize how offputting the idea is when you don't have all the facts," Zee quickly began. "Growing human biology, even brains, is a simple matter. But all you get is inert flesh, capable of absolutely nothing beyond involuntary life processes. Consciousness can't be created from nothingness. Artificial intelligences are just that, artificial, not truly alive. Do you follow? A clone is empty. It is only alive in the sense a tree is alive."

"I know some trees that would object to that," Emily said dryly.

"Only a full-scale neural transfer will turn an empty clone into a truly living *person* as you or I would define it. To put it in religious terms, since those invariably arise... we aren't God. We can't create a soul from dust, and to pretend otherwise is unthinkably dangerous. But we can move the mind around, pouring from one extremely similar vessel to another, to save it from falling away. One vessel dies in the process, unable to sustain without its neural matrix; the other truly comes alive as consciousness takes root in a new home. ...look! It's happening now!"

The process was rapid. Now, there were two of the patient... one unhealthy, failing. The other pristine but lifeless. She even had her original hair back. *Red, like mine,* Emily thought absently.

Doctor Zee keyed in a final sequence of codes... and a white flash of light made Emily see spots. The healthy girl was now breathing, and sleeping peacefully... while the other lie still at last.

"...I can't... I mean... okay," she said, trying to figure her way through this. "I can't even begin to fathom the bottomless pit of philosophical horrors you just described to me."

"To be fair, neither can the Orbitals," Zee said. "It's a frequent topic of debate. But when given a choice between the abyss and continued life... many choose this. Some don't. Either way, the decision is respected."

"So you DO inform your patients of what they're in for, right...?"

"Absolutely. I am being fair with you, Emily, honest and forthright," he promised. "I cannot be anything but honest and forthright with my clients. They sign non-disclosure agreements, of course, even if they decline the procedure. The miracle needs to remain a secret. But many have already turned to other failed methods, some adventurous ones even looking to the Fae. In the end, the ones who are desperate enough or determined enough will proceed. None of them have complained of feeling like anything other than who they are afterwards."

No matter how uneasy the prospect of the 'cure' made her, Emily was glad to hear that. If he was creating Frankenstein's monster without informed consent, well, that'd drop him squarely into the same category with cackling mad scientists that the peasants typically attacked with pitchforks and torches. As is, he was merely highly suspect.

"...what do you do with the old body?"

"It varies, depending on patient request... but most of the time, respectful incineration. The organs usually are unsuitable for donation to patients in need. I certainly don't harvest it for crazed genetic experiments, if that's what you're wondering."

"Thought hadn't crossed my mind," she lied. "Alright. Two more questions to determine if you're a psychotic madman drunk with power or simply someone with good intentions and amazingly spooky methods. One... why did Doctor Stevens say the procedure isn't always effective? Do some bodies reject the transfer?"

"...no."

"Uh. Then, why...?"

"Camouflage. The need for secrets. Because--"

"Because a miracle can't be too miraculous, or else people will start asking hard questions," Emily finished, Insight suiting her. "I get it. Some have to die. Otherwise, they'd worship you like some kind of saint, or they'd steal your hypertech and control it like Graves did, or who knows what? ...but... if that's the case, if you need some failures-- no. Wait, you said you didn't want to sit idly by--!"

"I don't! I wouldn't... no. I would never pretend someone was incurable when I could cure them. I wouldn't let them die," Zee clarified. "Instead... I find patients who want to start a new life. I can sneak them out under another name, and say the original patient expired -- complete with a dead body as flawless proof -- and compensate as generously as I can manage for the trouble. ...the failure rate is still lower than I'd like, drawing attention, but the alternative is unthinkable. Unacceptable."

"Alright, then. It's your problem to deal with, as long as you aren't being neglectful. The last thing I'm wondering about... are them. The oompah loompahs."

"...the... oompah...?"

"Sorry. Old movie my Nana loved. I mean them," she said, gesturing to the multiple O.R. techs who were, in the background, tidying up the room... including wheeling away the sealed egg that contained the former shell of the patient. "Because I can't help but notice they're all the same height and the same build. Oddly enough... your height and build."

"...ah. That is.. another matter."

"Honest and forthright," she reminded him, waving a finger.

"No no, I will be. ...you've seen the lengths I go to to conceal the secret. Even my colleagues who pose as me in the 'front office' I keep carefully in the dark, at great expense. That does not mean I can go without help in the 'back office'. Without them, I could not--"

"You cloned yourself to make your little helpers."

"I.. suppose that would be accurate," Zee said, fidgeting in place.

"You said you couldn't make a soul!"

"I can't!" he protested. "But I did say artificial intelligence was possible. Artificial, but possible. They are... organic machines, nothing more. They have the most limited task-focused intelligence I could create using these tools... they know nothing beyond how to assist me in my work."

"They're six inches away from lightning coils, neck bolts, and cackling during a thunderstorm!"

"I know not of these 'neck bolts' of which you speak, but they are totally harmless. It's my genetic code to do with as I please -- I exploit myself, and no one else. A dozen or so of them stay quietly in special quarters the rest of the time, and need only subsist on a specially prepared cube of compatible biomatter now and then. It is the only way I could ensure a fully trustworthy, secret-keeping staff to handle the hypertech. ...I have always intended them to be temporary, once I could find trustworthy persons. But I worry. I play it very conservatively. You have seen the dangers when hypertech ends up in the wrong hands. I will not cause any more pain than I already have!"

Emily rubbed at her forehead, feeling the headache coming on. This was beyond her, completely beyond her...

"I'm not gonna bother passing judgment on what you're doing here," she decided. "There's fifty glittery little failure-points where it could collapse around you, but... I'll admit that if we shut down your operation, it'd be worse than a failure. Failure means you tried and screwed up. We stop this, and you don't even get to try -- people simply die because they never get a chance at a future. Jeez... this is craziness incarnate, but... fine. I'll thumbs-up your freaky experiments into what horrors man hath wrought. Just don't expect me to ask for a new body when I get the sniffles. That's not my way."

"It's your decision, of course," Zee said, swinging the glass control panel aside. "We should rejoin your companions. So, you will recommend to Una to leave my hypertech be...?"

"Hey, it's your bed to lie in, not mine," Emily said. "We've got bigger fish to fry. It's the original cache that worries me. ...Esrever said 'things have changed'. Did you know that a Summer Court witch had access to hypertech? This isn't just about the infection vector linking Graves to you, no way. So, I'll leave you to tend to your own soul. There's something nastier afoot. ...oh. One thing. You know the boy we came here with?"

"The quiet one? Yes, what of him?"

"Don't try this on him," Emily said, gesturing to the cloning eggs. "I'm hoping Una has more sense than to suggest it, but if she does, turn her down. It's probably just my Insight, but I think we don't want to see what happens when the darkest magic of the Winter Court butts heads with the science of the Orbitals. Not unless we're three miles away and behind lead shielding."

Unease is a common feeling in a hospital. Patients waiting for test results, doctors trying to pin down the cause for an ailment, visitors hoping all will be well with their loved ones. To be in a hospital is to be in an ongoing state of unease about your immediate future.

Scout was uneasy. Even aside from his issues of self control over his Winterhound self, issues he was trying to grapple with now that he wasn't hunting solo and had good reason to pay attention to them... Una seemed keen on unsettling him, on pushing those boundaries of emotional control. But beyond her prodding and poking, there was that odd moment where he felt what she no doubt would immediately label as "hope"... and his first instinct was to flee and rejoin Emily.

Una was uneasy. She had been trying, trying and trying to reach Scout, as she had promised she would to Emily... and as she wished to do so, herself. A wish growing in impatience by the hour, it felt! But something about it wasn't ringing true. The awkwardness wasn't just in his skewed reactions... something inside her told her it was wrong for other reasons. --no! Hope for a wonderful tomorrow, that is the way! Any feelings of wrongness are just Pragmatic conservatism. The bold move forward! ...even if they feel strange when doing so, like they must tiptoe forward.

Emily was uneasy. First of all, an alien had just challenged everything she knew about existence, consciousness, and even the human soul. Of course, such 'transfers' were possible with some of the stranger and darker Fae magics, but... that didn't make them any less strange and dark. Was it right? Was it her place to declare it right or wrong, when she wasn't the one staring down the barrel of a tumor-loaded gun? Shove it all and flee back to what she knew, that was the only way...

Zee was uneasy. He had to prove his life's work to these strangers, had to justify the things he had done... when even he himself never felt fully comfortable with it. There was no choice, he had to go on, because to do otherwise would be to remove what little safety net he could provide this world. Such a waste it would be, to do nothing when he could do something! They would let him continue, he trusted, even if they had reservations... but having to reveal so much, to face up to it and need to examine it again himself, wasn't comfortable by any means.

The unease was not helped by macaroni and cheese and hospital gelatin from the cafeteria they were currently sitting in. The desserts wobbled with uncertainty, for instance. The cheese looked suspect. All was bleakness and despair, particularly the pasta, which was tough and rubbery. It was a grim metaphor of microwaved dining, truly.

Una was the first to break the silence.

"This is unacceptable!" she declared.

"I know. It's a mortal sin to charge five bucks for this crap," Emily grumbled, letting some of the orangey-yellow starch tubes plop off her spoon back into the bowl.

"The unacceptability extends beyond the food," Una clarified. "I speak instead of the mood that has settled about us. Friends! We are united behind good causes, and what's more, I have discovered one of my countrymen! This should be a time for joyous celebration, not misgivings! ...I would like to make a proposal, which should assist greatly."

"The fish special?" Emily guessed.

"No! I speak of... THIS!"

And the cheaply printed flyer she had torn off a community bulletin board outside the cafeteria was slapped down on the table, like the throwing down of a gauntlet.

Emily leaned across her dinner tray, to read it. "One night only, post-curfew horror movie marathon at the Theatres at the Mall of America. Doors close at eight PM sharp, reopen at eight AM. You'll scream until you drop. ...uh. I'm not really in the mood for screaming, Una."

"Ah, but horror movies are part of the lexicon of teen relations, and our varying ages from eighteen to twenty fall within the proper brackets for such activity!" Una said, seemingly brightening the table itself with her sudden cheer. "Horror is false danger, which helps us process and deal with real dangers in our lives, in cathartic reaction. It is tension relief, and you no doubt agree that there is far too much tension here. So! We shall journey forth, and cavort with our demographic peers, as teens of old once did in ancient times!"

"I was never a teen from this world's ancient times," Zee reminded.

"I hate movies with rubber monsters," Emily grumbled.

"I don't have fun," Scout noted.

"Given the alternative is to return to our respective residences and mope while waiting for Esrever's reply, I myself am going whether you are or not," Una declared, folding her arms. "I originally came to this planet to enjoy its culture up close, instead of from afar, and I intend to do that even amidst the 'Serious Business' as your Internets describe! Emily, you wish to help Scout transition from being a lone wolf to a social creature? This is the method! Zee, no doubt your life consists of little aside from your work, yes? This is an escape! So! Friends! Are you with me?!"

The shells slumbered in their steel crypt. Empty bodies, warm and inviting... not hollowed out, not exactly. They were never filled with the spark of life in the first place. Such ideal conditions!

It was so easy, like slipping into a suit of soft clothing. The Hungry Ones took hold effortlessly. They were shown the way to their new accommodations, channeled through the spirit-sky on this eve of chill and darkness... a path illuminated by the one who rules over all things frozen and dead...

Tonight, there would be eating, and murder.

"I can see the zipper," Emily complained.

"Shhh!" a girl in the row behind her hissed.

"Look, they didn't even blend the makeup in at the edges. You can see his ears--"

"*Shhh!*"

Emily grumbled, and sank deeper into her seat. No amount of popcorn and icy beverages was worth this, she had pre-decided. "The People Eaters" was so deep in the hole that if she had three thumbs to rate it down with, she would.

The problem wasn't just with the movie, though. It was the company. Somehow, in the darkened theatre, they had managed to get split up, with Una and Scout sitting alone two rows behind and Zee and Emily off to the side. That meant she was surrounded by her so-called 'peers'. Emily rarely felt like she had peers. Not in a "I'm more awesome than you" sense, just in a "I can't relate to you" sense.

The girls from her ye olde country village weren't her peers... not anymore, at least. They were barely at the edge of memory now, anyway, aside from Jesse. Nobody from her Witching School counted, absolutely, positively not. Especially Jesse. Few folks she'd met along the way when she journeyed out on her own counted... most of them were either running in terror from the pointy hat, trying to light her on fire, or throwing rocks. Whee.

...actually, in retrospect, this crowd had treated her nicer than most of those people combined by virtue of ignoring her in favor of watching the screen. Here she was, surrounded by young adults from all walks of urban living, and she was just another one of them. ...kind of comforting, actually.

Dammit. Emily hated it when Una was right.

Even Zee was relaxing, judging from how he whispered to Emily about why the (obviously latex) organs being pulled out of someone's abdomen by fleshy claws had been arranged in all the wrong places and were all the wrong colors. ...a play-by-play which was kind of fun, actually.

Dammit *dammit*. She didn't WANT to be having fun! It had been a day of stress and decisions and strange new concepts that needed heavy thinking, not... not sitting around with the bread-and-circuses crowd cheering as naughty teenagers who snuck off to drink and smoke and have sex got beheaded by lawnmower blades! (Even if they totally deserved it for being a bunch of ill-dressed strumpets chasing after empty headed manwhores.)

Like it or not (she didn't want to like it, even if she did in fact like it very much) this was going to be her activity for the next eight hours or so, between naps in a special crash room in Theatre Three. The curfew had fallen shortly after the four of them arrived; the streets would be barren now, patrolled by roving citizen watch vehicles.

Staying indoors for an all night movie marathon was how young people in this town defied both the city authority AND the nebulous menace of the Winter Court, who occasionally stalked the streets at night. It was a way they could feel alive, together, in the dark.

...which made her like it even more. Curse you, Una. She made it hard to get properly witchy and grumbly about things.

"Emily?"

Speak of the devil.

"Have you seen Scout?" Una whispered, leaning over some movie patrons to talk. She was holding a box of popcorn in each hand, one clearly intended for him. "He is no longer in his seat... did he leave?"

"Well... maybe he had to use the bathroom?" Emily guessed. "Look, go back to your seat before someone steals it, and I'll head out and look for him. He can't have gone far, the mall's a big place, but it's shut for the night. This won't take long."

"Are you sure? Maybe I should come with you--"

"I need a break, anyway. ...oh, and, uh. ...um. ...thanksforsuggestingthemovie."

"What?"

"I said I'll be back before the next movie's up. Zee, don't go nowheres, either."

Slip through the canyons of metal and stone. Not yet, not yet, they were warned, the leash tugged away whenever they were drawn to the lights that skittered about. The one you want is not there. You will be shown where the one that slipped away is hiding, so that you may finish a meal begun long ago...

The theatre playing endless scenes of teenage wastrels being gnawed on by toothy things from the grave may have been as dark as the night beyond, but the Mall itself was alive with light.

It was the largest manmade structure Emily had ever been inside, and it made Harbor Place in Baltimore look like a sad little flea market. Four floors, shaped like circular rings around a giant open-air amusement park in the center, were lined with shops and restaurants and more.

In fact, Una had spent the time prior to the curfew shutdown of the mall shopping rather than heading straight for the movie festival -- she felt less of a need to hide her jetpack and its questionably larger on the inside than outside luggage storage compartment when several of the shoppers were visiting Faeries.

Una looked downright normal next to them -- the Fae were also young, which meant flamboyantly human clothing, anti-authority punk against the pomp and circumstance of the higher Court members. Unfortunately, they dressed worse than Una did, and this was a woman who picked out clothing based on how "interesting" it was rather than how appropriate it was.

(Emily had even picked up a "WELCOME TO TWIN CITIES" snow globe when nobody was looking, ringing it up at the register after Una had moved on to obtain yet more shoes. Not that she could keep the fragile thing when flying about on a broomstick from city to city, but she'd have enough time to memorize it so that it could appear in her FaePlace. Why she wanted to remember this filthy pit of a city she didn't know, but she'd bought it anyway.)

So, even though the mall spanned four circular floors and one basement featuring a massive walk-through aquarium... once curfew went up the only place actually open was the theatre. The rest had been shuttered down for the night. Given he wasn't in the theatre lobby, or in the restroom (although she only dared a peek, not proper to stare at boys like that), he was likely downstairs by the one entrance that remained unbarricaded. Not that anybody would be leaving, but sometimes the kids would step outside to have a smoke anyway.

It felt good to be out in the light. Something about the theatre's dark had given her a sudden urge to relocate.

One quick elevator ride later, and she was with Scout. He was leaning on a railing, looking out at the still-life amusement park, its roller coasters depowered and its various whirl-and-puke attractions neither whirling nor puking. She stepped up next to him quietly, assuming a place on the railing as well, propping up one leg against it.

"Colorful, huh?" she observed. "Bet it'd look cool in motion."

"Wouldn't know."

"Ah, right, you don't have fun," Emily smirked to him. "Y'know, if we end up in town more than today, I should drag your ass back here in daylight. Roller coasters can be exciting, I'm told. Always wanted to try riding one. I'm sure it doesn't compare to stalking wild zebra or whatever it is you do in the forest, but you never know..."

"...why do you two keep doing this?"

"Eh? What?"

"This," Scout repeated, gesturing to the fun park. "Trying to make me do human things."

"Uh. That'd be because you're human, Scout. This is one of those A to B logic things--"

"I'm not. I'm dead. I'm something else."

"Something you don't want to be, yes? I'm pretty sure we covered that ground."

The boy had no reply to that, likely because it was true. Instead he resumed gloomily looking at the kiddie funpark.

"Y'know, you don't get to have it both ways," Emily chided. (Scout needed a guiding hand, but a firm one. She'd decided that days ago.) "Either you're some 'graarghraaffllesnarl!' beastie of the Winter Court that tears things apart on a whim, or you're an aspiring human who wants to do what it takes to man up. Dancing around in the middle's worked well for you so far -- 'I'm not a wolf' letting you stay true to your code, 'I'm not a human' letting you avoid anything uncomfortable. You can be whichever you feel like. Well, I'm not gonna allow that anymore, got it?"

...did.. Scout just smile? It was a brief flash. Maybe it was just the glaring lights of the mall.

"You're very different from Una," he said. "Similar, but different. Rougher."

Emily scoffed. "Yeah, well, we can't all be Little Miss Pretty Perfect Panties..."

"She's not like that. She hurts."

"Oh, really? Pull the other one, it's got bells on--"

"I'm serious. I'm always serious," he reminded her. "You shouldn't look down on her."

"...I don't. Honestly, she is a friend, I just... y'know. I'm just being flippant," Emily apologized, backing off. "Let's bring this back to you, okay? You want to be human, yes/no?"

"Yes." No pause, no hesitation, just confirmation from Scout.

Emily stepped away from the railing. "Then let's get your ass upstairs and engage in horrible, horrible movies with your fellow humans. I swear I'm gonna get you a life even if it kills me."

Scout didn't move. Not a muscle.

The young witch rolled her eyes. "Oi, let's get going--"

"Quiet."

Not a command, not a rebuke, just... what had to be. Emily silenced quickly.

Something was wrong. She could feel it without knowing how or why. Scout had picked up on it before she had, that's why...

...nothing should move that quietly. Moving that quietly was almost like a siren's wail in and of itself. She could see the figures running at the glass doors, the only unbarricaded entrance to the mall, clearly pounding feet on pavement of the parking lot hard enough to leave dents. Gaunt figures, emaciated, horrible... and all bearing the same *face*...

Scout was in action a moment before she was, as before. He slammed his shoulder into a long bench, shoving it up against the doors just before they impacted, sending fractured chunks of safety glass into the mall. And THEN the howling was finally audible.

Wendigoes.

Her spellbook snapped open in an instant, instinct bringing her to the section she needed. "ǝʇɐɯᴉuɐ!!" Emily yelled, touching the nearest trash can with her free hand. Garbage spilled out as it flew through the air, guided by a thought, to add itself to the barricade Scout had begun. "ǝʇɐɯᴉuɐ ǝʇɐɯᴉuɐ ǝʇɐɯᴉuɐ ǝʇɐɯᴉuɐ ǝʇɐɯᴉuɐ..." Chairs. Tables. Anything within reach, anything with some heft to it. She had to be careful to maneuver the objects around Scout, busy using his own blinding speed to stack item after item...

Soon, the wiry arms of the Wendigoes were trying to pry away the objects. Unsuccessfully... for now. Only for now.

"Winterfae," Scout recognized, stepping back to join her. "A dozen of them. All identical humans. They look like--"

"I know. And I know why. Dammit, DAMMIT. I hate being right as much as I hate being wrong," Emily hissed. "We need to warn the others. Then we've got work to do if we're going to survive tonight."

There wasn't enough time for a proper council of war -- they had a matter of minutes, hopefully in the double digits, before the enemy stormed the gates. Still, this was going to take coordination. Step one was to pulling Zee and Una out of the theatre into the quiet lobby, and then tell them in honest and reasonable terms exactly what was happening.

"The Good Doctor's clones are here to eat everybody in the building," Emily explained. Her glare at Zee could carve holes in sheet rock. "You say you fed them 'compatible' biomatter, correct?"

"...er.. what? Wait, what--"

"Focus, Zee!"

"Y-Yes, it's.. well, for maximum concentrated nutritional needs, I created their protein supplements using my own genome," Zee explained quickly. "Um. ...is that bad?"

"Oh, gee, let me check. You create a dozen empty, soulless human bodies, you feed them human flesh or some scientific equivalent thereof. A pack of pissed off Wendigoes -- spirit Fae who possess and mutate cannibals into walking murder machines! -- Wendigoes who you escaped years ago for some reason drop in on you tonight, and what do they find but the most flawless weapon of revenge imaginable. Yes, that is bad! Didn't your father study these things?! Were you paying attention?"

"Wendigoes? Here?! ...we'd heard about the whole 'evil spirits' myth, but figured it was... err, primitive superstition..."

"Right. Well, now we've got a dozen superstrong, lightning fast primitive superstitions here to eat Zee and likely everybody else that they happen to find, including a theatre full of horror movie buffs," Emily continued.

"Run for it!" Zee suggested.

"They're pounding on the mall entrance doors right now. No dice."

"The mirrors, then! ... except Esrever's busy searching his reflection space for us and won't be back until... oh, no..! Can we fly out the window? Una, your jetpack--"

"And leave behind a theatre full of human popcorn for them, Doctor?"

Emily paused in her scorn, when she saw how much Zee was shaking. Okay. Maybe she'd been a bit harsher than she should have. This was his fault, yes, but at the same time this was the menace that ate his entire family...

Taking on a more reassuring voice, she got down to business. "I have a plan," she said up front. "No arguments, no panic, no TALKING, just listen to me. We can sort this out. Scout and I are going to kill-- no. We are going to *try* to kill these things and likely just slow them down a bit."

Una spoke up. "I have my defensive firearm in my jetpack's storage. I will assist you in the fight, correct?"

"No. You can do more good here. In the time we're buying while holding off the nasties, Una, you are going to personally jetpack as many people as you can to safety through the nearest window. Next, Zee... you know this city's people and you're a more accomplished liar. Can you impersonate a Citizen Watch patrol type guy and keep the crowd calm while Una does her work? Make sure they don't try to get out through the mall itself?"

Zee worked his mouth up and down. "I... I don't know, I mean--"

"Yes or no!"

"Y-Yes. I mean, not much choice, so... yes. ...assuming I can keep myself calm. Yes. I'll do it."

"Good. We'll --SCOUT! Atten-SHUN!"

The boy froze, in the middle of slipping away.

"You are not going to try and solo these bastards in hand to hand combat," she ordered.

"...this is what I do," Scout reminded her. "The Wild Hunt. I can *feel* them, Emily. I must hunt the hunters. It's--"

"Yes, that's very nice for you, but use your damn brains! This is a puzzle, not a brawl! Let's say you play bloodcrazed Lone Wolf and gut a few Wendigoes with your bare hands... then one rips you in half. You lie dead on the floor while the rest of them nosh on our spicy brains. Oh sure, YOU wake up awhile later fresh as a daisy, but I prefer my brains unnoshed! Scout, think less like a Winterhound, and more like a SCOUT. Be your own master!"

One set of words led to another set of words within his memories, ones spoken years before. Despite their age, they rang out just as pure and true as Emily's wisdom.

You master yourself, and you'll be able to find peace one day. Swear it on my honor.

...Scout pushed through the battle-instinct, the pulsing of his unpulsing heart that sang *kill kill kill*, and... agreed. "...a puzzle. We can use traps. Ambushes. Frontliner strategy. There's a wildlands survival supply shop on the third floor. I'll get a scoped rifle; Scouts are trained snipers. Precision weapons. But we'll also need some munitions, explosives, nothing incendiary or the mall burns around us... right. Good. I've done this before. This will work. Wait here, and--"

"Nuh-uh. I'm coming with you."

"No. You'll die," Scout noted. "I won't let that happen."

"Well then, if you won't let that happen, I've got nothing to fear, do I? Besides... you haven't seen me in my element," she said... cracking her knuckles, before flipping through her spellbook. "You give a witch enough time to prepare, and she can hold off an *army* of angry villagers waving torches!"

The inside-space the food lusted for was awkward to them, confining. The Hungry Ones already felt confined enough in these fleshy forms, even after adapting them to their needs. Confinement-withinin-confinement would be agonizing. Hunt on the plains of their ancestors, across the frozen wastes, that was the way of the Wendigo -- but their long lost food lie within the inside-space, this vast shaped cave. The hunger mattered more than the discomfort.

The Whisper of Ice told them the way, led them to the flesh-eater forms they now wore, spoke of how to avoid the food that would fight back and delay them, instructed them to hide in shadows until they reached this place... and at last, to enter this place, and devour the missing meal. If only they could get IN--!

The barricade gave way after a half hour of scrabbling, pushing, and ramming the doors at full speed. Copies of Doctor Zee, twisted by the Wendigo curse, poured into the gap. Despite being "human" in shape, their limbs and joints were hypergrown, bones visible through taut-drawn skin, fresh blood pooling around them from the cuts received during the gateway assault... dripping red as they prowled the foyer, sniffing the air.

The meat was high above!

Climbing was out of the question; it might have been possible, but to do that you'd need a working knowledge of man's architecture, where the footholds could be, where you might be able to grasp and swing. It was all a pile of incomprehensible stone and metal to them. Even the elevators were foreign and unrecognizable (not that this had stopped Scout from slicing the cables with a torch from the hardware store, dropping them to the ground floor as a precaution.)

But the primitive sloping inclines, the 'stairs', these could be used. The pack howled in joy, spotting the way up, loping and lumbering and scampering--

On setting foot on the stairs, they flew out from beneath the mangled feet of the Wendigoes. The stairs, more aptly named 'escalators' ignored their default mechanical state thanks to a well placed Animate spell, and were now running downhill at Unsafe Speed. Wendigoes piled up at the bottom, hurtled backwards each time they tried to climb... until finally the mechanism gave out, and the escalator failed in a catastrophic manner, parts and step segments and belts flying free.

It was a momentary distraction. Which was all it was meant to be, really.

The Animated products from the fine people at Sweet Cravings Kitchen waiting for them on the second floor, now, THAT was more of a threat.

With the Wendigoes in 'sight', they became a deadly cloud of stainless steel. Knives advertised as being able to cut a tin can in half were able to slice right through arms and legs of the gaunt beasts -- a cloud of carving blades slammed into another Wendigo's chest, turning it into a glittering pincushion. Even the crockery got in on the action, cookpots slamming over heads to obscure vision, soup ladles banging mercilessly on them to drive a ringing clamor eight feet into the Wendigo's eardrums.

This had more of an effect. One Wendigo, its left leg lopped off at the thigh and right foot chopped away at the ankle, dropped and started thrashing on the floor helplessly...

...until the fallen one was devoured on the spot by the remaining beasts, their flesh healing itself when supplanted by the meat of scientifically grown clone bodies. Knives were pulled out, pots knocked aside. Now, there were eleven of them.

The next wave of defense came from Just Play It! Sporting Goods. Animate bowling balls were first, one bounding off the tile floor and impacting into the chest of a Wendigo hard enough to shatter its rib cage; others simply tripped or stunned the monsters. Lawn darts were next, little vicious things that went right for the eyes, tiny geysers of blood spurting on impact. Jumpropes snarled around legs, while croquet mallets beat down anybody on the floor, some taking time to pound sharpened U shaped gate stakes into their backs.

The assault disabled only one of them, too blinded to proceed. He was promptly devoured. All told, the chaos and the eating did slow them down enough for Emily to finish one last trick up ahead, before flying off the edge on a freshly stolen and enchanted broomstick, to rejoin Scout above.

Snarling in anger, the Wendigo loped forward, picking up the pace. It was perfectly clear between here and the next staircase, with only the black and white tile floor of the Food Court in their way. The first one took a step in that ring of culinary workstations--

The Shock enchantment spell is applied to discrete objects, and the electricity only discharges when the object comes into contact with another living thing. Much to Emily's delight, it seemed that each little square tile of flooring counted as a discrete object.

The effect was like walking into an electric minefield. She'd left no recognizable pattern to which square was "lit" and which one was safe -- she didn't have to, since she had been hovering on a broom while setting the traps.

Watching from one floor up, Emily let out a cheer to see the blue sparks of lightning snarl from Wendigo to Wendigo. This, now THIS worked well. It was an attack to the nervous system, the core of the bodies they used. With voltage rammed up your spine to fry your brain, the meat would be useless, even if the Fae spirits could've gone on. Two of them dropped dead on the spot, limbs twitching and crisping up nicely. The others caught on, leaping past the minefield, onto the stairwell itself. And thus, there were eight of the original dozen remaining.

The third floor seemed clear. The pack moved on, more cautiously this time, instinct-minds finally cluing in that the opposition was devious and a clear floor may not mean much.

The braincase of a Wendigo splattered across a wall, the explosive-tipped sniper round fired from across the mall's open courtyard taking off half its head.

Howling in rage, the creatures broke into a run. More shots snapped off, hitting arms, one scraping a back, but they were moving with superhuman speed now. Explosions triggered around them, grenades on tripwires, which knocked them about even with the rapid movement through these death-gates. One Wendigo was hurled over the railing, screaming as it flailed through the air -- crashing spine-first against the indoor roller coaster track, an audible CRACK sounding as it was broken in half.

The final series of blasts toppled a portion of the fourth floor onto their heads. 'A portion' meaning a full fifth of the Mall of America's fourth floor. The dust cloud kicked up by falling rubble, the deafening noises of collapsing structures, those alone would've been enough to knock them flat... being buried under hundreds of pounds of debris did the rest.

Emily peered up from behind the sandbags, while Scout kept his rifle trained on the cloud.

"Did that do it?" she asked, immediately wishing she hadn't said that, because people who say that usually see that it did not in fact do it.

Six shadowy shapes were slowly pulling free from the wreckage. Scout picked off one of them with his rifle, then set it aside, out of the expensive explosive ammo. Regular bullets wouldn't do much here.

"It'll have to be enough," he said. "They'll be up to the theatre soon. We need to fall back."

"...Scout? I don't have a Plan B," Emily said, in a smaller voice. "I was kind of counting on Plan A here. Can you fight off five of the things by yourself...? Maybe with Una providing fire support?"

I want to, Scout thought. He still had the itch to go tangle with them in true Winterhound fashion, even when his Frontliner training told him that would be suicide. *I want to fight. Want to kill. Bathe in their blood. Howl. Dominate and conquer--*

"No," Scout said. "You were right. I could take a few and then I'd be killed. ...we need a Plan B? ...hmm."

"We could burn down the mall?"

"It'd take too long. Una might not have all the hostages out yet."

"The building has a basement aquarium. We could let the sharks eat them."

Scout looked at her. "You want to face Wendigo-sharks? The fallen ones still have spirits out there, seeking ravenous flesheaters to possess ...Hmm. Drown them, maybe. Or..."

His eyes drifted down to the Food Court, and its enchanted tiles.

Two minds clicked as one. The snarling, murderous Winterhound and the calculating soldier. There was possibility for slaughter here that would satisfy them both.

"Theatre, now. We need Zee. And you need to copy a spell," he said.

Eat them! Devour them! Curse them!!

A Wendigo is not naturally an angry thing. It just moves and eats. Its body language is easily interpreted as rage, when really, it's just ravenous hunger.

When you've got them ravenously hungry AND utterly enraged, then you're really in for it.

The five remaining Wendigoes devoured what parts of the bodies they could find in the mess. They would need the strength to carry on, to finally assault the food they had been waiting years for. Other food was around the main course... it would be a feast. Blood to drink and muscle to tear and bones to crack...! But they would eat slowly, keeping the food alive and in pain, for the pain that they felt right now. It would be glorious...

Picking their way out of the mess, they reached the stairs to the fourth and final floor. The dark-caves ahead had the food--

The meal! It flies!

"H-Hey! You!" Zee called out, sitting on the broomstick behind Emily... with Una hovering next to them on her jetpack. They had zipped across the open courtyard, hanging in the air, luring the Wendigoes. "Here I am! Come get me, you.. you bastards! You ate my father, you ate my mother, now come EAT ME!!"

One Wendigo jumped the gun, leaping, trying to cross the distance in a single pounce... and came up two feet short when Emily hastily made a course correction. It plunged to the ground, neck snapping in an instant against the floor below.

The last four, they would not make that mistake. They scrambled down through the obstacle course again, "following" the three flying meals, which for some reason were slowly descending as the Wendigoes descended. Were they offering themselves willingly? Unusual. Not that it would grant any mercy, but--

When they reached the ground floor... all three meals were off like a bullet. They fled!

The remaining clone cannibals roared, breaking into a full run across the funpark in the center of the mall. Follow! Chase! Straight through the mall... to another staircase, this time leading down into the ground. They ignored the signs reading "UNDERSEA ADVENTURE" and "World's largest tunnel walk-through aquarium!" and "Closed for renovations"...

...water?

They were underwater. --no. They were in some sort of air-space, a long, long bubble under the water. A transparent surface surrounded them, keeping millions of gallons of water from crushing them. ...and at the end of the tunnel was the food. Standing. Waiting.

The pack moved faster than ever before. In less than two seconds, they-- slammed headfirst into a glowing dome of light.

"The shields are charged, but the kinetic impacts are draining my capacitors quickly!" Una spoke to her companions. "What is the signal? How will we know when Scout is in position? I cannot see anything through the water..!"

Knock knock.

Scout flashed a thumbs up through the plastic tunnel, slapping a small wad of C4 on its glass surface, before swimming away with a powerful kick of his legs.

"That's it!" Emily said, looking down at the hastily scrawled spell on the back of her movie ticket. "We're gone! ǝdɐɔsǝ!!"

--the Wendigoes staggered forward, the barrier they were pushing against having vanished in a flash of light. The FOOD having vanished in a flash of light.

If they'd run for it, rather than stand around howling in rage, they might have escaped before the explosives shattered the tunnel. They were buried at sea... an artificial sea, but a sea nonetheless.

And just to be absolutely sure... because it had worked so well on the tile floor... Scout unplugged the mainline trunk of the mall's electrical system from the central aquarium filtration unit, and held onto the cable as he dove into the water.

Escape wasn't a reliable spell. All it did was remove you a good distance from the current danger... where it dumped you was scattershot, beyond that. Fortunately, luck was on Emily's side tonight. The spell sent her right where she needed to be.

Safely standing on the roof of a building two blocks away, the rescued moviegoers and their rescuers waited to see what would happen. None of them knew what was actually going on -- back at the theatre, Zee had told them the situation was in hand, the Winterfae were being contained in the mall, and then the girl with the "experimental personal flight pack" brought them here, one by one. Then Una flew off, and didn't return. What was--?

A flash of light signaled the arrival of Emily, Una, and Zee. But that wasn't what caught their attention.

The teenagers, human and Fae alike, were now staring out at the shopping mall as all the lights in the building flickered, then went out for good.

"Whoa!" "Did you see--?" "Cool!" And the sound of tiny portable camera / phone / music player gadgets snapping pictures followed. The shots would be on the Internet in microseconds.

Emily did not think it was cool. She only had one thought on her mind. "It had to work. It had to," she whispered to herself. "It was so crazy it just might work, which means it had to work. He'll be popping out of a shadow any second now, giving me a big 'ol thumbs up. Mission accomplished. ...any second now."

And nothing happened.

Nothing continued to happen.

"He was to meet us here, yes?" Una asked, joining Emily at the edge of the rooftop. "Assuming that the monsters were slain, I mean. ...you don't think--"

Emily mounted her broomstick, flying off without a word, and without sparing the speed. Wordlessly, Una fired up her jetpack, its localized gravity manipulation carrying her off into the air to join the rescue.

The Light spell could barely penetrate the smoke. Parts of the building were on fire... Emily held a cloth to her mouth, coughing as she proceeded. Una turned on the personal buffer she normally used during high speed flight to improve aerodynamics, giving her some breathing space.

The basement aquarium had been flooded. Only a small platform, the top of a large turtle display tank, was safe to stand on... the water was still electrified, judging from the way the fried Wendigoes twitched now and then, floating upside down in the dead sea.

Judging from the way the fried Scout twitched now and then, floating upside down in the dead sea.

Emily fought back her panic, using very, very controlled motions to poke at his corpse with her broomstick, trying to nudge it towards this island in the electrical storm.

"I.. ah... I will attempt to turn off the power," Una said. "Please don't touch him yet. ...he will be fine. He *will* be!"

Emily stayed there, sitting on the top of the turtle tank, eyes locked on the body. His uniform had been fried, smoking strips of cloth... exposing his scarred back. So many whip lashes... one for every time he 'failed' his mistress, she knew, as all Winterhounds had. So many--

Another one snapped across his back, the crack inaudible, but blood welling. Scout screamed underwater, returning to life -- only to be electrocuted anew, his limbs thrashing in the water. ...and going still again.

Another whip crack. More screams. Another death.

"Stop it," Emily said, her knuckles white as she grasped her broomstick. "Stop it. STOP IT!!"

He is mine to do with as I please.

The voice was speaking to *her* now. She'd never heard Lady Winter before... but knew immediately whose voice it was.

This is the heavy price he pays because you will not leave things be. You were forewarned of that. Do you remember? Words in a mirror...? He suffers for you. And simply because it suits me, naturally. He should have hunted as a true--

"STOP IT!" Emily screamed again, getting to her feet, as if shouting at the ceiling would somehow reach the ethereal queen of ice's ears faster. "I command you to leave him alone!"

Command? How amusing! But as said: my pet is not your concern. Fly away, little witchling, while you can.

"I'm MAKING him my concern," Emily... warned. "Mine. Not yours."

You would defy a Queen of Faerie...? For this little scrap of manflesh? Interesting. What is he to you...?

"Th-That's none of your business," the little witch replied, instinctively.

...and Emily... HEARD a smile, from the nonexistent lips of Lady Winter. Felt the icy delight in her bones...

I chose my pet well for the trials that lie ahead, it seems.

...and it was over. Not that she was ever really there, but Lady Winter had withdrawn. Scout no longer twitched in pain.

Three minutes later, Una returned, slightly smeared with grease and soot. "Wonderful news, friend!" she announced. "I have disabled the building's power gr..."

Una stopped in her tracks at the sight of Emily cradling Scout's unconscious body tightly in her arms, rocking back and forth. Sobbing.

The remainder of the evening was a bit of a blur for Emily.

Scout recovered in mid-flight to the rescue rooftop. The shock of pain as he awoke nearly sent Una's flight path spinning away. ("He cannot safely ride your broom in his state, Emily. I will carry him." Una said, when Emily had tried to insist otherwise.)

Upon returning to life... he groaned. "...I liked my uniform," were his first words, on seeing the tattered and burnt remains of his clothes.

The teenagers had cheered their heroes on when they returned. Zee played his part, still pretending to be a government official, thanking them and telling them to wait here until dawn before heading home.

Zee was then silently returned to the roof of his hospital under cover of darkness. The basketball he had dropped when he first met them was still here, having rolled up against the wall.

Three very tried adventurers landed on the roof of their hotel, making their way to their FaePlace'd rooms. Scout slumped off into the eternal dark of his strange room. Emily said "Just give me a minute" before sitting in the rocking chair by the fireplace and passing out.

Una returned to her room and did not sleep.

This is wrong.

I want him!

The timing is bad. We're all completely exhausted. I shouldn't make decisions within such an emotional state.

I need comfort. I'm alone tonight, tired, and afraid. I want him to hold me.

She cares deeply for him. I've known it for days, and tonight, I saw it myself.

That's why it felt wrong.

She's made no actual claim. She has not acted! I could be his! I could find love, at last!

Neither of them are very good at expressing their feelings. Neither am I.

Optimism says I must persevere in the face of hardship and failure. I must try!

There is something dangerous in him. I want to find the human in him, just as she does, but I could risk much by disturbing the hound at this hour.

It is a mystery that intrigues me, a fear I want to conquer. Like a horror movie. I want him!

This is--

I WANT HIM!!

Back and forth Una went, unable to rest.

She'd made her attempts at alluring Scout, at finding that bond she now craved so. She had been awkward, sloppy in approach. This wasn't like the Earth romances she had snuck several looks at in the anthropology databases, the ones recovered by cultural studies teams. Those seemed easy. (Certainly easier than her failed attempts at Orbital romances over the years.) On Earth, there were the requisite fumblings and misunderstandings, especially in the comedies, but in the end it simply... happened.

The idea had come to her right as she was trying to forget the night's chaos, trying to slip away into unconsciousness. The idea prevented that sleep.

It would be so easy to give in to that impulse to slip over to his room, and...

...and in the end, she couldn't resist. Curiosity led the way, mystery and desire mixing up in a way that felt more intense than childish poking at cultural databases. She wanted to know, to experience, to *feel*. Letting an opportunity to learn slip went against her core self.

But what she saw in the main room of the FaePlace nearly stopped her. Emily was still asleep in her rocking chair by the fire.

She's made no claim. She claims to the otherwise every time I ask her!

Lingering might stay her hand. Her bare feet pressed her onward. Just a few short, silent steps. Una steeled herself before walking through the magical darkness of Scout's room... but in the end, it wasn't cold or terrible as she had assumed it would be. It simply was... dark. Comforting, in a strange way.

Still, it took a few moments before she could raise more than a mere squeak in her voice.

"S-Scout...?"

A sniff. Breathing. He was still awake, as she was! But where was he in the room? --behind her. He was behind her. When did that happen?

"Why are you here?" he asked.

"I.. ah..." Una trembled as she stood, finding herself unable to speak.

Another inhaling noise. "I see. That's why," he decided. "Can smell it on you. Smell your need..."

It was in his voice, Una realized. That lower tone, moving around her body, as if stalking her... *That's not the voice of the Scout I know.* It was... huskier. Inflected with something else, something that could relax in this room of darkness, when nobody was around.

"I'm.. not afraid," she insisted.

"Yes. You are. I'm dangerous."

"...I won't run from you," she decided, even if she did tremble at the thought. Whether this was from fear or excitement or both, she wasn't-- both. It was definitely both. The danger was enticing, pinning her where she stood, ready for what would come...

Hands grasped her shoulders, her cry was one of surprise, and then he--

You have my blessing, pet. Take her.

--paused. Not that Una could have heard that voice, that death-whisper in his ear. She wouldn't feel the chill breath of Lady Winter, but he certainly did.

Long have I waited for you to find a mate. She's clearly willing and ready to lie with the 'big bad wolf'. Your hound-self is eager, as you see! Claim her. Today you denied yourself every other pleasure of being a Winterhound, but there's no reason to deny yourself this. Break her down and make her the alpha male's pet. It is the way of the thing you are.

...you know I don't want that. I don't want that any more than I want to enjoy killing people!

This is destiny, boy. Sooner, later, you will want it. You will one day be Consort of the Winter Queen, as I told you long ago. Consider this your training to please your destined bride, if you like. You will WANT to pleasure your Lady, one day.

NO. I will never want that!

But you will! And you do have such needs, even now. You desire the Wild Hunt just as much as you desire this one's delicate form. You resisted the hunt so long tonight, you have little will left to resist this with... so do not. Use her! So very pretty, these people of the stars! Do you not enjoy her with your eyes?

That is not the point at all--

Or perhaps you crave the Summerling outside? You find such relief in her compassion. You could find relief in her flesh, as well! Her fire-red hair, her smile, her simple folk beauty. A fine pairing with the other's exotic touch! Make them both your playthings. It is our way. I would do the same, in your place.

Leave her be!! Emily is no threat to you!

Amusing. Did I threaten her? You are the threat to them both, boy.

...this is a sick game. You're tempting me. Or phrasing it in a way you know will shock me back to reason.

I simply explain the facts of your death-in-life. The choice ultimately is one I leave to you. Be thankful for that; I could force you to save yourself for your bride. Very well. If you are so certain... do as you truly want.

--and he carefully, carefully distanced her away from himself. Turned her around, to face him. Somehow, the light level of the room raised ever so slightly, just enough to make out his features. His sad eyes...

"The danger," he explained, in a much calmer voice, "Isn't just to you. It's to me. Both of us."

"Y-you have nothing to fear from me," Una insisted.

"This isn't what I want."

"Am.. am I not pleasing? I have made myself pleasing for you! I think. I have done my best--"

"Not what I mean. You have no idea how hard it is to resist," he explained. He had to find the right words, had to make her understand... "Do you remember Zee describing the Fae who ambushed Graves...? They were Winterhounds. Fully Winterhounds, given over to the hunt forever. ...I give in sometimes, when my control slips during a fight. But it's not just violence. It's... everything. Dominance. Cruelty. Power. Control. ...if I did this with you, keeping that from leaking in'd be nearly impossible -- and it'd leak into you the other way. Breaking you down. Reshaping. Wouldn't even realize until it was too late and you were... made passive and adoring, diminished. Both of us twisted up into something else..."

The fear returned now in Una, pushing past the allure of the mysterious and dangerous. It was just fear. But not fear of Scout himself... fear of the consequences he was describing.

"I.. believe I understand," she said. "Beyond the biology of your condition, it's the magic. The nature of what it wants you to become, yes? It doesn't affect you alone... you maintain control of it for our sake as well."

Scout sighed. It seemed to deflate him. "Yes. That's why this can't be. ...sorry."

He expected her to leave, to abandon him. That would be the best outcome, after all. It would preserve both of them. It was one of the many justified reasons he had for keeping himself apart from people, and if she understood that, she would leave.

"...I believe my resolve to help you is redoubled," Una said, standing her ground, but smiling at last. "You deserve happiness. A true happiness, not the cruel pseudo-happiness you describe. As you wish, I shall withdraw and leave you in peace, but I will not withdraw fully from your life. ...I suppose this silliness I attempted tonight, however, was indeed the wrong thing. I should have trusted my reasoning rather than my instincts. Pragmatism has its purposes as well. I apologize for that. Good evening, Scout."

She started to moved past him... and paused.

"...a hypothetical situation," she proposed. "If somehow my science was able to lift this strange curse, if you could love and be loved without it turning into something terrible... would you love me?"

It was the first actual use of the word 'love' he'd heard all day, even through Una's strange interactions with him.

"I, ah... it's..." Scout's voice fumbled, failed. "I don't.. know. She... I mean..."

One finger pressed to his lips.

"I think I understand," Una said. She was still smiling, although for some reason, there were tears in her eyes as well. "Very well. I suppose you shall not be my dearest... but you shall be dear, nonetheless. And with her help, I have no doubt we will find a way for you to be happy. There is always hope, Scout. Always. Please don't forget that."

end.a03

re-flec-tion [ri-flek-shuhn]
-noun
1. The act of reflecting, or the state of being
reflected. Such as: The return of light from a surface.
2. a realization occurring in careful consideration

Esrever the Mirror-Fiend, the Imageless One, the Silver Specter, King of the Empty Lands, the Outsider Reversed, Estranged Noble of the Winter Court was quite nervous.

Today, he would entertain guests, in the truest sense of Fae hospitality! Him, the reclusive one, perpetually hidden just out view, would be socializing as a proper individual should!

All thanks to that fateful decision years ago to reach out and talk to the mirrorchild known as Zee. He'd never talked to anyone outside the Winter Court before then, and even his own kin were more strangers to him than his newfound friend. By his shapeless, imageless nature, he was at once a member in good standing of the Winter Court and also distant and untouchable.

Tonight, that would all change. He had plans. No longer would he be a lonely hermit of the mirror world! He would be observed, and observe in turn, and... well. That was getting ahead of ourselves, yes.

First, he needed attire. He tried on various shapes... not needing a mirror, of course. He was a mirror onto himself. He tried male shapes, female shapes. He tried beasts and creatures of legend. What would make the right statement about him to his guests? What statement did he WANT to make? "Self" was rarely a question he had opportunity to consider. What a glorious opportunity this would be!

Eventually, he settled on a male shape, as Zee had come to see him as a brother. He wanted a shape that the humans would know and appreciate... something comfortable, familiar. After some brainstorming, he decided on a shape that was stately and quite well known across human civilization; often he had seen humankind trading the image, wanting to have as many copies of it as possible. Pretentious? Well, maybe a little. He could tune the shape later, if it made a poor impression, but for now it was all he could think of--

They were here! He could sense them five rooms over within his looking-glass world. Quickly, he reflected his way into the antechamber connected to Zee's bathroom mirror... and after making a grand appearance, in a shower of light and sparks, he took a deep bow.

"Welcome, honored guests," he spoke, in a formal voice he imagined his image as having. "I am Esrever. Ah... nuvus ordo seclorum...?"

Why was the Summerling laughing?

"Is.. there something wrong?" Esrever asked, adjusting his wig slightly, wondering if he had gotten some detail wrong on the image.

"You're *George Washington,*" Emily pointed out.

The evening had not started as well as he'd hoped, no.

a04 reflections

He fumbled around quickly for a replacement shape, settling on the long-gone Canadian boy he'd met Zee as originally. It was familiar to him, age appropriate, and less of a grand display. After that embarrassment, he felt the need to express humility.

"Is this more suitable?" he asked, his voice much younger.

"That works," Emily decided, marching up to him, sparing a mildly interested glance around the antechamber. (It was a reflection from some political building's foyer in New York, the polished granite of the floor having provided Esrever with enough of an overview to duplicate it in his lonely world. He'd spent a lot of time getting the flags right.) "Hi. I'm Emily the witch. That's Scout, that's Una. Which way to the hypertech cache? Let's get moving."

"Ah... the way has been prepared, yes, as was promised," Esrever said. "And the price paid, true, but--"

"That'd be the Wendigoes, then? Lady Winter sicced them on us."

"It.. it was not my intention to harm you, Summerling!" he promised, as he felt this social situation spin merrily out of control. "I had to go to great lengths to re-open the long-shut ways to what you seek... and my Mistress's price was steep, yes. I was bound by oath not to warn you, as much as I wished too--"

"We dealt with the little bastards. We're fine now. And we'd like to get on with this quest of ours, so if you would kindly show us which direction to go...?"

"But... but... dinner?" he suggested, voice weak. "I can prepare meals. I am extending my hospitality, honored guests, and welcome you into my world of--"

"Do you think we're stupid?" Emily asked, peering askew at him, lips a tight frown. "We're not sitting down to eat at a Faerie table. I'm not indebting myself to you by accepting your gifts. Don't think I don't know how devious the Winter Court can be, and given it's already tried to have me killed once in the last two days--"

"This isn't what I wanted," he pleaded. "Not at all...! I must... I must collect myself. Must rethink. Excuse me!"

And the boy winked out of existence, his stolen image flickering once before angling off into the distance in the form of a beam of light.

Emily grumbled. "Typical. Alright, folks, one-eighty, we are marching the hell out of here," she said, making 'shoo'ing motions to her friends. "Hup hup. I'm not spending one minute in this crazy Winter Court wonderland if I don't--"

"Emily!!"

The witch paused in mid-shoo, as Una tapped one foot, arms folded. It was a posture she'd learned well from Emily, after all.

"You're being quite rude," Una told her. "This fellow invites us into his home, he wishes to express himself in the manner of a gracious host, and you accuse him of subterfuge? For shame, my friend, for shame! This is not the diplomatic mindset you espouse, is it? You told me yourself you sought to improve Human/Fae relations..."

Emily groaned, palming her face. "Una. Winter... freaking... court. They're universally bad news, even when they're trying to be nice to you... especially, even! Faerie gifts *always* come with a price tag. They trade on favor and debt, and have no compunctions tricking people into falling right into their pockets!"

"Scout has ties with the Winterfae sociopolitical structure, and he has not attempted such ruses on us," Una reminded.

Said boy coughed once, to clear his throat. "...I'm with Emily," he clarified. "Winterfae are dangerous. Myself included--"

"Oh, none of that, either! Emily and I have been working very hard to improve your outlook and get you out of this mindless rut of self-loathing, you know. Neither of us truly fear the risk you represent, and neither should you-- wait, I am engaging in sidetracking. --my point! Yes, my point is, you are assuming too much. Hear this fellow out, at least!"

"...we could always follow some other lead to get at the hypertech cache. Maybe go bug Graves again; he got out of there alive, remember? We don't have to waltz through spooky mirror boy's magical mystery world."

"I want nothing more to do with Graves, or with his... associate. Ever again," Una said. "Now. We are going to smile, and be polite, and accept the help we have been offered. Or I'll consider possibly maybe going on alone although I would really prefer not to but I will consider it if that is what is required to normalize your behaviors! Am I expressing myself in a manner which is understandable to reasonable degree?"

Emily stared, bug-eyed and speechless. "Angry Una" was akin to "Adorably Annoyed Pouty Cuddly Thing Which You Feel Instantly Chastised For Upsetting." Some paranoid impulse made her wonder if Una was capable of some sort of psionic glamour spell, but no, she was just shiny and expressive.

"Now, then. Let's try this again," Una said, before turning to address... well, the walls of the antechamber. "Ahem! Mr. Esrever! I apologize for our conduct, as does Emily. Is that not correct, friend?"

Emily sighed. "Ah... yes, okay, I apologize. ...I was being a bit catty there. I've had bad experiences, and-- look, nevermind. I apologize. ...I'm sorry? Okay?"

The mirror-boy reappeared. If he looked humbled before, he was positively cowering now.

"I... intend no harm, I swear this," he said. "I would never hurt you. My food, my drink, my hospitality are offered freely to you. I offer what comfort I can, with no debt incurred, such that you may rest and be well before undertaking the path. ...please, ma'ams, sir, I suggest your acceptance. The path will be difficult, and as night has fallen, you will not want to go that route until daybreak."

After picking through the words, looking for holes... Emily nodded, in approval. "Right, then. ...y'know, I am actually really hungry. I told you guys we should've stopped off at a restaurant or something..."

Esrever smiled, pleased. "Yes, food! Come. I have prepared a feast of dreams! Ah, I myself do not need food or drink, but I've seen both consumed many times at many banquets, so I know what is required. This way. The dining hall is through the bathroom and the fishing pond and the dance hall."

"...huh?"

"Ah... this is a space of rooms, each with reflective surfaces in them, each connected by magical means. Navigating it can be a bit... tricky. But fear not! If you are lost, just look in a mirror and say my name three times, and I will come assist you. ...I suggest holding hands, to be sure we are moving together--"

Scout wobbled in place, finding each of his hands had near-instantly been grasped by one girl apiece.

The dining hall was quite lavish... a mirror-copy of a long abandoned palace, somewhere in Russia. It seemed to be constructed entirely from diamonds in silver inlays, with mirrors all around. It was quite possibly the most expensive room Emily had ever visited in her entire life. She almost felt bad eating a country biscuit, corn on the cob, and fried chicken in here. It was the sort of room you *dined* in, an activity defined by caviar-and-wine rather than burgers-and-soda.

The food was also a reflection, somehow tuned to look and taste like what they most craved to eat... but unlike her primitive FaePlace objects made of weak dreamstuff, these were solid and satisfying. Emily had a good home cooked dinner complete with the little wooden corn holder pegs she remembered as a kid; Scout was eating some sort of Texas rib eye steak, medium rare. The only telling difference between this and the original food was the logo on Una's New York pizza box, which had been reversed; apparently it now hailed from "azziP s'iccunaP".

Esrever sat at an empty plate, with forks and knives lying unused at either side. He did try to be polite and summon up an illusory goblet of wine to swirl around now and then, which looked a bit odd on the casually dressed teen whose image he wore.

"I don't understand why this human meal appeals to you," Esrever asked Una, watching her carefully nibble away at the gooey sausage and pepperoni special. "From what Zee has told me, your people have mastered nutrition in food pills. He had difficulty adjusting to human foods when he first got here, but you seem to be fine..."

"Off, iff.. ahh..." Una started, before realizing talking with a mouth full of cheese was counterproductive. She swallowed before continuing. "My mother and father used to have 'Earth picnics' every weekend, when I was young. Food pills are more satisfying, but... this food is much more enjoyable!"

"Then you visited Earth even as a child?"

"Oh, no, we'd go to the Arboretum on Arcology #BE12. You see..."

And on and on. They'd been at it for over twenty minutes now. In fact, Esrever hadn't paid the least bit of attention to Emily or Scout after the initial conflict had passed. No, he was more focused on chatting with the "mirrorchild," as he called her, asking about her people, her culture... and herself.

Emily flicked her eyes from the Winterfae to Una to the Winterfae and back again.

Oh, hell.

She set down her knife and fork. "I need to hit the bathroom," she announced, somehow managing to pull Esrever's attention away for a moment. "Where's the nearest one?"

"A third of the chambers in my home are bathrooms," Esrever noted. He gestured to a wide set of double doors that clearly should've lead to some vast ballroom. "There is one through there."

"Good, good. Also, Una, I'd like to introduce you to an ancient and proud Earth cultural tradition!"

Una's eyes glittered. "Ooooh? Yes, friend?"

"It's called 'girls going to the bathroom in groups for some reason.' C'mon. Won't take long."

"Ahh! Yes, I have heard of this! Very well. Please pardon us, gracious host. I am required to powder my nose!" Una announced, sliding her chair out. "We shall return promptly. Oh, this is exciting!"

The girls vanished through the double doors, which somehow revealed an ordinary looking apartment bathroom on the other side.

Esrever looked at Scout looked at Esrever and back again.

"So... ah... Scout," Esrever attempted. "You are.. a Winterhound, yes?"

"...yes."

"Ah. Good. ...how is that... going for you?"

The boy stared flatly at him. Esrever coughed once, and swirled his wine, glancing away.

"What? No, no, that's absurd," Una protested. "He is simply--"

"He's hot for you, dammit! 'Oh, Una, tell me of your native peoples!' 'Oh, Una, do all your people have white hair?' 'Oh, Una, that's such a fascinating dinner!' 'Oh,

Una, your eyes are like starlight!'"

"Ah... I do not recall him comparing my eyeballs to visible-spectrum solar radiation..."

"Yeah, well, give the guy a few minutes and I'm sure we'll be knee deep in the poetry," Emily said, while adjusting her hat a bit in the mirror. (She felt an irresistible urge to preen and primp a bit, now that she was in the ladies room with a friend. It was uncanny. Even Una was reapplying a shade of blue lipstick.) "...hmm. I need to patch that rip at the brim of my hat. --look, I'm just saying, watch out, alright? This guy is socially awkward, inexperienced, and apparently super keen on you. ...you're not into him, right?"

"Into...? Ah..." she paused. "Well... he is a curious person. But.. I... well. I have been thinking on that subject lately, and perhaps... I am not ready. ...I still believe in the spirit of love and romance, but, umm... I just... well--"

"Right, right, whatever. I ask because the last thing you want to do is have a Faerie suitor. I don't care how nice a guy he is, it's an alien culture with its own twisted little rules and skewed morality. What he thinks is generous could be horrific, and he'd never know. Trust me on that."

"I really don't think--"

"You know, it's funny to hear you say you're not in the market, because the other day I could swear you were making a play for Scout or something."

Una's lipstick tube clattered to the sink basin.

"Oh, hey, you dropped this," Emily said absently, passing it back, not noticing Una's briefly terrified expression. "Anyway, I guess that was just me reading too much into things, as always. You're not some kind of interstellar playgirl, after all."

"R-Right. Nothing like that. ...um. Friend?"

"Yeah?" Emily said, putting the finishing touches on her hat-adjustment. (She didn't wear makeup and had none to futz about with.)

"Are you... 'on the market,' as you have named it?"

"What, me?! Hah!" Emily replied, laughing out loud. "No way. A witch is always a busy little bee, you know? Go here, go there, do that, run away from that mob, use your magic to save the day, that sort of thing. It's a big responsibility! Who's got time for something stupid like chasing after boys? ...now we'd better get moving or they'll think we fell in, or something."

"Ah? Fell? What? Oh. Right. Better get moving," Una repeated. "...right."

Any place with access to a reflective surface was fair game for importing into Esrever's domain. Bathrooms, mostly, but also bedrooms aplenty -- luxurious ones, he promised, fit for royalty, which would provide comfort and rest for the travels ahead.

But the night was young, and he had more surprises for them...

The group emerged on a grassy riverbank, under a starry night. Emily fought to find some night vision, blinking several times, before spotting torchlight ahead...

"...I know this place," she recognized. "It's... Lilith's Henge!?"

It was a simple little thing -- a stone circle, in great Faerie tradition, erected on a hilltop at the edge of the wildlands forest. Five torches ringed the structure, with fresh footprints in the dirt above, circling around the central altar. The Henge overlooked a river of sparkling clear water, which Emily had once gone fishing in, before being chased away by a school prefect...

This was a place of memory, not all of them good, but above all a place of magic. Still, something was different, something amiss...

"...where are the tigers?" she asked, taking a step back, in case she needed to be ready to run. "They should be charging out of the forest to disembowel the trespassers by now..."

"My magic doesn't copy anything living, unless I deliberately do so... and at great effort," Esrever explained. "So, the guardians of Lilith do not prowl *these* forests. It is a safe place, Emily. She can't find you here, and you can enjoy familiar ground in peace. I, ah, hope this gift is to your liking...? --again, free of favor, of course."

Emily bit her lip. She should object, on general principles. It was a waste of magic, irresponsible. A sentimental gesture, too. Not the sort of thing a proper witch should go in for...

"I.. guess I could stay awhile," she said. "You know, for nostalgia's sake..."

"I would like, tonight, to provide all three of you with fond places that you will enjoy," Esrever explained. "Your road has been difficult. Let me ease your troubles. My mirrors have... a limited ability to see within you, but I promise your secrets to be safe, I merely wanted to glean what you might enjoy. Una, I have prepared a place of your own choosing as well, and, ah... Scout...? ...I couldn't seem to find any place of joy for you. I apologize."

Scout offered a shrug. "I don't have a lot of happy places," he said, honestly. "Not anymore, at least."

"Then I shall offer you this."

Esrever cupped his hands, breathing into them... and a silvery ball of moonlight floated from them. It shaped as it touched down on the ground, in the loose shape of a deer, the suggestion of one. It bounded left and right, as if to say 'chase me!' before dashing into the forest.

"I offer a guilt-free hunt, a chance to enjoy yourself without fear of the dark," Esrever suggested. "Harmless. I know you resist your Winterhound nature, and I will not deny you that, but perhaps you might enjoy this as an alternative to the constant strain of holding it in...?"

Scout.. twitched. He took one step forward, before realizing he had done so. Oddly, he found himself looking to Emily, to check her reaction.

"Eh?" Emily said, surprised at the look. "Well... hey, your call, Scout. It's just a different sort of game. A puzzle. Go for it if you like, or don't."

He considered... then nodded once. And braced one foot behind himself, before pushing off on it, breaking into a sprint. Once in the shadow of the trees, he was simply... gone.

"Think I'll scope out the old rocks, myself," Emily said, allowing herself a smile. "I bet they left a spellbook out when you copied it, if the torches were lit at the time. Maybe I'll learn a new spell! 'course, I'll have to copy down the Word reversed to make it work, but I can swing it..."

Esrever smiled, relieved. "Excellent. Now then, Lady Una, if you will join me...? I have prepared--"

"Juuust a second."

He froze.

"This is exceptionally nice. Extraordinarily nice. As in, EXTRA-ordinarily," Emily emphasized. "Your promise holds true? You aren't charging us an arm and a leg for the star treatment?"

"I... I have said I intend no harm. I will not hurt you or your friends."

"That's not what I asked."

Una sighed. "Emily, please! Mister Esrever, sir, I'd be happy to accompany you. I can't wait to see what wonders you have in store! I am here to learn Earth's culture, and I believe that of the Faerie should count as well, yes? We shall reconvene at the resting quarters within two hours. You recall the way, yes? Two rooms forward, one to the left."

"Una--"

"This way, please," Esrever said, offering his arm. The white-haired girl accepted it graciously, as they stepped onto the surface of the nearby river-- and vanished.

I want to be wrong, Emily thought. *Please let me be wrong.*

Instead, she turned her attention to the Henge. A smile leaked back in, thinking back. Those were good memories, some of the few she had of this place. Learning spells... listening to lectures... and... oh, right, that...

Una stepped from moonlight to earthlight.

At first, she wasn't sure what this new place was. It looked decidedly dreary, so gray and featureless, save the occasional pockmarked crater awash in a fine dust. She turned in place, to take in the lay of the land. There were footprints here -- large ones, from boots, left behind in the dust that covered the ground below. In the distance was some sort of odd golden spiderlike thing, a platform of some sort, and oh yes, there was an Eastusa flag, how curious, and beyond that--

"--the Earth!" Una exclaimed.

"The moon itself reflects light, as does the planet," Esrever explained, turning to face her. "It is distant... I had to find a telescope first, so I could look at it, understand it. It's so far away. That's why I couldn't copy your amazing mirror-cities, I can only dream of them... this is as close to home as I could get you. ...do you like it, Una-mirrorchild?"

Una took several light hopping steps, the dust shuffling as her shiny boots walked across it. So light... she was so light here, like a feather...

Esrever floated nearby. He didn't need to walk, or bounce.

"I know it's not the real thing. Nothing in my world is real... it's all just a lonely copy of the original. But... I'd like to think you are the only woman in history to set foot on the moon. I wish I could give you that honor..."

"It's... it's so beautiful," Una said, softly, honestly. "I've seen it from an observation deck on my Arcology many times, but it's just... I thought it was just a lifeless rock, a simple planetary satellite. But from here, seeing everything... EVERYTHING..!"

"We can stay as long as you want," Esrever said. "Explore it. Visit the dark side, scale one of the craters miles wide. We could... picnic here, if you like. There is air because I want you to be comfortable. It's not too cold, because I want you to be warm. ...I want you to be happy, Una-mirrorchild. Dear Una..."

Her bouncing slowed, until she stood on her feet again.

"Ah... Esrever..."

"Your people fascinate me," he was quick to explain, floating closer to her, looking in her eyes. "People of mirror-cities, people who shine like the stars! Zee opened my eyes to a world beyond the tangle of the Courts, beyond the harsh structures of man. I've seen your technology. It's so beautiful... so perfect. Just like you, Una. I've longed to meet a female of your people, and you do not disappoint! Delightful, delicate, wondrous Una. Teach me. Please, show me your ways! We could have all eternity to share between us. I can make it be!"

...she sighed. It would have been a shock, if not for Emily's sharp senses. Now, she'd had time to think about it. Time to know how she would react.

"Esrever... I'm sorry."

"Sorry for what, Una?"

"I can't stay with you," she said, offering a sad smile. "You're a fine host, a gentleman... and I sense goodness in you, no matter what my friends think of my judgment of character. But I just can't. I'm happy to talk with you, to tell you about my people, but I have a responsibility to them. I need to find the hypertech cache, so that we no longer indirectly hurt the people of your world. ...and... I don't think I'm ready for what you want, beyond that. So. I'm so sorry."

...Esrever floated down gently, his feet touching the moondust.

"I've approached it wrong. I know I have," he tried to explain, in his defense. "I needed to study how people relate to each other more. I have no experience. I don't know anything. But I could learn! I could... learn how to love you. I know if you give me a chance, I can find what makes you happy. ...is it my shape? I can wear another!"

"Esrever, it's not that, I--"

He shifted, to a handsome man in his twenties, a fashion model. Then to a stately Fae baron, in a large fur coat, with smoldering good looks. Then to a woman, then to a young boy band singer from the cover of a teen magazine, desperately trying to find something that would change that sorrowful look in her eyes.

"...ah! I have it!" he declared. "It's him, isn't it? You want him."

--and Scout was standing there. --yes! Her eyes widened, and the mirror-sense, his innate magic could sense the need. Just as it had sensed the pizza, and the Henge!

"I can be his reflection for you," he promised. "I can hold you and love you and make you mine. He is handsome, yes? Or are you attracted to his Winterhound nature...? I can do that! I can be intense, passionate, even cruelly so! Or, or would you want myself AND him? I can arrange it with Lady Winter! It would cost me, but his leash could be yours, anything, anything you crave--"

"NO! S-stop it, please..!" Una exclaimed... stepping back awkwardly in fear, slowly falling to the ground, arms ahead defensively...

...Esrever shifted back to his first form, the teenage boy, although more hazy and transparent than before. Distraught.

"I.. I didn't mean to..."

"You don't understand at all!" Una replied, harsher than she wanted the words to be. "I want Scout to be well, and... I want him to find love, the one I can tell he needs, even if it leaves me lonely, and that means even if I desire him it's not what I *want*, you're just mixing it up, and, and..!"

Too strong, too cruel. Una dialed herself back some, before he could fade away completely, as he had done when Emily originally scolded him.

"I... I meant it. I meant what I said before, Esrever. I have a responsibility, and that is the one reason I can't stay with you," she clarified. "It's not your fault. ...I'm not very good at romance, either, I won't fault you on anything of the sort. But none of that matters -- the responsibility *must* come first. For the sake of the mirror-people."

"...for the sake of the mirror-people," the Winterfae repeated, his image solidifying again.

"I owe this world a great favor. We've hurt it, by letting our technology fall into the wrong hands. ...I need to leave in the morning, on the path you made for us. Do you understand now?"

His eyes were downcast, scuffling a toe on the dusty surface. "I understand. ...I'm sorry to hear that."

"I know you're disappointed--"

"That's not what I mean. I was hoping I could convince you to stay... even though I knew you would need to move on. But you have to stay. ...that's the favor you owe to Lady Winter. She's decided."

Una cocked her head, trying to understand that. "What? Favors? I owe her nothing that I know of..."

"Not you, specifically. Your people," he said. "It's the hypertech cache. It... trespassed into her domain. It doesn't matter if that was intentional or not, it counts as an insult against the Winter Court, and there must be a leveling of the scales. She has held onto the favor for a long time... and told me yesterday that the payment your people will make is you. 'The mirrorchild will stay with you, forever.'"

"But... but you said you wished us no harm, that the hospitality was free!" she protested.

"It was! ...but this is another matter, something distinct and separate. I was honest, even if I could not be forthright. ...this is out of my hands, Una! I must obey Lady Winter. When morning comes... your friends will have to proceed without you. I am able to force them through the path, if need be. But you must be at my side, and remain there, or the debt is not resolved. ...please don't make me force you to stay. I do not wish to abduct the woman I adore so much."

"Then... then don't make me stay! Come with us. That would fulfill the contract, yes?"

Esrever shook his head. "This is my realm. I cannot leave. I can summon people or things through the looking glass, but I remain trapped here. It's a lonely world... all the more reason I wish you could be happy here. You must stay. Neither of us have a choice in this matter."

"But... but I can't--!"

"You must. I'm sorry."

She tried to protest again... and stopped.

No. This is a problem, Una recognized. *Solve it like a problem. When the Wendigoes attacked the mall, Emily made a plan, right on the spot. How clever my friend is! I must be clever, as well. ...even if I have fallen into another trap. I must be clever and save myself as she would have.*

"Esrever... please, this is of critical importance. How did Lady Winter phrase the payment that the Orbitals must make?"

"The mirrorchild will stay with you, forever. Those were her words."

"Ah, but I will one day die, won't I?" she asked, oddly hopeful. "Or... does your world keep me alive, somehow?"

"...no, it doesn't have that power. Only reflections are eternal."

Perfect! Una thought. "And if I did die, then my body would have to stay with you forever. You would need to be in the company of my corpse for all time, or you would be breaking your vow!"

The Winterfae was aghast at that thought. "I... I would trust my Mistress not to require that of me--"

"You would? But her wording implies it. She might never release you from that! She is cruel, is she not?"

"Yes, but--"

"So, the way I am observing the situation is that you require 'the mirrorchild to stay with you forever.' Which isn't something I myself can realistically do. ...tell me. Your reflections, even if they aren't real, they are the things they are, yes?"

"I.. I don't follow."

"A reflection of a pizza is a pizza," Una explained. "Otherwise, how could I eat it? A reflection of a bed is a bed. Otherwise, how could I sleep on it comfortably? A reflection of the Moon is the Moon! I can feel its dust in my boots, even now! And therefore...?"

"...you can't possibly mean..."

"It is possible! You said as much to Emily -- that it would take great personal effort, but it could be done. What's more, it would fit Lady Winter's words flawlessly... perhaps more than what you think she intended! A true 'mirror-child', one that is forever! My understanding of the Fae is that wordplay and fulfilling the letter of a request if not the spirit are quite common, yes?"

"...my people do like to make a game of oaths and promises, yes. This skirts very close, however. Lady Winter may exhibit a terrible rage... or she could be terribly amused. Her mood is difficult to predict..."

"I realize it's a risk," Una said. "But... if the only other option is to abandon my people... I'm sorry. I can't do that. And I'd rather not have to fight the Winter Court for my freedom, but I will, even if it would mean my death. I suspect my friends would do the same."

"You can't--!"

"Then you agree to my alleged cleverness?"

Esrever looked pensive. "Una... although I can promise the process would leave you unaltered... are you sure about this? The implications..."

"I realize there are, ah... philosophical issues," she said. "Similar to ones our biologists have dealt with in our healing methods. But... I'm willing to brave them, if you are. ...if it must be done so that I can continue, and so that I am not putting my gracious host in an untenable position with his lord and ruler... I'm willing."

"...your generosity is... it's... I am unworthy of it," he spoke, adding a grateful bow to her despite his nervousness. "Very well. I would need to, ah... study you, extensively. Your form, your shape, your self. It will take some time..."

"Then my time is yours," Una said, arms wide in acceptance. "Forever, it seems."

At last!

"At LAST!" Emily shouted to the moon. "It's mine! All mine!"

She felt like laughing, dancing, running about. So, she did. The world spun with delights, and Emily spun with it...

It was just like the best days of her life... awash in magic and camaraderie. Here at the Henge, all the troubles that went with learning the art would fade. It was just the witch, the wood, the Word, and the Way. The Joy of Hex.

She circled the altar, twirling as she went. It was the first time she'd danced in... well, since those halcyon evenings. Now, ordinarily Emily didn't hold to dancing, she'd decided in her 'old age'. It was frivolous, the sort of thing silly girls normally did to excite boys. But the feet knew the steps and the body knew the motions, she was finding on this strangely reflective evening... it wasn't just prancing about or moving according to formal steps to some silly old three-fourths time tune. This was a celebration of discovery!

Yes, just like those evenings with her coven-sisters.

Which meant that she was in fact dancing naked in proper witchy tradition when Scout emerged from the forest.

Emily spun out of control from the shock, crashing into the altar and scraping her knee. This didn't stop her from scrabbling behind it immediately, trying to use the thin stone column to keep anything unseemly from poking out into the open air.

"Don't you KNOCK?!" she shouted at him.

"...on what?" Scout asked.

"I don't know... a tree, or something! You move too damn silently-- QUIT STARING!"

"I'm not staring..."

"Quit... looking, then!"

Scout averted his eyes. Good.

It was the fastest Emily had ever dressed in her life. She didn't skimp the details; petticoats, stockings, everything had to be in place to cover up her red-hot embarrassment. The hat made her head feel hotter, but she didn't care. The entire process took a little over a minute and she probably tore her stockings in the process. They could be mended.

"...alright. You can look now," she decided, allowing the boy to once again gaze upon her witchiness, now that it was properly clothed witchiness again.

Scout un-averted his eyes. Good.

"That was just me following the very respectful and traditional dance of magical, er, learning," Emily justified immediately. "It's very ancient and time-honored. Totally normal and ordinary and in fact quite a serious ritualistic, ah, ritual, and NOT simply stripping off and running around nakers for fun, no matter what you may be thinking!"

"I.. wasn't thinking anything one way or another," Scout decided to say.

"Well, good! Just as long as you understand I'm not some sort of, you know. Girl who takes off her clothes and dances around for no sensible reason."

"...what was your sensible reason?"

"Ah! I was just getting to that!" she said -- pointing to the open book of magic on the pedestal. "Behold! The manifold mysteries of the arcane have been realized in mine eyes! I now hold the long-sought spell of Perfectea!"

She lifted a teacup that had been left next to the book, whispering a twisted Word from one of many paper copies she'd made, in the Way of Faerie magic. The cup glowed briefly... and with a tiny 'sloop' noise, the cup instantly filled to the brim with warm, steaming tea, rich in colour and emitting an aroma promising flavour. You could practically taste the U in those words.

"I could never find a copy of the Perfectea spell," she explained. "Books of spells are jealously guarded by their owners. I met an elven lorekeeper who offered to copy it for me, but I didn't like the way he was leering, so I turned him down. But now, I can make my OWN perfect cup of tea, any time I want to! Oho! My witchy ways are amazing, are they not?"

"Yes," Scout said, clapping lightly, as he felt she wanted the appreciation. "Amazing, Emily. Yay."

Sipping gracefully at the Tea of Victory, she let its flawless brew warm her, head to toes. Even if she was already quite warm. "Ahhh... at last. I've been waiting to get my hands on this spell..."

"I don't understand what tea has to do with dancing without your clothes on."

"...now, look. I've gone and spilled my tea," Emily complained, shakily setting the cup aside after. A forced change in topics was required. "Let's get back to the fancy pants bedrooms Esrever's picked out and hope he hasn't somehow locked Una up in some crazy Fae debt. ...and not a word to her about what you saw, understand?"

"...'kay."

It was the second time in twenty four hours that Scout had been subject to nude girls. At least he could be thankful that there were no more of them around to confuse him like this. And that Emily had been too startled and manic to trigger any sort of Winterhound's lust reaction from him.

Even if, for some strange reason, he felt like he wouldn't entirely dislike the idea of once again seeing Emily like that.

The night had passed uneventfully.

They had been given adjoining bedrooms, each one flavored to their needs, each one clearly from a different building entirely. Scout had a military barracks of some sort -- amazing, how the entire room could be duplicated despite the only reflective surface being a shaving mirror on an open locker door. Emily had been given a cozy little second floor cottage bedroom, with a window overlooking someone's farm; it had a lived-in beloved auntie sort of feel, which suited her. Una had a hotel room decorated with some sort of weird mix of furniture that clearly was what 20th century people thought the 22nd century would look like, and they had gotten it hilariously wrong.

Except Una wasn't in fact there. Emily had peeked in a few times, just to confirm this. Una was still out somewhere in the mirror-realm with Esrever. Well, that wouldn't stand.

She returned to her bedroom, looking in the full length dressing mirror. "Esrever, Esrever, Esrever. I summon you. I don't have a candle but you'd bloody well better show up!"

After a minute without reply... a hazy, indistinct light appeared in the mirror. Silvery, like the moonlight deer he had crafted earlier that evening. His voice was distant, as if coming to her across a long ways.

"My attentions are elsewhere; I apologize for my inability to attend to your needs directly," he replied, muffled as he was. "How can I assist you, Summerling?"

"Where's Una?"

"She is with me."

"Right. I had a feeling. Well, don't think this sort of funny business is going unnoticed -- if she's not back in five minutes I'm going on a tear, you understand? You got a lotta pretty mirrors around here. Shame if anything *happened* to them--"

"Emily, please... I'm quite fine," Una's voice replied, from within the mirror. "There's no need... for threats..."

"...you okay? You sound out of breath."

"If you must know... I will be spending the night in the company of Esrever. I will rejoin you in the morning so that we may continue on our way."

Emily groaned. Figured. "Una, we talked about this--"

"What I do with my time is my decision. I'm a big girl, and I can handle myself," she protested. "I appreciate your concern, my friend, but... I do not require a chaperone. I'm just as old as you are, you know! Have a little trust, please..."

"Fine! Whatever!" Emily exclaimed, holding up her hands in surrender, as the silver light faded from view. "Don't blame me when you end up with a litter of snowmen or something in nine months! If you won't listen to your resident expert on all things... hey! Are you even paying attention? Get back here! You.... ooooh!"

Frustrated, she turned back to her bed, and threw herself on it. Grumbling and cuddling a pillow. Once again, everything would just be so much easier if everybody did what she told them. Why was she the only person to realize that?

Despite their host's intentions, an evening's rest hadn't put the three at much ease. Scout was the closest to relaxed. He'd managed to find a Frontliner's uniform in his 'bedroom', complete with the Scout's crosshairs logo on the shoulder. It was the wrong shoulder, since everything in this realm was reversed, but it suited him far more than the simple black t-shirt and pants he had come in, his old uniform having been scorched badly in the mall incident. Still, he was busy working out a crick in his neck.

"You'd think you'd be used to military bunks, given you were an army brat," Emily had commented.

"You would think that," Scout chose to reply.

Emily, of course, was not relaxed at all. She'd composed herself well, true, making sure to look her best -- it wouldn't do to be seen in a post-worrywart state. She'd washed up and had a quick breakfast. Slotted some new empty pages into her spellbook and copied a variety of utility spells, in case the challenge ahead of them needed, well, anything she was capable of. Despite living the motto of "Be Prepared," her nerves were far higher strung than she'd have liked them to be.

Una... looked exhausted. Her hair wasn't fully combed, just tussled a bit to put it in some sort of workable shape. She'd smoothed out her clothes as best she could. Dark rings under her eyes betrayed a lack of sleep, and her slow reaction time to Emily's frosty "Good morning" call showed she had much on her mind.

"Aaaand did you have a fun time last night?" Emily asked.

"I take care of my own problems," Una chose to reply. Oh no, not ominous at all, that.

Their host... well, their host could look like anything he wanted, with no wear and tear. He had kept to the form he left with Una in. Still, he looked troubled... serious in intent and tone.

"I... ah... realize that my goal of helping you prepare for the journey ahead may not have gone as I wished," he said. "If you'd like you could wait another day, before continuing--"

"I'd really like to get out of here," Emily stated.

"--right. Then let me explain. The place you are going to is in... dispute. I am oathbound not to explain, and for this I must apologize. Ever since it was brought to light following the incident with Quicksilver Security, the way has been shut to me. I have opened the path, at an expense you paid in enduring the trial of the Wendigoes. By conquering them you have earned right of passage, but the way is dark, and not without its defenses."

Scout cracked his knuckles, trying to get limber and ready. "We can handle any fight you've got," he said. "Don't worry."

"This is not a fight in a physical sense. What you are to face is... yourselves. You will be made to reflect upon yourselves and events that brought you here. Three mirrors you will cross in front of on the path -- a Mirror of Beginnings, a Mirror of Difficulties, and finally a Mirror of Suffering. ...I don't doubt that you can face them, as they hold no surprises for you. But just as someone can observe another in a mirror... your companions will see you for what you are, as well."

Scout's left eye twitched.

"Well... alright, then," Emily said, doing her best to look nonchalant and confident. "So, we learn of each other's mysterious and spooky pasts. So what? We're friends. It's not like we've got anything to hide. ...even if we don't talk much about years gone by. Whatever. That's your big challenge? Fine, we're up to it. Which way to the mirrors?"

Esrever gestured, and a distant door swung open. "The hallway lies through there. Walk the path of mirrors, and you will find an exit into your world at the very end. From there, you are on your own. ...I wish I could have been a finer host for you. I know you were not satisfied with your time here. But... I will miss you, when you are gone."

"Lonely life, huh?"

But Esrever only smiled, at that.

The group tentatively walked on, led by the witch who strode firmly ahead, and were through the door. Gone.

"...I don't think they're ready for this," he whispered aloud.

"I think it's for the best, actually," a voice from mirror-shadow said, before joining at his side. "They need to know each other better. There's too many things left unsaid between them. I remain optimistic that they'll emerge as better people! And now... we can know each other better, as well."

Esrever turned to his companion, with a hopeful look. "You wish it...?"

Anu smiled to him. "All that she valued is reflected in me -- and she is willing to share as much as she can of herself with those who wish to join her bright future. I am free to be with you, to teach you."

"...and to love me?"

The true Mirrorchild offered an awkward smile. "Well... maybe. We'll have to learn of that subject that together. We're both a bit new at all this, you know. ...hmm. Now that the journey is left to my sister, and I've my own path to consider... what will Lady Winter think of me? Can you, err, I don't know, phone her and make sure she isn't going to--"

Oh, I am amused.

Both boy and girl froze at the sound of that icy voice. But it wasn't a sarcastic statement... there was glee there, like the play of light off an icicle.

This was one possibility. A clumsy dodge, hardly the stuff of legendary Fae trickery, but satisfactory for an amateur. I will accept the gambit Una has played. After all, in the end, I still obtained what I desired.

"...ah," Anu said, not quite sure yet if she should be relieved. "And... what is it you want?"

I want them to walk the road they are on. I want them to walk it all the way to the doom at the end of the journey. And beyond that doom... I want her memories, her knowhow, her connection to the other-worldly ones. How useful for the days ahead! Such purpose it can be put to!

After all... that wonderful outsider knowledge is now bound within a Winterfae form, sworn to obey the Crown of Ice by nature of what it is. A shame the silly girl didn't realize that. In the end, you will serve the Winter Court well.

Now... you will kneel, my pets. Kneel before the Crown and swear fealty.

Esrever and his eternal companion slowly bent knee to the presence of Lady Winter, eyes downcast, while laughter whipped through their heads like a chilling gale.

Meanwhile, the three were facing a long, dark hallway.

The hall itself wasn't very menacing. It had been copied from some ancient manor house -- here and there were doors, although they didn't want to risk going off the path by exploring them. An occasional small wooden table held a vase of flowers, or an old rotary dial telephone, or other odds and ends. Portraits of people who were likely important for some reason hung on the walls.

Between the portraits were mirrors. One directly ahead, another farther down, and one on the edge of the darkness at the end of the hallway.

A grandfather clock nearby rang out the hour, nearly making Emily jump out of her skin.

"--right. Well. Okay," she said, composing herself again. "We walk in front of the mirrors, get treated to a magical peep show, and move on. ...who's going first?"

Una raised her hand. "I volunteer. I believe in exploring new frontiers, and--"

"No way. If the mirror gets teeth and tongues and eats you alive, we'll have nobody to disable the hypertech at the end of the hallway. So, Scout goes first," Emily decided shortly after asking for volunteers.

"...don't want to."

"Err?" she said, checking to see if that mousy reply really came from Mister Tall, Dark and Spooky.

"I... don't want to go first," he said, clearly trying not to look scared. Emily could only tell because fear wasn't something she'd seen in Scout before; the slightest hint of it was therefore obviously different and strange. "...sorry. Maybe dangerous. But... I, ah..."

She almost said 'Oh alright, you big baby' but stopped herself. "Ah. Well, then--"

Before they could debate it any further, Una stepped in front of the first mirror.

Una point zero one of Arcology #A076 was born to Ono (an up and coming Optimist and anthropological studies protege) and Lea (a no-nonsense Pragmatic engineering apprentice specializing in shift engines).

It wasn't entirely unheard of for such opposites to come together and produce an offspring -- genetic planning systems could produce unusual pairings, owing to the minute details of DNA combination that would be all but invisible to an Orbital laymen. As long as the resulting child was of strong breed, the parents mattered not, and often rarely took part in raising the child beyond donating their genetic material.

It wasn't even entirely strange for two people to unite and declare bonds of love for each other, producing a child without the assistance of the eugenics program. In a culture with plenty of free time to ponder the nature of the universe and the truths of beauty and art, love was sometimes seen as a silly indulgence for liberal minded types, but certainly not disallowed. Celebrity bonding ceremonies made for excellent gossip, after all.

But put the two together -- a pairing of opposites, who somehow fell into an emotional bond of love? That was entirely unheard of. It was the talk of the Arcology for years after Una's birth. Not that she was aware... all she knew was her father loved her, her mother loved her, and she had no wants in life. Those days were perfection. Happiness.

In her seventh year, her parents took up new societal roles. Ono was promoted to be Master Council Anthropologist of Arcology #A076 (Eastusa Specialist), and Lea was the new Engineer Superior in charge of maintaining the great shift engine and its many interlinked systems. They moved outward -- the districts of the Arcology core were cramped and unappealing, compared to the outward components of the city. Specifically, ones with windows.

It was when they introduced Una to her new bedroom that she got her first taste of Earth.

"Pretty!" she exclaimed, pressing herself up against the transparent surface, wanting to be as close to that wonderful blue and white thing as possible. "It's so pretty! That's Earth. I've seen pictures, but this picture's the best one!"

"Do you want to go there, one day?" father had asked.

"Oh, yes! Very much so! What is it like, father, to walk on a planet? How do they not fall off?"

Ono chuckled. "Well, if you'd do your physics homework, little lady..."

"It's so booooring," Una complained.

"But if you complete your tasks... I will teach you all I know of Earth, and expand your database access so you can learn as you please. Is this satisfactory?"

Una showed her satisfaction through hugging. It was an appropriate and well received gesture.

Not everyone was happy with the arrangement.

"Earth is savage," Lea had complained. "I'm not sure I want our little one exposed to them. She is too dear to me to allow such risks. Earthlings are liars and thieves, and will use her if they are given chance."

"Oh, come now, dear. You must have faith in the essential decency of people, regardless of their origin-world. We were not unlike them once, yes? So very much like them, in fact..."

From that day onward, they would picnic in the Arboretum of Arcology #BE12, a short flight from #A076, every week-rotation. And Una would study, and learn, and prepare. And hope one day to walk the surface of the strange and mysterious place of her dreams.

...and Una staggered forward once, her memory snapping back to the present. She glanced over to the mirror, hesitant... but now it was just a mirror again. Just a mirror in a hallway, and nothing more.

"Ah... well. That wasn't so bad," she said, confidence rising. "Quite nice, in fact! I wonder if I can have another go of it? Oh! Did you see...?"

"...you were right about the pictures."

"Pardon?"

"Pictures of Earth," Emily said, quietly. "I've seen it in books, from back when people still flew into space. Just looked kind of flat and blurry with lots of clouds and water. ...it IS pretty, the way you saw it. ...good gravy, Una, you had the best bedroom window of anybody that's ever lived!"

"Ah, well, actually, a few blocks down the view was a bit better. Mine was occasionally blocked by a set of broken and drifting communications satellites..."

Emily stretched out a bit. "Alright! I'm doing this next. This is really amazing! I can't believe Esrever thought we'd hate this--"

"Mirror of Difficulties next," Scout reminded her. "And then, a Mirror of Suffering."

"Yes, well, we'll burn that bridge when we come to it. Now, what do I do? Do I just walk in front of it like--"

Emily Moonthistle was born in a humble little village which made other humble little villages look like Xanadu. By and large, her family farmed dirt, because little else would grow. Some corn, some cabbage, that was it. They'd raise chickens and hogs for slaughter, but had no room for larger animals.

Still, it was a pleasant place which saw no struggle or strife, partly because it wasn't worth the effort for raiders to stampede over it and take everything they had, partly because of Nana Moonthistle.

Nana was an ancient woman, old as the hills themselves and twice as wise. (A saying which never made sense to Emily, because the saying "dumber than dirt" implied the hills couldn't be very bright.) The council of the elder farmers made all important decisions... but often after much deliberation and debate, when they'd finally reached consensus... they'd give a sideways glance to Nana in her rocking chair, and wait for a brief nod of approval before moving on. When traders came to town, Nana gave a brief nod or a brief shake of the head to any offers made. Even when brigands threatened the town, all it took was a sharp glance from Nana Moonthistle to make them immediately reconsider.

Nana was godmother to all the children of the village. At their birth, she'd be there, to bless the child: "Be strong and capable and may your crops grow tall." It was tradition.

But when Emily was born -- the direct female line descendant of Nana Moonthistle, her great-granddaughter -- according to legend she had started to say the blessing by route... but paused. And then changed it.

"May your eyes be sharp," she'd blessed, "May your mind be sound. And may your path be your own."

This made Emily a bit of an "alpha girl" whenever the village girls got together to play their games. When the boys played games like Frontliners and Faeries, Emily would often interject herself, and they knew they couldn't say no to her. (Oddly, she always wanted to play a Faerie, even though they were the bad guys.)

It was even said that Emily had the Insight in her. It was always said that way, with a capital I, some sort of supernatural insight into events around her. When she was very young, you couldn't spell things out like B-A-T-H or B-E-D-T-I-M-E around her; she'd know what was what in a flash, even before she could properly spell. She also picked up on things others didn't, like how old man Winters was probably seeing old widow Marigold, even if she didn't know why. It was a talent Nana had in spades, able to make a connection when others couldn't -- a guess, not something you couldn't make if you had the facts, but a guess that usually turned out to be correct.

Still, despite Emily's ranking status as Senior Junior, she didn't play with her peers too often. Much of the time, she was holed up in her room, reading the books her Nana had given her. Reading about how to mend clothes, how to churn butter, how to take care of ailing pigs, but more interesting to her was a single book accidentally mixed into the pile about Faeries. Nana didn't like Faeries, and shooed them away whenever they came to trade... which only made them more and more interesting to Emily.

This is why when it was announced that the village had, at tremendous expense, traded for a portable solar-powered media player with some passing merchants, Emily immediately insisted that the first village movie gathering be the Wizard of Oz. She'd heard about it from other children who passed through the village with trader parents -- it was the most commonly cited movie about magic they knew of, since most of them didn't care about that stuff and were more keen on watching Death Bloodfist IV and Adam Sandler Is The Girl Scout and things like that.

That movie was the single most wonderful experience of her childhood.... a tale of wonderful magic, and clever girls who learned how important your home really was, and silly boys who couldn't get by without the help of a brave young girl. And a little dog, true, but she was more interested in the flying monkeys than the dog.

But one thing didn't click with her.

"Are witches really wicked?" she'd asked her Nana, the next day.

"Mmmm. The movie said she was, so she was, wasn't she?" Nana asked, looking up from her knitting.

"But there was a *good* witch in the movie, too. She flew around in a bubble and wore a pretty dress and everybody liked her," Emily pointed out. "So, there have to be good witches, too."

"It's just a story, Emily. The way of things're different, they are. Mayhaps there could be good witches... but mayhaps there are more bad ones than good. Ought to be careful, around witches. Around Faeries, in general."

"I think I should want to be a good witch, Nana. I'll wear a nice hat and will help people with their problems and people will like me, like you do for people."

"Oh? And you need magic to do those things, do you?"

"Well... maybe not, but it'd be a lot easier with magic."

"Ahhh. Makin' things nice and *easy*, yes, that's witchcraft," Nana said, laughing bitterly. "You focus on your studies, young'n. There's value in the work. You'll understand, one day."

Emily wasn't listening, by then. She was too busy picturing herself in a nice pointy hat. Probably one like the battered old hat Nana kept hidden away in her closet that nobody else knew about.

"--this...?"

Her next step sent her off balance -- arms pinwheeling to stabilize. She didn't want to run the risk of staggering ahead into front of the next mirror. After recovering, the brim of her hat flopping forward over her eyes... in a moment of sheepishness, she paused to adjust her hat, making sure it was pointed in a direction reasonably approximating up.

"...ahh, so... you always wanted to be a witch," Una said, evaluating. "And... the hat! That's your ancestral hat..!"

"...yeah. It's Nana's," Emily said, with a sigh. "When I.. graduated, I decided to wear this one, ratty as it may be. ...never dared to mend it with anything other than a spool of thread, though. In mirror-induced hindsight... I don't think Nana would've approved of me using magic to fix it when I was capable of just doing work..."

"I see! So, your 'Nana' was also a witch!"

"I figured that out later. Much later. But... yeah."

"But... she said she didn't approve of witchcraft...?"

"Look, can we just get on with this? It's embarrassing enough as is. Starting to see why Esrever was all antsy," Emily said, waving Scout along. "C'mon, you. I can't imagine your story would be as silly as mine was."

Scout hesitated. "...wouldn't be silly at all," he warned. "It'd be something else."

Frustration welled up -- and was shoved down deep inside Emily. No. He needed support, now, no matter what her witchy impulses told her to say. "Scout... it's okay. Whatever happened to you obviously wasn't sunshine and roses. But you know we accept you, right? No matter how you ended up like this, I'm not changing my mind about that. You're stuck with me, whether you like it or not... so you don't have to hide. Come along, now. It's going to be alright..."

The boy took a deep breath... and closed his eyes, as he stepped--

---

Surrounding him, laughing, jeering. He could barely see, the tears were so thick, but his ears picked up every little sing-song nuance of the chant, every mocking jeer.

"Crybaby crybaby cry all day, crybaby crybaby cry all day!" they sang. It was a popular song in the orphanage -- a fine way to pass the time, when none of the adults were looking. Sure to make the little boy shirk away into himself, sobbing pathetically. "Crybaby crybaby cry all day, all the day long!"

He was five, and had no mommy, had no daddy. He didn't know it at the time, but mommy had gotten pregnant when she was just in high school, and didn't even know which daddy was the right one, that's how drunk she was. Her parents were direly religious, and refused to support her wishes for an abortion -- she was kept out of the public eye, so that her shame didn't humiliate them in the small resettling community of San Antonio. The boy only saw his mother for a few seconds, before he was shipped off to the orphanage in Austin.

Off to grow up a scrawny, weak willed thing, easily picked on by his peers. Maybe they somehow knew he was a rejected child, something nobody wanted, even beyond their own sob stories. They learned quickly that they could make him suffer on demand with such simple prompting.

"Crybaby crybaby cry all day, crybaby crybaby cry all day!"

He covered his ears, trying to muffle the catcalls. Didn't help. He balled up his fists under his chin, looked down to the floor, tried to wish them away. Didn't help. Nothing could help. He couldn't do anything...

There's something you can do, a cold thought echoed inside him. But it was bad. Bad kids did that. Not that anybody cared if he was bad. Not that anybody cared about him, at all. If nobody wanted him... then why should he care if he was a bad kid?

"Crybaby crybaby--"

He already had a fist. He just needed to use it.

The small child knocked a kid a year older than him out cold in one punch. Not that this stopped him, no. Now the sorrow was rage, a simple twist to the left, redirected into something that he could use against him. Something that WOULD make them stop. He hit the other boy. He hit him again. And again. And again.

They'd stopped singing long ago and he kept hitting anyway.

Eventually an adult hand clamped over his arm, dragging him away, the other hand still flailing in the air. The tears had dried up now, and would not return for years.

The three were quiet, after that.

Scout made no reaction whatsoever to the projected memory. It was the sort of no-reaction that took an amazing amount of self control to maintain.

Emily spoke up first -- more to herself, than anyone else. "...kids can be little bastards," she grumbled.

Una tried to comfort. "Scout, I... I am sorry for the way your fellow young people treated you--"

"I found my solution, that's all that matters," Scout said, with a shrug. "Made them stop. ...wasn't right. I know that now, of course. I won't apologize, won't excuse or explain. Won't justify, either. I did it and I kept doing it beyond that day. That's all it was."

They looked to the next mirror. It was identical to the previous, but somehow felt... darker. Like the silvery surface that was lying in wait would not be a particularly smooth one.

"We should retain the ordering," Una decided, before Emily could start planning. "Give Scout some time. I have no problems going first. ...I doubt my issues will eclipse yours, so they would serve as a welcome pause in what lies ahead. I take no pride in that, friends, but perhaps it can be plied to your advantage, agreed?"

"...um... 'kay," Emily agreed. "If you want, Una."

Una turned to face the next mirror. *No fear! There is always hope!* she told herself, before stepping directly in front of it.

"I don't understand your query."

This wasn't going as she had imagined it.

It took Una days to work up the courage. She had reviewed the cultural recordings of Earth, learning the customs and standards, comparing and contrasting them against what she could find in Orbital poetry and style guides to such things. She'd obtained a new dress just for this, a slimming one with a shorter skirt compared to the simpler garment she had worn all year long.

If anything, she had to force herself to have patience. She wanted to walk right up to Dar and ask him outright, so eager was she to explore this new feeling, but knew that all good things came with careful study and planning. Her mother had taught her that. A thing worth doing is worth doing properly!

But all that work, all that forethought, summoning up her nerve to speak the words... and it was collapsing around her.

"I.. was wondering if you would consider it an attractive proposition," she tried to explain. "It is to my understanding that you appreciate the dramatic entertainments, and obviously, proper nutrition is the cornerstone of--"

"If I wanted to visit a drama, why would I need to attend it in your presence?" Dar asked, genuinely confused. "Discussion between audience members during the performance is discouraged. It's also unusual to consider company during eating, because by definition, your mouth will be occupied with consuming, not talking. Why would I want to go to these places with you?"

"Be.. because... it'd be... fun?" Una suggested, weakly.

Dar considered the suggestion, and rejected it promptly. "These things are more 'fun' to do by myself. Having you around would not improve upon them, and would likely detract, as you are a talkative person from what I have observed in our study groups. Also, your intellect is too low to properly interpret the dramas that I enjoy, so I don't see how you could possibly have anything to say that would interest me. Excuse me, I am late for returning to my room to study."

The shock and terror on Una's face did nothing to slow his departure.

"But... but..!"

butiloveyou, she couldn't say. *Every time I look at you, my heartrate fluctuates! Your insights given during class inspire me! I have imagined the times we could enjoy together for weeks now, I knew it was meant to be, that love will light the way, that...*

She hadn't considered for a single moment that he wouldn't like her. She hadn't thought he might think she was... stupid. Chatty. Boring. Maybe ugly, even...

Una ran all the way home, down hallways and corridors, brushing rudely past pedestrians who idly wondered what all the fuss was about. Through the communal area, past her mother enjoying a steaming drink, into her room and onto her bed to collapse into tears.

The chime sounded at her door, voice carried through the comm. "...Una, dear? What is the matter? May I enter...?"

"y-yes, mother," she spoke, desperate for some comfort.

Mother had just returned from her work with the engines. There was still liquefied mass stains on her jumpsuit; she rarely cared about such things, as preening and primping were not practical activities. She sat on the bed next to Una... stroking a loving hand through her hair. "There, there. In your own time, now. When you're ready, you may speak of what has transpired, and I will assist you in understanding the experience."

Several minutes later, the young girl slowly sat up... leaning heavily against her mother for support. And she described what had happened, in detail.

Lea-mother sighed. "Una, Una, Una... of all boys... why Dar? He's so utterly boorish..."

"He.. he was handsome," Una weakly suggested, unable to think of any other virtues. "I imagined much, mother. ...too much."

"He's also quite firmly a Pragmatist, dear. Even at this early age, he's selected his mentality. I suspect one day he'll be high on the Council, deep in their camp."

"But mother, you're a Pragmatist, and you love father..!"

Lea smiled, playfully. "Well, if I didn't help keep your father's feet tethered, he'd likely float off into space, wouldn't he? But Una, love is about more than complementary angles. It's about more than a pretty face. Pragmatism states that one should be familiar with your intended partner, very familiar, before considering the question of love."

Una pouted. "I don't want to be old when I find love! I want to enjoy the dating and the romance that the Earth children find so easily!"

"I swear, if your father didn't insist on filling your head with that surface nonsense..." Lea groaned. "Una. The young of both Earth and the Arcologies often rush in, guided by hormones and dreams. But I swear by all things reasonable... one day, you will know your love not by your hopes... but by your head AND heart. It will sneak up on you, unrecognizable. Perhaps in the form of a favored friend. But when it is *right*, you will know. Have patience."

Una nodded a little, between sniffles.

"You are learning well, dear. This experience may have been unpleasant, but through suffering we can find knowledge that may have otherwise escaped us. I hope you will one day look back on this and understand. But for now... would you enjoy some Cold Fun?"

"...will you add the decorative particles?"

"Blue AND pink," Lea promised. "As you like."

...Una looked at herself, in the now quite ordinary mirror. And from this angle, she could see Scout, on the edge of vision.

A lesson I should have learned better, she thought to herself. *One I had to repeat. Next time, I will be wiser. I promise, mother. I promise.*

"I like your mother," Emily said, with a big grin. "Now there's a woman with her head screwed on right! Y'know, when we're done with this madcap adventure, you think Scout and I could head upstairs to visit your family? I'd love to meet her."

Wordlessly, Una stepped aside, gesturing to the mirror. "You are next, Emily. I will hold out hope that your 'difficulty' be as simple as mine was."

"...I'm kinda doubting that," Emily said, having to consider it now. "But... guess we'll see. ...this is inevitably going to land straight in the suck zone, I'll warn you. I have a bad feeling what the next mirror will show, if this one doesn't show it first. You two ready...?"

Nods, all around. Emily slowly, slowly stepped in front--

The girl looked down into her sack, counting off the herbs, checking the colors. "Red sunset blossoms, six of. White pearl drops, two of. One wild sunflower. Are we missing anything, Emily...?"

Emily consulted the book, one of many Nana had given her years ago. "Hmmm. We still need the handful of peppergrass. ...I think... it's the grass that smells spicy. I read once that Faeries made that stuff, you know. Now it grows all over the place!"

"Ewww, Faeries?" Jesse said, wrinkling her nose. "Why do we want the stuff, then? Maybe it's got a horrible magical curse on it!"

"Don't be silly. Nana wants it for the remedy she's brewing, so it can't be cursed. ...maybe the magic in the grass helps the remedy? That'd be really neat! A magic potion, just like in the stories!"

"I don't wanna drink any magic potions! They'll give you warts, just like some ugly witch!"

"Witches aren't ugly," Emily insisted. "That's just made up stories, to scare people. Witches are... beautiful and powerful. They can fly through the air, they can make the plants grow, they can do anything! This world would be a better place with more witches in it, I suspect. Why don't more people realize that?"

"Because they're afraid, of course."

The voice made them jump. A few flowers fell out of Jesse's sack, which she was quick to recover from the dusty traveler's road... while Emily looked up at the stranger. And up.

She was a tall woman, wearing a stately gown of deep purple. Her hands were in soft, velvety white gloves, folded neatly in front of her. Her raven-black hair was finely combed and washed, highlighting the sharp features of her face, and her--

"Ears!" Emily said, pointing to the pointy ears.

"Why yes, they are. You're a very observant girl," the woman said, pleased.

"You're a Faerie! You're a real Faerie, like in the books!" Emily recognized, overjoyed. "Wow! Jesse, look, look, a Faerie!"

Jesse... took a few steps back, nervous. "We're not supposed to talk to Faeries," she reminded her friend. "We gotta go. We gotta go now..."

"Why're you here?" Emily asked, peering curiously at the woman, now. Insight connected some memories together, things she was told, things she reasoned out. "The nearest Summer Court folk live deep in the forest. We're near a human village. You can't be here to attack us, there's just you."

"Oh, but I'm quite powerful," the woman spoke. "Child, have you heard of the Archmagii?"

"Nnnnno. What're those?"

"I am Archmagus Lilith, of the Summer Court," she spoke, adding a polite curtsey to greet the little girl. "And I train witches. I wander your lands, seeking out bright young girls without fear of the Faerie, ones whose imagination and cleverness help them see past the silly old monster tales of their elders. You, I can see, are one with great curiosity. Am I correct...?"

"Well... yeah," Emily acknowledged. "I've got a book about you, but--"

"We gotta GO," Jesse insisted, tugging at her sleeve. "We gotta go...!"

"You teach girls how to be witches?" Emily asked. "How to cast spells, and ride brooms? Brewing potions and enchanting objects and protecting the world with magical powers?"

Lilith's smile was wide. "Oh, yes. All of that, and so much more. The secrets I could share would open your eyes wider than any mere human school possibly could. Do you wish to learn? Other girls like you are gathering at the circle tonight, to begin the path -- do you know where the Chalk Henge is? The stones, five hills away from your village...?"

Jesse was nearly in a panic. "We're not supposed to GO there!"

"Oh, but you should!" Lilith insisted, turning now to Jesse. "You, especially. You're a big girl, aren't you? Strong. Oh, how the boys tease you... but *we* wouldn't tease you because of that. Strength is a good thing, little one; it gives you power. I could teach you so much about power--"

"You'll do nothing of the sort, Lilith Goatmother."

Emily didn't see the Faerie turn. She simply... was no longer facing the girls. Facing instead the old woman behind her, standing between the Archmagus and the village of Emily's birth.

"...Moonthistle. I had wondered where you crawled off to hide," Lilith spoke, in a voice that was not very nice at all.

"These aren't yours. You'd do best to leave be, now," Nana Moonthistle warned.

"Oh? And you could stop me?"

"You want to find out?" Nana asked. "Don't forget the rock and the river, 'Archmagus'. Or I'll have to remind you."

The danger embedded in that pause could be felt by all of them, even the girl with spell-dreams in her head.

Lilith was gone. Emily hadn't seen her left. She simply... was no longer there.

"Come along, then," Nana said, gesturing with her walking stick. "Flower gathering time is over. Dinner's soon. An' we'll speak no more of this."

Emily tried to ignore the confused look on her friend's face. This was possibly by not looking back at her.

"So... your ancestor was against witchcraft, and against you being a witch?" Una asked. "But you--"

"It was stupid. It was the single stupidest thing I have ever done in my entire life," Emily hissed. "And looking back at it just makes me feel stupider for being so stupid as to make that stupid decision. We'd snuck out after dark. I'd gone and grabbed Jesse... I made her come with me. She didn't *want* to go! But no, I was the big girl around the village, and she'd obey if I said jump..."

"Jesse? The same Jesse who called herself the Runeblade, and attacked Olney?"

"Oh, she changed her tune fast once we got to school," Emily glowered. "All the little wide-eyed girls Lilith had snarled up in her net eventually fell in line. ...nevermind. I know what the next mirror's going to be and I am SO not looking forward to it, now. Let me explain the rest later. It wouldn't make as much sense now. ...and that leaves us with Scout."

This time, he took a step forward with less hesitation. "I... think I know what we'll see," he said. "It won't be as bad, if I'm right. But if I'm right... the next'll be bad. Like Emily said."

"I think that third mirror's going to stink on ice for all of us, so fine, we'll cope," Emily declared. "Let's move on. Step up, Scout."

It wasn't like clockwork, no matter how frequently it happened. There wasn't any predicting what could set the boy off. That's why, by and large, the student body stayed the hell away from him. It was better than being at ground zero when he went nuclear.

The brooding, dark boy would sit by himself, say nothing, and simply occupy space. There was something wound up inside him like a spring, though... and at least once a month, sometimes a few times a month, he'd get into a fight. The school staff were aware of his problems, the guidance counselor kept trying to reach him, the orphanage kept assigning him to new foster homes, but nothing could crack that shell. By now, in his early teens, they'd all learned just to stay alert and be ready to pull him away from whoever he'd decided to attack.

It was strange, though. He had all the earmarks of a sociopathic bully... but he never instigated. True, he could snap at even a perceived slight, but if left alone he wouldn't go out of his way to antagonize anyone. He never put someone else down, never fought to establish himself as the big man of the school. He didn't draw any followers rallying behind his strength. He just wanted people to stay out of his way, and they were happy to do so. To do otherwise was risky business.

Nobody knew what set him off, that day in the lunchroom. Maybe someone had bumped into the boy? Maybe a transfer student who hadn't learned the score had needled at him, making fun of him for his dark clothes and his sour face. Perhaps one of the school bullies got it in his head that if he fought the psycho and won, he'd be king of his age bracket.

It didn't matter, in the end. The boy came off the chain for whatever reason, and pounced. Kicking, punching, grabbing, even biting a boy twice his size.

Then he grabbed a metal fork from a nearby lunch tray, and swung it wide. Far too wide...

The doctors said she'd have to lose her right eye. It was far too damaged much to be saved. She'd be in the hospital for days.

The boy was dismissed from school for the day. For the week, even. Possibly forever. He took this news with no reaction at all, no anger, no rage. He waited patiently in the principal's office, waiting for his latest foster father to pull up in that ratty old pickup truck of his, and haul him back to what passed for a home.

He made no sound, as he sat in the passenger seat, buckled in while old man Saul drove along the streets of Austin.

But he did cry. It was the first time he had cried in many years. Not the wracking sobs of his youth, of sorrow and despair, but this time tears of regret.

"Principal tells me you're gonna be transferred to Sister-of-Mercy," Saul said, in that gravelly old Texas voice of his, to break the silence. He didn't comment on the boy's quiet cry. "Burned up your last strike today. That's what, eight fights this year alone?"

"...yes, sir," the boy replied, discreetly wiping at his eyes.

"Ahum." Saul rapped his fingers on the steering wheel, in thought. "Guessin' you didn't mean to hurt that girl."

"...no, sir."

"How you feel 'bout it? 'bout hurtin' someone who's never done anyone no wrong. Losin' control like that."

NOW the tears made noise. A quiet sob, but it was there.

"Ahum. Reckon I know how you're feelin'," Saul said, and said no more for the duration of the ride.

The home wasn't much of one. Saul lived in an apartment, a third story walkup, which did nothing for his old hip injury. This time... the boy lent a hand, helping support the old man with each step. When they reached the dingy homestead, Saul fumbled his keys, turned the lock, and entered. He kept on walking, right through the living area, and on to his bedroom. The room the boy had never been in before.

"We don't talk much, I know," Saul admitted. "By and by we stay out of each other's business. I help the state out takin' in problem cases like you, I get a check, we move on with our lives quietly. Think this is a time when I may have somethin' worth saying, though."

"...sir?"

"Kid, you were born with a fight in you. No sense denyin' it, or coddlin' you to wish it away. High time you found somethin' worthwhile to do with it."

Bending over carefully, Saul unlocked his old military-style footlocker.

Inside... neatly organized, in little rows, in careful piles, were medals encased in small glass boxes. Stacks of photographs, pictures of men in Frontliner uniforms grinning and holding up weapons for the camera. Newspapers, old and fading, of action securing Eastusa in the last echoes of chaos after the Pandora Event. Combat action, defending Austin against the Summer Court, driving them back to the midlands. Finally, a battered old licence plate with military bolts still stuck to it with rust, embossed letters reading: *Don't Mess With Texas.*

"Tomorrow I'm taking you to the gun range," Saul explained. "You're going to learn how to respect a weapon, how to use it 'stead of it usin' you. Next day we're gonna visit the old folks center, meet up with some of my war buddies. They're gonna scare the hell out of you, boy, but for good reason. Frontliners lead the way, not just in battle, but in showin' you how to be somethin' other than the random menace you are today."

The boy looked up at him... and it clicked, somewhere behind his young eyes. He didn't protest, didn't roll his eyes, didn't storm off in a teenage rage. He stood upright, focused on the old soldier. "Sir," he said. (The word felt like more than a simple formal way to address an adult, now.)

"Mark my words, boy," Saul warned. "This *will* be brutal, ayuh, very harsh. No easy thing ahead. You're gonna learn all about how to take that fight in you and put it to use defendin' folks like that poor girl you hurt today. We'll put a leash on that animal in you and make that dog hunt for just cause. You master yourself, Scott, and you'll be able to find peace one day. Swear it on my honor."

"--and THAT is how you joined the Frontliners, and became a defender rather than a brute!" Una concluded, smiling brightly. "I knew there was a streak of nobility in you, Scott! ... wait. Scott? Your name is *Scott*?"

...Scout coughed, once. And actually fidgeted in place. "I prefer Scout," he mumbled. "More purposeful. More of who I am."

"But it sounds just like--"

"I didn't join the Frontliners then. I was too young," he who named himself Scout explained. "Saul trained me anyway, taught me everything he knew. Stealth, close quarters, long range sniping, safe handling of explosives to ambush and trap. Counter-magic military tactics. Things that ran counter to the wild fighting I was doing, so could learn another way. He'd seen action, defending Austin. Believed in the city, so I believed in it too. The walls, the Frontliners, the cause of protecting it. Just cause. ...we fought so hard. In the end, it didn't matter. Cities fall. They're illusions. ...I reserve right to explain later. I know what's coming in the third mirror."

The third mirror. They turned to face it, now. The hallway was even darker, here. The portraits of random people of importance seemed to be staring down at them, glaring with eyes of judgment...

"...well. By now, we know what we are facing, don't we?" Una said. "That means we are prepared. We can endure this -- after all, we will face it not alone, but together. If you are here to help me, when I experience it all over again... I promise to you I will do the same in a reciprocal fashion. I will face this first."

Emily swallowed, nodding once... watching as Una stepped forward--

---

It was sheer random chance. It couldn't have been fate -- such things were absurd concepts. They were not practical.

Una had been walking along the outer wall of the Arcology, past the docking decks, past the airlocks where shuttles would come and go to ferry people between the great star cities. It was a common walk for her, as it had the most windows, and she so loved looking out at Earth. Earth, planet of wonder and mystery! Earth, planet of cities and forests, of men and magic.

If she couldn't fit in up here... perhaps she could fit in down there. It stood to reason.

She walked by airlock after airlock, casually noting the figure standing inside one, and on, and--

--back again, quickly. She pressed herself to the small viewport, eyes wide...

Una beat against the glass, screaming, not that Lea could hear her pleas. The depressurization cycle had already begun. The girl fumbled at the keypad, not knowing how to cancel it, not knowing if it COULD be cancelled... glancing up quickly, reassuring, making sure her mother was still in there...

Lea was still there. And now, instead of standing rock still in the center facing outward... she had turned. Looking at her daughter through the glass.

There was a smile. There were words, lip-motions. *I love you.*

And then she was gone.

They found the memorandum of self termination intent filed away on Lea's workstation later that evening, when Investigators came around to the empty-feeling home. Apparently, Lea had given into despair. "There is no hope left," she'd written. Nothing specific, no reason for dissatisfaction. She'd simply fallen away from them, somehow.

Common among Pragmatists, the Investigators decided. Lea was in a bizarre situation, married to an Optimist, having given *natural* birth on top of that. Surely such instability and inconsistency could break down her psyche. It was perfectly reasonable and nothing more needed to be said.

Father... had faded. He retained hope, he had his smile. But he also had his Council business now, and he sank into that, surfacing only now and then to offer weak support to his daughter. He didn't know how to comfort her. She didn't know how to be comforted.

Eventually, Una decided it was Earth. That was the answer. It was a place so far away, so distant, full of such wonders. A place like Earth could restore the hope of Optimism inside her...

Scout recovered last, his eyes hazy. Una had slipped to the floor, kneeling there, twin streams of her tears sliding down her cheeks. As he focused, Emily had started to move to Una's side, to hold her, to tell her she understood--

Crossing into the mirror-space in the process.

Witches school was a complete nightmare.

Emily was not the top girl of the village here. She was the runt of the litter. Gradually, as they settled into the study of magic... the other girls adopted that name for her, *runt*. They took great joy in the name, as it put her in an easily defined place, beneath them.

Rapidly, she learned that the Faeries loved a good social hierarchy. There was Archmagus Lilith, high above. Then the prefects, then the instructors, then the girls, then the servant-elves, and then finally Emily. The little witch who couldn't.

She tried so hard -- all-night cram sessions, desperately trying to memorize the magic spells that the other witches in training seemed to grasp so easily. Emily read every book she could, learning of the Word, the Will and the Way. She had mastery over them all! She could speak the Word, understanding the strange lattice of letters and lines that made up the Way, she could apply her Will with fierce determination... she could cast magic! And every time she did, she felt so alive, so true, that being a witch was her purpose...!

But she couldn't memorize spells. She was stuck on the 'training wheels' of spellbooks. Such a wasteful practice, that was! Each casting from paper burning up the pages. Emily had to spend hours each night copying spells, replacing ones she'd purged in her attempts to cast from memory, making copies for her own later use. But no matter how long she stared at the Words, she couldn't remember them when she pulled her eyes from the page...

The only solace she felt was during circle time, at the Henge. Where the only instructor to give her any sympathy, Instructor Elriel, would have infinite patience helping her cast the new spells they learned there. And each time the class had mastered a spell (well, all of them except emily) they would dance, oh how they danced in the moonlight, the simple joy of new magic filling them...

...and then she'd crash back to earth, unable to use the spell again without a fresh paper copy.

Two years passed away from her home village. Making no progress, showing no signs of ever being a "true" witch. Her peers mocked her, even Jesse, who had decided she hated the name and would one day take up a witch name more befitting. Cruel Jesse, who had gone from meek to fearless in short order. Short on temper. Quick to anger. All of them were, the trainees, each strange on their own way and growing stranger by the day...

After the two years, it was Graduation Day. A pumpkin carriage had been crafted by Lilith herself, to carry the trainees to the place of their final exam.

Emily was permitted to come along and take the test, even if nobody expected her to pass.

The carriage arrived at their destination... the Chalk Henge, the familiar circle five hills removed from her home. A dozen skilled witches, ready to move beyond trainee and take up their pointy hats at last, piled out of the Fae vehicle, Lilith laying down the rules of the test.

"A human settlement lies ahead," she explained. "By tonight, I want it a lifeless, smoking ruin. Then, you will truly be free of this dying world of men, and ready to embrace the Summer Court in full glory as a witch."

She had to be joking, except she wasn't. Emily stood still, horrified, as the eleven others in her class marched forward, ready to fight--

"You... you can't!" Emily protested. "No. NO. This isn't what a witch should do! We should be protecting our people, not--"

"They're not your people. You're a controller of arcane forces now, pathetic as your control may be," Lilith declared, pointing an sharpened fingernail at the girl. "They'll never accept you, now. They hate and fear witches -- as they should. We are the champions of the Faerie Court, and we will one day lay waste to this world, returning the glory of the Land of Faerie to its rightful place! What matter is one little mortal village, against the Forever Ones...?"

The would-be witch stood her ground. "I... I'll... stop you?" she said, not wanting it to sound hesitant, questioning. She had no idea how to 'stop' Archmagus Lilith. It was a stupid thing to say...

"Oh? And you could stop me?" Lilith asked, smirking. "Girls...? You may start with this one. Make me proud."

Emily backed down. She didn't want to, but the eleven had turned, and were advancing. Instinct said she had to run. "You can't do this, you can't," she protested.

"You can't kill people--"

Jesse drew her sword -- the graduation gift Lilith had given her, one day previous. "I can do anything I want now. I can fight anyone and beat anyone! I'm not weak like you are, Emily!"

"I can see the fire dancing already," another witch said, with a distant smile. "It's so pretty. It eats everything..."

"The voices won't leave me be," a witch spoke, skin shaking, little body twitches.

They're mad, Emily realized, her Insight giving her the horrible truth. *The magic ate them. Human minds weren't designed for this. When you cast a spell from a book, it burns away the page. When you cast a spell from your mind, it burns away your mind...*

Realization was little comfort as they beat her. They didn't use spells; Emily wasn't worth wasting good magic on. They simply beat her half to death, and left her at the roadside so they could continue on with their final exams.

It was dark when Emily was strong enough to get to her feet. It was deep into the black of midnight when she was able to limp her way into what was left of her village. As if the punch line of a sick joke, her home had been left standing, even if her parents were left nearby unrecognizably burned, having tried to flee the destruction.

Nana was here. She had fought, had worn her old tattered hat, had brought powers to bear she had forsworn to try and defend her family. They weren't enough to stop the destruction. They did keep her alive this long, however.

"...Emily," she recognized, through eyes already fading away. "Tell me. Are your eyes clear? Is your mind sound...?"

The birth blessing. She made me unable to memorize spells. It was there to protect me, and I was stupid all the same...

"Y-yes, Nana," Emily said. "I'm fine. I'm... fine..."

"Good, then. Good," Nana said, slipping into her last rest, relief in her features. "Your path WILL be your own, child."

Emily buried her family in the morning, and walked away from her failure forever.

But she wore her Nana's hat, and carried her Nana's broomstick. Emily would redeem the word *witch*, even if it took the rest of her life.

Now both the girls were in tears, with only Scout at the edge of that terrible threshold.

He had absolutely no hesitation, now. He stepped forward to join them.

The disappearances didn't start making headlines until several days into the hunt.

At first it was page three material. Then page one; mysterious killer strikes again, leaves no clues, body mutilated.

Two days later it was clear this was an attack. They were inside the Freedom Walls of Austin. The Frontliners watched the streets, but it was no use; every night, more bodies.

Eventually, scores of the dead were piling up, and the attackers weren't bothering to hide. They were Fae, strange and terrible Fae of a feral nature. They wore scraps of cloth, their eyes were wild, and whenever they pounced from shadow... they killed, and brutalized, and worse... sometimes dragged away the people, never to be seen again. A state of emergency was declared far too late, the population going down with every evening passed. Soon, with every day passed -- being indoors during daylight hours made you just as vulnerable...

Saul recognized the signs early on, and had stocked up. Scott's enrollment in West Point would have to wait; survival was the key. They gathered whoever was willing to follow them and fortified a school, taking advantage of cancelled classes to begin an unauthorized civilian occupation of the building.

By the week's end, when there were few people left alive in Austin despite Frontliner reinforcements being sent regularly from Philadelphia, their little gymnasium was still standing. The power grid was holding, keeping the overhead lights strong, banishing any shadows. Scott and Saul alternated watch shifts, alongside volunteers, and Frontliners who had abandoned their units in favor of uniting under Saul's banner. Saul, hero of previous Austin defenses. Saul, who had the Fae's number. Saul could get them through.

Saul died while Scott was asleep. He had been on patrol. The Fae left his mangled body nailed to the basketball backboard high above -- a symbol. There would be no hope here.

Scott barely got out of the gymnasium alive, when the final attack struck.

He survived a week more. He slept rarely, he fortified positions... he even took down several of the enemy, baiting them into the open, then blowing their heads off from afar through a scoped rifle. He snuck up on them, and slit their throats from behind. Just as Saul had taught him. Saul, who was gone. Everybody was gone but Scott.

Eastusa wasn't sending reinforcements anymore; they'd given up on Austin. Scott was the last of the Frontliners and he wasn't even officially a Frontliner yet. He'd found a Scout's uniform, and wore it when his own clothes were too shredded from a close encounter with the Fae. It suited him. He felt strength in the uniform, strength Saul would've wanted him to have.

The Scout lies in wait, the Scout prepares. Frontliners stand fast when an enemy is at the gates. Hunt the hunters. Just cause. Purpose.

The Fae stopped stalking him, since by that point, he could take them down in a one on one fight. Instead, they made it a dozen on one fight. And they didn't have the decency to kill him, to let him fall with the city he had been trained to protect. They didn't allow him his final failsafe, the vest of explosives he'd rigged so he could take as many of them down with him as he wanted. He couldn't even remotely trigger the atomic he'd found in the Frontliner shipments being sent from H.Q... couldn't complete the Pyrrhic Victory condition that they had sought. The Fae had taken his hand from him to be sure of this.

Scott was dying, pinned to the ground in the darkness by feral Winterhounds. He recognized their faces... faces he'd murdered, returned to "life." This was an unkillable enemy, and all he'd done is endure their onslaught.

Before he could slip away and find the peace Saul had promised him so long ago... their Mistress wanted words with him. She'd even showed up in person to do so.

Lady Winter was... a thing. A concept. She was ice and wind, shaped roughly like a woman wearing an elegant dress. She had no face, but an eternal snowstorm in the shape of one. Upon her head hovered a majestic ring... the Crown of Ice, crystals in the shape of a circlet.

Consuming your city was not personal. I would like you to understand that, before you perish, and fall into my domain of the dead. No, I took the life of your "Austin," so far into Summer's lands, to address an offense. Lady Summer trespassed into my lands of ice recently, you see.

An eye for an eye, an insult repaid. Now that we are even, the alliance of Summer and Winter may continue. And so shall you.

There is a beast in you. I can sense it, boy. Oh, what wondrous rage, what great desire it has...! But you have... contained it, channeled it. I can't imagine why you would do such a thing, but I will not argue with results. You stood against my hounds well. You deserve to be honored. Be joyful!

Scott didn't get a chance to reply to this. He had died.

And then he was awake again. His heart did not beat, but he was aware, he was... if not alive, at least akin to it. He had his hand back.

The Winterhounds withdrew, the growls of the feral undead Fae ceasing, as they gathered to their owner's side.

You will hunt for me now. You should be honored; few humans have been found worthy of joining the Wild Hunt. I will take the thing inside you and unleash it. You will run from forest to forest, truly free, killing and dominating any man, woman, or child as you please--

"No."

The Lady Winter's snowstorm-features blurred, a flash of lightning between the space where her eyes would be.

No...?

"I... I'll hunt the hunters," the Scout said... rising to his feet, his strength returning... as well as the burning rage that once dominated his days. So strong now, so difficult to control, but... he could point it. Saul gave him that much. "I don't hunt for you. Not for your way. I have a purpose."

Interesting; you can resist me, to some extent. You were trained to resist, of course, but to resist the purity of the mindless Wild Hunt, when I KNOW the core of you is a frightful thing...? Such strength! ...yes. Yes, you can be used as more than a mere dog.

I see where you will end. Yes. Yes, this will work. It is decided. You shall be consort to the Crown of Ice. You shall marry the Gale of Winter one day, boy. That is the ideal role for you, in events to come.

"...no," Scout repeated. "No. Nothing you say. I'll do nothing. My mission isn't over."

All learn to love the Queen of Death, in time. You will as well. I foresee this. But, as you like... run free, little hound. Restrain yourself as much as you can manage, if it pleases you. May your antics continue to amuse me, until the day of blessed union. Farewell.

The next day, Scout gathered supplies he'd need -- weapons, armor suitable for his new uniform. He set off into the wild. The city was a lie, the city had fallen... but that just meant the borders he needed to defend had expanded. There were enemies everywhere. This world would never lack a just cause. The Wild Hunt could be put to purpose.

Eventually, his military training and his discipline started to crack and fade. The beast loved to hunt with its bare hands, and the only thing keeping it from killing the undeserving was to at least allow it its favorite methods. The feral nature grew stronger, the brutality harsher... but all the while, he kept it leashed. Kept it from harming the innocent. So difficult, the daily battle with himself, and growing harder every lonely day...

All this struggle would be worth it... even if one day, the Queen would tire of him, and would bind him in some twisted nuptials, overriding him completely. He was now Winterfae, and would eventually bend knee. They always did.

Now all three of them were huddled together. It would be the third time Scout had ever cried.

Untold time passed, before anyone could speak.

"...I hate it here," Emily said. "I really hate it here. ...it's over, right? We're done? Three mirrors and we're gone."

Una blew her nose on Scout's offered sleeve. "Yes. It's over. But... Scout? What did Lady Winter mean, about being the... consort to the Crown of Ice?"

"She won't have him," Emily immediately said. "Whatever the hell that means, I won't let her--"

"She'll destroy me and remake me as a true Winterhound, one day," Scout whispered. "I think that's what it means. When she gets bored with my games, she'll take me. I'll still fight her, if she tries. I won't willingly become a monster again. ...you understand, now? The risk. The reason I kept warning you, again and again. Even before she got to me, I was dangerous. If I slip, even a little--"

"You won't," Emily sated. "Simple as that. Scott... Scout. You resisted a Queen of Faerie! In Twin Cities, you even reclaimed Saul's discipline and fought like you had back in Austin. Nobody's ever staved off her influence like that before! If you can manage such a thing... oh, hell, you could move mountains with that kind of willpower! No. No, I don't fear you, and frankly? I never will. You're your own master. ...I mean, jeez. I feel safer just being around someone capable of that."

"I as well," Una agreed. "Now, let us leave this place. The exit is..."

The exit was ahead. It was a strange thing, a rough patch of metal wall, polished to a reflective shine... with frost all around the edges. It didn't belong in this hallway.

Neither did the two mirrors, hanging on walls opposite each other, blocking their path.

"...no. Freaking. WAY," Emily growled. "Dammit, Esrever, you said three mirrors! Not FIVE! And... oh, for crying out loud, they're facing each other! Standing in front of one mirror, that's bad mojo enough, but being trapped between two, an infinite reflection...?!"

"But the way out is ahead--"

"We can turn around and go back. This wasn't in the deal! I don't know what he's trying to pull, but--"

"We'd have to cross the three again. We'd have to experience more memories," Scout reminded them. "No. The only way out is through. ...you trust me now?"

"Ugh. Scout, I've always trusted you, even when I didn't, okay?"

"We go on, then," Scout said, getting slowly to his feet. "I'll go first. If it's a trick, if it's deadly, it won't matter. At worst it can destroy me completely, I guess. Then you can turn around and leave. Find another lead. Continue the mission."

"Oh, NUTS to that!" Emily snapped. "Okay, fine, I suggested you go first earlier just because I was bossy and it was logical, but I am not letting you dive into certain doom out of some misplaced chivalrous--"

Una was already between the mirrors before Emily could stop her.

If I die, they'll still be together. It is practical, she'd decided--

They sat across a negotiation table, in the Council chambers. The rest of the Council wasn't here -- it was only the Optimist, and the Pragmatist. And both were Una.

"This is a strange thing," the Pragmatist said, studying herself, her greasy jumpsuit. "I'm sitting across from myself. It's not a rendition from living memory --

this is new imagery. These are new words. I don't think I ever said these words before; do you recall if I have?"

Optimist shook her head, her Council robes settling as she steepled her fingers in front of her. "I suspect the final mirrors are magical in nature. They are the ultimate self reflection, setting one image against another. It has a poetry to it. Do you think Emily or Scout can see this imagery...?"

They sat in contemplation, before both drew the same conclusion, shaking their heads.

"This is our business alone," the Pragmatist said. "It's not for them. It will be private. Don't ask me how I know this, I simply know this. This was set up by someone unknown, for purposes unknown."

"To destroy us? To stop the quest?"

"...nnnnno. I don't think so. Again--"

"You don't know why you know, yes. I feel that too," Optimist agreed. "So. There is hidden purpose we must discover. You are me and I am you, but we hold different views, represented by the mother-figure and father-figure. We sit in a place of discussion. The meaning is clear, we're to discuss some matter. What would that be, though...?"

"Well, we could start with how badly this journey is going, thanks to your childish impulses," the Pragmatist said, sitting back in her chair, leveling her gaze at the other Una.

"What? The journey is going very well! We have bonded with our friends, we have found a long lost countryman--"

"We've made missteps at every turn! We're too trusting, too quick to see people in good light. This is why we ended up chained to a chair and tortured in Baltimore! Mother was right. This planet is corrupt and it craves to exploit our weakness -- specifically, YOU."

Optimist shook her head. "I don't see myself as a weakness. I am the core of our belief, remember? Hope, despite counterexample. To lose that would--"

"You worry we'd jump out an airlock."

"--what?"

She scratched her chin, in thought. "That's the fear, isn't it?" the Pragmatist said. "Whatever drove mother to despair, whatever made her give up hope, ended her life. You fear that if we lose our hope we'll collapse as well, because the hope is all we have left. That bright future, the one we're desperate to share, desperate to make happen! Oh, how you cling to that silly dream! Yes... I see the purpose of this place. It's to make me talk sense into you!"

"I resent the accusation!" Optimist said, standing upright. "Yes, I cling to hope! Without hope, what matters what we do? Why do anything, if not in hope of a better tomorrow? That's not naivety, that's the driving desire of all mankind. Without it, we'd fall into absolute apathy! Why eat? You just need to eat again, after all. Why build a better structure? There's no point, the weather will erode it away regardless. Why live? Everybody dies. No! Hope is what gives life structure and purpose!"

"If you were this eloquent when trying to woo every boy you meet, maybe you wouldn't be so lonely," Pragmatist commented dryly.

"How... how DARE...?!"

"Didn't you learn mother's lesson?" Una asked herself. "Stop grasping so desperately, quit letting your drives lead you when your mind knows not to go! You went out on a limb for that mirror person, too far on a limb. You have no idea what the consequences will be! And Scout... where do I BEGIN with Scout?"

"You have no right to speak of him--"

"He could have raped you, you know," Pragmatist said, shuddering at the thought. "He *would* have raped you--"

The Optimist slammed her fist on the table. It resounded louder than it ever could have, if this was a real table, in a real place.

"No. Now, you're being cynical," she said, voice oddly calm. "I see that, now. The same cynicism mother often had, ready to assume the worst, even when actual logic and facts indicate otherwise. That's not tempering hope, that's inviting pessimism. You saw what I saw, just now... the iron will of Scout. He would never hurt us -- he stopped himself, remember! We'd made the perfect conditions for him to lose control, in his place of darkness, deliberately arousing him, even inviting a beastly encounter... and he resisted. And THAT is the rock I can anchor my hope to."

"...that's a small rock, you know. It doesn't even belong to you. If he is to be anyone's love, it's going to be hers, not yours."

"It doesn't matter. It's proof by example that there is good in this world, and that I have every right to look for it even in the darkest places. Don't you see? THIS is what the mirrors want me to know. That my optimism is well founded... tempered by pragmatism, I will agree to that. But not to the point where we ignore the good in favor of the bad."

Pragmatism considered this. "...you haven't won, you know. But I suppose there are no winners or losers here, just an ever-shifting viewpoint. ...very well. I concede. ...but there is something else here you should see."

She rose to her feet, smoothing out her jumpsuit, and beckoning Optimism to follow. Curious at why the vision hadn't ended yet, the robed Una tagged along.

"This is pure hindsight, understand, but I think it's accurate hindsight," Pragmatism explained. "We were too young to understand what we were seeing. The facts weren't there, yet. ...do you know where we are, now?"

It hurt to be here. It hurt to look. The sealed door. The little window. The figure inside...

"Look at her," Pragmatism said.

"I.. I don't--"

"*Look at her.*"

Una looked in at her mother. *I love you.* Lips in a smile...

...a thin, thin trickle of red touching her lip. Leaking from her nose.

"What...?" she said, confused--

"LOOK AT HER!"

A silver headband, peeking out from between her bangs, almost invisible. Just like the simple tool that teachers used, to share information with their pupils, a mind link. It was harmless, really.

Unless you used it on a mindless creature like an ogre... controlling them, from afar.

Unless you used it on a mindful creature like a person... turning up the gain, beyond safe levels, using it in terrible ways no Orbital had ever considered.

Controlling them, from afar. Making them kill themselves.

"Do you see?"

"DO YOU SEE?!"

Una collapsed to her knees, hands over her ears. It helped muffle out the sound of her own scream. This time... her friends weren't so quick to jump in, to help her. If this pair of mirrors could kill--

--but Una threw out a hand, to hold them back. Speaking quickly. "It reflects you on yourself. You see and know things. It's safe... even if it hurts. It's *important*..."

Slowly, shakily, she got to her feet and stepped out of the way.

"You need to know that it's a private thought-space, a series of visual metaphors that teach you about yourself. You need to be open to what you see and hear, don't run from it. I... think that the magic is telling us things, here, things we wouldn't otherwise know. I don't think it's malicious. You'll see for yourself. Emily...?"

"M-Me...?"

"You are next in rotation," Una reminded her, with a tiny smile. "Come on. I'm here on the other side, waiting. I swear to you that you will endure."

Swallowing hard, Emily glanced left and right at the menacing mirrors. And she stepped--

---

Pencil scratching against paper. She didn't need a straightedge; she could draw flawless lines, a finely practiced skill. One spell copied, then another, then another. With each new spell committed to paper, her power grew, her confidence rising with it. Everything would be fine as long as she had enough magic and applied it with precision.

A single candle lit her drawing desk and absolutely nothing else. Which was fine -- nothing else mattered.

"Emily."

Slot in another piece of paper in her ornate, leather bound spellbook. Another spell. Mending, this time; she had several copies already, but it couldn't hurt to have another. A witch should be prepared. It's important not to approach a situation and not be ready. If you do that, they'll see through you, they'll know you aren't a witch. It would break the *witchiness* of the shell--

"Emily!"

She ignored the voice, moving on to the next spell. There would always be more paper, always more work to do. A loaded spellbook was power, not just for the spells, but for what it looked like. You knew when you saw a witch with a proper hat, a proper broomstick, and a properly full book of spells that she knew what she was doing. There would be nothing she couldn't--

Her hat tugged itself down over her eyes. Since the room was pitch black beyond her writing desk, and all she cared about was the writing, this vexed her.

"Child, listen to me. Time is short. You--"

"No, you listen to ME," Emily commanded, pulling the hat back up. "Everybody should listen to me, because I'm a witch. I have the hat. I have the plans! If everybody would just listen to me and do what I say, I could save them all. That's what a witch is."

"Oh, is it now?" her hat spoke, in its elderly tones... somewhere between gentle and gruff. "It's the book, right? Well, no more book, then."

Emily stared at the space where her book was.

"Well... the broomstick, then," she said, pulling it to herself. "They know I'm a witch when they see it. Not some silly little girl, just some passerby, but someone who--"

The broomstick went away, next.

"Are you still a witch, without your broomstick?" the hat asked, cloth rippling as it spoke. "What is left, then?"

"...m..my fashion, of course. Very proper witchy fashion. No nonsense, no fooling around," Emily said, crossing her arms. "They know I'm above such things when they see--"

The clothes were gone. Panic started to rise -- no! She had to be presentable. She couldn't run around like this, it wasn't what a proper young lady should do..! It wasn't how witches behaved!

Except they do. In fact, they do that among other witches, which is as witchy as you can get...

"And all that's left is me. Your hat," the hat reminded. "When that is gone, are you still a witch? Can you still order people about, are you still the picture of witchiness you strive so hard to project...? Let's find out..."

"NO!" Emily shouted, grasping the brim of the hat. "No, don't take my hat! I need it! Please, Nana, don't take it away...!"

Her hands were grasping at nothing.

"Strip it all away, Emily," the voice spoke, from nowhere. "The trappings, the symbols of office, the attitude, the false fronts, the little lies you repeat over and over. Every defensive shell that keeps you from accepting your friends, like that outer space girl you call silly and immature, and the boy you schoolmarm every chance you get--"

"She IS silly! She chases after boys, just like some doe-eyed little farmer's daughter...!"

"Una chases after love. She wants to make her dreams come true. There's nothing silly about that," Nana spoke. "You want the same things she does, you just tell yourself that witches don't have time for such things. That it's all beneath you. And here you are, no spells, no broomstick, no hat. Can you still hide without anything to hide behind...?"

"I... I d-don't..." Emily stammered. She found a place to duck behind -- a topic change. "I only 'schoolmarm' Scout because he needs it! He's broken and needs to be mended. Witches mend things! Without his homework assignments to keep him distracted--"

"Distracted from his problems, oh yes, funneling his needs into something else. Does that sound familiar, child? He doesn't take comfort in those games and puzzles -- he takes comfort in *you*. Which is amazing, considering how cold you are."

"I am not--!"

"Are you a witch, child?" her Nana's voice asked.

Emily looked around desperately. Her broomstick had to be nearly. Her spells. But even the desk was gone, now. There was nothing, not even her fine ankle-length skirts, not a single thing... not even the persona she'd built up to show the world. The mask of a perfect, no-nonsense woman who is here to save the day. She was too bewildered and afraid to keep up that facade.

"Are you a witch?"

"I... I don't have..."

"Are you a witch, foolish child?!"

...a witch is not to be cowed by such an insult. Not because it hurts the dignity cultivated over the years, a threat to your public image, but because a witch was a witch. Period.

"YES!" Emily screamed back. "I don't care if I don't have my spells, or my broomstick, or... or even the hat! I don't care what you think of me! I'm a witch! I want to help the people I care deeply about -- and even the ones I don't care for, if they need help! That's what a witch does!"

There was a soft, felt-y feel around her head.

"In all the years you knew me, rarely did I use magic, but I was still a witch at

133

heart," her Nana spoke, voice no longer a tower of accusation and anger. "I didn't need to sling spells around all day to prove that. I blessed you at birth, and that was enough to save you, that one little thing."

"...the right spell, the right place, at the right time," Emily recognized. "Practical magic, nothing more. Just like the spells I use the most. And the village feared and respected you without much magic at all."

"Feared? Oh, heavens no, child! Lilith is the sort of witch that wins respect through fear. I didn't demand the respect of the village, shouting and ordering them about; I earned it, through compassion and wisdom. I didn't win the hearts of my friends by solving all their problems, I did it by sharing their problems, and sharing myself with them."

Emily dug into her memories. "It was more than just giving the elders a nod when you agreed with them," she recalled. "You listened to people. You listened to me, a lot. You told stories, too..."

"A witch is not an island. A witch is a *nation*," Nana spoke. "Sharing in the ups and downs, one with the people. A shaman lives beyond the village, called on in need, but not part of the village -- the witch lives life with the lives of others. A witch *lives* life. Hah. Child, how could you have been born, if I was 'above' all the silliness of life's simple pleasures? If my nose was constantly in a book, if I kept my skirts down, you wouldn't be here today!"

"GAH! Nana--!"

"Compassion, Emily. Compassion with wisdom. If you have both those things, you will be a fine witch. If you suppress your heart behind walls of what you THINK a witch should be... you may never be able to climb out again."

And now Emily had her symbols of office back. A broomstick, a book, her simple clothes. But she didn't need them anymore. They were welcome, as they kept her warm against foul weather, they gave her tools to approach problems with, but a witch simply *was*.

"...I think I see why Una liked this whole vision quest thing," Emily said, feeling more in tune with outside herself. "Thank you, Nana. ...and... I miss you, Nana. ...are you really her? Or just some aspect of me that's identifying as her?"

"Hah. What fun would magic be without its unending mystery, child?"

"Uh... 'kay. Ah, I can't promise I can shuck all my old habits overnight, but... well, I know what to look out for now, don't I?"

"Indeed you do. Which is important, as time is short," her Nana-hat warned again. "The times of trouble're coming faster than you realize, great-granddaughter. A time when the hat will weigh three times what it weighs now. If you don't learn how to live with it instead of letting it live you, the burden will be crushing."

"...wait. Since when can I predict the future? Insight doesn't work that way," Emily Insightfully said. "It just makes connections, and I don't recall anything that would point me towards knowing about some sort of major trouble ahead... other than, well, the usual trouble I tend to get into..."

The hat's voice was deeper now, richer. Almost like two voices in harmony. *"That's because this truth is not from within you, witchling. This is prophecy from hats yet to come,"* it identified. *"A dire responsibility is waiting for you. Take your ancestral lesson to heart, or you will doom all you hold dear. And that is all you shall be told."*

"...that's crazy. Wait, no, that's... come on! I'm just some wandering busybody!" Emily protested. "I'm not the sort of person vast prophecies happen to! What're you going on about, then?"

134

But to that, the voices stayed silent.

"My wacky head-trip experience is going to end before you give me any concrete details, isn't it," Emily realized, slumping her shoulders in annoyance.

Nana's voice chuckled from within the depths of the hat. "Unending mystery, child. That is magic."

Emily emerged from the vision... not resolute, exactly. No stiff upper lip. But she was calm, and satisfied.

"Alright," she said. "That wasn't ALL that bad. Although if I ever act like my hat is talking to me, you've got permission to smack me back to reality. Also: I want to lie down sometime very soon. ...Scout? Let's finish this."

The boy nodded once, and proceeded forward.

This was exactly what he was expecting.

On one side, the stoic warrior monk. Control. Willpower. A Man of Stone, honed and carved by a master craftsman named Saul, ready to stand guard against all that would clash blades against him.

On the other side, the rampaging animal. Rage. Desire. A beast of impulsive craving, wild from years of unchecked aggression and suppressed urges, waiting to overtake him and...

No. It was staying still, not challenging the Man of Stone.

"We need to talk," the animal spoke.

The Stone considered this development. "...talk," he spoke. The Stone only spoke in simple phrases, as its maker once did.

"This isn't some puppet play of metaphors. You and I both know we are quite literally of two minds," the insatiable beast of madness calmly stated. "One being the hyperdefensive little monster we once were, twisted up inside Faerie magic into a dog of nightmares. The other, well... you. The leash and almost nothing else."

"...listening."

"I want. I *want*. I want to run, to howl, to be free," the beast explained. "I want more than the table scraps you've thrown at me over the years, using me for YOUR wants. I want to kill and bathe in the blood, to eat the flesh. I want to take all the human urges you associate with the darkness and explore them. I want your women. I want the fine one, the porcelain girl from space, and I want to break her in half while I enjoy her. I want the earthen one and I want to reshape her clay. I want--"

"Disgusting," the Man of Stone spat. "Pathetic."

"Yes, I know! That's my entire point! Without you, all I am is the mindless little wild 'id' that Lady Winter seeks!" the animal replied, snarling in anger. "This is what you aren't understanding, what you're deaf to outside of this magical space. I. Do. Not. Want. What Lady Winter wants. Hers is just another leash, worse even than yours, because it's one I have no hope in hell of shaking!"

The stone turned its head, a grinding of granite echoing. "...undesired...?"

"I don't want her leash any more than you do. But at the same time, I hate you, because you're so... limited. You see my problem? I'm caught between a rock and a hard place!"

"Limited. Bah. I limit you, you hate that--"

"YOU are the limited one. See, this is what I have to explain to you, in the limited time these mirrors allow," the animal said. "Haven't you noticed? You're... thin. You've got nothing. All you have is the leash. You can't feel anything, you distance your emotions, because you've attributed them ALL to me. There's things in you that you'd actually enjoy, things that could give you the peace Saul claimed you'd have, and you think they're from me! You limit yourself. Oh, I'm a danger! Oh, don't trust me! All because you forked out some poor bitch's eyeball. All because of some silly magical curse you know damn well you can fight. Over and over you hit the same worries. Even the women have noticed."

"...maintain control. Check desire. Otherwise--"

"That's all you have. You could have so much more!"

"Won't hurt."

"I am not asking you to. And that's where we come to my proposal."

This was new. This was strange. The stone was listening...

"We have the same goal -- get out from being Lady Winter's groom-to-be. Now, obviously I'd love it if you weren't around, and I could do as I pleased. But you are here, and if I'm going to have any chance at a future... I need to compromise. --because YOU haven't been willing to! Do you see that? You deny yourself everything, but you don't have to. I would be willing to... restrain myself. To work with you, in a partnership. Not just you using me or vice versa, we work this together. We've got to do it, if only to see us become SOMETHING more than this pathetic wretch!"

The stone.. cracked, slightly. "Can't believe that. If I let down my guard--"

Clenching a fist... the animal drew blood from his own hand, dripping out between his fingers. "I swear to you on the blood of everybody we failed to protect in Austin. You will have your way, I won't argue with it. Oh, I'll push your limits nice and hard, I'll feed you urges, I'll show you desires... testing you. Otherwise, you'll never get out of your rut. But you'll always have final say. We take this slow, and maybe we can both get used to the idea of being something other than a mindless fighting machine."

"...unsure."

"Do you want love or not?"

"--what?"

"Without me, you don't get her," the 'animal' said. "There's no love without passion. No LIFE without passion. Okay, yes, you obviously don't want to indulge in the wild pleasures I could show you, as much as I think you'd enjoy them... but without me, without letting some of me through that damned thick skull of yours, you'll be incapable of love. Affection, maybe, a strong knight complex, but you can't *love* her. And I bet eventually, she'd realize she couldn't love you, either. Is that what you really want to be...?"

The leash wavered.

"We can be more. We CAN grow. ...yes."

"And about damn time," his Drives and Desires agreed.

When he came to, he had someone in his arms. Not a death grip, not pouncing an enemy. He was holding Emily.

"...uh... Scout?" she asked, a bit confused.

"Thank you," he said. "Thank you."

"You're welcome. ...um. What are we thanking me for, again?"

Una looked over to them, as she started to prod at the icy metal, the polished surface at the end of the hall. "Friends, I think I know what this is," she said. "I think that--"

And they were gone.

end.a04

flow-er [flou-er]
-noun or -verb
1. a plant, notable for its blossom or cultivated for its floral beauty.
2. to emerge into full development; to mature.

The city was frozen. That one word encompassed the sum total of it.

There was ice, of course -- it slicked the roads, it formed icicles on signs, it added a layer of frosty haze to the windows. Nothing moved, everything locked in by the permafrost that had settled over the entire city; a solid layer of glaze applied by God's brush. It made the city resemble some sort of 1:1 scale model railroad, full of carefully designed little buildings that were both real and unreal.

But ice brings water with it. Any ordinary city, under assault by wave after wave of permafrost, would have collapsed on itself by now. Food would spoil, batteries would corrode, glass would shatter, and buildings would be reduced to mere skeletons. It doesn't take much time for nature to reclaim its territory, and two hundred years would be more than enough to reduce any city to an unrecognizable pile of twisted metal and collapsed structures.

This city hadn't collapsed at all. The buildings were pristine, the cars unrusted, and the food in the grocery store windows looked fresh if a bit chilled. That's because the city of Edmonton, in the consumed nation of Canada, was frozen in more than ice. It had been frozen in time.

When Scout started exploring, he knew right away what was going on here. He dared not make a salvage and supply run until he talked to the one who had laid claim to this eternal place.

He found her bouncing along merrily on a pogo stick down a central highway, between long-abandoned taxis and city buses.

Her ponytails bounded along with her, as did the frilly little olde-worlde style dress she wore. She was, however, also wearing an MP3 player complete with little white earbud earphones, the dangling wire bouncing up and down as she pogoed across the impossibly slick ice surface, somehow able to keep it from turning into a bone-breaking disaster. The earphones were neatly plugged into a set of pointed Faerie ears.

Scout stepped carefully into her field of vision, hands raised. Fortunately he had no weapons -- there weren't any in Esrever's copy of a Frontliner bunker, just uniforms and flak vests.

The girl pogoed in place a bit, considering him, before she hopped off her toy, and pulled out the earphones. Upbeat acoustic guitar from some long-dead Canadian comic book author silenced as she tapped the pause button.

"You're dead, aren't you?" she asked him, cocking her head to the side, one ponytail dangling.

"Winterhound," Scout clarified. "And you're Halcyone."

"I like Hally," the Winterfae who called herself Hally corrected. "I don't like Winterhounds much. They snarl too much and get annoyed that there's nobody here to kill."

"I don't snarl, and I'm not killing anybody today."

"Living people are messy. I don't like messy. I like tidy and pretty and cold, just like I made this city," she said, with a gesture and a little smile of pride. "Do you like it? When I first got here it had lots of noisy, noisy people. I got rid of them. Now I have all the toys I want. I watch a lot of their movies. I eat ice ice cream. There's even a building here where they made games with dragons in them, I like those games a lot. They remind me of where we came from."

Scout shrugged, noncommittally. "I didn't come from there."

"Yeah, you were human once, weren't you? It's a funny sort of thing. Lady Winter never makes humans into her pets," Halcyone said, cocking her head to the other side, now. "You're special. I bet she has all sorts of plans for you. If I give you ice cream, will she owe me a favor for treating you nice?"

"Probably not," he said, honestly. "We don't get along well. She thinks I'm going to marry her one day. She's wrong."

"You're not afraid of me, are you? You aren't really one of us, and you don't like our Mistress much, but you're not scared I'm going to get rid of you like I got rid of the other humans."

"I'm dead. You only turn living people into nothing. Dead people aren't a bother."

"That's right! You're smart!" she said, clapping for his cleverness. "I think I like you. Where did you come from?"

He pointed off to the east.

"Oh," the Faerie said, disappointed. "The *living* place. I don't like that place. Summer had no right, invading my city like that. When that silver thing fell on part of my city, I decided to keep it because it was shiny and looked like it'd fun! Especially after I got rid of all the people inside it. It was mine for a long time before *they* came here and filled it with those stupid things. Didn't have the decency to get rid of them when they left, either. Now I can't go there. Isn't that sad?"

Scout decided not to tell the truth about how he felt about her killing everybody who used to live there. He needed to stay on her good side, after all.

"How long ago did you say that Summer invaded...?"

"Oh, I don't know. A few years? Time isn't something I like very much, so I don't allow it to do anything," she said, with a beaming smile. "Nothing changes here. Everything stays as perfect as it should be. Not like those other yucky rotting cities! Hey, hey. You should stay here. You'd like it, it just goes on and on, forever. There's nothing to hunt, but we could play hide and seek. I'm REALLY good at that..."

"Would you mind if I take some things from your city?" he asked, wanting to get on with this. "Some food, supplies, things like that."

"...why would you need that stuff? Sure, Winterhounds like to eat because it keeps their tummies from hurting, but you'd be okay."

I need to tell her. She could find out anyway, if watched from afar, he thought. "Got people with me. Humans. Don't worry; they're staying in the living-area. Just for a little while, I promise. They won't mess up your city."

"Ewww, messy people! Why would you wanna hang around-- oh, I get it! They're your pets, right?" she asked. "Winterhounds do that, sometimes. They drag away the silly humans and enthrall them. Then it gets REALLY messy, which is stupid, but hey, if it makes you smile... okay. You can feed your pets. But don't bring them into the city, okay? Unless you want me to get rid of them, I mean, like, if you're bored with them. That could be fun. I once knew this Winterhound who had a dozen females, and--"

"I'll just be about my business," Scout said curtly. "Thank you for your hospitality, Halcyone."

"Hally," she reminded him. "I'm bored now. Goodbye."

She plugged her headphones backed in, cranked up the music, and bounced away.

What a strange Winterhound, she thought, as she pogoed her way through the business district, heading to her favorite toy shop. *Why would Lady Winter coddle him and let him have so much free will and keep little human girls, if she was going to marry him?*

Hm. Maybe she's waiting for him to come around. Lady Winter's playing a game with him, a really long one. That's like her. So many pawns placed on so many spaces. One big forever game, so her children will always be happy and perfect.

Just like my city.

a05 flowers

The icy winds that rushed past him chilled him to the bone. It also kept the food and supplies he was hauling away in a pair of thick paper shopping bags chilled... probably for the best. Once he got back to camp, he wouldn't have long to cook them.

Around him, Edmonton gradually shifted from pristine ice to askew, damaged buildings, right up to the edge of a blast crater.

The weather shifted, as well. The icy winds warmed up the instant he crossed from the city proper into the circular zone of the Summer Court's lingering influence. Within 50 feet, the dead and blasted ground around him had sprouted grass. Then, flowers, vast fields of butter-yellow flowers, in a ring around the enormous silver dome...

One city had crashed into another, long ago. The original city was Edmonton, one of the many shining jewels that Canada used to own, a towering metropolis of steel and glass. The icy touch of Halcyone had preserved it nicely.

The other city was an Orbital Arcology. An alien city, fallen to Earth from the skies above.

Its vast silver dome was covered in flowers, vines, and other mossy overgrowth... but here and there, silver peeked out, like a vast mirrored hemisphere. It was through this gleaming surface that they had emerged this morning, emerging from a patch of metal that was iced over for only seconds until they had arrived, before the frost had evaporated into the air. After all, in the flower-fields around the Arcology, the temperature was a sweltering 99 degrees fahrenheit.

Camp had been established at a sealed airlock door, one Una had been unsuccessfully trying to gain access to for the last few hours, while Scout was, well, scouting out the human city that surrounded the crashed Arcology.

"Can't set foot outside the crater," he warned them, after setting down his shopping bags. "There's a powerful Winterfae out there who hates all living things. She'll leave us be if we leave her be, no sense pushing it. I got food, tents, other gear."

Emily was unsuccessfully fanning herself with her left hand, the heat causing her multiple layers of clothes to stick to her in a huge sweaty clump. "Please tell me you found some decent clothes," she begged. "Not all of us have all-weather techno fetish dresses..."

"If I could only open this external port, we could go inside and obtain you a hypertech laced garment," Una said, without much cheer. Her upbeat attitude had faded after the fiftieth attempt to open the doors via the remote keypad and display. "Until then, I could always remove mine and allow you to borrow it, but that would not solve the issue of having only one set of suitable clothing. --blast! Another layer of lockout! I thought I had it that time..."

Emily dug around in the shopping bags, while Scout gave his report.

"Got a guess as to what happened," he said. "The Arcology crashed into

Edmonton awhile back. Halcyone, the Winterfae who owns the city, killed everybody inside. ...she doesn't have much perspective on mortality or morality, for that matter. Then, some years after... the Summer Court invaded."

"This far north? No way," Emily disagreed. "Even with the alliance in place, making them all cooperate -- which in Faerie terms means wider smiles while hiding the knives behind their back and lying in wait -- I can't see the Summer Court venturing this deep into Winter Court turf."

"Flowers," Scout reminded her, pointing a thumb over his shoulder to the ring of fields that covered the downslope of the crater. "Deep Faerie magic, certainly not Winter's. ...besides, I know how it went down. Summer insults Winter by coming up here. Winter exacts revenge and kills Austin, Texas... a city Summer had wanted for years, thinking it was hers by right. ...Lady Winter said she attacked my city because of a Summer trespass. This is the place."

"So... Summer risked breaking the alliance when they found out Lady Winter had a hidden cache of off-world technology," Emily speculated. "Presumably after the incident with Graves. Hell, odds are Graves crossed over Summer's turf on the way back to Baltimore with his stolen hypertech, and that's how Lady Summer found out about this place. They come up here, seal off the place against Halcyone's influence, do their research... uh. That could mean they're still in there..."

"I rather wish they would allow us access, then," Una protested. "I feel quite silly, poking away at this. I am not much of a security expert, even knowing father's Council codes. ...ah, I wanted to find out what he got me for Life Day one year and looked into his acquisition logs."

Scout had a seat nearby. Normally he'd just stand at ease, but even with his stamina, the heat was oppressive. "Halcyone said they left. The flowers are just a defensive measure, in case they want to return, I suppose. ...guess Lady Winter was gracious to let the insult slide."

"Uh... Scout. She killed everybody in Austin, remember?"

"She was balancing the scales. Alliance could've collapsed otherwise. A full-on Faerie civil war. World might not've survived that. ...not that I forgive her. Ever."

Emily pulled a tissue-paper wrapped bundle of cloth from the bags, starting to unpack it. "So, we go in there and figure out what they were up to, report it back to Una's dad-- Scout, what the hell?"

"...what?"

She held out the too-wide shorts, glaring at him. "I *told* you my waist size, yes? Please tell me this was the only thing you could find."

"Thought you were exaggerating. Don't girls do that? Didn't want to have to make another trip, figured bigger could at least be worn, but smaller would be problematic..."

If the temperature were any lower, Emily would be fuming. As is, she didn't have the strength to bother, already boiling internally. She shoved the clothes under an arm. "I am going around the long way to find somewhere I can change in decency," she informed him, as icily as the heat would allow. "And you *will* see how svelte and ladylike I am, or will poke your eyes out. Ahem. Excuse me."

He watched her go, with no small amount of confusion. If Una was the sort to kick puppies, and she wasn't, she'd have recognized the post-kicking look. Sort of a What'd-I-Do? expression.

The befuddled silence was interrupted by Una letting two sneezes out in succession.

"...guh. Pollen, I believe," she said, trying to discreetly wipe her nose. "The plant life is quite thick here. ...ah, I believe I may need a full day to gain access. Some sort of security protocol is in place, a bit like father's authentication systems, but... not quite. ...perhaps therein lies the key to this mystery."

"Key?" Scout asked, wanting to shift to thinking about something other than Emily's disappointment.

"Something is very strange here. An entire Arcology has crashed on your world! That should not be possible!" Una said, pushing the fold-out keypad back into the surface of the ship for now. (It sealed itself, leaving behind only a smooth and seamless surface.)

"Machines break," Scout suggested.

"True, but... this is a catastrophic failure! We have systems and subsystems and more designed to prevent this sort of thing. In addition... I would have known if an entire Arcology fell on your world. Even if it happened before I was born, it's so impossible, so unheard of, that it'd be common knowledge in the fleet, yes? And it certainly wouldn't be left here to rot; it would be recovered or destroyed immediately. Otherwise..."

"Hypertech leaks. Just like the ones we traced here."

"Exactly. This is the absolute worst case example of interference in another world's progress! It... ah... *achoo!* Ah, it is beyond reason that this could have happened, or if it did happen, could have stayed here like an unexploded explosive! ...although... ah..."

"...although?" he prompted.

"It could have shifted in from another world," she suggested. "Another cataclysmic failure, if it shifted onto the surface instead of into high orbit. ...but the crater suggests it fell! So... I'm uncertain."

"Shifted...?"

"Oh, yes. It's how we move from world to world," Una explained. "Arcologies are fitted with shift drives, like the kind my mother attended to. It crosses the divide between worlds in less than a second. Whenever a fleet moves from one world to another, they shift. When a new ship being built on the surface of a world is sent along on its mission, it shifts. It's quite impossible to move from world to world using the gravity thrusters, after all!"

"But... the crater. Couldn't have just appeared. Might've appeared *through* the ground, but still wouldn't be a crater..."

"Teleporting, huh?"

The two looked over at the... well, you could tell she was a witch from the pointy hat. Emily refused to take that off, no matter how hot it was.

She'd taken the too-large shirt Scout got her and tied it up in the middle, making an impromptu halter. The shorts, (simultaneously too baggy and too short for her tastes) had been secured in place by tightening her spell-holster belt several extra notches. This, plus the sweat from the sweltering "summer" sun, resulted in a lot more of Emily being shown off than usual. Notably, far more than head, ankles, and hands.

The only sensible part of the ensemble was the footwear, tramping along the flower-covered grasses beneath them.

"...not one word," she warned, up front. "Not one damn word. It's functional and that's all there is to it. ...I do approve of the hiking boots, though. Good call there, Scout, considering the terrain. I might keep these when we get the hell out of here. ...so. Una. Your culture teleports from world to world?"

"Ah... sort of, yes," Una continued, despite distraction. "I guess shifting could be considered a kind of teleportation. Not that I have seen it done -- I was born well after we came to your Earth, and our mission of cultural observation was to last another seventy years or so before we moved on. ...I suppose shifting is irrelevant to this mystery. Please, disregard. ...ah, we have food, yes? My physiology is strongly demanding proper nutrition..."

On cue, Scout opened the second of the shopping bags -- revealing an array of plastic-and-styrofoam wrapped steaks, some small bottles of seasoning, fresh vegetables, and more. "It's safe to eat. The city they were in is locked in time. I also brought utensils and cooking tools."

Emily peered in the depths of the bag, at the assorted groceries. "What, no military rations for you?" she joked.

"...thought I'd try something with a bit more flavor today," Scout explained. "For a change."

Emily knew how to cook various varieties of Nomad's Vittles... simple dishes that took whatever you could get your hands on and made it edible. Back home she was too busy reading books to bother learning how to cook, despite chowing down on a number of country feasts prepared for her whole village... and when you wander the Fringe, never quite sure where your next meal is coming from and occasionally having to make do with the old hunter/gatherer routine, gourmet cooking was a rarity.

Scout, on the other hand, had a few years with Saul to learn not only military tactics and weapon proficiency, but also the ins and outs of good Texas barbecue cooking. It was one part of the union that absolutely knew what to do with a slab of meat to make it more than chewable, but delectable.

"Haven't done this in a long time. Haven't bothered," he forewarned them, before dinner was served from the simple cooking pit he'd crafted up. "Don't know if I got the mixtures right or anything."

It turned out to be needless humility. The food was utterly satisfying, especially after a tiring day in the baking sun. As that sun started to sink below the horizon, with bellies full, the three fell to repose... Una turning in early, complaining of headaches, while Scout and Emily sat and watched the sunset, eating from two small cups of yogurt with plastic spoons.

"What I don't get," Emily said, between spoonfuls of yummy goodness, "Is why you don't cook more often. I mean, why forage? Why eat raw deer, for that matter?"

Scout sat back a bit amidst the flowers, considering. He'd barely touched his yogurt, in contrast to Emily gobbling it down. "Never wanted to. A Winterhound can eat nearly anything to make do. Don't have to eat at all, really, we can survive even when starving... just do out of habit and to silence any hunger pains. So, I didn't bother with anything fancy after... y'know."

"And tonight...?"

"I didn't make that steak for me. I made it for you. Us. ...y'know."

Emily nodded. Sh'knew, indeed. She had one last helping, emptying out the little cup, and set it aside while watching the last gasps of sunset.

The temperature had started falling, as the sun slipped over the horizon. From the lower vantage point inside the crater, the 'setting' was a bit early, but the effect could be physically felt. The night wasn't going to be as cold as the dead city around them, but it would bring welcome relief all the same. As the light slipped away, the flickery, badly damaged battery lantern Scout had brought back would have to make do -- although that was fine by her. It reminded her a lot of the candlelight she usually read by, back home.

"Probably for the best that we're getting a night to unwind. Once Space Girl gets that door open we'll be in full forensic investigation mode," Emily thought aloud. "After that, I guess Una'll call her dad and they'll send in cleanup crews. She can't tidy a city-sized mess all by herself."

"Right. And then...?"

"...then... I don't know. I guess we go after whatever tech the Summer Court took, although I'd rather face Graves again then that lot," she said, with a grimace.

"Aren't they the 'good' Faeries?" Scout asked, as his experience with the other court was quite minimal.

"Aren't you and Esrever the 'bad' Faeries? There's charlatans and saints in every camp. If you're very lucky you'll find the latter before the former, but nobody who gave Jesse that hypertech counts as a saint in my book. Honestly? This could get bad. And I don't have the foggiest idea how to approach it beyond just stomping around the giant expanse of middle America looking for Faeries with zap guns."

"I'm sure you'll think of something. ...and after we deal with the Summer Court? What then?" Scout asked, tentatively.

"Uh... I don't know. I guess that's it. Una goes home, maybe the aliens fly away. It'd be over."

"What will you do...?"

Emily shrugged, not quite picking up on Scout's implied concerns. "I haven't thought about it much. Same as I always do, I guess. Wander around trying to help people, run away from mobs with pitchforks and torches. Try to find more spells. Do witchy things."

"...you wouldn't have to worry about the torches, if you didn't want to."

"Why? You know how to make hats fireproof?"

"No. I could go with you," Scout said, quickly, to get the words out. "...if you want me to, I mean. If you don't mind."

Emily slowly turned to look at him, curious. She leaned on one arm, lying back a bit. "So... what, as my bodyguard...?"

"If you like. If you want me to be," he suggested.

"...it's damned boring roaming around by myself. Lonely, too. And you cook a mean steak," Emily justified.

"I could be your chef, if you want me to be."

The wandering witch offered a playful grin. "So, what, you're saying you'll cook for me for the rest of my life?"

"...if you want me to," Scout said, his seriousness now sharply contrasting that amusement.

The difference in his voice hit Emily a bit too late. She quickly shook off the giggles at the idea of Scout in a chef's hat, realizing the mental joke image of a "Kiss the Cook" apron had... other implications. ...but after a moment's consideration, she had an answer.

"I.. could go for that. I think it could work," she decided. "You and me, I mean. Us. --wandering around. Two beats one for long journeys, after all. Right."

Emily pondered.

Something was different about him.

No doubt it was in aftermath of the mirror experiences, of course. That didn't take much Insight. But he seemed... more connected, maybe. Less likely to sink into the background. Maybe this was just because Emily didn't have some mercenary king or miracle doctor to yammer on with, someone to distract her while Scout slipped away from them, but... it didn't feel like he'd do that again, even if they were distracted. He was *here*. With her.

And, according to his suggestion, he'd be here with her for a very long time. It was an idea she found it unusually easy to get behind. Before starting Ye Grande Adventyre, she'd been perfectly happy to shuffle from village to village by herself, but... the prospect of returning to that, now that she'd had a moment to sit down and consider it, wasn't very appealing.

...of course, that also brought up why Scout was with them in the first place, when (until now) he hadn't particularly seemed to enjoy having company. Why did he tag along with them after they left Olney? At the time, the best he could offer was one of his dismissive shrugs, and Emily hadn't bothered pursuing it. If asked, he'd probably just ignore the question, she felt.

Maybe he wouldn't ignore it now. Although... it could also break whatever strange spell was in the air tonight, if she asked...

Nuts to that, Emily thought. Sentimentalism shouldn't get in the way of being informed.

"Scout, why did you join us on this trip in the first place?" Emily asked him.

"...Lady Winter ordered me to."

Night had brought calmer climates to them, but a chill deeper than that ran through her.

"I don't know why," Scout said. "She never explains these things. Winter wanted me to follow you. At the time I didn't know or care why, it didn't matter, so I did as she commanded. ...I won't hurt you. I don't care if she orders me to. I'm good at saying no, lots of practice. But if she wanted you dead, she might be able to force me to do it. Told you one day she'd probably destroy and remake me, to be her consort. ...do I need to point out I'm dangerous to you, again?"

"No. Absolutely not. Obviously I'm not going to turn you out over a thing like that," Emily said, firmly. "Neither of us will let that come to pass without fighting it with everything we've got. Besides... that's an assumption, that she'd want us killed. There were plenty of opportunities to do it before now, after all."

"Emily. Wendigoes."

"Which we overcame. I don't think that was an assassination attempt, it was just... some sick kind of test. Like the mirrors. She's playing silly buggers, is what she is... not trying to stop us, but... I don't know. Trying to mess with us? ...egh. No, no. Now I've gone and ruined the mood, see. And it was such a lovely evening until now--"

"Blueberry."

"--eh?"

"I found a blueberry in my yogurt," Scout said, pointing his spoon to the plastic cup. He'd been eating it more slowly, in little bursts. "There's a big one in here. You should have it. I don't need the vitamins as much as you do. Say ahh."

"Wha--?"

Plop. Emily went crosseyed a moment, the fruity nugget having been placed on her tongue by the boy's spoon. Instinct kicked in after that.

"Good?" Scout asked, simply.

"...muhhh. Umm. ...yeah. It is. Thanks, Scout," Emily replied, a smile coming back. She shook off the last of the rattled nerves caused by Lady Winter's vague schemes, getting to her feet, stretching arms over her head. "Y'know, I'm pooped. Think I'd better turn in. Thanks for bringing sleeping bags, by the way."

"Mhm. I'll keep watch. I don't need much sleep."

Although his eyes covered the horizon of the crater's edge, he did linger whenever he passed over Emily, back turned to him as she slept on her side. Visually checking now and then to make sure she was sleeping well, soundly, no bad dreams.

It was all a lie, of course. Wandering with her forever. Eventually, Emily would die. And well before that, Lady Winter would grow bored with his antics and recall him to her side, to shatter him like ice and rebuild him to be lover to the Crown of Ice. She'd promised as much when he was brought back from the dead. It would simply... be.

But hopefully, that day would not come for a very, very long time. Long enough to explore the new feelings that the animal side of him promised he could now safely access. Feelings that very much involved his new companion.

This wasn't how Emily had envisioned a Shiny Jetpack Future City would look like.

Everything should be made of gleaming, flawless chromed metals, white plastics, colored glass. There should be light everywhere, maybe with holograms or something, like in old sci-fi movies. And people... there should be equally shiny people, flawless and pretty like Una, wandering around talking about high intellectual concepts without a care in the world...

This was rather the opposite.

From the moment Una broke through the complicated security on the airlock, they were hit in the face with a heat wave MORE intense than the one outside. Like the flowers outside, the inside had been completely overgrown with plants... vines, this time. Moss. Ivy. Covering every surface, choking the air thick with their scents. The power was on (otherwise the airlock would never have opened) but nothing was shiny, nothing was lit up properly -- plants had broken most of the overhead lights, others left flickering away, still others strong but so covered in fungus that they were dimmed to nothingness. The only consistent light came from Emily's handheld light spell.

As for people... if she didn't know about Halcyone's fixation on 'cleaning up' messy people, she'd have assumed the place was never occupied. No people. Not even bodies...

Una coughed violently on the pollen and junk in the air. Wading through the ankle-deep indoor swamp was not helping her allergies. "The... guh... the Council Chambers will be not be far now," she said. "A half hour's walk, hopefully, at most. We are halfway there already. Every Arcology configuration is different, but the engines and the chambers are always in the center. Judging from the size of the ci... the ciii... ahhh... ghkk. ...I believe I have swallowed a sneeze..."

"Maybe we should get out of here," Emily suggested. "We're hardly crime scene investigators, you know. Just call your pop and have them take over..."

"No... no, this is my task. I want to know how this... this impossible thing has happened," Una said. "I'll be fine, friends. I love... ghlrk. I love plant life. I used to take picnics in the arboretum on Arcology #BE12, remember? Plenty of floral lifeforms there, from all manner of worlds, and they never bothered me. I'd run around watering them, and I'd give them names, and we'd have Earth-style meat sandwiches, and..."

Emily sighed, and pulled a hanky from her back pocket. (A good witch is always prepared, even when she's abandoned her nicer clothes in favor of Deep Jungle Harlot Shortpants.) "Una? Less talking. Just... wrap this around your mouth, breathe through it. We'll go on if you insist, but no sense not taking precautions. ...Scout?

You holding up okay?"

The boy glanced to her sharply. He'd been twitchy ever since they got in here... seemingly.. prowling, at their side. Keeping his gaze flicking left and right. "I'm alert," he said. "I'm fine. ...Summer Court. This place is thick with it, even thicker than outside. It disagrees with the lesser half of me. That's all."

"This is over the top, even for the Summer Court," Emily recognized, tugging a vine away from the wall, trying to find some sort of shiny under it. All she got was mottled, slightly crumpled metal paneling. "Sure, they like the whole green motif when doing interior decorating, but they rarely go for the entire Creature From the Black Lagoon flat pack kit..."

"...thought you hated rubber monster movies."

"I do. You have no idea how many I had to watch as a kid. All the *boys* in my village loved them," Emily grimaced. "I think the whole big ugly woogums bonking teenage girls over the head and dragging them away thing appeals to the male trouser jockey mentality. ...um. No offense."

Scout didn't take any. He was too busy being squirrely. "There's a reason Winterhounds are usually male," he agreed. "And I know better than most. ...I've come to terms with that, though."

"Keeping the Big Bad Wolf on lockdown, huh?"

"...not completely," he admitted.

"Eh?" Emily asked. Not alarmed, not shocked, just... not expecting that answer.

"Long story. I'll explain later. No danger, though. I swear it."

"We've got time for long stories, I think," Emily said. "It was the mirrors, right? The introspective ones. I know my own was enlightening, if a bit nutso crazy bonkers..."

"Talking's too risky for you, not just Una."

"Eh?"

"You should stop talking and breathe through a mask," Scout indicated. He tore part of his sleeve off, offering the thick fabric to her. "Hold this over your mouth. Una's an alien, not used to Earth plant life, but it is could hit you soon enough. Better not to inhale the junk as much."

She couldn't argue with the logic. She accepted the cloth, nodding once before pressing it to her mouth with her non-lit hand. Soon, the only sounds around them were the squelch and splash of their feet tramping through the hallway muck.

On the whole, Emily would've preferred conversation to that sound of life amidst the dead.

The air within the vast Council Chamber wasn't quite as musky and horrid-smelling. Instead of cramped corridors, the oval-shaped room was spacious with a high domed ceiling... it showed the sky above the Arcology, although clearly this was a projected illusion, as the sunny skies flickered now and then like a television screen on the fritz.

Everything here was just as ruined as the rest of the ship. Chairs were knocked aside, the table they previously surrounded sagging after one of its legs had been corroded through by a heavy strain of mold. Holographic displays showing current system states were fuzzy, indistinct... ghost numbers tallying up themselves forever, with nobody to relate their info-dumps to.

Fortunately, the walls hadn't taken the plant life very well. Whatever the ivory-colored metal alloy was, it resisted the corruption that had soaked through the rest of the city.

Acid-etched carvings of some kind crawled along these walls instead. These depicted proud looking Orbitals, gazing and/or pointing towards the bright future horizon... vast sky-ships soaring through the stars... and worlds, endless round planets representing the eternal journey of knowledge the Orbitals had chosen to undertake.

Una couldn't resist describing the history to her friends, despite a promise to keep it brief.

"Ages ago, we launched from our homeworld," she explained. "The shift drives were the invention that freed us from a solitary existence on one little world. Now, all worlds were ours to observe, to learn from, and to contemplate. It's a quest for infinite knowledge. An Observation fleet hovers over a world for some time, learns what they can from it, stores it in our vast networked databases -- that's depicted here, in the mural, with the fleet surrounding this world, see?"

"...I see," Emily said, studying the shape, the lines etched into the wall. "And... how do you find these worlds?"

"Oh, we have Surveyor fleets for that," Una continued. "See, this one here shows them shifting into orbit over a new world, rich with life, vast untapped potential knowledge! It takes some time for them to find life-sustaining new worlds for Observation. We come across many lifeless worlds, or ones where life perished long ago-- here, here!"

She moved along the edge of the Council Chambers, pointing to a world that was... no longer circular. It had been broken down, disassembled into precisely geometric chunks.

"Even dead worlds can be put to good use. It's a cycle of life!" Una said, beaming with pride (despite the watery, red-streaked look in her eyes from the pollen around her). "Mining fleets shift above these expired planets. From there, planetary mass is extracted, compressed down, and stored in capacitors, to become a wonderful source of energy! Continuing in this way, the Orbitals will never lack for worlds to observe. Our scientists have predicted there to be an infinite number of life-sustaining worlds out there... so many opportunities for learning! ...friend? You look.. unsettled. Is the pollen getting to you, too?"

Emily looked left, right... up and down the span of the mural. She had to be sure, before she brought the point up.

"Okay... this world on the very far left. That's the original Orbital home planet, right?" Emily asked, pointing to the engraved image.

"Ah... yes. As I said."

"Right. And this one here, representing a typical Observation fleet. That's a different world, correct?"

"Well, of course! What use would observing our own world be--"

"And the one being broken down by the miners, that one's yet another different world."

"...er. Yes? I'm not sure I understand. Why would it be the same?"

A finger traced along the wall carving, following the grooved lines in the metal. Tracing around, a lumpy sketch of a coastline. South, and west... then around a little outreaching peninsula...

"Una," Emily said. "All three of those supposedly different worlds have the same exact continents on them. They ALL look identical to Earth. Look, there's Eastusa, and there's Florida... that other one, that's showing Africa. The mined planet, I think that's Australia in the corner of what's left... for crying out loud, the one being 'Surveyed' is showing Eastusa again!"

She could have pointed out that water was wet and the sun was bright, for all the shock and surprise that registered with Una. "Yes, and? Why is this strange?"

"They're ALL Earth!"

"Well, of course not! Your world is Earth. The others almost always have different names."

"...almost always...? Una... are you saying every populated planet in the Milky Way is identical to Earth, just with funny names?"

"Milky...? --OH! Oh, I see! The name you have attributed to the galaxy itself. Ha ha, I see, yes, just like your science fiction movies!" Una exclaimed, happy to have figured out the puzzle. "No no, there's only one planet in this galaxy that supports life, as far as our scientists can tell. We don't cross interstellar distances -- we *shift* through layers of reality, visiting different incarnations of the same world. I suppose... yes, I see! I am indeed from a version of your Earth, and thus biologically human, despite being of the Orbitals. ...well, technically, I was born in orbit over *your* world, so that does make me an 'Orbital-Earthling' native to this reality, I guess--"

Emily stamped her foot in frustration. Fortunately, there wasn't an inch-thick layer of floral sludge here to splash around.

"You said you were an *alien from outer space!*"

"Well... I am," Una said. "Our ships remain in high orbit, which is under scientific definition 'outer space' in relation to the surface. Obviously I am not from your country, nor an immigrant with proper paperwork, and therefore I am an illegal alien visitor. It seemed a more appropriate word than 'foreigner', and less vague than 'outsider'... did I choose the incorrect term? Is it important? Sometimes I have difficulty with Earth language..."

"Is it important? *Is it important!?*" Emily raged. "IS IT--?!"

...and she paused.

"...actually, I'm not sure if it is important, but it feels like it ought to be," she said, catching herself. She was tumbling the idea around in her mind, now that the surprise had already popped out of its little box. "I mean... I guess it doesn't change much of anything, being a 'shifter' instead of a 'deep space alien' or however you'd call it, but... agh. I don't know. Now I'm getting a headache."

"Could be the pollen," Scout reminded her, speaking up for the first time since offering his sleeve. "Let's get the information we came for and go. Doesn't matter right now how the Orbitals move around. Matters more how and why this Arcology crashed, and what's become of it since the Summer Court took over."

"Right, right," Emily said, shoving the revelation aside, ignoring her intellectual bafflement at it. "Gotta stay focused. Thanks, Scout. Una, you have your dad's council codes, right? Can you dig up, I don't know, meeting minutes or logs or something out of that table's computers...?"

"Ye-- yuhghkaaaff," Una gurgled, the cough she'd been trying to keep down finally rising to the surface. She moved her hanky back to her mouth, muffling herself slightly as she moved to the table. "It shoulf be eafier than the airloff doorf, I hope..."

She carefully brushed aside a layer of pollen and dust from the surface of the table, sure not to sweep it up and into the air, just push it aside. Fingers played over the featureless surface, somehow finding buttons that Emily couldn't spot upon the smooth and flawless metal surface -- lights flared at each touch of her fingers, the only indication she wasn't uselessly poking at the table randomly. It took several minutes of this poking, judging from Una's muffled curses of "Oh, shoot" and

"Darn!" and "Such a bother!" before--

The image was 3-D. It was a slice of the room itself, or rather, a narrow viewport into the council chambers, a perspective turned around and replayed in midair. It focused on the head and shoulders of an elderly Orbital, the rest of his body not in the recorder's frame. He was bleeding from a gash on his forehead, raised and swelling, and the distant sounds of panic and alarms could be heard beneath the tinny representation of his voice...

"Elder Pwq's errata to the day's logged decisions," he spoke. "Our city has fallen to the world below. We don't yet know what has happened -- we were on schedule to leave the fleet, a routine shift of resources. But instead of shifting into the orbit of another world, we shifted directly into this world's atmosphere. We have Chief Engineer Tyr to thank for his quick work using the gravity thrusters to prevent massive damage to the ship, but both thrusters and the shift engine were severely damaged on impact. I'll append more errata when I have more information to append."

The image flickered. His forehead wound was now gone, although the alarms were still going... figures in the background were attending to the wounded, sharing information on small square tablets of some sort.

"Elder Pwq's errata, continued. We are unable to contact the fleet for assistance. The same unusual, contradictory error messages we get when trying to access the engines are popping up on our communications arrays. Tyr says that the error is completely illogical, and should be quite impossible, but somehow it crippled every failsafe in place to prevent this sort of disaster. Councilwoman Rew is suggesting we send scouting parties outside of the city, but I've decided to seal the airlocks, for the time being. Non-interference must be held -- our people cannot leave, and the natives cannot be allowed inside. ...I fear how far I may need to take this ruling. Message ends, for now."

Hovering pictures faded away. Una worked the keypad, trying to find the next one. "There is a gap -- no missing data, but no further logs. I, ah, aahh... ACHOOGhhk... excuse. I assume they were too busy to sit around recording--"

The next log entry appeared. The imaged version of the Council Chamber was darkened, now... and Pwq had fear in his eyes. Other men, in more tattered silver clothes, were hunkered down behind fallen chairs, with energy weapons drawn...

"If someone finds this entry, I want it known that I have done what I have done with no regrets. I support the highest law of Orbital culture," he spoke, quickly. There was some echoing sound in the background... some sort of pulsing electric sound. "We must remain sealed. No one in. No one out. The risk to this world is too high. Pragmatism dictates that if we are stuck here, if the city will never move again, at the very least it must remain an unbreachable artifact that will never yield its secrets. The Earth city beyond appears to be empty, and the surrounding terrain frozen and lifeless, but we cannot take chances. I have heavily encoded the airlocks, and should the... factions within the city now that insist on leaving ever breach them, they will self-seal moments later."

A sinking feeling began high in Emily's throat, rapidly dropping to the bottom of her stomach. "Self-sealing airlocks...?"

"I have locked down all shuttles, although if they are taken, I suppose an exit could be blasted through the walls," Pwq spoke, some bitterness now in his voice. "Assuming my fellow Orbitals have truly gone mad, mad enough to attempt such a thing. ...why did we have so many damned weapons lying in our cargo holds? I've held a seat on three different Arcologies and I've never seen one so well armed! I can't find the supply transfer logs for these terrible things. Suppose it doesn't matter now. This is a war, a war for our ideals, which must--"

"Sir! They've breached an airlock!" a voice from off-camera shouted. "They've... what's that noise--?"

All went quiet.

And then... a little girl's giggle.

The recording ended.

"...Halcyone," Scout said, darkly. "That was her. She ended their civil war. I see, now. They crash, reasons unknown. Sabotage, likely. Seal up, pick sides, fight each other, kill each other--"

"No. NO," Una declared, weakly pounding a fist on the table, kicking up some of the mold. She resumed typing at the keyboard, intense, trying to search for more files. "This... this can't be. A war? It's preposterous! Even if there was disagreement, there would be... discourse. Analysis. Reasoned contemplation! We are not savages!"

"Nobody's saying you are," Scout spoke, voice far calmer. "But anyone can kill, in the right circumstances--"

"Impossible! We are.. we are enlightened. Not like the worlds in conflict and strife that we have observed! Orbitals do not murder! They... they..."

...her mother, the silver headband, the nosebleed...

Una's breathing was rapid. Her handkerchief had been left aside, now using both fingers to type. There had to be a file, had to be some data which disproved Scout's theory, something that would make all of this fit in with everything she knew to be true about her people...

The keyboard was closer, and closer still. Was it rising from the table? No. She was falling to meet it. That was the more logical conclusion. Yes, she was in fact falling, hitting her head against the table, because gravity was a law of physics. Consistent, reasonable, sensible.

At least something makes sense, she thought, before falling unconscious.

"...the thingy is below the other thingy now. And it's beeping in a way I do not approve of, not one bit..."

"What would happen if we pushed--"

"No pushing anything! Not that thing, or the thing below it, or the other thing. We've got no idea what would happen!"

"Gotta do something."

"I know. I know! I'll do something. Just give me a moment to *think*, okay?! Give me a moment, here!"

"...sorry."

"I should've taken some damn notes. I saw Zee do the whole procedure, end to end, and I was so busy pondering the morality of it I didn't bother learning anything useful! I wouldn't even know where to start, or if it'd even work..."

I'm scared, Una thought. She heard voices, distant -- her friends. *Help me. I'm scared. Emily, please...*

A shadow crossed her vision. It was a person, she reasoned, simply between herself and a light source high above. Above? Yes, she was lying on her back. A medical bed. They'd found a medical bay, and brought her here, she remembered that now through the fever pounding in her head...

"We're going to help you," Emily declared. "Don't be afraid, okay? I'll fix you. One damn way or another. A witch makes things work out, in the end. It's what we are."

"I'm not afraid," Una mumble-lied.

Emily declined to correct her. Odds are, the girl didn't even remember saying it aloud.

She wore the confidence of the witch, despite knowing it was false... even if she was trying to avoid those pretensions, after her little mirror experience, she knew they had a purpose here. They would reassure her friend that everything was being taken care of, even if nothing was in fact being taken care of. Hope was the cornerstone of Una's life, and Emily was *not* going to dash it to little bits if she could help it.

Mending spells did nothing to stop the infection. The rash, the same green color as the plant life around them, had started spreading the moment Una collapsed and wasn't stopping. By now, it had nearly covered half of her perfect, pretty skin, leaving Una mottled and sickly looking. And if Mending wasn't doing a damned thing to repair the damaged tissues... that meant this wasn't some ordinary malady.

It was magic.

"Scout, I want you to look around the ship, and in your own speedy little shadow jumpy way," Emily decided.

"Understood. Looking for a way out? The hole Graves made when he left, maybe?"

"Not yet. If we get her out of here that won't change anything. She's been exposed to whatever this is. So have I, but I'm not sick in the slightest... I have a feeling it was put here specifically to take out any Orbitals who dropped in on Summer's little project," she explained. "There's got to be a source. Find me a plant. Something large, growing, living. The root of everything that's filled this city. Trust me... you'll know it when you find it. It's gonna positively reek with Summer Court magic and set all your Winterhound hackles a-risin'. Come back when you've found it -- don't take any action. We'll go confront it together."

The Winterhound stretched, flexing his joints, ready to move... and moved. He stepped into a dim corner of the lab, and was gone.

Emily didn't loosen up, in contrast. She was wound tight, but a good tight. The sort of tight she felt when there was a problem to grapple with... a situation that needed the wise witchy wiles she had in surplus. This tangle could be untangled. Una would survive this. There had to be no doubt whatsoever, about that--

"I'm going to die, aren't I?" a weak voice spoke from the egg-shaped medical bed.

"Absolutely not," Emily quickly replied. "This is magic. I AM magic. We'll fix it."

"I've never been loved. Not like you are."

That made Emily's coiled internal springs creak slightly. "Huh...?"

"I tried, and I tried, but nobody wanted to love me," Una spoke, quietly, in an odd and sad calm. "I never looked in the right places. I made mistakes. All I wanted was the kind of love my mother and father had. And I'll never feel it, now. I'm so scared, Emily. I don't want to die unloved..."

"Cut that out, NOW, girl. You'll be up and eating New York pizza in no time! ...look... we love you, okay? You're our friend. We've had some bumps on the road, but all the crap we've been through, it'd be impossible not to come out the side caring about each other--"

"That's not the kind of love I mean, and you know it. ...you have to make me a promise, Emily. Please. This is very, very important."

Emily bit her lip. "If this is some kind of cheesy melodramatic deathbed promise, forget it. It won't matter--"

"You have to love him."

"--huh?"

"Scout loves you," Una whispered, very carefully, very quietly, trying to make sure she got the right words through the fever-haze that was blurring her senses. "Not me, you. He'll never find peace until you return that love. If you two go on without me then you have to do it together, with love. Please. Promise me that, Emily. I can't die without knowing he'll have what I couldn't have. Promise me."

"I," Emily started.

"Uh," she continued.

"..." she failed to say.

Well, he DID want to cook for you for the rest of his life, some no-nonsense part of her recalled. *To journey with you even after your business with the Orbitals was finished. And you liked the sound of that. A lot.*

"I found it."

If it was physically possible to jump out of her skin, she would have. As is, she simply knocked over a tray of silvery medical tools, arms flailing in surprise.

"The plant. It's definitely Summer Court magic," Scout confirmed, leaning his head towards the door. "Not far. It's in some kind of preserve. Let's go."

"--right. Let's go," Emily agreed, straightening her pointy hat. Witch time. "Una, we'll be back in minutes, and we'll have the solution. All three of us are getting out of this deathtrap, or my name is not Emily Moonthistle, Witch at Large. Lead on, Scout."

Una tried to raise a hand, to protest. To say something. Too weak. *Don't go. You need to promise me. You can't leave until you promise me...*

And they were gone.

Her head rolled to one side... eyes falling on a silvery handheld device, that had been knocked onto her bedside by Emily's panic reaction.

Even with her blurry vision, she noted two things about it. One, exactly what it was used for, based on her early internship as a biologist. And two, the serial number, indicating which Arcology medical bay it was assigned to.

Pouring all her hope into the action, she forced her arm to move, to reach, to grasp. To thumb the button at the end of the stimulator.

If the Council Chambers were vast, this new place was vastness upon vastness.

It was pressed up against the surface of the Arcology, near the top... Emily could tell because several of the windows high above had been shattered high above, bringing in fresh air. They weren't simulated skies, like the Council Chambers had... no flickering, no telltale signs of images. Just the rush of air and true sunlight. Both were quite important, considering the plant life.

While the entire Arcology had been stuffed to bursting with plants, this room WAS plants. Emily couldn't even see the walls. Various bits of Orbital technology were strewn about, often tangled up in the layer upon layer of twisted plant life that ran through the mulch beneath her boots, but that was about it when it came to artificialness. Nature had found a haven and taken root to it, quite literally.

The pair approached the center of the room cautiously. A good idea, when a gigantic, mouthed flytrap the size of a Baltimore city bus was writhing and slavering and waving menacing looking tentacles with vicious barbs on them. That's not something you want to bumrush. Unfortunately, it also wasn't something you could sneak up on, given it was the centerpiece of the entire room.

This was definitely the right place; Emily could see, as Scout led the way, how the vines and ivy through the halls all seemed to originate from here. The lines of life followed straighter paths the closer they got to this Faerie vision of Eden... emerging through open hallway entrances to join the chaos of nature, all roads leading back to that one giant plant...

"Talk or fight?" Scout asked, in a low whisper.

"Talk first," Emily suggested. "Assuming the thing is sapient, I mean. I'm... really not relishing the idea of trying to 'fight' that thing. Let's see what we can manage through diplomacy alone--"

[Winterling. Summerling.]

The pair stopped in their tracks. It would've been bad enough if the giant flytrap had lungs and vocal cords; instead, it spoke directly into their minds. Never a good sign.

[Winterling-out-of-favor. Smell of beast, but not-smell of anti-life girl,] the flytrap continued... its leaves twisting outward, unfurling, angling as if to 'watch' them. [Summerling-out-of-favor. Smell of human-mage, but not-smell of Archmagus. Both fall outside of the Lady-geas. Not-welcome. Not-unwelcome. Uncertain.]

"Ah... hello there, Sir Plant," Emily said nervously, falling into a curtsey despite having left her nice skirts behind. "As a wanderer, one familiar with accorded bonds of wild forests, one respectful of nature's innate power and with respect due in turn, I hereby request peaceful parlay until--"

[Not-dryad, witchling. No-code. No-parlay. Only the Lady-geas.]

So much for that idea, Emily grumbled internally. *New tactic.* "Explain the Lady-geas," she said, simple and direct.

[Life-reward, mind-reward. Unfurling leaves. Unfurling mind. Favor-exchange, Lady-geas,] the plant continued, its broadcast thoughts like tiny green shoots emerging through Emily's senses, ordering themselves into simple patterns. [Silver-people, if-return, not-leave. Must-purge. Spread-self, spore-cloud, grow within. We-grow. We-grow.]

"You were ordered by Lady Summer to kill any Orbitals who come looking for their fallen city," Emily translated, in case Scout didn't pick up on that. "Correct?"

[Sunlight.]

Scout looked upward. "Sunlight...?"

"It means yes," Emily explained to the side, before turning back to the plant. "We haven't found any bodies. Halcyone got rid of them all before you were animated by Lady Summer. ...hrm. Have any returned, since then?"

[One. Silver-girl. Returning to soil now.]

"Right, then. Silver-girl is with us. We'll leave, peacefully," Emily promised. "No trouble, no fuss. Pull back your spores from her, leave her in good health, and we'll be out of your, er, leaves. I swear it by the laws of magic, by Court Doctrine, with--"

[Lady-geas. Sun-above-all. No other laws, nothing. Unfurling leaves, the favor, the price. No. Silver-girl returns to soil.]

Emily nibbled her lip. "...I'd threaten you, but I'm guessing since your marching orders come from Lady Summer herself to defend this place, we can't scare you into letting Una go, can we?"

[Sunlight.]

"You're a living thing, with its own mind, now! You have free choice. Favors can be defied," Emily tried to reason. "Even ones owed to her. Granted, there's repercussions, but you don't have to do this!"

[Darkness. Favor, mind unfurling. Gratitude. Will obey Lady-geas.]

Scout braced one foot back, ready to break into a sprint. "Fight?" he suggested, again.

"Go for the roots," Emily said quickly, drawing her spellbook from her belt. "I'll put darkness around it to shut it off from the sun. Move!"

The fight was on.

Scout took eight steps and promptly collapsed, screaming in pain. Emily was casually knocked backwards by a flailing vine, the thick green cable striking at her arms, to knock the spellbook away before she could manage a single syllable of casting.

The fight was off.

Emily tried to scrabble for her book -- overriding an instinctive urge to rush to the fallen Scout's side, to see what was wrong. But the single vine that disarmed her had been joined by its brothers now... a dozen of them, snarling and twisting, forming a living blockade. She tried to push through it anyway, only ending up tangled up in the mess for her efforts. The vines effortlessly lifted her off her feet, holding her aloft, far away from her book, far away from the boy...

Screams of pain slowly silenced, as mushrooms began to rapidly grow from Scout's open mouth. The ever-present pollen, spores, and microscopic bits of plant life had found something new to take root in -- his body.

[Dead-flesh. Good-soil,] the plant said. [We-grow, we-grow. Fill death with life. Incapacitate the Winterhound. Summerling, questionable. In-exile but still Summerling. Hold. Call-Summer. Lady-children will know what to do with the witchling.]

This can't be happening, Emily thought for the first of what would prove to be two times that day. She struggled, pulling at the vines, which now had completely immobilized her. She couldn't even talk -- one had been wrapped around her head, to gag her, preventing spellcasting from memory. (Not that she was capable of spells memorization.)

There had to be something she could do, some way out of this. A witch is never helpless. A witch can't afford to be helpless when her friends are in trouble...

"AUDREY!"

Emily instinctively tried to twist to see the source of that voice. She could barely move... but managed to turn just enough.

The silver-girl, Una, stood uneasily at the edge of the room. In her hands, she held one of the many fallen pieces of Orbital technology... a small, gleaming garden watering can. Even the simplest of machines were flawlessly chromed in Orbital society, it seemed.

"Bad flower. Put her down now," Una commanded.

...and the vines slackened around Emily, just a bit.

[...Water-girl?] the plant asked, confusion in the way its psychic tones grew through Emily's mind, not sure what to make of this strange thing...

"I gave you your name!" Una reminded the plant. "I came here every weekend with my family. I watered the plants and I gave them names. You looked like the funny plant in that movie father showed me, so I named you Audrey. I cared for you when the garden workers didn't really care, when they just went through the motions of their assigned tasks. I left crumbs behind from our picnics, for the insects, for your soil. You are a good plant, Audrey of Arcology #BE12, and you are going to release my friends right now!"

One silent pause.

Emily felt her feet make contact with the ground. The vines that had caged her were retreating now, carefully, gently. If she could read floral body language she might have interpreted it as apologetic, even.

The heaving, sickly noises nearby indicated Scout had a less pleasant time of it, on the other hand -- he was coughing up plant matter and mushrooms, emptying his stomach on the ground. Fortunately, the soil soaked the sick up, to put it back to good use afterwards.

[...Water-girl. Remembrance. Care. Comfort. Nourishment,] Audrey recalled. [Like Summer-Lady, care and comfort. ...but... Lady-geas--]

"Do you want me to die, Audrey? Because once this stimulant I have pumping through my body wears out, I think that's exactly what's going to happen," Una said. Already, her limbs were starting to twitch, the color in her face was starting to drain. Whatever she'd found in the medical bay may have given her the strength to walk all this way and confront the plant, but it would do little beyond that...

[Darkness! Water-girl must grow!]

This time, Emily didn't have to resist the instinctive urge to rush to the fallen Orbital's side, as Una sank to the ground. (Even collapsing and near-death, she managed to be graceful.) Scout was there, as well... despite looking sickly and horrible himself, he found strength to join them.

Una's purging process made Scout's look like an impolite sneeze in public. Emily tried to reason that plant life had no problems with massive expunging of waste matter and bodily fluids, that in the end it was all part of the cycle of life and death, and therefore a beautiful process of the natural world.

The rest of her just felt like it was going to be violently sick from the sights, sounds, and *smells* of Una's body being cleansed of the corruption that had infested it. It was like having a terrible stomach flu coupled with irritable bowel syndrome and slamming your way through a full week of the experience in the span of a single minute. By some divine miracle, none of the combined biological horror managed to splash on her beloved pointy hat.

If there was any mercy, it was in a large flower opening up high above them -- pouring out accumulated rainwater, washing all three of them down after the episode was over, cleansing them fully of the aftermath. The water actually smelled vaguely sweet and perfumed, like daisies.

Carefully, Emily and Scout helped Una to her feet.

"...I need new clothes," Una decided.

Audrey was silent, after that. Whether the plant had been subdued by the effort of restoring Una's health -- or perhaps as punishment for going against Lady Summer's wishes -- was unknown. The three had bigger concerns at the moment, regardless.

"We need to get the information we came for and get the hell out of here," Emily decided. "All those in favor?"

"Aye," Scout spoke, after coughing up another mushroom.

"I want new clothes," Una insisted. "I still smell like a waste reclamation unit."

"You'll live. I say we go to the engine room, figure out why this place went splat, then find a shuttle and leave. Notify Una's father of what happened here, then if there is a just and righteous God out there, we'll be able to retire somewhere sunny and pleasant to rest for awhile before we look into what hypertech the Faerie Court's snatched up. But right here, right now, I have no intention of spending one more minute in this stinking pit of doom than we have to. Again. All those in favor?"

With a sigh, Una raised her hand in consent. "The engine room will be in this direction," she indicated, nodding down the hall. "It may take some time to access the security logs, however..."

"Screw that. No more pushing buttons. I have Plans," Emily declared.

Apparently, the fallen remains of what was (also apparently) Arcology #BE12 had three rooms that could be described as vast, and they had now visited all three. Council Chambers, the Arboretum, and finally, the Shift Engine Room.

Of course, it felt a lot more vast with critical portions of the central machinery missing.

"There should be a large gyroscopic device in the center!" Una exclaimed, moving from computer display to computer display, surveying the damage. (Despite losing a portion of her body mass recently, she'd managed to regain some energy. Probably Faerie magic again, Emily reasoned.) "And this... the mass capacitors, most of them are gone. There's a few left, but half of those are damaged. There's no way to shift the ship away, it'd be too much matter to transport at once..."

"There goes the idea of beaming the wreck into space to clean up the mess," Emily said. "Drat. We'll definitely need a team from your home Arcology down here to deal with this. We'll have to figure out how to keep Halcyone from eating them, but--"

"And look, look here! All the navigation systems, and the error logs, everything's under encrypted lockdown," Una continued, furiously pounding at invisible keyboards. "It's definitely going to take me hours to unlock this. It's just as bad as the security the Council put on the airlocks..."

"Yeah, well, we're not doing that," Emily spoke, pulling out her spellbook and flipping to the section she desired. "Stand back, both of you, and hush. I have no idea if this is going to work. I guess at worst, we'll just have computer dancing and flopping around the room..."

Curious, Una stood back -- so she could look over Emily's shoulder. Scout stood on guard, just in case something went horribly wrong, ready to intervene between the computer and the two girls.

This is going to take one hell of a Will focus, Emily considered. *Especially since I want a specific effect, not just some spoon floating through the air or something...*

She closed her eyes for three minutes. Odds are Una was saying something, sort of an "Ooo, what's that, what's happening?" but Emily ignored it.

Magic wasn't like pushing a button on a missile launcher and watching it blow something up a mile away -- pick your implements of destruction, do one simple gesture, and kablam. Magic was more like shooting an arrow... it took skill to make the arrow go as far as it needed to go, to make sure it hit the target you were aiming at. Strength in the pull of your arm. Focus and talent to direct the energy. Give an identical bow and arrow to a half-trained archer, or a skilled one that was in a rush or putting in a sloppy effort, and you wouldn't get the same results.

The Word was the same, always. The Way of speaking it was the same. It took the same amount of time to cast. But the Will Emily poured into this casting was another matter entirely.

With a voice of absolute confidence, she cast a spell upon the computer banks. "ɘɟɐm﹐uɐ."

It felt like someone punching her in the brainpan, when that spell fired off. She reeled on her feet, wobble left, wobble right, wobble-- into Scout's arms.

"Uhh.. thanks," she said, trying to get back on her own two feet. "Did it work? I'm all blurry for a few seconds after a heavy duty casting like that--"

"Excuse me, but... what's going on?"

It was a man's voice.

Emily shook her head lightly, forcing it to clear. Her eyes would remain sharp.

They settled on a gray figure... a man made of machine, looking slightly perplexed, as he studied hands assembled from various bits of hypertech... super science equivalents of diodes, wires, and circuits.

"This is a very strange experience," the computer spoke. "I seem to be sentient at the moment. I don't recall any sort of AI installed during past program operations..."

"...you animated the shift engine control systems?!" Una exclaimed. "That's... that's...! ...well, that's actually quite clever, really. Hello, Computer!"

"Er, hello," the computer replied, waving his hand before realizing he was waving. "Odd. A social greeting gesture. I suppose I absorbed quite a bit of Chief Engineer Tyr through his customizations and tweaks to my software over the years, didn't I? Yes, that makes sense... this is his voice, from the voiceprint files, and the shape matches as well. ...oh, no. Am I going to need to eat and breathe like an organic lifeform now? I'm not sure how to do either of those things..."

"It worked?" Emily asked, slower on the uptake. "I mean, ah, of course it worked. I AM a witch, after all. ...so. Tyr, is it?"

"Well, not really, but I guess that'll do for now," Chief Engineer Tyr / Primary Shift Control System replied. "Can I help you, miss...?"

"Emily. That's Una, that's Scout," she introduced. "We need to make this fast, because the Animate spell won't last long, especially not after such a strange casting of it. Uh. Sorry about that."

"You mean... this state of advanced consciousness will end and I will return to non-sentience? Oh, thank goodness!" Tyr exclaimed, relief on his silver face. "Here I was worried I'd be like this from now on! Thank you. How may I be of assistance today, Miss Emily?"

"We need to know why #BE12 crashed. Yes yes, there are security protocols... but you're a living thing, with its own mind, now. ...for the moment, anyway. You'll find that you have have free choice. So, if you want to help us, you'll be able to. Right?"

"...huh. Funny, that. Yes, I can open the files for you. But that's not the real problem -- the reason for the Arcology's fall is not something I know for certain," he said. "There was some odd evidence, some theories, but he Council could only speculate..."

"Sooo... speculate. Time's ticking," Emily reminded him.

"Right, right, sorry. Well. We were intended to change fleets, but the shift drives sent us into this Earth's atmosphere instead," he explained. "A program was injected into the system, source unknown, which redirected shift navigation. That should be impossible, of course, we have extensive safety logic to prevent this. Tyr attempted to figure out how they breached those protocols, but every time he did, he got a strange and illogical error message..."

Una spoke up, next. "Ah, the error, right..! Can we see it?"

"Oh, certainly. Here, I'll display it for you... "

Holograms flickered above Tyr-Computer's head. Red error symbols appeared, one after another, in a strange encoded machine language -- glyphs that meant more to Orbital engineers than they would to anyone else.

"Oookay. Una? Can you read those?" Emily asked.

"...no," Una said, staring up at them.

"Damn. Alright--"

"But I've seen them before."

"What?"

Una pointed. "These two, they're contradictory. Errors that shouldn't appear at the same time, like, 'a thing has occurred' followed by 'a thing has not occurred'. I... think I saw this before. I was scanning Scout using Zee's equipment, back in Twin Cities... and when the machine tried to parse the spells that kept him animate... it threw up the same symbols. The same pattern."

"Uh... so... that's not normal, is it?"

"Emily... I think that Faerie magic crashed Arcology #BE12," Una concluded. "This is the same signature."

Tyr started to look nervous. "Er. Excuse me, but--"

"That's crazy. The Faeries can't even reach high orbit," Emily argued. "Esrever said that the Arcologies were out of his reach! ...I don't... THINK Lady Winter could've reached out and touched someone that far away... I can't say I know for sure, but..."

Scout spoke up. "Winter's a goddess of nature," he reminded them. "Manifests where she likes, in person or simply touching one's mind. Bet the cold, bleak death of space vacuum'd be within her grasp, even if one of her children couldn't reach that far."

"Exactly! This makes much more sense! What happened here wasn't strictly some Orbital internal affair. I KNEW my people were incapable of this kind of madness!" Una said, latching onto the idea, anchoring hope to it. "There was an external influence -- the Faerie Court! Somehow, they hexed the engines! But... why? Once the Arcology crashed in her lands, Lady Winter didn't exactly do much with it... that we know of, I mean..."

"Ah, I don't mean to be a bother, organic persons, but..."

"Relax, you'll go back to normal soon," Emily dismissed. "Alright. I'll take it as a given that Faerie magic was somehow involved; you know this tech more than I do, you know how it'd react. But we don't know enough to guess who really did this, or why. Just *how*. Okay. So, we leave through either the Arboretum ceiling, or better yet, go find a shuttle, and--"

"I really must insist that I speak up at this point, ma'am!"

The three looked at the panicking computer. The computer was not enjoying the fact that it was now capable of panic.

"I.. ah... I was trying to point out, the moment I displayed the error to you, I believe some dormant self-defense program injected behind the error codes activated," Tyr-Computer said. "In fact, I'm sure of it. The shift engines are activating. Worldbleed opening within twenty seconds. I strongly suggest you run in order to preserve your lives. Eighteen. Seventeen--"

Una glanced around at the ruined equipment, unbelieving. "But... but there's hardly anything left of the engine! It can't possibly move the entire Arcology--"

"The navigation sensors have been inverted. It's like nothing I've seen before. Something is coming *here*," Tyr said, "And I highly recommend your swift departure. Eleven. Ten. Adequate hostility levels to destroy intruders determined, subject lock complete. Seven... oh dear, and there goes my sentience. Good luck, all."

The silver components of the computer man fell apart on the spot, parts and bits collapsing into a less man-shaped pile.

Scout stepped in front of the girls. "We can't run fast or far enough," he said. "We fight here, where we have open space. Get ready."

Spellbook and energy blaster were drawn. Emily tried very hard not to let her hands shake as she flipped through the pages, trying to find something that would be of any use in a fight. "Scout... we've gone through hell today. We're not exactly in fighting shape--"

The flash was not blinding. It was a spray of misty light, a featureless white cloud of illumination... accompanied by a sound of displacing air. Like a cork coming out of an ancient bottle...

The room may have been yet another in a series of vast rooms, but the creature that now stood before them made it seem positively cramped.

Emily had seen one before, in her book on mythological beasts. Strong hind legs, leathery skin, a head with massive jaws filled with razor-sharp murdering teeth. Tiny little arms...

It was a Tyrannosaurus Rex.

Wearing a leather military overcoat, emblazoned with a symbol like twin jagged lightning bolts.

And carrying what looked like a gunmetal gray plasma rifle, already charged with the wide nozzle glowing a sickly green light.

This can't be happening, Emily thought for the second of what had proven to be two times that day.

"Was ist dieser platz!?" the beast growled, in a voice like thunder scattering the clouds. "Wer sind diese entgangenen Zootiere? ACHTUNG! Alle feinde fallen vor dem Reptilreich!!"

The rifle began to make a loud hissing noise.

"Scatter!" Scout shouted, diving to the side. Instinct kicked in, and Emily ran the other way, looking for something reasonably sturdy to hide behind.

She came up a foot short, forced to scramble along the ground, before tucking into a ball behind a metal computer console. The room rocked, green light flaring all around, but she dared not peek out to see what was happening...

Other worlds, other versions of Earth, Emily's Insight mused, heedless of the encroaching doom. *Of course. Presumably there would be one where dinosaurs became the dominant species, adopted values of the ancient Nazi regime from those old war movies, and then developed super science weapons. It stands to reason. IT IS COMPLETELY INSANE but it stands to reason.*

And if I don't do something, we are all going to die at the tiny, tiny hands of this completely insane thing.

Blast marks scored the wall in front of her, as the dinosaur fired high. It howled in rage, stomping around the room.

"SCHMUTZIGER AFFE!" the monster roared, twisting this way and that... Emily daring to peek out from her hiding place, only to see Scout on its back, having looped some stray computer cable from the ruined machinery around its neck. Not that this seemed to be having much of an effect, other than enraging the already enraged beast... but it did leave the creature wide open to attack.

"Una! Shoot its weapon!" Emily called. "It can't possibly have a good grip on that thing!"

...Una hesitated, her gun wavering. "I've... I've never actually fired my blaster before," she admitted, knowing full well what horrible timing it was. "It's just standard issue for surface excursions--"

"No time like the present to learn! SHOOT!"

The Orbital energy weapon fired.

It wasn't a particularly impressive effect, not like the weapons demonstrated long ago in Baltimore. There was a quiet hum, and a beam of pure white light lashed out from the wobbly tip of Una's blaster... smacking not the rifle in the T-rex's hands, but his hands themselves.

The creature howled in pain, limbs going limp from the stunning energy shot. The plasma rifle clattered directly to the ground at its feet.

Swift as a wolf, Scout released his leash, sliding down the leathery body of the dinosaur -- landing on the ground in a crouch. Within a single bound, he sprung between the beast's legs, twisting around as he grasped the fallen weapon... ending up on his back beneath the enemy, with the business end of a plasma weapon pointed up from above...

Green fire lashed out, and the alien tyrant's head went away.

Melted fleshy slag sprayed out in all directions... before the headless creature slumped forward, collapsing to the ground with an impact that shook the entire room.

Scout rose from the floor, keeping the plasma rifle aimed away, before wiping some splatter from his face.

"I think we should leave now," he suggested.

They decided to take jetpack and broomstick out through the Arboretum ceiling. True, they had no way of leaving Canada yet, but the consensus was that they didn't want to stick around to search for transport.

However, transport was awaiting them on arrival at the airlock campsite.

The mounted knights rode war unicorns -- two of them had lions on leashes, snarling and ready to tear out throats on command. Apparently Audrey had indeed managed to send word to Lady Summer about the "stray witchling" before being pacified.

"By order of Lady Summer of the Faerie Court, you are charged with trespass upon her grounds," the Faerie Warchief declared, reading from an official scroll of decree. "As payment for this insult, the Winterhound, Witch-in-Exile, and Orbital are to be shown Hospitality. In short... you are hereby required to attend Her Majesty's Solstice Ball. You will come with us."

"Oh, we're going to a party?" Una asked. "How exciting!"

We are now officially boned, Emily thought.

In a flash of sunlight, the entire group vanished from the flowery fields, leaving them rustling in the wake of their departure.

Once more, Edmonton and Arcology #BE12 fell to silence.

end.a05

in-vi-ta-tion [in-vi-tey-shuhn]
-noun
1. the act of inviting.
2. incentive or allurement.
3. a provocation: Her comments were an invitation to
rebuke.

There is a house in New Orleans.

It's also the only house in New Orleans, at least in the sense that any human would recognize something as a 'house'. Faeries have some very peculiar ideas about architecture, usually involving gigantic treeborne villages of majestic spires, or living structures made of wood and leaf, or strange cathedral-like buildings half made of living rock and half made of mysterious glassworks, and so on, and so forth. The higher in your Court you sit, the more beautiful and majestic and unearthly your domain shall be. Emphasis on 'un-EARTHly.'

The exception to this is the House of the Rising Sun. It was crafted to resemble an Earth-ly mansion... a design throwback to the Victorian era, with majestic ivory spires, bedchambers upon bedchambers, and an opulent ballroom with the world's most majestic chandelier. It took the elf-servants hours just to light all its candles, using delicate little Light spells. Having a home in human design was the peak of decadence, of wallowing and playing about in low foreign motifs -- and the house was no stranger to various manners of decadence.

Of course, the house was a new structure, raised by Lady Morgana of the Summer Court using a strong weave of building spells and glamours. Before her arrival, there was nothing here but the ruins of some ancient human city, still loosely bearing the name "New Orleans." A hundred years of abandonment led to most of the city to be overgrown, flooded, or otherwise simply collapsing from old age. Without humans around to maintain and repair their structures, nature will fiercely and swiftly retake any city, after all.

The new owner of New Orleans, appointed by Lady Summer herself, ordered the soggy remains of the city pulverized to make room for her plantations. Her business was medicinal herbs and roots that grew well in swampland, cultivated by her legions of lowly indebted elves. The few standing structures of the French Quarter fell within a day to destructive spellwork; the above-ground graveyards had their stone crypts ground to dust. Within a week the slate had been wiped clean, ready to be remade in the Faerie image.

But Lady Morgana refused to make her own home in the resulting muck and ruin... she considered herself a modern Faerie. So, she built the House of the Rising Sun on the edge of the city, in the spitting image of human opulence -- mostly because it seemed like a good idea and she was bored. In time she came to enjoy the strange comforts humans idolized, like canopy beds and fresh linens and what they once called "chambermaids." Her new mansion was now named after an ancient folk song she'd once heard her slaves singing, about drunkenness and gambling and endless crushing debt, which seemed quite fitting to one such as her. After all, Lady Morgana *adored* the art of the gamble.

When the agricultural industry bored her (which was frequently) the Lady would throw a lavish party of games -- various Faerie styles of gambling would act as centerpieces. They could be word and imagination, games competitions to outmaneuver your opponents, or all manners of combat-by-proxy with creatures (and even slaves, at certain special occasions). Faeries didn't care for little laminate cards and plastic chips. They went for the thrust and riposte of intellectual fencing... or betting on games of brutality that they rarely took part in themselves. That was the style of decadence the House of the Rising Sun was famous for.

Naturally, it wasn't considered a place for *proper* Faeries, or even proper witches. Nobody sensible would go there. Not that this stopped sensible Faeries from going there in droves, even while steadfastly denying they had visited it.

Emily had heard of the House, of course; it was a subject of frequent excited yet whispered gossip, about how so-and-so would never go to such a place, honestly, really. If she'd had her druthers, Emily wouldn't be there now. Unfortunately, her druthers were quite disregarded by the Summer Court.

They had committed the crime of trespass. (This was a strange crime, given the 'turf' they walked on embedded within Edmonton was stolen from the Winter Court in the first place, but you didn't want to argue legal semantics when a Lion of Summer had his lance pointed in your face.) The penalty chosen by the Summer Court was Hospitality.

"But why is being invited to a fancy party with the elite of Faerie society a punishment?" Una asked.

"Because it's a trap," Emily explained, while pacing back and forth in one of the many guest bedrooms of the House.

The three of them had been brought to this room by a Lion of Summer, ordered to stay put and wait for further instructions -- and not get any of the muck and dirt and other horrible fluids they'd collected from the fallen city of #BE12 on the furniture. After that, they were left alone... and given this would be one of the few times they could speak without eavesdropping, Emily felt the need to give her companions the thumbnail sketch of the Hospitable doom in front of them.

"A trap? A party is a trap?" Una wondered, not quite grasping it.

"Faerie parties aren't just about wining and dining and dancing and polite conversation," Emily continued. "Even without any actual declared games currently in play, the party itself is an elaborate game of cat and mouse, where the politeness is a defensive technique. Nothing a Faerie offers is free unless they expressly say so, and even then, you're going to want to watch the particulars. That means the appetizers could come with a heavy price tag, a poorly chosen word could insult your host, even the dress you show up in could be enough to lock you into owing some massive favors. It's like being offered a fresh apple pie that just happens to be sitting in the middle of a big rusty bear trap."

"But... why would the Faeries enjoy anything like that? It sounds horrible!"

"For many of them, attendance is mandatory. If they owe the host, the host can collect by insisting on an RSVP. Plus... well. You have to understand, the Faerie mindset is not the same as a human one, certainly not an Orbital one. Many Faeries *enjoy* the cat and mouse game, especially as the mouse who manages to outwit the cat. And the higher court Faeries, if they do slip up, well, they've got plenty of favors in their back pocket they can spend to avoid any real penalty. It's a kind of gambling. Only instead of losing your shirt you could lose your life -- in the sense of getting killed or in the sense of being enslaved in bottomless debt."

"Sooo... we're being forced to attend a party... in hopes that we'll fall deeper into their clutches?"

"Exactly. Now, not all Faeries are vicious bastards about it -- remember, I was assuming Esrever was a sneaky bastard at first, until he went out of his way to assure us his 'hospitality' wasn't malevolent and freed us from any possible obligation. --but this is different! We're in the *House of the Rising Sun!* It'd almost be better if we were in some wealthy pervert's orgy palace, compared to the kind of playful "fun" they can have here without even needing to take off your clothes. You don't want to hear the stories I've heard of this place...!"

"How distasteful! I can only imagine what sort of foulness transpires here."

"No, actually, you can't. You've led a sheltered little utopian space life. No, that's not an insult, I wish I *didn't* know about this place, frankly. I envy you that. ...so. Now that I've tuned you in to the nasty, let's go over the rules--"

Scout counted them off, from memory. "Don't eat or drink anything," he said. "Indebts you to come to the host's next party. Don't insult anyone. You do that, your only hope is they insult you worse and tip the scales in your favor. Blend in, move with the crowd, don't stand out or create a scene. Don't be an awkward loner. And don't say anything about what we're really up to here."

"Yes, thank you, Scout, that just about covers it," Emily said, nodding along.

"Very well! I shall be cautious and careful," Una promised. "...what are we really up to here, then? Oh, wait, I know -- trying to find out more about the hypertech that Lady Summer stole from Lady Winter. ...but can we really do that, when we're under such stringent self-control?"

"Prrrobably not," Emily admitted. "But if you see an opening, a *safe* one, take it. We need to get as far away from this place as fast as possible and as soon as possible, so if there's any investigation to be done it has to be done tonight. Once the party's over and Hospitality ends for us we need to clear out. So. Any questions?"

"Yes. Why would Lady Summer utilize such a terrible place for her Solstice Ball?"

...that had been nagging at Emily ever since one of the Lions of Summer that dragged them here let it slip.

There were two problems with it.

One, the House itself was all wrong. Lady Summer was a Faerie's Faerie, the Queen of the Summer Court, bearer of the Crown of Flame. As the ultimate expression of what it is to be Faerie, choosing Lady Morgana to host her yearly Solstice Ball made no sense whatsoever. The House's dis-reputation meant it was the least likely of the great houses to be given this honor.

Two, Solstice was June 21st this year... which was actually five days away. They were celebrating too early -- the yearly ball was always held on the longest day of the year, without exception. It was the height of Summer's power, when the Summer Court was at its greatest strength. You don't shuffle up the date of the party like that and still call it "Solstice," and yet, that's exactly what was going on.

"I have no idea," Emily admitted. "And that scares the hell out of me. Something's very wrong here. The only positive upshot is there won't be any obvious games of chance in play, since the Solstice Ball is a formal affair. ...which means the games will be non-obvious, which is probably worse. Jeez... as if things weren't wrong enough with magical creatures toting energy blaster rifles..."

Scout kept his eyes glued to the closed doors of the guest bedroom. "We're being kept waiting. They're preparing something, or hiding something. You know Summer Court more than I do. What comes next?"

"Next... I suspect we're going to be given a gift," Emily said. "Probably no favor attached, thankfully, to avoid an incident. That's because if we don't accept it'd only deepen our insult against Lady Summer worse, AND make things very bad for our host to boot. Not that I'm going to enjoy this gift at all...

"What is it?"

"In all likelihood? Two very beautiful dresses and a fine suit of clothes. Going to the party in these yucky rags would be suicide for all involved. We're going to end up being the belles and beau of the ball, whether we like it or not."

a06 invitations

The dress was indeed beautiful. It would be the finest garment Emily had ever worn, and she hated it with a burning passion.

"Can't you de-glitz it more?" she asked the young Sprite who brought it in for her. "Less shiny bits, less frilly bits? I'm going to look like a disco ball at this rate!"

"Ma'am, I've already tuned the glamour-stones down as far as they'll go," the Sprite protested. "This is as dull as it gets, I'm afraid..."

"Well... can you tint it an earthy tone? Something boring. To go with my hat."

"Oh, you can't wear that old thing to the ball...!" the Sprite protested. It produced a spool of thread in one hand and an enchanted needle in the other. "At the very least, let me patch it up some--"

Emily yanked the hat off her head, and held it behind her back, protecting it. "You touch this hat and I will grow very cross. Is that understood? This is a priceless family heirloom. I'm wearing it as-is. I know the accords -- wearing an old hat isn't going to be enough to count as an insult against the host."

The Sprite considered that. It was a flighty little thing, as all Sprites were... a cross between a tiny, tiny little Pixie and a human-sized Faerie, 'standing' about a foot tall and hovering on gossamer wings of iridescent silk. They had a tendency to take things that looked shiny, regardless of legal ownership... meaning quite a few of them ended up owing rather severe favors.

This one wore the usual ragged, leafy one-piece garment afforded to servants of Lady Morgana's house; something simple that could be grown from a seed. No sense wasting good hand-crafted clothing on a serving-slave, after all. The only piece of finery was a velvet choker, with a a silvery pendant engraved with Lady Morgana's silhouette. Rather like a neo-Victorian dog collar.

"If you insist on wearing that hat... then yes, I suppose an earthy tone would be more appropriate," the Sprite decided, after searching its constantly-bouncing thoughts for some workable logic. A few words of a glamour spell were mumbled, and the dress Emily wore shifted to a light brown tone, with sandy beige highlights. "Hmm... it'll do. That and the adjustments made to, ah, de-emphasize your figure have flattened out its impression considerably. It does look very unimpressive now, my lady... are you certain that is your wish?"

"I'm certain. I've got absolutely no reason to show off," Emily said, turning this way and that to study the plain-ified dress in a mirror. She put her hat back on, reasonably assured it was safe now from spontaneous repair and glamourization.

"I understand. No doubt you do not wish to outshine your companion!"

"--eh?"

"The one with the snow-white hair, yes? Such a fair maiden, she!" the androgynous little Sprite spoke, swooning in midair. "I've not a doubt she will make a wondrous impression on the Court tonight, especially with that handsome lad on her arm..."

Emily cleared her throat. "Ex-CUSE me, but that 'handsome lad' will be on MY arm tonight," she corrected. "...I mean... not that I've asked him, but it's likely. Y'know. Bound to happen."

"Ah, I see. Please forgive my mistake, ma'am. ...but while factually that may be... no doubt those at the party will assume him to be *her* fancy lad, what with you appearing so utterly ordinary and forgettable. My lady."

The young witch studied her gift-dress in detail. And in thought.

"Maybe turn up the glitz a little. Just a little," she said, making a pinchy gesture with her fingers. "Maybe this much. ...little more. ...little more than that. --right, there. ...oh, and about my figure..."

While Emily was being fitted with an now-increasingly pretty dress, Una was relaxing in one of the many guest baths.

The inset ivory bathtub was far larger than she would've expected a simple hygiene apparatus to be. It had gold and silver inlaid into the taps, the knobs, and even decorative trim. The little dishes that held soaps and sponges were also solid gold. While it was quite lovely and reminded her very much of the self-polishing metals of her home, it seemed a bit too much for what she knew of Earth. Metals like these were valuable, and rare. Why waste them on a device for routine cleansing of foreign contaminants?

She'd asked this question to her attendant.

"Lady Morgana has expectations upon her," the young elven girl explained, while carefully scrubbing Una's back with a sponge. "Guests come to expect this sort of finery when they stay at the House. It would be an insult not to provide a customary level of luxury."

The girl's name, or at least the one she had given, was Nel. She was an elf, with light brown hair and (when they weren't downcast) matching brown eyes. She wore a simple leafy green tunic Una thought was quite lovely, a collar of some sort, and little else. Her purpose in being here was to make Una presentable, which was a harder task than Emily or Scout faced, given hours ago Una was busy being violently ill in every conceivable way.

The first step was a bath, of enchanted oils that would utterly dissolve anything repulsive. Later, Una would be fitted with the exceptionally wonderful-looking silver dress provided (free of favor) by their host, Lady Morgana. Nel explained it all in simple tones, then set about helping 'Lady Una' cleanse herself... but Una insisted on conversation during the process, which Nel was not prepared for. She tried answering the first questions, but that just led to more questions, and more questions...

"An insult...? So... while the party is a trap for guests, it's also a trap for the host. Such a strange way to live," Una pondered aloud, while washing her own arms. (She'd also insisted on doing the lion's share of the bathing, eager to experience Earth cleansing techniques after years and years of boring nano-cleansing.) "But even beyond the strange system of debt and politeness, this bath itself is overdesigned! I suppose aesthetic appeal has a much stronger value in Faerie culture. Not that Orbitals are any less keen on the art of aesthetics, but dipping that art into even the most mundane of activities would be unusual... but I will admit, the scents on these soups are exhilarating! Smell this, smell it!"

The servant elf blinked a few times in surprise, and sniffed the back of Una's wrist, as requested.

"Isn't that great? I wonder what's in it? Pressed flowers, perhaps. I wonder if I could get some to bring with me before we leave?" Una talked and talked on. "And to think, you get to enjoy these bathing methodologies every day!"

"...I do not, ma'am."

"Huh? Why?" Una asked, turning in the bath, despite being mid-back-scrub. "Are the soaps a conserved resource? Perhaps bathing only occurs on a longer temporal cycle?"

"No, ma'am. The perfumes and soaps are kept plentiful at all times."

"Then... the water is in short supply? I know obtaining clean water can be taxing, and is one of the reasons humans build cities primarily along rivers and oceanfronts..."

"No, ma'am. Spellwork keeps a steady amount of clear water available."

"Ah... why, then?"

Nel lowered her eyes a moment, while wringing out the sponge. "It's not my place to use this bath. I use the water pump and bucket at the servant quarters outside the House. Now, ma'am, lift your arms please, so I can finish washing--"

"Ahh, wait, this is a concept I know!" Una said, recalling Emily's discussions. "Servants, I mean. They are hired by people to perform mundane, routine tasks, freeing them to focus on their areas of expertise. We don't really have them, where I'm from. I suppose servants are needed when the group, be it familial or professional, lacks a strong enough membership to distribute tasks among the collective. But... if you're part of Lady Morgana's collective, why can't you use her resources?"

"...because I'm her servant."

"Yes, and?"

"And... and I'm her servant," she tried again, not sure how else to say it, voice increasingly unsteady.

"I'm not sure I follow-- ahh, Nel? Why do you look relatively alarmed...?"

"I... I am not alarmed," Nel protested. "We should finish your bath. You need to go. I need to go..."

Una pointed out various signs. "Your eyes are darting back and forth lightly, and you've been nibbling your lip. It's my understanding these are stress indicators. Is something wrong? Should I call for a biologist?"

"N-no, there's no need to call anyone for anything!" Nel insisted, horrified at the idea of the Lady causing a scene on her behalf. "I... ah... please, a thousand apologies, ma'am, but... I'm not used to being asked so many questions. I don't understand all the things you say. I'm trying to answer to the best of my ability, but... I'm sorry! Please, forgive me! Don't hurt me!!"

Una cocked her head, curious and confused. "Er, forgive you for what? Hurt you? You've done nothing wrong. Why would I want to hurt you? Ah, I'm the one who should apologize -- your culture's quite unfamiliar to me, mostly I engage in human sociology studies, not Faerie, and... oh, dear, I'm upsetting you more...!"

She quickly climbed out of the bath, wrapping a nearby towel around herself, and tried to steady the shaking elven girl.

"Please... I mean no harm," Una insisted, keeping her eyes on the girl's, despite the servant trying very hard to avoid a direct look. "I just want to understand you better, that's all. ...ah, I know! Let's try this from another direction. Nice and simple! What sort of things do you do here for your employer?"

Nel tried to steady herself. "Emp...loyer?" she asked, unfamiliar with how the term applied here.

"Ah, for Lady Morgana. What sort of routine work tasks are you employed to perform?"

The elven girl told her what sort of routine tasks she performed.

More importantly, she found herself telling Una about what happened whenever her tasks weren't done to the Lady's approval. Which was always.

This wasn't the first time Scout had been imprisoned. It was certainly the most pleasant cell he'd been held in, given it was shaped like a luxurious fitting room. If you looked very, very carefully, you'd still never see the bars... but the bars were there, all the same.

He was Winter Court. This was a place of the Summer Court. That put him at unease, but it was one he could control, despite his inner Fae self's desire to run wild and tear down the building. He was getting better at selective control every day... more practiced at deciding what he would or would not feel, not just what he would not feel.

So, he decided that rather than taking his usual "patiently wait for a moment to strike" approach to imprisonment, he'd make the most of his time. He did some warmup exercises, stretches, a few martial forms. It was a different sort of lying in wait for the enemy, true, but it was one that kept him focused and sharp, rather than simply coiled tight and waiting to spring.

Scout was studying the wooden beam in the closet normally designed for hanging suits, wondering if it was structurally sound enough for him to do some chin-ups on it, when the Lion of Summer entered.

The Lions were the counterparts to the Winterhounds. Where a Hound was a wild thing, a creature of mad violence and lust, a Lion was a noble warrior of poise and strength. (Oddly enough, the sort of thing Scout had shaped himself to become, to counter the Hound within.) They wore ceremonial battle armor at all times, emblazoned with the flaming sun of Summer. And rumor had it they too could not be killed.

Seeing this warrior-priest put to task as a laundry errand boy was a strange sight, as he came not bearing arms, but bearing a neatly folded and pressed uniform. He did casually dump it on the floor at Scout's feet, as a token gesture of dissatisfaction with his current role.

"You can abandon that tattered suit you have on," the Fae soldier suggested in a way that implied it was not a suggestion. "I can see from the shoulder insignia's reversed text -- and from the smell of the thing -- that it's likely some product of Esrever the Mirror-Fiend's false empire. Unacceptable for a guest of Lady Summer to wear, of course. Be thankful the Sprites were skilled enough to weave you something similar to replace it."

Scout picked up the pile of uniform from the floor, shaking out the top, to study it.

The uniform consisted of military dress blues, in a Frontliner cut. Similar to his old uniform, similar to the mirrored one, but of a far finer fabric weave, with more piping and decorations. Even the patch on the shoulder, the old familiar crosshair and embroidered title of SCOUT, were of superb craftsmanship.

"What I can't comprehend is why a bloodhound of Lady Winter would want to wear a human soldier's clothes. But you're no ordinary bloodhound, are you?" the Lion spoke. "A Winterhound of human make. The Scout. I've heard of you. Specifically, of how you've hunted my kind, from time to time... and even your fellow Winterfae."

"I hunted the hunters," Scout explained. "Those who had it coming, for preying on the innocent and weak. That's all."

"Harumph. I won't defend the behavior of others; my charge is strictly to defend my Lady Summer," the Lion said, with a rolling shrug of armored shoulders. "Nor will I absolve you of any past deeds, however. Frankly, right now, you are not my concern. I suggest you continue to not be my concern, Wintertouched. I intend to see this evening through in peace and security. Unlike you, I am willing and ready to die to protect my Lady."

"As am I," Scout said, as he started to undo the buttons on his mirror-uniform.

"So you are oathbound to Lady Winter, then...? The rumors of your wild streak, of the beast off its leash, are false?"

"I didn't say that was my lady," he clarified. "Do you mind? I'd like to change. Get this evening over with sooner."

The Lion nodded in agreement. "The sooner you are gone from here, the happier I will be. Agreed. But I will be in the ballroom, waiting, and watching. Mind yourself, Winterling."

Nel the house elf was crying.

Partly, it was from her recounted stories of her time spent in the House of the Rising Sun. How she tended to Lady Morgana personally, as her glamour specialist... tuning and fine tuning and re-tuning her Mistress's appearance near endlessly each morning, until Morgana was satisfied with the results. Which was almost never, no matter how much effort Nel put into covering up the Lady's fading beauty. That "failure" always resulted in some sort of punishment, from mundane to creative...

Partly, it was because she knew she was now raising a scene -- the worst kind of scene, with someone who didn't truly understand why it was becoming a scene. This would not end well for Nel.

Una felt supremely bad about this. Her inquisitive nature had turned some simple questions of an anthropological interest into a full blown interrogation. But once the answers started coming... she couldn't STOP asking. Partway through, Una realized why. She was purposefully building a rather impressive amount of rage. Not an emotion she was familiar with, rarely feeling actual *hate* towards anyone or anything... which fortunately let her stand outside it, recognize it, know what it was by virtue of how alien the sensation was.

"I... I still miss them. I barely remember my family but I miss them," Nel was saying. She'd kept talking, minutes after Una had stopped asking questions. "I'll never see them again. I try, I try so hard, I do everything I'm asked, but it's never good enough. It seems I'll never be out of my debt to Lady Morgana..."

"Nel?"

"Y-Yes, ma'am...?" Nel asked, between sobs...

...and Una reached over, to dry those tears with her the corner of her towel.

"I'm going to ask you to do some things you'll be hesitant to do," Una said, being very careful now with words. The plan had been forming behind her eyes... piecing together, component by component, like software. "But I promise you... if you do as I request... you will see your family again. I think I know how I can make it happen. I cannot stand by my principles as a Optimist and allow this... this *madness* to continue, this frivolous causation of despair. ...do you trust me?"

It would be completely insane to put any trust in this stranger, of course. Nel recognized that. She came from a people that clearly had no idea how anything worked. One which had absolutely no concept of the word 'slave' and even a shaky grasp on the idea of asking someone else to do something you could do yourself.

The white-haired stranger had no concept of the word 'slave'...

Once her Lady found out about this scene, about upsetting a guest of the House regardless of the nature of that upset, Nel would be doomed, regardless.

One doom was as good as another.

The sun had set on the House of the Rising Sun, and the guests were at last arriving for the grand Solstice Ball.

They had gathered to pay homage to Lady Summer, the all-mother of the Summerfae, the goddess of that which is green and grows. It was one of the few times they could be assured she would make an appearance... although all Summerfae bent knee to the Crown of Flame, many would live their entire lives without laying eyes upon it. That honor was reserved for the Lions of Summer, high noble attendees of the Solstice Ball, and those who Summer took a unique interest in (for good or ill).

Two by two, the guests would be introduced by the Herald, a dapper old fellow who stood today in a human tuxedo-style suit, as befitting the House's motif. Always by twos... it was considered a great insult to be invited and not bring a guest with you of some sort.

It was a trap that Emily had unfortunately let slip her mind, when she was giving her friends the mission briefing. She waited in the antechamber, trying not to be noticed by the Herald, letting other arriving guests brush past her in their Faerie finery. Emily would be fine... provided Scout got here in time to be announced with her. But what would happen to Una...? Would some Faerie unfortunate enough to go stag snatch her up to get through the door without incident, and if so, how would the favor play out in that scenario? Perhaps one would cancel the other out...

She tried not to fret too much. Fretting would result in sweating. Sweating in a dress that was once beautiful and then homely and then, at her insistence, just SLIGHTLY more beautiful but not too much to be considered extravagant but still quite beautiful and honestly she felt very silly in it but on the other hand did kind of like the idea of wearing a nice dress even if the circumstances weren't to her liking and hopefully she hadn't gone too far in the tweaking particularly with the artificial corset spell which made her actually have a noticeable bust which she noticed a bit too late but went with anyway despite knowing she should have reservations about that sort of thing and--

No. No fretting. It was a survival tool for the ball and nothing more. ...even if it was also very lovely.

A figure without pointy ears approached. She was relieved to identify Scout on sight... even if on second sight, his uniform seemed considerably nicer than before. It had *epaulets*, of all things, and what looked like soft white gloves. A formal dress saber, a gilded weapon designed only to look macho-yet-stylish, had been placed at his hip through a blue sash.

They'd also combed his hair, properly combed. Emily couldn't recall the last time Scout bothered to do more than slightly de-wild his hair a little.

"Wow, Scout, you look--" "You look especially--"

"Ah, you first--" "No, go on--"

"Um." "Hmh."

The two paused, not sure what to say next.

"I do feel a bit silly," Emily decided, to take some wind out of her own sails. "I've never owned actual jewelry before..."

"This sword doesn't even work," Scout complained, tugging at the hilt, which was simply attached to the scabbard with no blade within. "No reason to wear a weapon that doesn't work."

"Stabbing people is the last thing we want to do tonight, Scout. We need a low, low profile if we're going to get through this," she said. "Alright. Let's get announced. Hopefully Una'll be along soon, if she's not in there already. We're going to have to meet Lady Morgana after. Don't let her rile you up."

"And the same to you," Scout agreed. He offered her his arm, bent just so, and Emily tentatively slipped her own arm through it...

"**Now announcing!**" the Herald called out, his voice magically boosted for the evening, ringing across the already crowded ballroom. "Emily Moonthistle, Summerwitch in exile, and Scott Reinhold, rogue Winterhound! Both attending within Hospitality, by order of Lady Summer!"

Emily desperately tried to ignore the wide-eyed stares of dozens of Faerie nobles, as the magical candles of the grand chandelier swerved their lights to illuminate the couple.

"... ...Reinhold?" Emily whispered. "Your last name is *Reinhold*?"

"I prefer Scout," Scott 'Scout' Reinhold grumbled.

As the two descended the staircase to join the party itself, Scout scanned the surroundings, memorizing where the exits were. There were hallways off to the left and right, which presumably would lead out... large floor to ceiling windows, which he could jump through if need be... and of course, the double doors they had entered through. Tables lined the walls, with chairs suitable for taking a rest when you were tired of mingling, as well as being good for kicking over if you needed cover. The center of the room, just in front of the enormous overhead chandelier (which could be dropped with a VERY well placed shot to the rope that held it in place, good for a distraction) was covered in a wooden ballroom dance floor... a bad place to be if a fight broke out, although human... well, Faerie shields were a possibility...

His view was blocked by a six foot tall woman, a vision of apple-red silk and blood-red hair in cascading waves. Despite her looming height, she managed a practiced poise, one that screamed elegance and grace. Screamed it in such a way as you'd better agree she was elegant and graceful, or it might start screaming something else, maybe starting with "off with her head."

(Little did they know, but this vision of beauty was a veneer applied by one Nel the house-elf. If they had caught Morgana as she rose from slumber that morning, they would hardly be facing a well-groomed lady of confidence and power.)

"By order of Lady Summer, by order of Lady Summer... well, well. You two make a very interesting couple," Lady Morgana, Mistress of the House of the Rising Sun stated, smiling in an allegedly welcoming manner. "And here I was concerned this crowd of nobles would be far too droll an ensemble for a proper party, the kind I am famous for. I welcome you, Summerwitch in exile, and you, rogue Winterhound. My word, an actual slave of Lady Winter in my house...! They'll speak of this for *years!*"

Emily dropped into a formal curtsey; Scout took a deep bow, following her cue. "We are grateful to be here, Lady Morgana, in your lovely House," Emily blatantly lied. "We are grateful to Lady Summer for this opportunity to repay her for our unfortunate trespass on her private domain. I can think of no more wonderful a way to--"

"Oh, do stifle the false enthusiasm," Morgana said, rolling her eyes. "You don't want to be here, it's all over your face. But it doesn't matter, does it? You ARE here, and for the next hours, you are going to be quite popular. I'll be marching all sorts of dukes and duchesses your way, to show off my lovely and interesting guests. I'll cement my reputation, or rather, my disreputation off of you, girl."

"As you like it," Emily said, through gritted teeth. The host was allowed *some* leeway with insult, particularly of the verbal sort... she didn't dare snap back at that.

"My very own relics of the old world...!" Lady Morgana exclaimed, clasping her hands to her chest. "How exciting! You know... soon, your kind will be irrelevant. It would be best to study you before you are made obsolete--"

"**Now announcing..!**"

The eyes of the room turned again to the doors, as was custom when a new couple arrived...

If Emily and Scout opened eyes, these two opened eyes and caused jaws to drop. Even the Herald stumbled a bit over the introduction.

"Una zero point one of Orbital Arcology #A076, daughter of Primary Council Leader Ono, and, er... Nelliwyn Myfanwy, servant of the House of the Rising Sun..."

The attendees looked from one girl to the other. It wasn't easy figuring out which one was which.

One was wearing an elegant silver dress, something befitting of an Orbital dignitary -- it was crafted by expert Sprites, able to weave tiny rainbow glimmers of Faerie-metal between the layers of silvery silk, spun by expert spiders. It was a dress to turn heads, a dress to grant an aura of mystique and allure to the wearer.

The other wore the rough leafy tunic of a house-elf slave, an ordinary organic thing, of no importance whatsoever. The velvet choker sealed the image of person as property.

However, the one with the pointy ears was wearing the beautiful dress.

Una, wearing the servant's uniform (along with her usual silver bracers and her small jetpack, oddly enough), led the reluctant and red-faced servant girl Nel in the lovely garment down the stairs, stepping along in her bare feet, all smiles like the cat who had swallowed the canary. Una paused in front of Lady Morgana, curtseying formally, even if she didn't have the proper bustle and skirt to do more than ape the gesture. Nel's bow was considerably more sincere and severe, nearly scraping the floor with her knees in a desperate attempt to show her servile nature...

Now, we are COMPLETELY boned, Emily thought, far too shocked to dive into the fray and try to salvage the situation.

"Lady Morgana, I am pleased to visit you in your lovely House, of which I have heard many a tale," Una explained, all smiles and good tidings. "I bring the well wishes of my people with me, as the chosen representative of Arcology #A076--"

The creak of Morgana's fist closing around the decorative vine-and-thorn whip at her side was audible from across the room.

"What. Is. The meaning of this," she asked, allowing her rage to seethe through in her words. "Miserable, pathetic little... little NOTHING! You have taken the dress intended for my guest--!"

Una kept her arm locked around Nel's, to prevent the elf from immediately diving to the floor to beg forgiveness. "Nothing was stolen, gracious host," she clarified. "I was given the garment, as was your intention. A fine gift, which the Orbitals show deep gratitude for! And in turn, I gave it to Nelliwyn, in thanks for her assistance in my preparation for this evening's festivities. Of course, I could hardly attend in the nude, as I did not wish to insult you, so I requested her dress in exchange. It is a simple matter, yes? All quite above board."

"Simple? *Simple!?* You disgusting little alien freak--!"

Nel wrenched herself away from the arm hold, diving to the floor, a deep kneel with her forehead pressed to the floor. "No, mistress, not her! I confess it all to be my idea. She does not understand our ways! If anyone is to be punished, let it be me, not Lady Una! Please--"

Scout was in motion before the whip of thorns was uncoiled.

And Emily blocked him with an arm, quickly shaking her head, *no.* Not this time.

Lady Morgana reared her arm back, pouring all her outrage, all her mindless fury into the strike. She would tear that dress from her disobedient slave's back piece by piece if needed, and then tear HER apart piece by piece, and then...

She got two strikes in, before realizing that she wasn't whipping the miserable little speck of an elf.

The whip had repeatedly struck Una, who'd interspersed herself between the two. A bleeding gash had opened on her shoulder... and one ugly, jagged line had been drawn down her left cheek.

Una could have used the energy shield in her bracers, Emily realized. *Could have deflected the blows. She didn't. She was playing a gambit against the Mistress of Games, one that she won handily...*

"To harm the beauty of a fair maiden is unforgivable," Emily spoke, quoting from her knowledge of traditional Faerie insults. "To lash out at a guest, particularly one under the Hospitality of Lady Summer, who had done no true harm to you is deeply unforgivable. And most importantly... to enact violence against a diplomatic representative, one here on a mission of peace and cultural learning -- to do violence despite her harmless and understandable faux pas -- is to bring the entire wrath of the Orbitals upon this House, if not upon all of Summerkind. Utterly, completely, and totally... unforgivable."

The air pressure in the room reduced sharply, as the guests inhaled, tension rising. They were smiling, of course. Attendees to the House certainly loved a good gamble... and one played against the host herself was truly drama of the finest caliber...

Lady Morgana had realized the severity of the situation even before Emily started running down the list of offenses. The whip had fallen from her trembling fingers, coiling neatly and magically in a little spiral upon the floor.

"I believe you owe Lady Una of Arcology #A076 *considerable* favor," Emily concluded. "Una, you've an idea of what you'd like in return for this insult, don't you...?"

Una looked up, from cradling the sobbing elf, consoling the trembling girl. She locked her eyes sharply on Lady Morgana... so fierce that the Faerie mistress actually took a step backward.

"You will release Nelliwyn's service, transferring it to me," she said. "She leaves this House with me, never again to glamourize you, or to feel your wrath. That will repay your debt. ...I'm correct about that, right, Emily? It seemed it'd be a a fair exchange, so--"

"Yes, very fair, thank you," Emily said, before Una could explain too much of her plan.

...it was a slow shift, but within moments, Lady Morgana had regained her poise. She shrugged it off, a dismissive gesture. "This miserable creature is of no importance to me whatsoever," she said, as if that was the only factor involved in her decision. "She is a failure at the only form of magic she knows. Why should I want to keep such a worthless thing? Take her away, if you desire her so. I've plenty more elves in my stable who can do her job, and with far greater skill. ...what are the rest of you all staring at!? This is a party! We are here to celebrate, to mingle and be merry! So mingle, damn you!"

The conversation level of the room resumed normality immediately, as Lady Morgana stomped off into the crowd, determined to mix socially. Preferably at the furthest point away from this scenario.

Emily quickly opened her small spellbook, flipping to a Mending spell, closing up the cuts in Una's skin before they could scar over. Una nodded briefly, grateful, before helping her companion rise from the floor.

"...what.. what just happened?" Nel asked.

"We've won!" Una declared, smiling brightly. "I promised you would see your family again, and you shall! I played a game, winning your services. Now you can leave this terrible place! You'll never have to face her wrath again. ...ah, how was my performance, Emily? I had to absolutely insist on how the Herald announced us, make sure they understood I was more or less an ambassador--"

"Una... that was very noble of you," Emily admitted, impressed. "Very courageous, very noble. ...and utterly stupid. There's any number of valid, legal interpretations of your position here that would've given her every right to smack you around. You're lucky she had an audience and needed to save face!"

"Well... I suppose, but... but we won," Una insisted. "I've struck a blow for Optimism! No longer will my new friend need to live in hopelessness--"

"Very good, very nice, have a cookie. Now can we *please* get back to work tracking down the hypertech?" Emily insisted. "You know, the thing we need to do before we're booted out of the house if we're going to have any hope of stopping Summer from using it...?"

Una sighed. "Yes, Emily. I understand."

"Right. ...and Una?"

"Ah, yes?"

"Good work," Emily said, offering her a smile. "I meant it when I said that was noble of you. Crazy, true, but... good work. Your mother and father would be proud."

After that incident, the group avoided further contact with their host, and the host avoided further contact with them. But much as Lady Morgana had predicted, they were officially the topic d'jour, and highly sought after by the various nobles in attendance.

High-court Faeries of all stripes were eager to talk to the four of them, although only two were talking back, Una and Emily. Scout stayed on alert without looking like he was on alert, never leaving Emily's side; Nel, the latest addition to their merry band of outcasts and madmen, was doing her best not to be noticed. She was arguably even better at it than Scott "I Fade From Your Short Term Memory" Reinhold, having years of practice at going about her work without being a blemish on the landscape that anyone important would find worthy of ill attention.

But conversation after conversation passed, dancing in and around and through the hoops of smalltalk, without any real progress on their investigation. They couldn't come right out and ask "So, seen any big piles of hypertech lying around, being used for nefarious purposes?" That would be a Very Bad Idea. So, instead, Una would talk up her experiences Orbital society in hopes of intriguing curious onlookers and getting them to admit what they may already have known about it... meanwhile, Emily talked about being a traveling witch, a mobile problem solver, who happened to run across Una's path, oh didn't you know she's from outer space, isn't that interesting, have you ever met someone like her before, etc...

The Faeries either were forewarned about this sort of thing, or were simply playing it coy to avoid admitting ignorance. They'd give little knowing smiles and looks, the graceful magical creature version of "I see what you did there." But they'd admit nothing. Oh, they weren't the least bit surprised at the concept of aliens from space (although it was impossible to tell if they knew those 'aliens' were from a parallel Earth) and had clearly heard OF the Orbitals, but how, why, and where they learned... those remained secrets. A good tangential topic could be deployed to deflect any questioning, direct or otherwise.

As the party wore on, Emily found herself facing another problem. Her body was being quite rude, in the form of a growling stomach. She hadn't eaten anything since breakfast back at the campsite in Edmonton. Eager to get off her feet and conserve her energy, she led Scout off to an unoccupied side table, slumping into the chair.

"Do you think if I pulled a blank page from my spellbook and wrote 'FREE FOOD' on it, planting it by those appetizers, I could trick them into feeding us without indebting us to come back to this horrible place?" she wondered.

Scout shook his head. "Doubtful. I could go steal some bread from the pantry... they'd never see me."

"I don't trust Lady Morgana not to have anti-theft tracking spells on everything she owns. No way. Ergh. I wish I knew how long these stupid balls lasted..." Emily complained. "And I doubt there's a fast food place anywhere within a hundred miles we could visit after finally being set free. Maybe you could, I don't know, wrestle an alligator and we could eat it."

"Una's new servant might be willing to bring us back to her former quarters, find us some food there..."

"It'd still be Lady Morgana's. I'm not giving that bitch any chance to get her hooks in us. No doubt she's already started planning some massive, multi-year revenge scheme. ...why did Una have to pick NOW of all times to take up the cause of liberating slaves?" Emily groaned. "Don't get me wrong, I loved watching her stick it in and break it off, and I hate the practice of indentured servitude... but... I don't know. It's just lousy timing."

"Battles choose you. You do not choose battles."

"Very zen of you, o warrior priest. ...where is Una, anyway? Haven't seen her in awhile--"

The melodious strains of a harp cut through the air, amplified by a series of hollow gourds positioned at each corner of the room. Excited tittering flowed through the crowd, as couples relocated from their conversation pits, migrating inwards... to the dance floor.

Trying to avoid panic, Emily consulted her limited knowledge of Faerie balls. "...I'm.. not sure if it'd be an insult to the host not to take part in the dances," she said, quickly. "Crap. I have no idea how to dance. Do you?"

"No," Scout admitted.

"We could risk it less by playing wallflower. If we go out there and stomp all over some baron's toes it could get ugly... maybe we should stay put. "

"...no. No need. Come on."

The boy rose to his feet, offering a white-gloved hand to his lady... although his eyes were on the dancers, on their feet, quickly memorizing the steps. As he led the perplexed witch out to the floor, he'd already gathered the basics by the time they reached a suitably open space.

Scout fell into the pattern of the dancers, doing his best to lead Emily along. Quick glances left and right confirmed his predictions of the enemy-- of the guest's movements. It wasn't all that different from engaging a foe with a unique combat style, adapting quickly, read the footwork until you could know exactly how to flow along with it...

The two pressed in close, a half-turn making Emily slightly dizzy, as she grasped onto Scout's hand for support. "Uh... Scout... you sure about this--?

"Left, then right," he whispered to her. "Like this. Then a turn. Repeat. Relax your body; move with it, don't tense. It may shift later but this should do for now. I'll keep an eye out for changes. Don't worry."

"Left, then right. Right. --correct, I mean. Okay, got it..." she said, glancing down at her own feet, making sure everything was A-OK down there. She followed the patterns in silence for a minute, until she felt confident enough to move along with her partner without fear. ...the lovely Faerie music wafting through the air, enchanted notes from enchanted instruments, certainly helped soothe the anxiety.

Here she was, wearing a lovely dress, dancing with a handsome boy, enjoying pleasant music, surrounded by beauty and majesty. Why did it have to be such a horrible thing...?

"...if it wasn't for all the secrecy and doom and the Faeries screwing me over years ago, I might've enjoyed things like this," Emily pondered aloud, in a voice like a resigned sigh.

"Fancy parties?" Scout guessed.

"Yes. God, yes. I was a silly little girl, once," Emily admitted, with an awkward half-smile. "I was all about ponies and pretty dresses and rainbows and big romantic dances with magical, graceful Faeries. I'd read a lot of books about that sort of thing, had a lot of daydreams. ...it's all crap, of course. I know that now."

"...wouldn't say that. That's just a viewpoint."

"Eh?"

"It is what you make of it," Scout said gently, before doing a sweeping turn, changing direction, Emily held close. "Assume it's one thing and it will be. There is objective truth, but the larger part is perceptive, in how you choose to approach it. ...hmmh. Example. Figured life would just be one fight after another, so it was. An endless battle. Seemed true at the time, it got me by, but... I'm opening up to other possibilities, now. Maybe I was wrong. If I can see it another way, maybe it'll be that way. Perspective changes."

"Uh.. huh. This is you and the mirror, isn't it -- that last one, where we all got weirdly introspective. Kind of like when you actually enjoyed cooking dinner, yesterday night..."

Scout nodded, acknowledging it. "Right now, it's just little things. Here and there. Practicing. Keeping control, as always... but not ignoring it all anymore. Trying to keep an open mind."

"So... and correct me if I'm wrong... while before you might not have been able to... right now, you're enjoying dancing with me," Emily concluded, despite the levels of pink that rose to her cheeks at the thought.

"Yes. I am," the boy spoke, in honesty.

The two danced in silence, for one long moment. That unspoken mood lasted somewhere between the length of no time at all and all the time in the world.

"...hey," Emily prompted, to get his attention.

"Hey?"

"Una said something to me, back in that wreck. I've been.. thinking about it, and..."

"Yes...?"

Emily took a deep breath. "...and I should warn you, I think I'm about to do something that goes against all my former instincts as to what a prim and proper witch is supposed to be doing with her life. Brace yourself."

"Wh--"

She had to pull him in close and rise on her toes an inch to do it, but Emily managed to firmly place her lips on those of Scout.

It wasn't her first kiss. There was a boy back in the village, but he ran away screaming something about cooties. And there was an elf who lived out in Florida, but that had been a mistake.

This, despite the hesitancy that had kept her at bay for so long, was not a mistake. Not in the slightest. It was the best kiss she'd ever experienced in her life, even if it was only the third one, best by far...

If there was a 'mistake' aspect to it, it'd be how she forgot to pay attention to the music. Because it had cut out several moments into the kiss. And the enchanted chandelier lights were now spotlighting them. And all the nobles were grinning and offering light applause...

She broke contact when she realized nearly the entire room was watching. That sucked all the romance out of the moment, replacing it with a feeling of icy dread. They were making a Scene. An amusing scene which the crowd approved of, but a Scene nonetheless.

Oh god, oh god, be graceful, don't make a fuss, don't insult the host... Emily thought in a panic. Scout picked up on her worry, stepping away from her slightly... mirroring the sloppy if grateful curtsey she gave the crowd with his own bow. And then they fled for the tables, to sit the next dance out and hopefully fade from view.

The two sat very awkwardly, in an awkward silence, on awkward chairs at the awkward table. Emily was hoping to shrink down enough to hide inside her hat. Scout had chosen to toy with a napkin at the place setting.

He's not saying anything, she thought. *I'm not saying anything. I ought to be saying something. I'm pretty sure the standard thing to say here is "I love you." I'm more than pretty sure I want to say that. I am not stalling. A witch is neither early nor late with a love confession. A witch confesses love precisely when she means to. ...I think I should've said it a minute ago.*

She took a second deep breath. "Scout--"

"Emily? Emily Moonthistle...? "

--that wasn't Scout. It was a familiar voice, though...

She turned in her chair, to get a better look -- and saw an elderly Faerie in a brown cloak approaching, his long white beard neatly braided in the way Emily had once taught him to do.

"Instructor Elriel?" she recognized, twisting that recognition into a question from the sheer surprise of it. "When did you...?"

"Ah, I was a bit late coming to the ball, I'm afraid," he said. "I misplaced my spectacles -- oh, bother all that! It's good to see you again, little one! Come, come, let me have a look at you. Oh, how you've grown...! And you still have your ancestral hat, very good, it pleases me to see that. --oh, I'm sorry, I've been ignoring your companion... err... am I interrupting anything?"

Emily nibbled her lip. Here was a friendly face, one of the few friendly faces she'd met within the Summer Court. Someone she was overjoyed to see, someone she could talk to (and maybe ask about the hypertech directly AND safely). But, there was still the aftermath of that kiss hanging in the air...

Fortunately, Scout picked up on the problem right away. He nodded once to her, confirming. "I'll catch up with you later," he agreed.

"I'll be RIGHT back," Emily promised him, quietly, before turning to Elriel, all smiles. "Sir, I'm happy to see you again. Come, come... let's go somewhere and chat. Catch up a bit! Oh, oh! Did you know I found a copy of the Perfectea spell...?"

Emily gathered up her skirt bustles, wandering off with the elder Fae. And left Scout sitting alone at the table.

Leaving him to finally let out a long, tension-releasing exhale.

It was such a strange thing, the sensation that had gripped him. Nervousness. He was actually *nervous* about something, a rarity in and of itself. Even before his transformation, Scout hadn't felt actual fear in a very long time... all that boiled away when he began to approach life as a series of devil-may-care conflicts, neatly locking fear away. This wasn't fear of death, or fear of imprisonment, or anything of that nature... it was a different flavor.

The best label he could put on it was fear that he was a bad kisser. He had absolutely no idea what to do, once Emily had started kissing him. He'd never kissed anyone before in his life. What if he'd gotten it wrong? Would she be disappointed?

Still, experiencing that little jangle of anxiety had to be a good thing. Scout knew he had to be willing to explore his feelings if he was going to--

"Ahem."

--he twisted in his chair, tracking the voice. It'd caught him completely unaware: a new and different sort of fear. Surprise. He'd been ambushed. HIM, ambushed.

The Lion of Summer stood, leaning casually against a wall, as casually as one could when wearing a formal set of armor emblazoned with the crest of his Lady.

"You were doing so much woolgathering I could've likely killed you before you could move a muscle, Mr. Scott Reinhold," he noted, lips curling around the name, as if testing it out for size. "...hmm. Still, I saw the incident that put you off your guard. If you weren't the least bit affected by her advances, I'd be damned disappointed. I suspect she would be, too. ...now. Come with me."

"An order from Lady Summer, sir?" Scout asked, curious.

"Call it a polite request. Yes, yes, no favor involved. I feel we should talk."

They'd found a stairwell off to a balcony, overlooking the main room. It was strangely private... even though everyone in the room could look up and watch them converse, nobody did. The main activity was in the swirl of social butterflies below, not in any aloof ravens of the rafters.

After arriving, Elriel reached into his cloak, and produced a cloth-wrapped bundle -- a finely baked piece of spiced bread, an elven design he knew Emily enjoyed greatly. He held it out, in offering.

"I never come to these parties without packing a lunch," he said, with a smile. "Here. I baked it myself. A gift to you, no favor involved. I figured you'd be quite hungry by now..."

Emily accepted the bread gratefully and tried very hard not to wolf it down on the spot. Tried and failed. She did manage to finish it off in about four quick bites, however, her body refusing to let her pause and chat politely until it was satisfied.

"I've been following your progress, little one," he said, leaning against the balcony railing. "Well, as best I can. After you were drummed out of Lilith's academy, you were persona non grata... but in visiting a human settlement while wearing glamour, I found your website."

"My whaf?" Emily said, trying to swallow the last of the bread.

"Your 'Witchipedia.' The one you started with that elven fellow from Florida. Such a clever name," Elriel said, with a smile. "I told no one, of course. I doubt my peers would appreciate your efforts the way I did... a shame, really. Why should one as old as I be the only forward thinker? We need more motivated young people willing to reach across those boundaries... oh, but I'm babbling, and there's so much to discuss! You are well, I take it? Although... why are you here, exactly?"

"We... kinda invaded one of Lady Summer's protectorates," Emily admitted. She felt safe discussing the truth with him, with the only teacher who seemed to care about her, back when she was studying magic. "Attending the party is our punishment. It's been touch and go, but I think we'll be able to ride out the rest of the event and then run for it."

"Advisable. Lilith will be in attendance," the elder teacher warned. "She is late in coming... but will be coming. And while she wouldn't be clumsy enough to break the barrier of insult with you, she will no doubt have cross words with you. Once she discovered that you survived the beating her chosen girls gave you, she was... inconsolable. If not for more important projects occupying her time, distracting her past her initial rage, she might have hunted you down."

Emily's good mood wobbled, darkening at the memory. ...she hated to ask the next question, but it HAD eaten at her now and then, ever since that day...

"Instructor... I'm sorry to be accusing, but... I have to know," she warned. "Why did you go along with her plans? The academy. Training the girls to be weapons for the Summer Court, knowing full well the damage they were doing to themselves. It... well, what I know of you, it doesn't seem like *you* to be a party to that..."

Elriel... sighed, his age finally showing as he slumped against the balcony railing. He couldn't meet her questioning eyes.

"We all owe fealty to someone or other, and ultimately, to Lady Summer," he explained. "I was ordered not to warn them of the dangers of Faerie magic in human hands. The mystique of the witch, the power and status we were offering, that had to be maintained. In my youth, when the program began to train human girls and burn them out on magic as disposable soldiers, I did try to lodge protest. I said that there were better ways, that spellbooks could serve as a buffer, a barrier against harm. But they would make our tools less efficient, and so, my plan was rejected."

"But you still taught me using books..."

"Well, you are the exception to most rules, are you not?" he spoke, eyes finally meeting hers, with a twinkle. "There was no other option, with your 'disability'. Your great grandmother was wise in her blessing. I could sense that hand in play... after all, I helped train her using the same techniques. It was my little rebellion, I suppose, to take one of the promising students and secretly show her another path. I was overjoyed to see my act of resistance bore fruit... and crushed, when I learned how Lilith attempted to purge her family line. ...when I then learned you had survived the destruction, I wept, girl. I wept with relief."

He might have wept a little at the very memory of it, the way he brushed one hand by his eyes, trying to make the gesture as casual and unimportant as possible.

"Emily... I see you as the future of witchcraft," he explained. "Not the wild and twisted creatures we have made, but someone who commands magic as well as she commands herself. A walker between worlds, one foot in the arcane wonders of the Faerie Court, one foot in the grounded rationale of the human world. You should continue your Witchipedia... perhaps one day it will carry forth the best of our ways, long after we are gone..."

"Instructor Elriel, you speak too highly of me! I am but a mere slip of-- wait, what?" Emily said, interrupting her practiced words of respect. "Long after you're gone? What do you mean?"

But Elriel had caught himself; the nervous look to him suggested he'd said too much. "I... ah. Emily. Please understand, I am oathbound... no matter the compassion I have for your unfortunate situation, there are some boundaries I cannot cross."

She considered this, measuring her response. "Is this to do with the stolen Orbital technology? The metal devices. The ones Lady Summer stole from Lady Winter.

...you can't tell me, can you. And silence is telling, too... drat. I've put you in a spot, haven't I..."

Elriel chose his own words twice as carefully. "My words to you are these: take your cleverness, girl, and hide it away. Survive. Something comes, something vast that will change everything. I wouldn't want you to be swept up in the madness that has taken the seasons. ...specifics, no, I cannot offer them. I've likely said too much, as is. But above all else... you need to survive. This is no world-shaking prophecy... I just couldn't bear to know that you came to harm."

Old joints creaking, he stood upright, adjusting his cloak. Making sure he looked presentable.

"I should join the party, at this point," Elriel decided. "I missed being properly announced. It would be unkind of me not to introduce myself to our host. ...no matter what I think of her ways. Be well, Emily Moonthistle, and may magic illuminate your days."

"Be well, Instructor Elriel, and may magic illuminate your days," Emily replied in turn, offering a curtsey.

"Hah. What few an old fellow like me has left to illuminate, indeed..."

"Oh, don't be silly, sir! You'll outlast us all!" Emily joked.

But the old man was thoughtful, and grave, in his reaction.

"Only by the grace of Lady Summer would that be," he noted.

Just outside the ballroom proper, a patio overlooked the plantations of New Orleans, and the many dirt hovels of the servants. They were hard to see, with the colorful array of magical herbs and plants arranged in neat grids -- sparkling fruit and vegetable matter, species of flora not of this world. Elves in green tunics moved through the rows, tending with watering implements, encouraging growth through spells, and killing the occasional pest. Even in the twilight hours, there was work to be done here.

It was a model of productiveness, and the true power behind the House. While it was known for its many games of chance, for hosting parties of a disreputable sort... the real reason it existed was to produce the crops, for use elsewhere in the Faerie Court. That always came first, even if Lady Morgana rarely paid attention to the harvesting.

Watching over the grounds, briefly scanning for any threats, stood the Lion of Summer. With him was a Winterhound. An unlikely pairing.

"I prefer this view," the Lion spoke. "Orderly. Organized. Put to purpose, rather than thrashing about in vice. A shame that the guardian assigned to this work should be such a bother, but Lady Summer's will is not to be questioned."

"Labors built on the backs of slavery, of course," Scout pointed out.

"We all bend knee to someone in the end, boy. There is no pure freedom. Even you, who wanders at will and defies Lady Winter, bend to forces outside you at times... or perhaps inside you. ...now, then. Let me regale you with a story. All it will cost you is a yes or a no answer to a question. Is that acceptable?"

"...maybe."

"I see you've raised your guard again," he acknowledged, nodding in some manner of approval. "Very well. I will continue regardless, and where it takes us is where it takes us."

He turned his back to the fields, to address Scout directly.

"Many years past, when my kind were more actively at war with your kind -- and by that I mean humans -- there was a city some distance from here," he explained.

"Which Lady Summer considered to be an insult, a human city surviving for so long deep in the deserts, in the warm places she wished to lay claim to. There had been efforts throughout the years to destroy the city, off and on, depending on Summer's whims. This latest one was not my first combat experience, but it was an early one.

"The difficulty was the human military. They fought hard, they fought well -- these 'Frontliners' had a firm backbone, not like the spineless, backward monkey men I'd assumed humans to be through years of military indoctrination. We tried every weapon in our arsenal to take the city... destructive magics, great towering beasts, airborne assault with winged pegasi. But these humans had a response for every tactic we used. Eventually, Summer withdrew her forces, as flailing about in futility was only draining our limited resources. The humans won the day.

"Now, understand that one man does not determine victory or defeat. The human commander was an import from the eastern shores, a pathetic man that even his own soldiers had no respect for. No, the real tactician who was quietly spreading his battle plans and methodologies through the ranks was another... a teacher, who prepared the humans for battle. He devised the many shields we broke our spears against.

"His name was Saul Reinhold. He is possibly the only human I have ever respected," the Lion admitted. "If more were like him, perhaps I'd have a better opinion of your species. ...so. That is my story. Now, the price comes in the form of a question I suspect you will be willing to answer. ...I heard the Herald announce your name, Scott Reinhold. You are the heir of Saul, are you not?"

It was with no small amount of pride that Scout answered.

"Yes," he said. "He was the closest thing I had to a father, sir. He's the reason why I could resist the Hound."

The Lion nodded slowly, that piece of the puzzle clicking into place, as his view on Scout solidified. "Good. Perhaps there is hope for you yet, then. ...I heard of the fall of your great city, you know. It was a disgusting thing, the way Winter strangled its life away. That's no way for such an endeavor to end. Your city deserved to be destroyed in honorable combat, not murdered in its sleep."

"I'd rather it have avoided either fate. But it is what it is," Scout spoke.

"Anyone with Saul's strength who would fight that enemy to the bitter end, and to fight it even now after being supposedly conquered, is admirable to me," the Lion acknowledged. "Perhaps you are disloyal to your Queen... but your loyalty to your code -- and from what I saw in the ballroom, loyalty to your woman -- that I will accept. ...that strength may be needed, soon."

"Sir...?"

"Change comes. I've known the tides of war often enough to hear the wave as it begins to crest," he explained. "Strange devices, things I don't trust, are in play within the secretive hands of Lady Summer -- and formerly, the hands of Lady Winter. I break no oath telling you this; you already knew, no doubt. But I tell you in my experience that the sleepy warm evenings of Summer can flare red hot like a desert wind, when she chooses to act."

"War between Summer and Winter, perhaps?" Scout asked.

"Perhaps. Or war with the humans. Or something else entirely. I wouldn't tell you, even if I knew. If you are wise... you will take your woman and shield her from the storm, in whatever shape it may arrive. For all I know, a time may come where I have to test my steel against yours. And while part of me relishes in clashing with old Saul one more time... you should know that I would likely be ordered the fell the both of you. Be prepared."

"I will stand fast, sir."

The Lion nodded. He didn't salute or offer his hand -- it wasn't the way of their kind. The nod would be enough.

"I'd have it no other way," he agreed.

Glamour is a style of magic quite popular with Faeries, as it enhances beauty, covers blemishes, and makes the unpresentable nicely presentable. Millions of dollars a year may be spent by humans on cosmetics, both mundane and surgical, which are easily trumped by an expert in glamour.

However, while the most common use of it is beauty... at the core, it's all about illusion. Illusion can be applied many ways, as a knife can do everything from slice bread to spread butter to cleave a man in twain. For instance, glamour can run the opposite direction from making you the most noticeable figure in the room... it can make you the most unnoticeable figure in the room, too.

Nel was used to wandering the halls without notice. She'd gotten adept at turning her magic inside out, to avoid being seen by guests, to avoid any undue attention. Other than her obligatory morning sessions prettying up her Mistress... her former Mistress, that is... and other daily tasks, she tried to avoid the gaze of any eyes. Which meant fooling others into ignoring her, not only in sight, but sound and even smell...

She hadn't tried doing this trick on anyone other than herself, but was surprised to find how easy it was to make two people completely and utterly unimportant. Not that different from one person of no importance whatsoever...

Despite being totally ignored by wandering party guests and the occasional House guard, she was just as terrified as she was during Una's other grand plan.

"We shouldn't be doing this, ma'am!" she pleaded. (No need to whisper, even as they stepped around someone who was walking right towards them. Nobody would hear them.) "The basements are off limits! If we're caught, we'll be punished severely..."

"Then we won't be caught," Una spoke, with a reassuring smile. "As long as this spell is up, you said we can't be seen! It's amazing, this magic of yours!"

Nel glanced aside. "If it was so amazing... then my Lady-- I mean, Lady Morgana would not be so dissatisfied with my glamours..."

"Now, that's just silly. She's a horrid old woman, Nel! I bet she envied your own youth and beauty," Una guessed correctly. "It's her failing, not yours. Have confidence in yourself, and your skills! You've done so very well tonight, acting despite your fears, and as a result of that bravery a bright future now stretches before you! This little act of rebellion against Morgana is your first step towards freeing yourself from this terrible House!"

"I... I don't object to working against Morgana's purposes," Nel clarified. "I will do as you wish. You own me, now, and I am yours to do with as you please, ma'am."

Una sighed. She could tell this was going to be a sticking point for some time to come... "Nel, I already explained--"

"Please, ma'am, you need to understand my objection! It's not fear of *Morgana's* wrath. ...what I fear is *HER* wrath," Nel whispered despite not needing to. Some things you can't say aloud. "Lady Summer. I can't hide from her beneath a spell! I've... seen her, leaving the basements to speak to Lady Morgana, once. At night, I can hear the sounds she makes within her secretive place! What if she's there right now? This is why Lady Morgana was allowed to host the Solstice Ball, so Lady Summer would not be far from her work. She will see us! Even one as important as you would not be spared from her anger!"

"Nel, I promise you, if it looks like we will be in actual danger... we can abandon the plan. Turn around and rejoin the party. I won't put you at risk, not for me or my causes," Una assured. "But this may be my only chance to see what's going on down there. My friends are counting on me. We need to at least try!"

The pair paused, in front of a heavy oaken door. Nel looked left, looked right -- glamour would hide them, even hide the effect of the opening and closing door, but her innate fear gave her a need to make sure there was no chance of being spotted, regardless. She took her key-ring out from the pocket of Una's donated servant's garb, flipping through the decorative iron keys until she came to the proper one... and carefully, slowly, turned it in the lock. She closed her eyes, focusing her magic to cover the sound of the tumblers, and the squeaky hinges...

For her part, Una pulled a pair of modified glasses from the storage compartment on her jetpack. She powered them up before slipping them on. They provided a perfect view down into the gloom... rather than showing visible light, they showed the shift-spectrum colors surrounding objects.

She'd developed this tool back in Baltimore, to see through walls, to find the distinct blue glow of Orbital hypertech. The color represented the dimensional shift, the signature which highlighted items of Orbital origin, with other colors representing different origins... yellow, for humans, as well as Earth-made objects such as the walls and support beams of the basement. Red, for Faeries and their artifacts brought with them from the World of Faerie. Una was looking at the spectrum of worlds, not the spectrum of light.

If Lady Summer was down here, there would be a brilliant red glow, no doubt... something purely and undeniably Faerie. Perhaps the glasses would even show the sequence of contradictory errors, which arose from hypertech trying to parse magic effects. But aside from a few odds tools and knickknacks, tiny spots of red... there was nothing alarming down there.

And a HUGE amount of blue.

"She's not there," Una promised. "I'd be able to see her, if she was. Let's go down there. It won't take long; I just need to verify what I think I'm going to find..."

"I can't see," Nel noted. "How are you able to...?"

"Oh, sorry... special glasses," Una said. "Here, just... hold onto my hand. I'll lead the way. Mind the steps..."

Una grasped her companion's hand tightly, offering a reassuring squeeze and a smile, as the two descended into the basement...

...and into most of an Arcology's shift engine chamber.

A huge gyroscopic assembly took up the center of the room, where a space had been cleared away, wine casks pushed off to the walls. It was the missing core component of #BE12's engines... unworkably damaged, but nonetheless hauled all the way from Edmonton down to New Orleans, to be hidden away in the basement of a disreputable house. Far from Lady Summer's core power base, far from anywhere a sensible person would expect her to be. The perfect hideaway to run experiments from...

A few computers were still active, operating off a pair of cracked mass capacitors, which hadn't yet lost the quantum field that kept their heavily compressed planetary matter generating power, rather than reverting to a useless solid lump of rock. Una memorized what screens were currently active, so she could return to them after doing a little poking around... and after erasing her tracks.

"I just need a few minutes," she explained. "Just to try and get an idea of what

Lady Summer's up to..."

Nel tried to see, in the dim lighting of the basement... making out lines and shapes of silver, the poor illumination reflecting off the objects in strange ways. "It's all made of... star-metal?" she asked. "Like your adornments?"

"These objects were created by my people, the Orbitals," Una explained, as she browsed the computer's active files. "They're... well. It's a science so advanced that it may as well be magic. Or maybe magic is just an advanced science... but either way, these things can be dangerous if misused. They're... anachronisms. Things which don't belong on your world, things which nobody here could have possibly invented yet. Maybe in thousands of years..."

"That assumes we'll live thousands of years, what with the wars and all," Nel spoke, as if resigned to it. "The humans have attacked New Orleans a few times since Morgana came here, trying to retake it."

"It's cooled off since then, though, hasn't it? I mean, not as many open attacks on each other..."

"I suppose, from what I've heard from the guests... but Faeries have long memories. It's been quiet before. It'll be loud again, and soon enough. ...I can tell, in their voices, while I serve drinks and move through rooms. Tensions are rising, ma'am. Something's coming..."

"Maybe something to do with all this," Una agreed, looking at the piles and piles of objects with blue auras lying around the glowing yellow floor, amidst the red spellbooks and arcane tools. Shift frequencies, superimposed over the real world, through her augmented vision...

Red and blue and yellow. Anachronisms from three worlds, three cultures, all overlaid on top of each other... but yellow was always here. The blue arrived by the might of Orbital science, using shift engines to transport Arcologies across the worldbleed...

But how did the red get here...? The Pandora Event was always assumed by Orbital anthropologists to be some sort of Faerie magical incursion. They certainly were hostile and powerful, *likely* capable of it, even if there was no direct evidence. Not that they'd gone looking for any. A simple theory and most likely correct, the scholars felt. But what if...

Una should have been browsing the files, paying attention to them. But something was tugging at her -- or rather, she'd found something to tug at. A loose thread in a weave of cloth. Something that had been there all the while, but had gone unnoticed. If she pulled at it just so...

"Nel...? What did the Pandora Event look like?" Una asked, her hands grasping in the dark for the idea.

"Er? The what?"

"When your people were transported to the human world. --yes, I know many Faerie believe it was the other way around, but... nevermind. My question is, what was the effect like, what did it look like they Fae arrived? Humans have shorter lifespans than Faeries. Your people might remember the first days of the chaotic age better than Earth records would."

"Ah... pardon, ma'am, but I'm still very young. I wasn't alive at that time... none of the Elders were, even. I mean, Archmagus Lilith is only one hundred and thirty! But... the stories do speak of it, yes," Nel clarified, trying hard to remember. "It was said to be a bright flash of light, and a sound, like... well. It's spoken of in the oral traditions, in poetry. My favorite way it was described was like a massive cork popping from a goddess's wine bottle, because it seemed more playful."

"Like... a sharp burst of wind? Filling in a vacuum, or pushing air aside?"

"Yes, I think wind was mentioned," Nel said. "Why, ma'am? Is this important?"

The flash was not blinding. It was a spray of misty light, a featureless white cloud of illumination... accompanied by a sound of displacing air. Like a cork coming out of an ancient bottle...

Of course, shift engines didn't work this way -- all they did was move Orbital ships from one world to another. Every good little boy and girl who took courses in the basics of planar mechanics knew that. Shift engines certainly didn't isolate lifeforms from one world and teleport them onto another. That'd be silly. It'd be like, well, like using classroom learning aids to create a mind controlled slave army...

Nevertheless, #BE12 had done exactly that, when its secrets were threatened. It shifted the lizard tyrant to Earth, a creature from another world. Called forth by a dormant self defense program, designed to ambush anyone who investigated the crash...

If she'd been wearing her glasses, what color would the creature have been? Purple? Orange? That strange monster, pulled away from all it had known and loved, shifted to this world by Orbital technology to be used up and discarded as a living weapon...?

And if that color could be pulled into Earth against its will by a crippled "ship transportation system," could something red not be moved by a wholly intact engine? A great deal of red, pouring into yellow...

Una's world reeled away from her. She grasped the edge of the computer, for support, as everything around her changed.

"We did it," Una said, the shock setting in. "My people. We caused the Pandora Event. It's just too similar to our technology to be a Faerie spell, or some Earthling's invention. I don't know how, I don't know why, but... the Orbitals overlaid the peoples of your world on top of this one, shifting the Faeries away from their homes... and gave way to centuries of bloody conflict. It's our fault. It's my fault..."

"...uh, my Lady..."

"It had to be an accident. It had to be," Una reasoned. "Shift engines gone awry, some glitch in the system. Maybe interference with Faerie magic, I know the two don't mesh properly. A mistake, that's all. Nobody would do this deliberately, this... this atrocity. It serves no purpose. It has no function!"

"My Lady! Someone comes!"

Una snapped out of her attempt to apply logic to horror. The stairs were creaking...

Regretfully her fingers flew across the keypad, erasing her tracks, despite having no time to truly study the files. The time for investigation was over; she had a promise to keep to her friend Nel. They would flee this place at the first sign of trouble. No more wrath of the Faeries for poor Nelliwyn, who had already experienced a Dennis-in-Baltimore of her own, so many times...

No more. No more suffering. Not for her, not for this world, not for anyone! Una declared within her mind, restoring the computer to its original state.

Moving quickly and with purpose, she led Nel out of the basement, sliding along the stairwell past a servant elf who had just come down to get another cask of wine.

The burly house elf felt as if something had brushed past him, but dismissed it immediately. It was probably nothing.

By some coincidence of fate, the four came together at the same time.

Emily was walking in from the hallway to the balcony stairs. Scout, approaching from the outside decks. A very pale looking Una (well, paler than her usual fair skin allowed for) accompanied by a confused looking Nel, from a servant's hallway. All four, arriving at an empty table in the ballroom, off to the side.

They took seats. Three of them did, at least; Emily raised a hand, to stop Nel.

"Y'know, I could just kill for a cup of tea about now," she said. "Nel, would you mind fetching some for us? I'm sure Una wouldn't mind, right?"

The servant girl looked to Una, for some sort of confirmation... but got no reaction whatsoever. For lack of a better option, she curtseyed politely, and slipped away to do as requested.

"Nel's not a slave anymore, you know," Scout spoke, not liking the taste of Emily's words.

"I know, I know," Emily said, sighing in apology. "But we need to discuss our secret clubhouse business, and--"

"I already told her," Una spoke at last, although her voice was barely over a whisper.

"...criminy. Una, we're trying to maintain a low profile. What if she goes back to her former owner and rats us out? Or Lady Summer, for that matter? Summerfae can't disobey the Crown of Fire! ...alright, fine, whatever. Look, I just got back from talking to an Instructor high in Lilith's circle, and he's told me some disturbing things. ...okay, some vague things that are also disturbing. I think he's worried about the Faeries dying out, or something... there's a madness overtaking the seasons. He told me to run and hide."

"I got the same suggestion from the Lion of Summer," Scout noted. "To avoid the coming storm. The Lion sees war on the horizon, although the sides involved in that war are unclear. He suggested we get out of the way, because we could become targets. He wasn't any clearer than your friend was, howev--"

"The Orbitals caused the Pandora Event," Una stated.

That effectively killed all conversation.

So, Una laid out what she saw, and what she deduced. About the shift frequencies, about how engines aren't supposed to do anything except move ships, and certainly not dinosaurs. And Nel's story about the impact of the Pandora Event.

"...we've been assuming all along that this... all of this, the crashed Arcology supposedly taken down by Faerie magic, the seasons plotting against each other... we thought it was all the Faeries. What if it wasn't?" Una asked, horrified at her own words. "What if... what if my people *murder* entire worlds? What if they're behind all of this?"

Emily cleared her throat. "Uh. Okay. ...look. Listen. Una. We... just know a few more things, that's all. We don't know anything for *certain*," she assured. "There's no damn reason to cause the Pandora Event on purpose. At least, none we know of. We don't know anything except what happened, not why. Let's not jump to conclusions--"

"What if everything I was taught was a lie? What if the Orbitals are... are the *bad guys?*" Una said, the last two words evoked like the name of the most terrifying devil to ever dig its talons into the imagination.

"Right now we've got no clue who the bad guys are, alright? Summer, Winter, the Orbitals, the Easter Bunny, who knows? We need to investigate more. ...any chance we can get into the basement again, to look at the files you missed? Summer's clearly up to something, here, and she sure as hell isn't an astronaut."

"I... maybe. I don't know. Nel could--"

"Emily. Five o'clock," Scout warned, leaning in to whisper. "Behind you. Real bad guys just showed up."

"What?" Emily said, turning instinctively to look--

At a phalanx of pointy hats, and the impossibly, magically beautiful Archmagus leading them. Lilith and her latest witch trainees.

Emily ducked her head, fast -- not that it would've helped, what with her wearing her Nana's hat. "Dammit. Dammit dammit. We could run. The ball's not over, not until Lady Summer makes her showing, but... it could be worth it to get out of here before anything goes wrong..."

"I won't let her hurt you," Scout stated.

"Yes, Galahad, that's very nice for you. Unkillable or not, Lilith could still splatter the walls with you in an instant. We need to *go*."

Una sat upright. "I won't leave Nel behind. She's mine, for better or worse, and she's experienced enough of this place. We have to wait for her to come back with the tea you wanted."

"Agh. Una, I appreciate your enthusiasm for the moral high ground, but--"

"Well well, what *have* we here?"

Too late.

Standing nearby was a woman who, if you'd rearranged the facial features a bit, would pass for a clone of Lady Morgana. They had the same attitude, the same stance, even the same fashion sense. The only difference was in headwear, as Archmagus Lilith favored the pointed variety, as did the slightly gaunt looking human girls in her entourage... facial tics and poor complexion in a smear across the entire group, more evidence of humans minds rotting away from magical addiction.

Pausing a moment to hate her life, Emily rose to her feet, pasting on her best faux smile of politeness. A curtsey. And if she ever had to curtsey to another one of these bastards again she'd likely eat her hat. "Madame Archmagus," she greeted. "How wonderful to see you again, on this the most glorious eve of Solstice, where--"

"Oh yes, it's been SUCH a long time! You've grown considerably, whereas I am, of course, unchanging and beautiful," Lilith spoke. "And I see you've adopted your ancestor's hat! Very good, very good. Your 'Nana' would have been proud. Although from the looks of it, you likely had to dig it out of her grave. Mmm. Well, I suppose I'm not one to judge; sentimentality can make us do unusual things, can it not...?"

Lilith smiled away all the while, dancing on the edge between punishable insult against Emily's Hospitality, and light conversation. This was how it would be -- little passive-aggressive turns of phrase, backhanded complements. All needling away, trying to get under Emily's skin. To make her make a mistake...

I shouldn't give her the satisfaction of riling me up, Emily thought. *If I want to survive this, I'm going to sit here and take it, let her chew on me for awhile until she gets bored and goes away. She's just a bully. I can endure bullying.*

"And look, you have friends now! Isn't it nice, having friends? It's a shame you couldn't make any at school, what with your deplorable learning disability and poor control of magic," Lilith said, with a mock sigh. "Oh, we tried and we tried, but in the end I'm afraid we failed you, little Emily. I blame myself, of course. A good teacher never blames her students, no matter how often they fail. Again and again, failing in everything they do. Failing even to prevent the death of their entire family and everything they have ever known. If only I had done a better job of it, maybe your Nana would be alive today..."

I need to sit back and let her do this. I need to bow my head and let her slap me across the face. She knows I need to do that if I'm going to get out alive. And she's taking joy in browbeating me.

...yeah. Okay. You know what? Screw this. Una's not the only one who can take a stand against them.

"Ah, Miss Emily, your tea...?"

"Yes, thank you, Nel," Emily said, accepting the cup of delicately brewed tea from off Nel's silver serving tray. "Oh, and Lilith? Up yours, bitch."

With a light flick of the wrist, the splashed the tea directly in Archmagus Lilith's face.

The light music being played through the ballroom warbled to a halt, the sound amplification gourds letting out a strangled little gasp before ceasing their platitudes. A similar silence fell over the crowd... as whatever they were talking about was suddenly far less important than the *scene* that was about to transpire.

For her part... Lilith didn't even react, despite the warm beverage dripping off her face. If anything, her smile grew impossibly wide, the glamour she wore conflicting with her expression, twisting it into a rictus grin of delight.

"I believe this ends your Hospitality," Lilith noted, for the record. "Runt, I am going to *enjoy* murdering you very, very slowly..."

A hand shot out to block Scout, before he could rise to his feet. Emily didn't even look to him -- her eyes were locked on her enemy.

"I declare a duel of magic, under the traditions of Summer Court vendetta," Emily said. "A drink in the face is a traditional device for opening combat, yes? Yes. You want a shot at me? Then we do this old school."

Now Lilith's smile faltered. But only for a split second; she couldn't lose any show of confidence. "You can't be serious, monkey-girl. You're not a standing member of this court. Why should I agree to duel you as equals instead of turning you into a pile of living agony where you stand...?"

"You'll be insulting your host, who if I recall is quite keen on games such as these. You'd be denying her audience the pleasure the House of the Rising Sun is known for," Emily reminded. "So, I humbly request that Lady Morgana be Arbiter of our duel, as is her right as host."

...Emily was fairly sure that wasn't the sort of laughter she needed from her foe at the moment. She especially didn't like the way the tone of it, the cadence, was an identical match for Lady Morgana... who walked over to join them, the crowd parting for her effortlessly.

"Big sister, what trouble have you gotten yourself into now?" Lady Morgana asked... directing the question to Lilith.

"Oh, nothing I can't handle. Just some little human girl too big for her britches, sister of mine," Lilith replied. "But I do thank you for your concern. So, how do you feel about this 'humble request' to play Arbiter for our duel...?"

The reason why Lady Morgana and Archmagus Lilith looked so alike wasn't simply because both were haughty noblewomen with eight parts attitude and twenty parts power. They apparently were family, as well. Emily's confidence in her oh-so-clever scheme started to wobble on its feet.

The rules, she thought. *Get them to stick to the rules. Play them in your favor...*

"As Arbiter, your role is to enforce the rules of the duel," Emily reminded. "Each of us gets to pick one, from the traditional list of duelist's conditions--"

"Oh, no need to explain the process, child. As you yourself noted... I'm quite keen on games," Morgana said. "And yes, naturally, each of you gets to declare one condition to be placed upon the duel. By my whim, I allow my dear sister go first. Well, Lilith? What would rule would you like imposed on the combatants?"

Lilith began systematically flexing her fingers, itching to start the fight. "I place the condition of Solitary Spell upon the duel," she decided. "Each of us gets to cast a single spell. No more than a single spell. I shouldn't need more than one word of power to completely annihilate the exile, after all... and I'll even be generous and allow the cripple to use her spellbook, provided she too only casts a single spell from it. That is my condition. After all, what could Moonthistle possibly do to me? She's never had an interest in dueling spells. Will she Animate a butter knife? Toss a Shocked napkin at me? Or maybe she'll just Escape. It would be like her..."

"Always with your pride, aren't you, sister? Very well. Human, declare your rule."

It took her a moment to find exactly the right words. She didn't want to lose on a technicality of declaring a nonexistent rule.

"...I place the condition of Heart's Guardian upon the duel," Emily decided.

This sent the crowd a-chattering. Some confused, some knowing... depending on who was present and paying attention earlier in the evening, during the dances...

"You can't be serious," Lilith said. "Clearly your mind is addled. Heart's Guardian is a tool for lover's quarrels, not a blood vendetta--"

"Two brothers were in love with the same woman," Emily spoke, reciting the fable from memory. "They began a duel, to see who would win her hand in marriage. But the clever brother spoke for the Heart's Guardian, that any who cherished him would be allowed to stand at his side during the battle... and the woman moved to his side. Heartbroken, unable to raise a hand against his love, the other brother withdrew. ...but the relevant bit there is that any who cherish the duelist are allowed to stand at the duelist's side, and take part in the fight."

"Very romantic, but you do realize you've sealed your doom, correct?" Archmagus Lilith spoke. She swept her arms open to either side, gesturing to the contingent of trainee witches. "I am the *Archmagus*, child. All these girls are ready and willing to die for me, if need be. I am cherished by all! In fact, I suspect at least a dozen nobles in this court owe me favor or fealty. By your own rule, now you face an army! Hah! Your little friends have no chance against--"

"Sister... I'm afraid that's not how it works."

"--what?" Lilith exclaimed, her prideful boast snapped in half by the ruling.

And now, Lady Morgana was the only one smiling. She did appreciate a cleverly played game, after all... and seeing her "dear" sister at the other end of a brutal gambit helped soothe the wounds she'd suffered earlier that night in a similar situation. Her own reputation's injury could be addressed if she oversaw a fine game of wits, restoring faith in her House as a place of wonders...

"There's no love in their hearts for you," Morgana explained. "The Heart's Guardian condition is very clear on this. Fealty is not the same as love. Favor is not the same thing as compassion. Therefore! I ask my guests, assembled here within my House: will any man or woman in this room stand by the Lilith's side, not because of her position as Archmagus, not due to any prior debt or obligation... but merely because she is Lilith, and she is cherished...?"

Absolute silence. Not even the gathered witches made a sound. But if smiles could make noise... a wave of amusement would've rolled across their ears. Because there was nothing a crowd enjoyed more than watching the underdog get an upper hand...

"Oh dear, oh dear... sorry, love, it seems you stand alone today," Morgana declared, in mock-sympathy. "And as Arbiter, I'm exempt, even if I do cherish you, my dear, sweet, wonderful, only occasionally very annoying sister. --now, then! Who here will stand by Emily Moonthistle, not because of her standing as a witch in exile, but merely because she is Emily?"

Scout stepped up next to Emily, unbuttoning the cuffs on his formal uniform, preparing for battle. He had no weapon... but rarely needed one, these days. He was a living weapon, after all, one now put to just cause.

"I'll defend her to the end of this world," he spoke, voice as firm as granite. "And beyond, if need be."

Una stood at Emily's other side, drawing the energy blaster from her jetpack's storage compartment, firing up the mass capacitor charges to prime the weapon. Her silver bracers were already starting to glow, ready to snap a force shield into place.

"Emily is my dearest friend. I'd sooner die than let her come to harm," Una agreed.

...and finally, Nelliwyn the slavegirl attempted to brandish her mirrored serving tray in a menacing fashion.

"I... I won't let my Lady stand alone," she said, with a bit less confidence. "That means I have to love her friend as I love her, so... I'm involved. ...despite being scared down to my toes, I'm involved..."

"It's four on one, Lilith Goatmother," Emily said... spreading her arms, in the same gesture Lilith used when gesturing to her now-useless flock of toadies and sycophants. "My advice is you withdraw. Despite all you've done to me, honestly? I don't want to kill you. It's not my way, no matter how much I hate your guts. Deal's on the table -- give up and I'll be out of your hair. Nobody stands with you, and all you have is a single spell."

...the crowd quickly began to withdraw, leaving the elder Fae and the young witch's friends with a wide, wide berth. The absolute rage burning behind the Archmagus's eyes suggested it would be a good idea not to be nearby when she finally exploded...

"I... HATE... that name," Lilith glowered. "You will call me *Archmagus*. You will call me Archmagus as the last thing you ever say! I need no one by my side -- all I've ever needed is my own power, whelp! ONЯƎℲNI!!"

The air in the ballroom exploded with a massive heat wave, as a column of solar fire burst from her outstretched hands. It was enough to make the tile of the dance floor curl and melt in its wake, enough to ignite the draperies hung over nearby tables. It was more than enough power to boil all four of them away and obliterate the ashes themselves.

That sideways pillar of flame slammed hard into Una's force fields, both bracers crossed, forming a protective dome. The four gathered behind it immediately, even if a shocked Nel had to be yanked in by Scout's grasping hand.

That's her one spell, the small, still part of Emily spoke. The Insight, the gift from deep within her grandmother's side of the family... *Lilith has to maintain the fire, has to break through Una's shield with it. It's draining her Will with every second she keeps the spell going. If she can't kill us before she collapses, it's over. But at this rate the convection will cook us well before then, so, we have to act...*

Eyes glancing around the brightly lit room fast, looking for resources, looking for...

"Una, blaster!" Emily screamed, over the roar of the fire. On command, Una dropped the gun -- she couldn't use it with all her focus on blocking the flame, anyway. Emily kicked it backwards with a foot, careful not to lose her balance and fall outside, where fire was streaming all around them... kicking it towards Scout. "Scout! Lights out!"

The Scout scooped up the weapon. He'd never fired it before... but he'd seen them fired before. Particularly the panic fire from a crazed highwayman, in an encounter that felt like it was years in the past... but not such a fuzzy memory as to forget how it worked off reflective surfaces, like the edge of a well polished chainsaw, for instance...

"Nel, please hold your serving tray up," Scout said, calmly.

Too shocked to do anything other than obey, Nel did so. And at the precise moment where it would give him the bank shot he needed... he fired.

The energy beam bounced off the mirrored tray, through the gouts of flame, off a wall-hanging mirror, and then finally slicing cleanly through the ropes that held the magically lit ballroom chandelier aloft.

The delicate structure of spellwork and glasswork dropped to the floor, spraying sparks and shards in all directions. Panicked guests scattered even farther away than they already were scattered, as the only source of light in the room went out in a piffle of failed magic...

That is, the only source other than Lilith's Inferno spell. Which now was casting a VERY sharp shadow from Emily and Una's bodies.

"Thanks for your help," Scout said to Nel, before stepping into the shadow and vanishing through the floor.

Less than a second later, and the fire had been redirected to the ceiling -- Lilith wasn't even screaming, as Scout slapped the modified anti-caster hold on her from behind, pulling her arms up while cupping a hand over her mouth.

NOW, Emily thought... swerving around Una's shields, sprinting across the dance floor, her spellbook out and open. One glance of the eyes to the page, to load up the Word and its Way, then apply the touch of a single to Lilith's exposed chest as she quietly spoke her Solitary Spell...

The fired died immediately, as the Will powering it collapsed. Scout let go, as Lilith began to thrash, to gag... collapsing to the ground in agony.

"One spell," Emily informed, snapping her book shut. "A spell I learned recently, which goes by the name of Perfectea. I just poured a cup of warm, steaming tea directly into your lungs, Lilith. You're drowning, and likely about to die. I've won the duel."

No haughty smile. No angry glare. This time... the Archmagus's expression was one of terror. And the entirety of the Summer Court nobility was there to watch it happen...

She fell unconscious, brain deprived of the oxygen it needed.

"I... declare Emily Moonthistle the victor," Morgana belatedly said, although without mirth. As much as she loved and hated her sister... the concern on her face was clear. "The... ah... death of the Archmagus is, of course, Lady Moonthistle's right, in payment for insult..."

But Emily shook her head, groaning at the thought of what was about to happen. "As much as I hate to do this, given, oh, she *murdered my entire family*... I said it before. Killing isn't my way."

The young witch got to her knees... and began chest compressions, followed by mouth to mouth breathing. CPR, to save a drowning victim.

It took several cycles of the process, before the doomed Archmagus began coughing up a tea slurry, her airway clearing. Emily rolled her, to let the fluid drain as best it could -- before being roughly shoved away by Lilith, who would not dare to be helped any further.

The assembly gathered in closer, wanting a good look, as the aftermath of the game played out...

"Sister... you are twice defeated, it seems," Morgana spoke, trying not to sound relieved. "Defeated in magic, and even saved from the icy grip of death by your foe. By Faerie law... you owe this girl *considerable* favor, now."

"nnhgh," Lilith choked, spitting up more tea, her robust Faerie constitution helping her fight off the effects... but not negating them. The fire returned to her glare, as she gazed at her hated former student. "...no. No. Never. I owe her nothing! I will do nothing for her--"

Do not deepen your humiliation, Lilith Goatmother.

The fallen lights of the chandelier, flickering and fading... began to brighten anew. They swirled away from the wreckage, forming a rough bell shape, which became a rough dress shape... which became the shape of a beautiful woman, with stray leaves and flower petals wafting in from open windows joining the light-form. The figure had no face, simply an eternal swirl of sunlight in the shape of one. At last, igniting point by point... upon her head hovered a majestic ring known as the Crown of Flame, a series of tiny dancing flames in the shape of a circlet.

"L... Lady Summer...?!" Lilith recognized, and expression of shock taking root...

Yes. As promised, I am appearing before my children during this, my glorious Solstice Ball... and what do I bear witness to, on this joyous evening? Your disgrace, Archmagus. You have disrupted my Solstice with violence and the stench of failure. So yes, you indeed owe the human child a boon. I suggest you grant it and be done with this foolishness. Be thankful I do not demand more of you than to fulfil your obligation.

"...she started it," Lilith mumbled, petulant to the end.

And you will end it. I've more important matters to tend to than to put up with your childishness...

With eyes like miniature suns, the gaze of Summer fall on the victor of the duel... Emily.

Well played, child. But don't think this will win you any more favor in my Court. The future comes closer with each day. The silver city will be mine -- you cannot change this destiny. Now. Speak your request.

"What do you mean, the silver city will be yours?" Emily most absolutely did NOT say.

It was a trap. Summer was baiting her -- she knew damn well what Emily was up to, what she was investigating. A little bait would be dangled, so that instinct would jump at the chance to ask about it... and the answer given in exchange would then count as the boon Lilith owed her. With the favor paid in full... she'd still be surrounded by Summerfae, and with no safety net. It'd mean game over.

So. Her request would have to be well chosen. But quickly chosen, lest the ire of Summer be raised...

"I request my friends and I be given safe passage to Orbital Arcology #A076," Emily spoke.

As you like it. Lilith? This is your boon to grant, in a method of your choosing.

Fallen and disgraced... but not without a streak of mischief, Lilith applied her trademark smile once more.

"As you like it," she agreed, speaking a Word of power...

Emily's eyes widened. *Oh dammit wait no I take it back I didn't specify not to be teleported directly into the vacuum of space--*

The four of them vanished from the House of the Rising Sun in a flash of sunlight.

end.a06

chal-lenge [chal-inj]
-noun
1. a call to partake in any contest, be it of skill,
strength, etc.
2. something that by its nature serves as a call to
special effort: *Space exploration offers a challenge to
humankind.*

Space. The final frontier.

In space, no one can hear you scream.

You ain't from 'round here, are yah, boy.

One of these three quotes from the ancient salvaged media empire of Westusa was applicable to the situation Emily found herself in. In a way, she was lucky it wasn't the first two -- being whisked away to a spot exactly ten feet away from Arcology #A076 would be nicely ironic and extremely fatal. It was hard to focus on the luck, however, when you were trudging knee-deep through the muck of some earthbound swampland.

"The mysterious expanses of outer space smell a lot worse than I thought they would," she complained, her muddy dress billowing around her in the brackish water, while she kept her spellbook and Light-spell charmed hand high and dry. "The Milky Way is also a lot damper than I was counting on. And possibly full of leeches and snakes and who knows what else. --oh, and mosquitoes! How could I forget those? No doubt deadly *Martian* mosquitoes, patrolling the canals--"

"Are you out of material yet?" Scout asked, his infinite monastic patience actually starting to wear thin.

"Oh, heck no! I've got plenty more where that came from! Have I brought out the Deliverance jokes yet?"

Una, who was almost fortunate to be wearing a short-cut tunic, remained puzzled. "I am not understanding how this location we have been brought to resolves the debt-condition that Archmagus Lilith owed you. There is no safe passage to my home Arcology that I know of here..."

"Yes, well, I suspect we're actually two or three miles outside of the House of the Rising Sun, dumped here on some legal technicality I haven't detangled yet," Emily explained. "So, to recap: We're starving after a full day without any food, we're wearing very fancy clothing, and we're in the middle of nowhere surrounded by hostile wildlife in both floral and faunal form. Did I miss anyth--"

"Emily, please. It's not helping," Scout said.

"Well, EXCUSE me for--"

"Not helping me keep my senses sharp. We're not alone here. Shhh."

The group froze in its swampy tracks. Nel instinctively vanished, along with Una; she hadn't quite gotten used to the idea of hiding anybody else yet beyond her current "Lady". Scout was actually thankful for that; a few less sounds, a few less heartbeats. There was Emily's. There wasn't his own, of course. And--

His hands reached out to intercept, as the alligator's jaws sprang from the depths just in front of him. He levered his arms firmly, snapping the jaws shut without getting his hands trapped in there; the animal had less jaw-opening power than jaw-closing power. It thrashed about in a panic, until--

The stereo roar of a metal monster sang high over the canopy of leaves. The alligator wrenched itself free from Scout's grasp, and quickly swam away, to escape the sound...

A figure wearing a fishing hat, overalls, and waders emerged from the trees. In its hands was a still-smoking double barreled shotgun.

Shocked, Nel's inverted glamour dropped, turning the party of two back into a visible party of four. And before Scout could size up the man to see if he was going to be a threat, the fellow slung his shotgun into a holster on his back and snatched off his wide-brimmed hat, to get a better look...

Without the hat, two pointed ears were visible.

"Emily?" the elf asked. "Emily Moonthistle...? Holy crap! What're you doing in this neck of the woods?"

For her part, Emily was equally shocked. "You're kidding me. Yavain? Weren't you hanging around Atlanta...? --oh, uh. This is Scout, Una, and that's--"

"Cousin Nelliwyn!"

"Cousin Yavain!"

"...wha? Wait, what? Cousins? You two...?"

"Excuse me, what's going on, thank you?" Una asked, quite bewildered.

Emily groaned. "Okay. Long story short. Friends? This is Yavain Minturn, my webmaster for the Witchipedia project, also known in online circles as SexyElf86."

"That's me, one damn sexy elf," the one who called himself SexyElf86 said, with a traditional double-finger-pointy gesture of dude awesomeness. "So! Who's up for some fried alligator burgers and brewskis?"

a07 challengers

There was actually someone picking at a banjo.

The music was nicely accompanied by the noise of the occasional mosquito meeting a horrible and tragic end within the bug zapper. Of course, with electricity at a premium this deep into the Florida Everglades, they couldn't spend it on an electrical coil -- instead, specially trained Pixies armed with lightning spells hovered in formation, drawing insects in with the pretty lights, so they could pounce en masse and annihilate the offending bug. In return, when the day was done, they'd be treated to a saucer of the finest microbrew the elves could make.

The last piece of the audio puzzle was the crackling fire, where Yavain was cooking up some alligator meat taken from traps earlier in the day. It was not exactly the tastiest thing Emily had ever eaten, but when you go a full day with nothing to nosh on other than a piece of bread, a gator grill was damned appealing.

The five of them gathered at fireside, while other elves sat around their trailers, working on various handcrafts, or playing cards. Each trailer was unique; some had heavy magical modification, being lashed to multiple broomsticks to make it a hovering home, while others were cobbled together from all manners of rusty industrial bits.

Yavain's home-sweet-home was in the form of a "Winnebago," whatever that was. It was certainly the most impressive mobile camper in the group. He'd promised them an extensive tour of his place, including his waterbed and disco ball, which he claimed was "chick catnip" -- and more importantly, promised them a ride the hell out of this swampy campsite at dawn.

"I'm only passing through, myself," he explained, taking a pull now and then on a sweet-smelling elvish beer from a recycled glass soda bottle. "Lake Okeechobee's okay, but I'm way too urban to hang in the sticks for very long. I'm on my way out to Palm Beach, maybe then down to Orlando. The recovery project on the Temples of the Mouse is going pretty well. I traded up north in Baltimore at a MediaCon for vacation videos of the various rides, which came in handy when the decorations were restored..."

"How fascinating! Clearly we should have paid more attention to this part of the country in our surveys. And does that mean all of Florida is elf territory?" Una asked, all questions and curiosity, to the point of neglecting her food. Some hungers took priority over others, it seemed.

"Well... the panhandle's more tightly aligned with the Summer Court. The east side and the Everglades, they're more modernist elves," Yavain explained. "Young folks like me who obsess over human artifacts, who try to dig into ancient culture to find a way forward, we're all over the place in this part of Florida, yeah. Eastusa maintains a heavy border patrol to the north, keeping us contained, but there are ways through if you know who to bribe and what to offer 'em. All you need then is a good glamour and you're free to go trading or salvaging for gear."

Emily managed to swallow the last of her food, actually thankful there was no more to eat. "Hrgh. That.. was nasty, Yavain. But you've got my thanks. ...oh, dammit, I forgot to ask what favor you wanted in exchange. Got anything that needs Mending? Or I could do breakfast, although all I know how to make is hotcakes and the like..."

"Nah, don't worry about it, my witchy hottie," Yavain said, with a playful leer. (Scout sat a bit more upright on seeing it, playful or not.) "All of you guys are in my cool book. Mi casa su casa, no favor implied, you dig? Yeah. That includes the road trip, and any clothes I can scrounge up to replace your slimed stuff."

"I have some clothes in my jetpack's storage compartment," Una said. "And Nel's about my size, she can borrow anything she needs."

"I like my uniform," Scout noted. "I don't want anything else. I'll just wash it."

"Weeelll... I've got a Laundry Basket you could use," the elf said, emphasizing each word, as if that explained enough. "But the fancy duds, those just are NOT road gear, you know? Sooo, that leaves just you, Emily. Don't worry, I can find you something."

"Uh-huh. Any chance you can find us a spaceship?" Emily said, dryly. "We were supposedly sent here to find one, but obviously--"

"Spaceship? Sure, if you want. I know a guy."

Bumping into a shotgun-toting elf driving a Winnebago in the middle of nowhere had already raised the weird-o-meter several notches. Being told casually that they also could have a spaceship pushed things over the top and down the other side.

"...I'm sorry, maybe I had swamp muck in my ears, but did you just say you 'know a guy' with a *spaceship*?" Emily asked, to make sure she hadn't suffered a stroke or something. "Spaceship. Space. Ship. As in, a ship that sails through space, by which I mean the airless void that comprises 99.9% of the universe. You know a guy with a spaceship."

"Yeah, he's pretty cool, I think he'd let you borrow it if you had good reason," Yavain said, using a pointed stick to stoke the campfire coals, before rising and dusting off his overalls. "...oh, hey, I get it. That's a surprise, right? It's only been flying for the last few years. We're actually keeping it a bit on the hush. I don't think Eastusa would like us having it."

"Ahh! I see, this must be another wayward Orbital!" Una recognized. "Tell me, sir, does your friend have white hair, as I do, and wear various devices comprised of a silver metal...?"

"Uh... no, he's got dark brown hair, glasses, and pointy ears," Yavain said, not getting it. "Y'know, an elf, like me?"

"An elf. With a spaceship," Emily repeated, still unsure of her sanity. "So. Lilith actually DID send us somewhere we could get safe passage into space... albeit very, very indirectly..."

"We can hook up with him out at Palm Beach," their host suggested. "Make your case, then we'll head north to the launch site. Everybody get some rest; the road outta the 'glades is a little rough. You don't want to tackle it without some shuteye, you dig? Humm... I can shack up someone on the couch in my camper, and hey, Emily, you know my bed's always--"

Emily got to her feet. "Just point the way to a tool shed or an empty camper or something, and we'll FaePlace up our own beds, thank you, 'SexyElf86'. I definitely want to crash for many, many hours..."

A polite little sound halfway between a cough and a clearing of the throat sounded from the easily overlooked elf girl, successfully hiding behind a small tin mug of beer.

"Ah, cousin..." she asked. "I wanted to ask..."

Yavain's expression swerved into seriousness, as he sat back down. "Your folks, huh."

"If you know where they are, yes," Nelliwyn asked. "I haven't seen them since I was traded to Lady Morgana... now that I'm finally free from that place and with the kind Lady Una, I'd very much like to see my family again. "

The elf boy leaned back in his ratty old lawn chair, unsure of how best to phrase it. "Nel and I go way back," he explained, first, for the benefit of his old friend and her new friends. "Her dad and my dad were bros, of course. Back when the family was a bit more together-like, out in the panhandle, and the Mississippi delta. But her uncle was a bit TOO into human flavors of booze... stopped being a connoisseur and started being a drunk, eventually... no offense, Nelliwyn. You know how I feel about the guy."

"...I take no offense, cousin. I suppose they need to know... continue."

"Right. Well, he also had a thing for gambling. I think you can guess how the rest of it went," he said, bitter at the memory. "We were just kids when he decided the best way to pay off his debts was to sell his own daughter to the House of the Rising Sun--"

"He had no choice, cousin! Lady Morgana--"

"Would have taken any variety of cleverly turned debt. Sure, she asked for you, but Morgana's not choosy. As long as she's amused with the offering, she'll take just about anything. Hell, he could have worked there himself, the selfish bastard! No, the old man didn't hesitate to cough you up, and for that I'm never gonna forgive him. Fortunately that won't be a problem, what with him drinking his ass to death a few years back, and good riddance!"

A tin mug clattered to the ground, spilled beer pooling near the fire.

Too late, Yavain realized his mistake. "Oh... oh, dammit. Nelly, Nelly, I'm sorry, look... your mother, she's fine, okay? I mean, she left after that, I don't know where she is now, but... it's not all bad! ...right? Right?"

Emily tried to find some sympathetic words... and found herself about to address empty air. Nel had vanished.

At first Emily assumed she'd run off... until she realized Una, who had put her arms in some odd position around thin air, was cradling her. Whispering far more sympathetic words than Emily could've managed.

"...y'know, here's you, and here's tact," Emily whispered to her elven friend, holding her hands very far apart. "Even if I'm with you on this one. ...point the way to somewhere I can FaePlace up, I'll go prep for bedding down while they talk."

It had only been... wait. How long *had* it been since Emily last stepped into her FaePlace?

They'd used it the night before leaving the Twin Cities. The following evening was spent in Esrever's place. The next day, Canada, working on the airlock door. Scout cooking dinner, then sleep under the stars. Finally, today... morning in the wreckage of #BE12, evening in New Orleans, and late night in Florida...

Two days. It felt like weeks, but it had only been two days since Emily was last totally at ease in her magical little home away from home. Amazing. Amazingly horrifying to think of how eventful and dangerous and VERY dangerous the last two days had been.

Just this afternoon, she'd told Una that if there was a just and righteous God out there, they'd be able to retire somewhere sunny and pleasant to rest for awhile after this mess. One sleep from now they'd be on the road to a place called "Palm Beach" which seemed to fit the bill. Maybe someone up there (not an Orbital) indeed liked her...

Or maybe not.

Despite all four of them being present during the casting, the FaePlace had changed. Change was expected, since the place had to accommodate Nelliwyn now -- but the three bedrooms, which should have now been four, were only two. One, a wooden door leading off to her favored rustic old bedroom. Two, a shiny metal door leading off to Una's high-tech rest chamber.

It was worth noting that the beds in both rooms appeared to have grown from twin size to queen size.

"Dammit. And now the spell's tied to this doorframe for at least a day! Maybe I should recast the spell somewhere else," Emily suggested. "It's late. I'm dead tired. My Will might not have been strong enough to get the thing working properly... although... it's never misfired like this before, even once months ago when I was near collapsing after a long day of witching. I don't get it..."

Una peered through her door. "What's wrong?" she asked. "Everything seems in order -- oh, you mean Scout's room being missing? Hmm. That is odd, indeed--"

"We're in the heavens?!"

Oh, right. Nel hadn't been here before, Emily thought, as she rushed past, to enter Una's room and stare at the wall-sized window. It was an illusion, of course, presenting Una with a view that would comfort her the most... no more than a glamour within the pocket space...

What would comfort them most. That's how FaePlace worked; it sensed what would help you rest, what would put you at ease. Scout had no room anymore. And Emily's bed was... wider.

"Um," Emily spoke.

"I think we should bed down for the night, rather than drain your energy further, Emily," Una suggested. "Nel and I will be fine as-is, and Scout can use Yavain's couch, yes? Maybe you can figure out what's wrong with the spell tomorrow night. Ah, Nel, that's not really a view from space... see, what happens is--"

The door closed behind her, one of those wacky science doors that slide shut with a hissy noise.

"Um," Emily repeated.

"Don't mind using your friend's couch," Scout said, with a shrug. "It's fine. I understand."

"Um."

"Don't want to make you uncomfortable. Goodnight, Emily. Sleep well."

"Um."

And Scout left.

Exhaustion tapped Emily on the shoulder, reminding her with some irritation that it really, really wanted to go to sleep now. Wordlessly (since there was no one to talk to anymore) Emily entered her room, closing the door behind her. She removed her muddy dress, put on some sensible FaePlace pajamas, and climbed into the oversized bed.

The bed felt very empty, now.

He's changed over the last two days, she thought, because even if she desperately wanted to stop pondering and fall asleep, Insight was having none of that. *Enough that he didn't want to be alone in the dark anymore, enough to subconsciously change the FaePlace to become what he needed now. Either that, or I didn't want to be alone anymore, or I didn't want to abandoned him to the darkness. Or both. All three.*

And now he's on Yavain's crappy old Winnebago couch with a loose spring digging into his lower back, because it's hardly proper and witchy to let a boy into your room, even if you wouldn't really have done anything improper. Even if all you wanted was to be held so you could sleep easier after being put through the wringer over and over again.

Wow. You suck, Emily.

Not a fun thought to have as you drift off, but that's how it was.

The young witch awoke with a sore neck and cranky disposition. This was a proper state of being for a witch, putting you right in the mood for a little turning of princes into frogs and luring of children into gingerbread houses, but all Emily wanted was some breakfast.

Yavain had woken up earlier and left a bundle of clothes outside her door, apparently -- he was always an early riser, a common trait in elves, as they're creatures of the dawn. Unfortunately, the clothes in question consisted of a pair of denim overalls, some sandals, men's boxer shorts, and a delicately spider-woven silken t-shirt reading "I'm With Stupid". Another fine product misfire from elves with a fetish for human culture.

At least she still had her hat. No self-respecting witch would be caught dead in that outfit without at least some token nod to her magical heritage.

Emily turned out to be the last one to join the impromptu going-away brunch. The other elves in the trailer park had pitched in, resulting in a buffet ranging from some nasty looking hamburgers and hot dogs up to intricately decorated elvish pastries, crafted from fine bread that could crumble away at anything but the most delicate of touches.

Scout was already up, and wearing a black t-shirt and jeans combo. He'd opted to skip the Laundry Basket, instead tearing the Frontliners patch off his muddy-yet-fancy dress military uniform, getting a weaver spider to secure it in place on the shoulder of his new clothes. Una was wearing one of her spare Orbital minidresses -- Nel, always at her side, was wearing a simple tank top and skirt also of Orbital fabric, judging from the way it shimmered as the cloth moved.

As for Yavain... he'd gotten dressed up for whatever was to come down the road. He was wearing baggy cargo pants with a wallet on a chain (not that he carried any money or credit cards of any sort), a shirt with what looked like a disembodied pair of red lips with a tongue rolling out and a caption of STEEL WHEELS '89, and a black leather jacket. It had to be a horrible combination for the heat and humidity of the swamp, but true to his elven nature, he looked impeccably sweat-free and well groomed all the same.

"Emily! Hey witchy woman, hey!" the elf greeted, waving her over. "C'mon, sit, eat up. We got grease, we got sugar, we got whatever you want. We've also got long hours on the road ahead, so also make sure you go take a crap after, you dig?"

With that appealing image assaulting her, Emily took her place at the end of the hastily assembled picnic table, next to Scout. "...hey," she greeted, taking a plate, loading it with some fried eggs. "You sleep alright...? I've crashed on that couch before, I know it's kinda lousy..."

"I've slept on floor mats in a high school gymnasium. An old couch is no challenge," Scout replied. "How about you...? Sleep alright?"

"Oh, yeah, totally okay," Emily lied. She glanced around, uncomfortable. More smalltalk, more would be good. "Una, how'd you two do in your... er, bed?"

Nel spoke up first. "I've never slept on a metal bed before, but it was the best night's sleep I've ever had!" she said, still with stars in her eyes from the amazing experience. "It was actually quite soft and malleable! I hope to one day visit one of Una's sky-cities. If they're anything like that small sampling of her people's works, they must truly be places of wonder and majesty...!"

"Honestly, I fell asleep straight away after getting undressed," Una said. "I was considerably lacking in stamina reserves and the rest did me well. And Nel, really, it's not all that amazing! I mean... it seems quite ordinary to me, at least..."

Something tickled at the back of Emily's mind. "Uh. Una...? So you two did share the bed, then? Don't you normally sleep... y'know... undressed?"

"Hm? Well, of course," Una said, reaching over to have another helping of bacon. "Orbital resting surfaces don't work very well without bioelectric feedback from skin contact, as I explained to Nel last night. Otherwise, your recuperation would be suboptimal! That'd just be silly!"

The FaePlace modifies itself to whatever the occupants would be at ease with, Emily thought. *Una had one big bed, too. Which means...*

There may have been more to tiny red tint on Nel's cheeks as she politely excused herself than just the spicy elvish pastry she was eating. Una remained oblivious, of course, too busy enjoying the various fried pig parts.

For her part, Emily immediately busied herself with her fried eggs. She had enough on her mind lately without taking Una's slightly screwy spacegirl social standards into consideration.

The last Winnebago plant had shut down in 2008, over two hundred years prior to their road trip. Not that Yavain cared; any parts that broke down or wore out simply got replaced with the nearest magical equivalent. For instance, before they left, he had to pop the hood and replace the glowing radish that was operating as his carburetor with a fresh one, from a UV lit grow-tank in the back that also housed some questionable green leafy plants.

The back roads of the Everglades also were barely roads anymore, after long term neglect; they were only rough corridors through the overgrowth of nature, where asphalt once might have held things at bay. Fortunately, his wheels were enchanted to cause plants to move out of the way, with a series of glowing runes instead of whitewalls doing their business with every turn of the axles. Still, even if they had a clear path, it was hardly smooth sailing -- the motor home bumped and lumped its way along, over rocks and deadwood and uneven terrain.

"I've got a guy who knows a guy who's working on a better kind of shock absorber!" he called back to the living area, where the girls were trying to learn how to play gin rummy to pass the time (and constantly dropping their cards when the Winnebago smashed over a dead log or fallen tree). "Sorry 'bout this! It'll smooth out once we high the highway. ETA at Palm Beach, two hours!"

The only one unaffected by the rough ride was Scout, perched in the navigator's seat next to Yavain. He instinctively leaned and moved with each lump the vehicle drove over, remaining upright and stable despite the unstable transport. He was half reading a cheap paperback copy of Lord of the Rings ("That Tolkein guy, he GOT us, you dig? We are *totally* sexy superhuman ninjas, all the way!"), half keeping an eye on the treelines left and right for any enemy ambushes. Not that he was expecting one, but if you were expecting an ambush, it wasn't much of an ambush.

"Dude, will you chill?" Yavain asked. "You've got that creepy Winterhound stalking thing going on. It's freaking me out. We are not gonna get jumped by some big evil woogums, okay? I mean, a big evil woogums other than you. This is elf turf."

All in all, Yavain took it well when Emily (in the interests of full disclosure) pointed out Scout's true nature. Instead of running in terror or attacking, he took it in stride. Even if he was keeping an eye on the boy as much as the boy was keeping an eye on everything else.

"You said not all of Florida believed as you did," Scout reminded him.

"What, the Braid of Dawn? They're harmless. I mean, almost always," Yavain said, veering left to avoid a turtle crossing the road. "They complain, they try to tell us off about how we're shirking years of tradition, blah blah blah. But they don't do much else. Be cool, alright? This isn't an APC and we aren't storming LV-426."

"What?"

"I'm just saying you're too uptight. I mean, you were all uptight last night, too! Barely got any sleep."

"Don't sleep much, anyway."

"Why ARE you hanging with Emily, anyway?" Yavain asked. "You're not her type."

"Her type...?"

"Frankly, I don't think Emily HAS a type," the elf said, watching the road. "I mean, I've known her for years and she's a total hottie, and there was that night we got piss-drunk in Baltimore and she kissed me, but I know better now. She's all business, all witchy business. No time for hip and happening dudes like you and me! Shame, really. I mean, I'm cool with the whole let's-be-friends thing, we talked it over a bunch, but... honestly, I think maybe she's content to just ride her broomstick, y'know what I--"

"I love her."

The RV nearly swerved directly into the trees. Yavain swore in elvish, swinging the wheel around right, then left, straightening out. Playing cards went flying in the background, as he called back apologies to the girls... and then settled in, ten-and-two on the steering wheel... even as he cast side glances to Scout.

After three minutes of silence, he said, "Seriously, dude?"

"Seriously," Scout responded.

"Holy crap, man. That's... wow. Uh. You told her that, right? And she didn't, I dunno, kick you in the junk? --Winterhounds HAVE junk, right? No, that's stupid, of course they do. They're well known for..."

The next pause was a dangerous one.

"Dude, tell me right now you're not just adding her to your harem," Yavain warned, playfulness gone. "I know what Winterhounds are like. How they feed on the pretty little flies they catch. You be straight with me or I swear I'll use my sexy elf ninja powers to boot your ass out of my car right now--"

"It's not like that. I swear it on my life."

"You're dead, though."

"I don't care. I still swear it. ...I haven't done anything with her like that. I don't want to risk it, even accidentally. One of the reasons I was on your couch last night. I'll never hurt her. I fought Archmagus Lilith at her side to keep her from harm, and if need be, I'd fight Lady Summer herself or Lady Winter. You have my word, Yavain."

"...you two fought Lilith? Like, the Lilith who killed her--"

"The same."

Yavain leaned back in his seat, digesting that. He let out a whistle, impressed. "Freeeow. What the hell has my little witchy woman been up to in the years since we last talked...? Man. This is just... *man*. ...alright. I'm cool, I'm cool. ...look, for the record, even if I still flirt, I know she's not mine and never will be. I won't cock block you, man, bros before h-- err. Y'know. ...I am glad to hear she's got someone. So. How long you two been at it?"

And now, Scout was the one to be taken aback. "...um," he said, trying to figure out a number. "Two days...? Been together longer, but not... been together. ...still not together, really. She kissed me, once. But... we've been busy. Fighting things. And stuff. ...there was a dinosaur."

"She kissed you once? And that's it? Seriously?"

"There was fighting. And stuff. ...we're on an assignment. The mission takes priority."

"Oh, bullcrap," Yavain said, shaking his head. "Alright, fine, you're busy beavers, but you gotta take some time to *woo your witch*, man! C'mon! --look, the concert we're going to tonight, you stick by her and show her a good time, dig? Let me do the heavy lifting on your quest, while you just roll with it. I'm holdin' you down, man, you go do your thang."

"...I don't know how to show her a good time," Scout admitted. "I don't really have fun. Although I'm trying to figure out how."

"You ARE hopeless, aren't you? Okay. I'm officially your new wingman, Scout," Yavain pledged. "I swear I will get you some of that witchy booty or my name isn't SexyElf86! We've got time to kill before we get there, and there's nobody better at romance than an elf. All the human chicks say so, after all. Let the education begin!"

They hadn't planned on stopping at a rest station.

"Does this thing have a privy?" Emily had asked.

"Well... yes and no," Yavain had explained. "The plumbing broke down a few months back, so I had a replacement unit installed. It's a little weird, but honestly, it works great! But I was figuring you wouldn't want to use it, 'cause, uh..."

"I think I can cope with some wacky magic toilet," Emily had assumed.

When she raised the lid, a long purple tongue slathered over the porcelain rim, and it emitted a deep and rolling guttural belch that smelled faintly of lilac.

So, they stopped at a rest station. The girls moved en masse for the restrooms, which fortunately were more mechanical and less monstrous. This left the boys behind, to munch on little gas station baggies of Cool Ranch Extreme Enchanted

Sunlight Crunchies (one of the first mass-produced elven snackfoods) and to continue the Education.

"And that's when I put my arm around her?" Scout asked.

"Yeah, but you gotta do it real casual-like," Yavain continued. "Y'know, like your arm wasn't really going there originally, it just sort of settled there. It helps if you yawn and stretch, then just HAPPEN to drape your arm around her shoulders. It's like you're saying you're too cool for intimacy but hey, here's some intimacy all up in your grill, girl. 'cause you deserve it for being so hot. Then, when the time is right, you cop a feel."

"Shouldn't I ask her permission first?"

"What? Gods, no. No, man. C'mon! You're the man here. You're taking valuable time out of your long hard work doing manly things like hunting wild animals and contributing to the gross national product in order to show your woman a good time, so hey, you just GO for it. I mean, like, obviously you don't wanna be a prick about it, but you don't have to beg for every little thing... besides, once you butter her up with the phrases I taught you, she'll be all for it."

"I'm suspecting Emily may not react well if I praise her 'bountiful, bodacious booty' or her 'awesome rack', Yavain."

"And THAT is what the beer is for. Look, we discussed this -- you go in the order of booze, schmooze, then cooze. You get that out of order and we've got a tragedy. You do it the way we say, and you'll be all up in them witchy drawers and you'll be her Prince Charming, verily."

Scout chewed thoughtfully on a Cool Ranch Extreme Enchanted Sunlight Crunchie.

"Where'd you learn how humans relate to each other, exactly...?" he asked.

"From the Internet," Yavain explained, tossing his now empty paper bag behind the driver's seat, onto an increasingly large pile of empty cans and bottles and wrappers. "It's the human methodology of courtship. I love courtship! I mean, Fae are also really into the whole casual sex thing, moreso than humans -- like, wink wink, you're cute, off we go. But when you wrap that up in a dance, a ritual, that's a lot more intense... it gives it some structure. Elves dig games. Now, the nobles, their courtship is kinda stiff and plodding and polite and slightly dangerous if you screw up and start owing favors... that's not our scene. All the happening elvish girls and boys learn how the humans get their freak on, and now that is how we roll, dawg!"

"I see," Scout said, processing that. "Your education will be... useful. Thank you."

Specifically, useful in doing the exact opposite of what you're saying, Scout didn't add.

Yavain snapped his fingers. "Damn! I almost forgot-- wait here. Hope they have some in stock... wait here!" And the elf was out the door of the RV in a flash.

When he returned, he pressed a small wax paper packet into Scout's hands.

"You're gonna need these," Yavain said, in seriousness. "Pack one into your wallet, keep the rest handy. Elves don't actually NEED them, they're just a prop in the human-style courtship game we play. Our women can control their conception... but from what I've learned, little humans spring up like weeds if you aren't packing protection. I had to guess at your size, but I'm guessing you're hung like--"

"Yes, thank you, I appreciate it," Scout said, jamming the small packet into a jeans pocket quickly.

Hm. Maybe not the opposite of EVERYTHING he's saying, he decided.

It's an axiom of the universe that rest area bathrooms will be horrible. It doesn't matter if they're a waystation between major Eastusa cities, or some backroad truck stop, or some sort of high science Orbital waste control chamber, or a restored gas station run by innately well groomed and stylish elves. It will always be horrible.

If anything, a bathroom originally constructed by men and then augmented by elves will be twice as horrible. Fortunately the toilets were purely mechanical rather than grotesque abominations, but the graffiti consisted largely of scrawled elvish runes about the easy nature of various elf girls, the mold growing in the corner had already sprouted smelly mushrooms that were currently occupied by a small colony of very rude pixies, and Emily's stall was out of toilet paper. Una had to pass her some underneath the wall.

The less time spent in here, the better -- but unfortunately, while Emily loitered around in her backwoods overalls looking cross, Una and Nel were busy trying to look pretty. Una was touching up her makeup a bit, using a strange chromed lipstick-like tool which adjusted the hue and shade of her various subtle cosmetic touches; Nel was working a glamour, trying to adjust her hair color a bit to be lighter toned and straighter, to better match Una's.

"What's the point?" Emily asked. "It's not like you two are going out clubbing tonight cruising for guys."

"I like looking my best, is all," Una said, capping her 'lipstick' and tucking it back in her jetpack's storage compartment. "The humidity down here alters the biochemical gels, makes them lose color..."

"And I'm just glad I'm allowed to be noticeable, for a change!" Nel said, with a bright smile. "I've never tried using my magic on myself before. I mean, except to tone down myself and look plainer and less important. This is really fun! Ah, Una, do you like my hair...? I can't seem to get it quite as white as yours..."

"Oh, it's so cute!" Una said, clasping her hands in front of her chest. "You know, you should consider pulling it back in a ponytail, maybe. It's nice and long, it could work that way, really highlight your cheekbones. Mine's too short to do much with, not as pretty as yours...! ...ah, Emily, if you want to borrow my Cosmetic Alterator or ask Nel to work some magic, you can. We're not trying to leave you out of the fun, honest!"

"Fun? This is fun?"

"Well, of course! I mean, it'd be moreso for you, since you actually have a boy you're trying to romance," Una said, with a knowing little grin.

Emily palmed her face and faced her palm. "I should never have told you two about that kiss..." she grumbled.

"I think it's sweet, Miss Emily," Nel assured her. "A Summerling witch and a tall, dark, handsome Winterling rogue, finding each other through struggle and strife, yearning for each other during a long and dangerous quest...! Oh, it's so romantic!"

"Oh yes, right up until the point where we all die horribly. Very romantic."

"I still say we should be calling for reinforcements," Una said, folding her arms, as she leaned against the counter lined with sinks. "I haven't contacted my father since we visited Edmonton. He should be told of our findings! An entire city, doomed through Faerie magic, with the Summer Queen likely having her eye on another city... we should be warning him, perhaps getting a team of specialists here. We've done well in our investigation by ourselves, I'm proud of our successes, but there's no shame in asking for help... and why GO up into space, for that matter? What purpose would it serve?"

Emily paused a moment, trying to gather her thoughts. It wasn't easy; there were a dozen workable theories that'd fit the sketchy evidence to date, none of them very convincing... so, she went with that.

"We have no idea what's really going on," she said. "I can't say 'all signs point to' this or that. All signs point to some weird ball of craziness going on with the Faeries and maybe even the Orbitals. Fae spies in your Arcologies, scheming and causing these events? Faeries colluding with Orbital Councils? Or just a wild string of coincidences and accidents? Honestly, by this point, it doesn't matter who or why or how. All we know is that something very bad is probably going down on the solstice, and all fingers point towards the Orbitals."

"Emily, I don't believe for a minute my people are behind any of this madness!"

"And the Pandora Event...?"

"...it could have been accidental," Una said. "Some unforeseen side effect of the shift drives. I do not doubt that Orbitals are responsible for the troubles your world has been through, but as you said... we don't know who or why or precisely how. I can't imagine malice behind such actions, even if I can't explain what happened..."

"Exactly! We don't know. We *can't* know, not from here. And in that kind of fog of war, we can't trust that your father isn't compromised."

"Emily--!"

"Hear me out," Emily pleaded, raising her hands. "I'm not saying he's the enemy. You know him, hell, I know him from those mirror memories of yours. I'm saying that he could act against us without realizing it. He could be under an enchantment, or simply lied to and tricked into doing things that the Faerie Court desires... and we've already seen examples of Faerie mind control using Orbital technology. If you call upstairs and he finds out what we know... then the enemy could find out through him, one way or another."

"So... you want to go into space... so you can find out what's going on firsthand?"

"Yep. We go up there and confront this head on, whatever it is. I know it's crazy, but it's the only thing we can do; there's no more we can do down here without getting dangerously involved with the Queens of Faerie. It's bad enough that Lady Summer now knows we know that she knows. You know? ...anyway, I'd rather take my chances with a bunch of scrawny juxtaterrestrial intellectuals. At least those guys I think I could take down with a well placed kick in the nuts. ...Orbitals have testicles, right?"

"Errr... yes. At last check. Not that I have checked. Or would have had any opportunity to check. ...erm."

"I don't care how fancy and shiny their energy guns are, a kick in the junk is a kick in the junk. And Scout's good at kicking, and I can Animate a boot, and so on. So, we go upstairs, and we figure out once and for all what's going on. Assuming we ever get out of this bathroom. The boys probably think we fell in by now. C'mon. We've got an RV to ride, before we start thinking about rocket ships."

Most of Palm Beach was in ruins. Over a hundred years of abandonment will do that to any urban metropolis; throw in the occasional Floridian hurricane and the sweltering heat and humidity, and things accelerate.

However, as the RV rolled through the empty streets, signs of repair started to show. Buildings gradually went from shaky looking skeletons and crumbling facades to restored shopfronts and homesteads. More cars were on the streets, including classic Detroit iron, and magically crafted replicas of classic Detroit iron done with such style and flair that it'd have made the original manufacturers break down weeping to gaze upon them.

In fact, that was one of the earmarks of elvish restoration: elegance and beauty in things that had no business being elegant or beautiful. Rough road hawg motorcycles with exhaust pipes that glittered like moonlight across a still pond. T-shirts being sold at roadside vendors with obscene slogans and flawless spider-silk weaves, the kind of garments which would be suitable for nobility. Street toughs with pointy ears and leather jackets that were so flawlessly crafted it wouldn't be surprising if they started mooing.

"Posers," Yavain complained. "You gotta rough your gear up some, make it look more authentic. Don't use so many magical band-aids, either, unless you can't avoid it. The newbies just don't understand how to grasp the essence of human urban living."

"Which is...?" Scout had asked.

"Everything is a pile of crap -- but it's loved all the same, because it's YOUR crap. Like the Rock Show."

The Rock Show was going to be their destination that evening, as dusk started to fall across the half-restored city. (The trip had taken longer than planned, thanks to several road blockages, the rest area, and traffic delays due to a rampaging swamp dragon.) As Yavain had explained it, the Rock Show was a yearly event, a gathering of Faerie musicians from all over the lands of the Faerie Court... but all under the universal banner of rock music, the human style of backbeat and rough and ready beautiful noise.

He was re-explaining the concept to the girls, as the group piled out of the RV, joining other elves gathered in the parking lot outside the stadium. Some were having impromptu tailgate parties, with grilled meats and spectacular demonstrations of expressive glamours. All of them were wearing human fashion styles, and usually with more rips and inconsistencies than the smoother looks of the elves they'd passed on the way here.

"You remember me complaining about how I couldn't figure the connection needed to link an electric guitar to a sound-carry gourd, right?" Yavain asked.

"I remember you dragging me to every music shop we could find in Baltimore," Emily recalled, as the group started to move through the crowd, towards the entrance. "But I was more worried the glamour you had cast before we breached the Freedom Wall was going to drop at any time than about why you were on a shopping spree..."

"Right. Well, eventually we cracked the problem -- use the real gear. Real human amps, real human instruments. Once you start tossing magic stop-gaps into the mix, you just lose the whole thing. It could work, but it'd *feel* wrong," Yavain continued. "Rock music, the sound we'd heard from the media we'd scrounged up, that's what we wanted. Faerie music is too ethereal, too delicate and beautiful. We wanted it to sound like the kind of wildfire we heard in human music, so, we had to go with totally human instruments. And we had to un-train all our musical skills."

"Faerie methods didn't work with human instruments? Strings were all wrong?"

"Oh, it worked. But it sounded too *good*. Like if you gave Mozart a modern guitar, he'd write something wonderful, but it wouldn't sound a thing like Joe Strummer, yeah? You'll get it once we're in there and experiencing the real thing; no posers to be found here, no ma'am! We--"

"Reject the ways of the outsiders! Embrace the ways of Faerie!"

Their progress was promptly blocked by a small group of elves, wearing robes of forest green and with long braids down their backs. Their expressions were stern; that alone would've set them apart from the freewheeling young elves, who were all smiles and laughter and chatter around them. The young ones seemingly paid no attention to the contingent in green, completely ignoring them in favor of their own social circles.

One pressed a pamphlet into Emily's hands. Too surprised to do anything else, she glanced at the rough woodcut printed paper; "The Braid of Dawn: A Return To Glorious World of Faerie," it proclaimed, with a watercolor illustration of a stereotypically beautiful and mystical Faerie woman casting spell-lights from her fingertips.

Before she could say anything in response, the group had already moved on, to assault other newcomers to the parking lot with colorful brochures. One cast a reproachful look back at her... specifically, at the non-pointiness of Emily's ears.

"Uh... who were they?" Emily asked, flipping the brochure over and over. It was printed in an ancient Elvish rune-language, something too complex for her limited understanding to broach. Probably too complex for many of the young elves to read, for that matter, having been raised on English and more modern forms of Faerie language.

"Panhandlers," Yavain grumbled. "Conservatives. Traditionalists. Just a bunch of self-important busybodies. Didn't think they were this far east, though..."

"If they're a threat to your ways, why do you allow them in here?" Scout asked.

Yavain shrugged -- but offered a smile, too.

"This is America, man," he said. "Everybody's got a right to free speech. So sayeth Kennedy."

"Who...?"

"You'll see."

The gathering made a cult movie night at the Mall of America look like a church tea social.

The arena was packed with music fans. Most of them were elves, but some human teenagers and twentysomethings had managed to slip away from their communities in the fringe to make the journey down south -- even a few from Eastusa, from the sounds of it. The only difference between them and the elves was in ear shape; everybody was dressed for the event, wearing shirts proclaiming blood allegiance to one band or another, with plenty of leather and denim and piercings to go around. Emily, in her elf-redneck overalls, felt terribly out of place.

They'd been abandoned by their Cultural Instructor for the day; Yavain said he had to go "make some arrangements" and set them up with some seats on the edge of the arena floor, as they waited for the concerts to begin.

Emily had no interest in mingling with the hundreds of folks in what was apparently being called the Mosh Pit, and Scout from his limited knowledge of concerts (mostly overheard in various high schools during his wild years) agreed it would be wise to stay out of there. For their part, Una and Nel didn't really care where they sat; they were busy being wide-eyed and curious about everything.

"I had no idea there was such a modern elvish enclave in eastern Florida!" Nel spoke. "Yavain and I grew up out west, where nothing like this was going on. Faeries in human garb...? It's positively scandalous! ...er, do we stand out? Should I try to glamour up a band logo onto our clothes, Lady Una?"

"Hmm? Oh, no need -- someone back there said we had 'sweet raver clothes,' which I take to be at least tangentially theme-appropriate," Una said. "I can't wait to hear this music! I only heard a few 'rocking roll' recordings in the anthropology database, but I predict they will hardly compare to a live performance! Orbital musical culture is so... restrained, so simple and graceful, in comparison. I once attended a recital of various sound-shapes, but honestly, I fell asleep halfway through. This outpouring of affection for acoustic creativity and fashionable style is delightfully energetic!"

"It's all just noise to me," Emily complained. "Aren't we here to get ourselves a ticket on a spaceship? We've only got a few days before Lady Summer makes her move, remember... it's the 17th, and everything goes down on the 21st. Four days. No time to futz around."

"I think we should try to enjoy this."

...Emily stared at Scout, looking for some sort of ironic smirk or outward sign of sarcasm. Instead, he was serious. As always.

"You're kidding me. I thought you said you didn't have fun," she reminded him.

"I didn't. Need to learn how, though," he said. "Lots I need to learn. This is human experience, so, I should experience it. Probably not dangerous. Maybe it'll give us a headache, at worst, so why not? There's no risk. We should try to enjoy it. Besides, if Yavain's space travel contact is here, odds are he or she will be busy enjoying it as well, and not ready to deal with our request yet. ...hmm. I appear to be fatigued."

Scout stretched out his arms, with a big, showy yawn. Emily ignored it, trying to scan the crowd idly for someone who might own a spaceship... and then noticed an arm had been draped around her shoulders. And now Scout was apparently closer to her than before. When did that happen...?

Despite having no heartbeat and being a creature of the Wild Hunt across the frozen planes of Lady Winter's deathscape, he was actually quite warm to lean against. Cozy, even.

Okay, obviously Yavain taught him that one, Emily thought. *It's one of his classics. I should call him to carpet on that, chide him for making such a blatant play. I should. I don't think I'm going to, though.*

The lights around the arena began to dim. Emily took this momentary respite in darkness to lean in against Scout, when nobody was looking -- they were all focused on the stage, now, a rising yell of anticipation coming from thousands of throats. Flashbulbs went off on pocket cameras, memory-fixing spells were spoken, everybody recorded the moment... when the first star of the evening took the stage.

Emily was assuming the first act would be dressed like Yavain, a 'band' that looked more like a street gang, all leather and chains and rock attitude. Instead, a solitary figure walked on stage, wearing a simple brown leather duster and elvish tunic, a young elf with human spectacles and a serious expression. Only a tie-dye bandanna around his forehead signified any allegiance to rock and roll... that, and a simple black and white electric guitar.

The few in the crowd who were still seated rose to their feet, when he took the stage... and en masse, the concert attendees placed their right hands over their hearts, the cheers going silent as the musician plugged into the amps, tuning up the guitar. Emily glanced around, surprised at the gesture... it didn't feel like the crazy crowd reaction a rock musician should get.

"What's going on?" she asked... before realizing Scout was doing the same gesture.

"National anthem," he replied, quietly.

"What? Eastusa's jingle? But... they're *elves*."

"They're American elves. Shh."

It was a song Emily had heard a few times before. Once, used as background music as a salesman claimed he had ordered too many cars from a Twin Cities manufacturing plant, and now Everything Must Go. She'd also heard it through a tinny speaker on television as a station signed off for the night. The third time, a wandering musician passing through her village had played it, albeit a bouncy, cheerful version on a flute.

This performance made the other three look like the sad little national embarrassments they were.

The elf on stage didn't perform beautifully, flawlessly, ethereally as elves often do. His instrument was coarse, his notes often skittering out of the way and back again across the melody. It wasn't a precision playback. It was instead a song directly from his heart... one which took the core of the Star Spangled Banner, the emotional punch it held for those who truly believed in the dream instead of giving it lip service, and pumped it out across dozens of amplified speakers for all in attendance to feel along with him.

All the while, his eyes remained closed... the musician was pouring himself down his fingers and into his strings, but it was a meditative act, an expression that would've remained just as powerful even if no ears were present to take it in. The old koan pondering if a tree falls in the forest makes a sound would've been annihilated in this case. His sound existed outside of the Rock Show, only touching down in this place by coincidence. It simply *was*, a statement of pure patriotism and faith...

His final notes, echoing the home of the brave, washed out over the crowd... which slowly burst into applause.

The performer finally opened his eyes, nodding once to the crowd, in thanks for listening. He reached over to a nearby mike stand, grasping it.

"Keep on rocking in the free world, Florida," he stated... before turning around, and walking away, as the thunder of an appreciative crowd pushed him along.

The next band started to set up their instruments, but waited until he'd left completely, out of respect. They were more of the leather and chains look Emily was expecting to see tonight.

Emily clapped along, even if her applause was a bit more unsure. She didn't want to say an ill word, not wanting to break the "spell" that the music had clearly cast over its listeners... so she kept her voice quiet, for Scout's ears only.

"I don't understand. I've never seen anybody in Eastusa play it like that, or even listen to it like that," she spoke. "Why here? Why with the elves?"

"It's the American dream," Scout explained, with no small amount of reverence. "Once this country was a gathering place for immigrants from a thousand nations, a place for those from other lands yearning to be free. Here, they could find a place where they'd belong. With the borders closed these days, many people living in Eastusa don't understand, so they won't hear the song the same way. They refuse to hear it as anything other than a war song or an empty comfort of tradition. The Faeries are outsiders, so it means something else to them. Odds are none of the elves here will ever live in America... but that doesn't mean they can't dream."

"...I didn't mark you for a patriot, Scout."

"Saul taught me," he said, with pride. "Before him, I didn't care where I was or why. But it's just a dream, Emily. 'Patriot' these days usually means mindless loyalty to Eastusa's government. Saul says you can take pride in the dream even if you have a hard time taking any pride in the place."

A squeal of feedback interrupted them, as the next act warmed up, ready to rock. The lead singer grasped the mike stand, pointing out into the crowd.

"Elves! Humans! Assorted Fae! We are The Ear Sharpeners, and we are here to rock your socks off!" he declared. "Our first number tonight is a dedication, going out to Emily, from Scout -- he loves ya, girl!"

Shock smacked Emily between the eyes, as the guitars started to warm up. Scout? Getting them to dedicate a song to her? SCOUT...? *'He loves ya, girl'?! Oh. Oh my...*

"...I.. ah... Scout...?" Emily spoke, trying to find the words. "Did you seriously ask that band to... I mean... really? ...heh. Actually, that's kind of swee--"

Then they started playing.

It was like someone smashed Emily's brains in with a baseball bat covered in porcupines. The elves, quite at home delicately picking at the strings on a golden enchanted lyre, were banging away on the electric guitars like they were trying to stab a man to death with a rusty hammer. The resulting noise would probably have been similar.

"What unusual lyrics!" Una spoke up, trying to be heard over the wave of acoustic assault and battery. "I'm not entirely certain the bodily insertion he's suggestion is physically possible, however..."

"ROCK ON, my friends, rock on!"

Yavain popped up behind Scout and Emily, the surprise of it causing Emily to pull away from him.

"Aren't these guys great? They've really nailed that human sound!" Yavain said, waving a handheld cigarette lighter in the air.

"Great?! It sounds like a dozen cats spot-welded to a kitchen stove rolling down a hill covered in broken glass!" she declared.

"I know! It's perfect! Oh, hey, I hate to interrupt your song dedication, but Kennedy wants to see you about that spaceship now," Yavain said. "I got you all backstage passes. C'mon."

He ushered them along towards the exits, distributing wooden charms on red lanyards as each passed by.

Scout went last, giving Yavain a questioning look...

"Did you tell that band to...?"

...which the elf returned with a wink, and a double thumbs up.

"We're bros, dude. Bros help bros out with their h-- with their girls," Yavain said, with a grin. "Did it work? Wasn't it totally awesome? Stick with me, bud, and you are TOTALLY gonna score yourself a witch!"

The sacred Backstage Pass is a thing of mystical power. It grants the bearer access to the hallowed service tunnels and back hallways of the arena, where the Lords of Rock prepare for their sermons to the people, usually delivered through amplifiers cranked to eleven.

(The elves were sure to modify all the speakers to go to eleven. It was said that this was the only true way to express oneself through human-style music, and that the legends of old frequently "went to eleven". They could have just made ten louder, but that may have been blasphemy against their ancestors of rock, and you don't mess around when you deal with ancestral spirits.)

Back here, the roadies ferried broken equipment around, casting Mending spells to get it back into the action. Burly looking elves wearing tunics reading SECURITY kept an eye on everything, ready to use various amulets and charms and bracelets to strike out against anyone who dared to disrupt the Rock Show. But the most noteworthy of the factions were the Groupies and the Bands, who were rarely seen apart.

Each band had their own set of groupies, usually dressed similarly to the band: the same colors, the same clothes. They were near universally divided across gender lines, with greasy looking male elves strumming away on non-amplified guitars in an effort to impress swooning elf girls. The whole scene of sexual pandering to someone just because they could bang away on an instrument left a sick taste in Emily's mouth... although she did note with some satisfaction a band of female punk elves who were teasing away at the male groupies that fawned all over them.

No group of groupies was larger, however, than the one they were approaching. It crowded around a dressing room door with a simple gold star on it, locked shut, flanked by the burliest and meanest looking security elves in the building. Nobody got in, nobody was going out... but when Yavain waved for attention, pointing to Emily's pointy hat (the only part of their group visible over the gathered girls), the guards moved to part the crowd. Apparently, Emily and company were going to be allowed in, much to the jealous glares of the gathered fans.

"You realize we're going to be lynched by this guy's fans once we leave the stadium, right?" Emily mumbled.

"Nah, it's cool, it's cool," Yavain insisted. "Look, I've got arrangements to make and people to see and autographs to snag, so I'm gonna take off now. The guards'll show you back to your seats when you're done, dig?"

"We don't even know this guy, though! You're our middleman."

"I explained your sitch to him. He gets the basics, just tell him what's up and it'll go okay, yeah? Yeah. Be cool and everything'll go fine. Later, witchy woman."

It was a bit like shoving a cork completely through the neck of a bottle, but somehow, the security elves managed to hustle their group of four through the door. It slammed shut behind them, latching and cutting off the plaintive whines of the fans, protesting their admittance to see the star...

...who was an unassuming looking fellow in a brown duster, reading from a book. He idly glanced up from his page, peering over the top of his spectacles.

"You're the one who played the national anthem," Emily realized.

"Kanthi F. Kennedy," the elf greeted, after closing his book and setting it aside. "I'm an Astromagus, and the organizer of this concert. And you're Emily Moonthistle, the Summerwitch in exile who defeated the Archmagus. Which makes you the rebel Winterhound known as Scout, and your companions would be Una the Orbital who gamed with Lady Morgana and won a house elf's debt... although her name, I'm afraid I don't know. The rumors didn't seem to care much about that."

"Ah... I'm Nelliwyn," Nel greeted, with a proper curtsey. "Yavain's cousin. I'm pleased to meet you. ...ah, your music tonight was very beautiful. Thank you for playing for us. It did seem quite... er, different, from the band that came on afterwards..."

To this, Kanthi F. Kennedy offered a wry grin. Emily got the feeling normally he was quite a serious-minded individual... except when it came to music.

"I play to express my feelings, miss -- not simply to try and recreate music from years gone by. My days are filled with mathematics and spellcraft, organizing and executing space missions. Music gives me an escape... and lets me show my feelings about the nation I admire so. I've taken on the name of my idol, the Martyr of Democracy, to further express my idealism. Speaking of which, thank you for telling me your name. That nicely completes the mental picture I've had of the events at the House of the Rising Sun... and it feels quite appropriate that a child of Florida has been rescued and returned, at last."

"Word moves fast, huh," Emily said, disheartened. If the rumor mill was spinning this fast, then they had no chance of outrunning it before the Solstice...

"We have the Internet, thanks to my work, Miss Emily. Your exploits were posted to various Fae-only social networking sites within minutes. Apparently some attendees of the Solstice Ball were from our camp. Now, then. Yavain tells me you need a ride into space, to visit an Orbital city?"

"Err... excuse me, but... how do you know about our cities?" Una asked, slowly raising her hand, as if meekly asking a question of the teacher. "For that matter, how do you know of the Orbitals...?"

"The official line is that you do not exist, of course," Kanthi said. "But it's been harder and harder to conceal the fact that the Summer Court and Winter Court have a bit of a spat going on over ownership of technology that fell from the skies. That, and I have some firsthand observational data... I saw one of your cities. It's in geosynchronous orbit over Miami. I believe the markings identified it as #A076, if that code means anything to you."

"My home? But... but that's impossible! Arcologies operate using cloaking technologies," Una protested. "Impossible to observe through a telescope, or even up close with the naked eye... impossible to detect using radar or any other scanning methodology--"

Kanthi mumbled a power word, gesturing with two fingers -- and in a flash, Nel's hair became more colorful, the glamour of paleness she had cast on herself wiped away as if a beam of light was aimed at a shadow. When he lowered his fingers, her spell reasserted itself.

"Orbital technology isn't very good at defending against magic," he explained. "I could spot the city through my enchanted glasses, even if my instruments hadn't detected it. I very nearly crashed into it, in fact... fortunately I realized they couldn't sense that I could sense them. I played it safe and carried out my mission to launch a comm satellite, pretending nothing was out of the ordinary, and they let me go about my business. I didn't want to stir up a hornet's nest... but I became curious about what I saw afterwards, and started checking the Faerie rumor mills about them. I've learned much since."

"Then you know Lady Summer wants more Orbital technology," Emily said. "We're hoping to prevent that. We need to get up there to learn more about what's going on, and put a stop to it. Can you give us a lift?"

Kanthi nudged his glasses up, sliding them along the bridge of his nose. "It's not a matter of 'giving you a lift.' Space travel is a complicated business, utilizing interlocked layers of science and magic. The earliest I could possibly launch our craft is the early morning hours of the Solstice day itself, and that's assuming the weather mages back at NASA are able to clear us a safe atmospheric window in time. On top of that... how exactly do you plan to enter the Arcology? Especially if you suspect a potential enemy lying in wait for your arrival."

Emily did not start to explain her brilliant plan, because she did not in fact have one.

"Okay, I've no clue. I admit it," she agreed. "But we *have* to act. I know that much. You say we're not going to be able to leave until Solstice morning...? It's cutting things close, but maybe that's for the best. It'll give us time to make a plan of action. ...assuming you agree to get us up there."

"Technically speaking, acting against Lady Summer's wishes -- even covetous ones for strange off-world power that could unbalance the seasons -- is high treason," Kanthi noted. He considered the point, scratching his chin in thought. "...but by helping you, I also help maintain the stability of the world, and ensure the safety of my fellow Faeries. ...very well. Assuming that you can figure out a plan of attack, I can get you up there. I need to launch the next ElfStar communications satellite, anyway; I was going to wait another week, but I can move the mission up a few days."

Kanthi offered his hand, a very human gesture of agreement and respect. Relieved, Emily reached out and accepted it, shaking on the deal.

"Give me two days to prepare the facility -- and my team, who will not be happy about this -- for your arrival," he requested. "No sense going there sooner, you'd only be underfoot as we scramble to prepare. Yavain will drive you up to the Cape the day before the Solstice. We can plan your mission that evening, and launch afterwards. It'll be cutting it close, but as you say... we have to act. My Insight tells me that this situation left unattended can only end in doom."

"Right. --wait, your what?" Emily asked.

"Insight," Kanthi spoke, making sure to emphasize the word, as a stand-alone concept rather than just a noun. "Have you heard of it? It's a magical trait, often misunderstood as telepathy or prophecy. Insight is the ability to *feel* the present, extending one's senses deep within a single moment in time, and jump to the right conclusion about the nature of a situation. It's how I'm able to fly my missions in space without a full crew, I can extend my Insight throughout the ship itself. It's a rare Faerie gift, I'm told. Only one in a million Fae are born with it, and only in certain family lines."

"...or have it enchanted on them, right?" she asked. Despite feeling absolutely no Insightful confidence about that.

"No, it's a birthright only. ...and now my Insight is making me wonder why you're so curious about this," Kanthi said, studying Emily head to toe, in a slightly disquieting way. "Are you saying that--"

"We won't take up any more of your time... we've all got work to do if we're going to carry off this plan," Emily interrupted. "Thanks for helping us, Mr. Kennedy. ...as much as my ears are protesting the idea of it, we should get back to the concert... then get a hotel room, since we'll be here for a little while. The rest should do us good, I think."

For a second night, the FaePlace hadn't responded the way Emily wanted. Instead of four rooms, there were two.

Nel and Una were totally at ease with the concept, by that point. (Correction: Una was at ease, and blissfully unaware of Nel's increasing discomfort with the situation.) Scout and Emily weren't quite there yet... Scout offered to sleep out in the main room, by the fireplace. Emily accepted his offer without a lot of protest, because she felt awkward at protesting the idea that the boy not sleep with her.

("Sleep with her." That was such a loaded phrase, one which Una's people had no problems with, because they assumed it meant "sleep with someone" and not "make tawdry nasty freaky fun with someone." The Orbitals, Emily decided, had a far simpler life in the stars than people on the ground did.)

Fortunately, all awkwardness surrounding their situation faded with a big, hearty breakfast at an elvish food co-op, followed by a day spent trading magical services along the boardwalk in exchange for supplies, clothes, and other goodies... and then, an afternoon on the beach.

Yes, technically they were supposed to be planning for a daring raid on an alien city facing an unknown opponent which would decide the fate of the entire Earth, but that wasn't until a few days from now. Until then, it was impromptu summer break, a vacation amidst the surf and the sand. Not a bad idea when you consider you don't have long to enjoy life before impending potential doom hammers you like the fist of God.

Una and Nel had, of course, chosen matching bikinis. Rather, Una had selected a bikini, and Nel immediately selected an identical copy of it. Both were a snazzy white that looked entirely too shiny when wet, and both were entirely too indecent for Emily's liking, particularly from behind. To lodge a silent vote of protest against their perfect little bodies bouncing all over the beach like that, Emily picked a wholly unremarkable black one piece swimsuit. And kept her hat on, of course. And hid under a sun umbrella. And wore gigantic sunglasses.

So, while Nel was trying to teach Una how to swim (since Una had never been *fully* submerged in water until today for any reason whatsoever), Emily contented herself with building a sandcastle, playing volleyball, flying a kite, and reading a book. All at the same time.

Scout (wearing camouflage-patterned swim trunks) returned to her side, carrying a pair of freshly refilled water bottles -- and did a double take at the various invisible persons enjoying traditional beach activities. A bucket and shovel were gleefully scooping up sand and slapping together a rough approximation of a castle-esque structure, a ball was mysteriously bouncing back and forth across a nearby net (although it came dangerously close to the sand several times), and a kite was in constant danger of just soaring off into the sky as the spool wobbled and bounded about in midair.

"Animate spells," Emily explained, flipping to the next page in Yavain's well-thumbed copy of Lord of the Rings. "I'm practicing my magical multitasking, trying to see how much I can keep going at once. I'm up to four different things. It's harder than wild swarm of kitchenware, or a herd of identical chainsaws..."

"Day's far from over. You shouldn't exhaust yourself too fast," Scout suggested, setting her water bottle next to her ratty folding metal beach chair.

"Whatever big woogums is waiting for us in space isn't going to let me sit around getting a second wind. This is my training," she said... pausing a moment to wipe sweat from her forehead. The concentration of her Will was a bit draining, admittedly. "As nice as the weather is, I don't have time to sit around having fun in the sun."

"I'd say you're having plenty of fun."

"Eh?" Emily said, looking up from her book -- just as her kite gave up and went rocketing away. She pouted a bit at that, but figured she could collect it after it crashed down to the beach.

"You enjoy magic. You love casting spells, learning spells, even copying spells," Scout said, while unscrewing the cap from his plastic water bottle. "You could just juggle objects, or move the sand around. Instead you're doing fun beach things. Nothing wrong with mixing fun with your training, y'know."

"Ah, right. This from the guy who's trying to learn how to have fun," Emily recalled. "And... well, okay. You got me there. This seemed like it'd be less boring than the usual drills we went through back at school. ...maybe you can lend a hand. See the volleyball net? Go be player two. We'll play to ten points. Give me a challenge; playing chess against yourself's no fun at all."

Scout flashed her a brief grin, before getting to his feet and stretching out.

Those are two simple actions, but deserve more detail.

For starters... he *smiled* at her. Scout wasn't a smiley type guy. That alone was enough to make Emily's jaw sag downward; the way he casually tossed it off, like...

well, like a normal person might do, not even making a big deal out of the fact that he'd smiled...

Also, he was stretching out. Flexing. And it wasn't even some Yavain-suggested overexaggerated action; he was just warming up before strenuous physical activity, in that uniquely efficient Scout-like way. Elegance in motion, simplicity in action. And coincidentally also a very... *interesting* sight, as he was only wearing a pair of trunks and the sunlight was doing wonders with the suntan lotion he'd applied to himself.

Emily had several very un-witchy thoughts, interrupted only by Scout coughing politely to get her attention. He was at the net, and ready to play.

Remaining where she sat, Emily focused her Will... and served the ball.

Right away she was thrown for a loop, as Scout immediately leapt into the air and spiked the ball down hard, pegging it directly into the sand on the empty side of the net. One point. Emily gritted her teeth, refocusing, determined not to lose... the sandcastle building got far sloppier, as she kept her eyes on the game. And on her opponent.

This wasn't some silly back and forth follow-the-bouncy-ball trick anymore. This was a real counter force working against her, one which took her best efforts to counter. She adjusted the ball, pounding against it with an impact of Will, working through the mental link the Animate spell provided her.

This wasn't just a matter of physics -- she had to work with the shape of the ball, with the purpose of it. Objects want to be Animated in a way that suits their design... the object had a "memory," if you will, of games such as these. If she didn't play by the rules, if she tried to spike or serve in ways a human could not, it'd fight against her. If she tried to cheat and adjust its speed, slow it down or speed it up in any way other than applying a single falsified impact, it'd wobble and the spell could break down...

Scout returned volley after volley. He was scoring too many points, slipping past her concentration, as his muscles shifted and his body slid around the space, shuffling along the sands to reposition well before the ball ever reached him. It was too easy for him.

Fine, Emily thought. *Let's see how he handles everything I've got...*

The shovel dropped, neatly sticking out of a sandy battlement. The book fell to her side. And every ounce of her Will slammed into the ball in one sharp jolt...

Which spiked it directly past Scout. He actually stumbled a bit, realizing his motions were already too late. Perhaps his instinctive urge to teleport through a shadow worked against him... it was late afternoon on an open beach. No shadows, no "home court advantage." So, one point for Emily.

Both players brought their "A" game, after that. Scout got the look about him of a hunter -- sharp, alert, focused. Oddly, he still had a playful sense to him, in the way a cat plays with a mouse, but also realizing this "training" was truly a friendly game as well. Emily for her part hadn't stopped smiling once she got that first shot past him, and was determined she'd beat the boy at his own game, using only her wit and her magic...

One point for Scout, catching Emily by surprise. Another for Emily, a trick shot which angled too far for Scout to reach in time. Back, and forth. Again and again, Scout applying his physical talents, Emily applying her arcane abilities, clashing and testing and feeling each other out...

Score, nine versus nine. Match point. Scout serving.

Emily tried very hard to both read his body language, watching the motions of his arms and the arc of the ball, without paying any attention to the way his flawlessly toned body shifted into action with a ripple of his muscular form. Just the ball. Only the ball. Look for an angle. Look where he isn't looking, and--

Strike.

The ball slammed down just inside the legal boundary, and past his ability to reach it. Game over.

"YEAH! I did it!" Emily proclaimed, pumping a fist in the air. "Summer rules, Winter drools!"

Scout staggered back to the sun umbrella, nearly collapsing underneath it, out of breath. He'd hunted through darkened forests, stalking targets and charging and landing his attacks, and even that hadn't matched this. "...well played," he summarized, unable to find better words than that, as he wrenched his water bottle from the sand, intent on taking a hearty swig.

Except that Emily had already reached for it -- it was her bottle. He accidentally grasped it around her own hand.

There was a pause, as the two very exhausted, very sweaty, very feeling things they rarely admitted to feeling couple glanced up at each other.

The bottle was left in the sand, as Scout made his move. It was only fair; Emily got the jump on him last time they did this.

It was hardly a delicate and gentle loving kiss. This was something borne of intense solar-powered passion. And after only a moment of shock, Emily was surprised to find herself returning that kiss with the same amount of primal lust that she was feeling in return.

The metal beach chair creaked in protest, as the weight of two people pushed its joints to the near breaking point. Emily found herself running her hands along Scout's sides, across his broad shoulders, tracing fingertips along--

Along the ragged whip-scars across his back, one for every time Lady Winter brought her favored hunting dog back to life.

Both of them stopped immediately. Emily out of the horrific reminder of that pain Scout had gone through... and Scout, realizing that he was very much feeling the same kind of crazed lust that his hound-self would relish.

After one protracted pause of absolute discomfort... the pair untangled from each other. Scout took a seat at the side of Emily's chair. Said nothing. Eventually, fetched the water he was originally going for, and drank down a full half of it to help him cool off.

"Sorry," he said, at last. "I... really shouldn't... you know. It's dangerous. If I lose control..."

"You shouldn't have to be sorry," Emily said, with some bitterness. "You should be allowed to... I mean... dammit! I'm tired of... of HER coming between us. Of her taking away the things you want from life."

"It is what it is, Emily. No changing it."

"Witches don't believe in destiny," she said. "We break the world, if need be, to protect who we care for. ...she won't have you. Dead serious about this, Scout. I'm not going to let her, that sick prophecy of wedding the Crown of Ice be damned. You're mine and no one else's!"

"Marry me."

"--whaflarglplah?" Emily replied, nearly getting whiplash from twisting her neck to stare at him.

"Cut her off at the pass. We'll get married," Scout said. "I love you, and you love me. I want to be with you forever; that's the only future I'll stand for. Break out of the cycle of mindlessly hunting evil down, again and again, as a lone wolf. I think I'd rather be dead than alone again. Marry me. And to hell with Lady Winter."

You may not get another chance, given all of you could die in the vacuum of space on the eve of the Winter Solstice, Insight was reminding her.

"I," Emily said.

"We, uh," she continued.

"This isn't. It's. I mean. That's. I... we... we were just playing volleyball," she protested. "We can't jump from that to this. It's absurd. Irrational. --that's not to say that... it's... the thing is, Scout, that... I--"

He pressed one finger to her lips, to cut off the stream of babbling.

"Not expecting a yes," Scout said, softly. "Not assuming a rejection, either. The timing's bad. I know. I'm sorry. But that's what my heart's telling me to say, despite how crazy everything is right now. Just... think about it. If we get out of this alive, you can give me an answer. ...focus on staying alive, on winning the day, and then there'll be time for anything we want. I'll go get us some food. You want a hot dog?"

The witch nodded mutely.

Her Scout leaned in, and kissed her cheek lightly. "Be right back," he promised, before getting to his feet, and wandering off in search of an early dinner.

Emily sank into her chair, tugging the brim of her hat down, as if to hide under it. Life was a complicated, tangled affair. And it just got loads more complicated. Scout was right... keep focus. Get out of the mess alive.

And then she'd answer him. She already knew the answer, after all.

Oblivious to all this were an elf and an alien, who were too busy enjoying their summer vacation to even notice madcap snogging action going down beachside.

Swimming was a bust. Una claimed to have experience maneuvering in zero-G conditions, thanks to a few jetpack powered spacewalks outside her home Arcology, but that wasn't enough to get her ready for the idea of being immersed in deadly salty watery fluid lapping up and down in waves. Nel, who was an experienced swimmer (largely because the only way to repair the water pump back at the slave quarters in New Orleans was to dive into a lake) did her best, but in the end, they decided to try something else for the rest of the afternoon. Namely, the carnival games.

After finding a picture book of Coney Island, an enterprising elf had decided that all beaches must in some way reflect Coney Island, and therefore boardwalk-side games of chance were a mandatory element of the experience. The end result was a series of ring tosses, milk bottle knockdowns, and watergun-and-clown-mouth affairs. Owing to an incomplete view of history, none of the games ended up being fixed, and the prizes were inevitably high quality hand crafted elven toys.

They also cost favors to play -- but Emily had planned ahead, spending most of the morning doing Mending and supplying vendors with thermoses of Perfectea, so the witch and her friends had free run of the facilities along Palm Beach. This included the games.

At the moment, Una was determined to win a prize for Nel, who had gotten all wisty-eyed at the look of the adorable little bunny rabbit doll that was on display in front of this game. The mechanics of the amusement were quite puzzling, however.

"By what cultural basis is it considered a good thing to turn a fire suppression mechanism onto a living person and attempt to drown them with a constant stream of water?" she asked.

"Can't say I know for certain, Lady Una," Nel insisted. "Maybe it's not really water. It could be-- er. Well. I heard some things from guests at the House, is all. Or maybe he's just really thirsty...? Are there clowns in the deserts of this world? Perhaps wandering tribes of them...?"

Una shrugged, and lined up the watergun, taking aim at the clown's mouth. Owing to the hybrid nature of all the games, it was a cheap plastic squirt gun, which happened to have a tank that could never empty due to the enchantment placed on it. She nodded to the attendant, ready, and when the bell rang... she opened fire with water.

The combined pressure from the nozzle as it cut loose nearly knocked her backwards. The stream was like a beam of pure H_2O unleashed from the trident of Poseidon -- after all, the game would hardly be fair if the stream wasn't consistent or strong, and the elves were assuming these games had to be completely fair. Unfortunately, it also meant far more kickback than Una was expecting, causing the beam to run wild... ending up with more water in the neighboring clowns than in hers, before the game was over.

"I seem to be having a great deal of difficulty with water today," Una complained.

Nel gave her friend a comforting squeeze around the shoulders. "It's alright, Lady Una," she insisted. "It's just a game, yes?"

"I suppose, but... well. I came to this world with a self defense blaster, and I've only fired it once," Una explained. "I barely hit my target at that time. Clearly, I require more practice... especially if, and I truly hope this not to be the case, we end up in a combat scenario once we reach the Arcology. We don't have long before Mr. Kennedy's ship takes us there, after all. I should train wherever and however I can, so I can help Scout and Emily, as they have helped me! ...ma'am? I'd like to try again, if you don't mind..."

The woman behind the counter emptied the clown tanks, dropping the fill meters to the bottom, and stepped aside. Very aside, as Una geared up for round two...

"Um, again, if you'd be so kind."

Round three.

"I think I almost have this," Una said, bracing the plastic rifle against her shoulder. "One last try...!"

Round four, and the tiny lightbulb atop the meter finally lit up. Nel applauded for her friend's success -- and then lit up brighter than the bulb, when the attendant passed her an armful of fluffy bunny rabbit doll as the grand reward for Una's efforts.

"I shall name him Hop," Nel decided, keeping her arms around the adorable floppy eared moppet. "Orbital names are all three letters long, right? It's appropriate. I can't wait to show him to your friends up in space!"

Una's smile froze a split second. "Ah... Nel, I don't think... um. Let's go over there and talk, okay?" she said, noticing for the first time the curiosity the carnie game attendant was showing. She offered a nod and a smile to the woman with the braided hair, then led Nelliwyn behind a Palm Beach community bulletin board, for a spot of privacy.

"Is something wrong, Lady Una?" Nel asked, equally curious, now.

Una sighed. "Nel... please, you don't have to call me Lady Una. We've been over this. I don't own you, not like that horrible Morgana woman did."

"But I am indebted, ma'am!"

"I released you from that debt, yes? Err, or is there some sort of form I need to sign first...?"

Nel shook her head... realizing that again, Una didn't have a complete grasp of Faerie custom. Her Lady would need it spelled out, which was fine. Nel was nothing if not patient.

"Lady Una... you misunderstand. The debt I speak of isn't the one my father incurred, the debt for which I was a token," Nel clarified, shifting Hop to rest in the crook of one arm. "You absolved that debt, as you say. But I owe you a debt FOR absolving that debt, one I give freely. I may be a slave no longer... but I owe you more than you can imagine, in thanks for my freedom."

"Ah... so... what does that have to do with referring to me as Lady Una?"

"Owner or not... you are my Lady," Nel said, with a bright smile. "I like calling you that. It gradually removes the stain from the word. No longer does it apply to Lady Morgana, a woman who hated me and made sure I knew it every day... now, it's a beautiful word again, applied to Lady Una, a woman who likes me and makes sure I know it every day. ...ah, not that I've known you very long, admittedly, but... I can only speak to how I feel things are. Still, if that word truly makes you uncomfortable, I can cease using it... but I mean it in all respect. For my savior... and my wonderful new friend."

Una considered fighting it further, or simply ordering Nel to stop addressing her so, but... it would be a losing fight. And she had a different reason for pulling Nelliwyn aside, one of more importance. She put on her best serious expression, before continuing.

"Nelliwyn... Nel. While I'm not aware of the particulars of Emily's plan yet... I'd prefer if you didn't come with us into orbit," she stated.

Nel's smile fell, eyes widening. "My Lady...? But... why? I mean... I could be useful to you. My spells, for instance--"

"Please, don't misunderstand," Una insisted. "I speak not against your... usefulness, or against our friendship. Although I suppose friendship is involved... ah. My point. Yes, my point is... the mission may be dangerous. If Emily's worst fears are true, if the Orbitals have been co-opted by the Faeries, or if... they've somehow gone rogue, then the situation will be dangerous. Perhaps even deadly. I won't put you at risk, Nel."

"But... my place is at your side, Lady Una. I want to stay with you..."

"I understand, but this goes beyond just helping a friend. The sheer scope of it...! Nel, this isn't your problem to solve. It's mine. These are my people, this is my legacy," Una explained. "The troubles of this world... for that matter, the troubles of the Faeries as well as the humans, all stem from the Pandora Event, something I believe the Orbitals accidentally caused. And now, more of their faults have put your people at further risk. ...this is my fault, indirectly. Therefore, I have to see this through to the end, no matter how much it scares me... and Emily and Scout have made the same pledge, for their own reasons. ...that doesn't mean you need to be caught in this mess as well. I won't see you harmed as well by my people's foolishness!"

The grip on the stuffed rabbit tightened, as Nel prepared to speak fiercely... a strange and alien concept for her, given years and years of submission to a fierce person's horrible words. That gave her pause. And fortunately so, as the moment to reflect allowed her to see between the lines.

Una didn't want her to die. Plain and simple. A warm feeling washed over Nel, realizing someone actually cared enough about her well being to keep her away from danger, rather than put her into danger as her former mistress often had...

"...if you wish me to stay behind, I'll stay," Nel decided. "I'll do anything you require of me, my Lady. ...but if I may make a suggestion?"

"Of course, Nel! You should always feel free to speak your mind."

"I think Emily should make the decision," Nel said, pleased internally at being allowed to voice her opinion... even if she felt it wouldn't be one Una wanted to hear. "She's the one who's planning your incursion, yes? If she thinks I could be a difference maker, that I could help you succeed... and survive... then I should come. I understand your heart, Una, but... I suppose our feelings are secondary to the mission. I don't mind being conscripted into service again, if it's for you."

It was a logic Una couldn't fight. As much as the idea of Nel being sucked into their problems was abhorrent... the reasoning was solid. A lesson that all of them had to learn, over the course of this journey. You did what had to be done, no matter what.

She felt oddly relieved at being so completely defeated. The responsibility for putting Nel on the firing line wasn't hers, now; it wasn't even Emily's, really. It was just the craziness of the times. Beyond control.

Impulsively, Una reached out, and gave Nel a quick hug.

"I'm really glad I met you, Nel," Una said, after releasing her. "And I'm glad I was able to rescue you. You deserve better than that terrible place. You'd make a fine Optimist!"

Nel went a bit stiff with surprise, when Lady Una embraced her. Despite being from the cold depths of space, the Orbital woman was very warm...

"Plus, I've got someone to talk to, now that, well, Emily and Scout are kind of busy trying to learn how to be a couple," Una admitted, after releasing the hug. "After all, a good friend wouldn't interrupt them! We should keep to ourselves for awhile, give them room. Tell you what -- we have some time before we have to deal with the trouble ahead. Let's make the most of it, together! Tonight, we'll find an interesting looking restaurant and consume its proffered foodstuffs! --oh, but we'll need proper clothes for a night on the town, swimsuits won't do. Shopping time! Let's go!"

That evening, the three groups went their separate ways -- Emily and Scout enjoying a relaxing evening together watching the moon rise over the waves, Una and Nel taking in some unique elvish cooking at Nel's suggestion followed by dancing at a hot and happening club, and Yavain totally failing to pick up one of the carnie game operators.

As a result, Emily and Scout came home well rested and calm, even if they parted ways soon after. Una and Nel were completely exhausted but giggly and happy, heading to bed right away to get a good night's sleep. And Yavain crashed out on his velour love bed with the mirrored ceiling alone (again).

The next day, the groups stayed apart. Emily and Scout practiced self defense techniques, Emily determined to be able to rescue herself if she got into trouble, with Scout acting as a willing and resourceful teacher by following Saul's many examples. Una and Nel visited an aquarium made out of a run-down deep discount department store, where magically encapsulated spheres of seawater held endangered species of both Earth and Fae aquatic life. The proprietor, a were-mermaid, offered hair care tips when dealing with sea water swimming. And Yavain totally failed to pick up a girl who was in town for the Rock Show.

And then... summer vacation was over. They'd be leaving the following morning for Kennedy's base of operations, and the day after it would be space or bust. Two days to just enjoy life and the company of each other, before it was time to turn back to the business at hand...

Nel wished it had lasted longer.

She couldn't sleep, not yet. She was resting on the oddly comfortable metal Orbital bed of the FaePlace room... feeling overwhelmingly lucky to be sharing a bed with her Lady. Even if her Lady didn't seem to understand the implications of, well, sleeping nude next to her... Una simply fell asleep, each of the two nights, straight away. Nothing unusual about it, in Orbital culture; and besides, Una was terribly tired after dancing the evening away, an activity she'd never engaged in before but found quite addictive.

...and perhaps Nel had encouraged that, so she would be so tired on returning home that they could simply bed down and have nothing more be said. No need to bother her Lady with what was on her mind, not when they had such a serious matter to tend to soon, not when Una was trying to live life to the fullest in the meanwhile. No distractions. There would be time to discuss such things, later... assuming there would be time.

But if there was to be anything of this, Nel thought as she smiled and rested next to Lady Una, there MUST be time later. Without that, there's no point talking about it. It make logical sense, and Nel was taking some pride in adopting the logic of the Orbitals to her decision making, lately.

One room over, and Emily and Scout were parting ways, as they had done for two nights running.

Except when Scout moved to have a seat in the rocking chair next to the fireplace, Emily didn't let go of his hand.

"No," Emily said, quietly.

"No...?" Scout asked, not understanding.

"Not this time. The FaePlace made a place for you, remember?" Emily said. "It's where you want to be. And if I didn't want it, it wouldn't be there. This is my spell and it won't do anything I don't want it to do, I say. So, no. Not this time. Come on. My room, both of us. We're getting some rest -- big day ahead of us, remember?"

Scout hesitated, despite the tugging at his wrist. "Emily... I can't. Told you. We can't... do that. I don't want to risk--"

"Excuse me, when did I say I wanted to do the horizontal bebop with you?" Emily chided, waggling a finger. "This isn't about sex. All I'm saying is I'm tired of you sleeping in a damn rocking chair. You deserve a comfortable bed... and frankly? I'm sick and tired of waking up alone. That's all there is to it. We are going to go to sleep, together, and feel the better for it. Now are you coming along, or do I have to chase you in there with my broomstick?"

For the second time in as many days, Scout allowed himself a smile. Instead of trying to pull his hand away, he clasped hers, and they walked in together, to enjoy one last peaceful evening together before the road ahead.

"Alright, I have had a crap couple of days in which I successfully hit on absolutely no hotties, my waterbed sprang a leak and I had to sleep with a couch spring dug in my back all last night, and I have a three hour drive ahead of me if I'm lucky," Yavain announced, as the Solstice Resistance Army gathered the next morning. "I've got takeout breakfast waiting for you in the camper and I hope at least one of you had a lousier night than I did, or I'm going to feel even more bitter."

"I slept great!" Una exclaimed.

"It was very comforting, yes," Nel agreed, shuffling in place.

"Don't think I've ever had a better night's sleep," Scout commented quietly.

"I couldn't fall asleep for an hour because Scout snores like a rusty chainsaw, tosses about a lot in his sleep, and lying next to him is like sleeping with a bag of sticks," Emily noted.

All paused to stare at her. Especially Scout, who looked vaguely sheepish.

"Hey, I'm not complaining," Emily said, trying to deflect the funny looks. "If anything it was kind of nice and humbling to know that he's a pretty ordinary dude with ordinary problems. Scout, I'm buying you some breathe-right strips next time we pass a convenience store. Meanwhile, let's get this wagon train rolling, m'kay?"

Yavain coughed, politely. "Right, then. All aboard, kids. Next stop, Cape Canaveral."

The Kennedy Space Center, so named both for legacy purposes and because Kanthi F. Kennedy used it as his base of operations, had been far more accurately restored than the rest of Florida.

He'd been very specific about this, as he directed the team of like-minded Astromages. No visible magic was allowed in the public areas. All displays and museums were to be restored to resemble their former glory as much as possible. The ancient spacefaring vehicles on display outdoors, rotted and discolored from neglect, were patched up using period materials where possible, flawless glamour where impossible. Kennedy was in personal possession of extensive photographs of the center, of the artifacts within, and of the byproducts of America's two-hundred-plus year old space program -- until the modern day view of the space center matched the yellowing photographs (sans yellow), he could never be totally satisfied.

The displays were on display, with no one to be displayed to. Tourists never visited. Even the few humans who snuck over the border from Eastusa didn't care much about these historical relics -- not when hot and happening locales like Palm Beach, Miami, and the Temples of the Mouse were around. The old of humankind didn't dare leave the safety and comfort of their settlements, and the young were too focused on the present day (and things from the past which the present day idolized, oddly enough) to care about outer space.

In truth, Emily and her friends were the first non-elves to set foot in the facility, browsing samples of moon rocks, walking past photographs of the first steps mankind took into space. They'd sort-of heard of these things, in dusty old history books and as footnotes in media culture, but seeing them up close... it was breathtaking.

"How did they not die horribly?" Emily asked, studying an Apollo moon suit. (It was only 14% of the original, owing to wear and tear and decay, but the elves painstakingly restored it to LOOK as original as possible.) "These materials are so... flimsy. Clumsy. And there's no air, right?"

"No air, yes. Just an immensely cold vacuum -- and of course micrometeorites capable of puncturing poorly designed suits, as well as intense cosmic radiation," Kennedy explained, as they slowly walked the facility. "The materials were primitive. Computers were barely as powerful as the weakest... well, I suppose people don't even use pocket calculators anymore, so it's hard to make a parallel..."

"But... it's so easy," Una said, not quite grasping the idea. "Space travel. I went on a space walk when I was five! We had a special force bubbler device which contained breathable air and a small gravity field, of course, but..."

Kennedy paused. "How do your cities break gravity and enter orbit?" he asked. "Ever since I learned of the Orbitals, I've wondered..."

"Er... they don't. Ships are assembled either on the ground or in orbit, then shift between parallel worlds right into place in high orbit. Why do you ask?"

"Another piece of the puzzle of your people. Achieving actual LIFT for a city the size of an Arcology... it's unthinkable. I suppose you would need to cheat to get them up there," Kanthi F. Kennedy said. "I don't mean that in an insulting way; an elegant hack, a cheat, is the ideal solution. Mankind had to make do with raw rocket propulsion, to fight gravity every inch of the way, and minimize the payload to what the rockets could handle. We use similar propulsion, but with strong Levitation spellwork and other tricks to make it slightly more feasible... difficult, no matter how you cut it. But we choose challenges not because they are easy, but because they are hard."

He paused, in front of a display of the Space Shuttle -- a large white airplane-like ship, mounted on a giant orange fuel tank -- in mid-ignition, lighting up prior to clearing the launch pad. Despite the inspirational nature of the shot... some sadness came to his eyes, as he looked upon plaque at the base. *In Memory of The Challenger.*

"One day... I want humans to come back here," he said. "To share in what we found. America deserves to recapture its legacy. We're going to outgrow this planet... soon, most likely. Faerie and human alike are having difficulty finding elbow room. My dream is to one day, through science and magic working together, establish the first off-world colonies. Orbiting stations, moon bases, even going to Mars if we can find a way to make the distance and inhospitable surface conditions more feasible. If both our peoples could lay down arms and join in such an endeavor in the name of peace, there's no end to what could be accomplished..."

"Mr. Kennedy... this is fascinating, I know, but... we've got a mission to plan," Emily pointed out, with a hint of regret. "I'm so sorry. I wish we had time for a proper tour, honestly. All I know about space travel I learned from horrible sci-fi movies. But we've got the real thing to accomplish, and my ideas for how to pull it off hinge on... well, on whether my Insi-- whether my guesses are right or not..."

Kennedy turned from the picture, raising an eyebrow. "And your 'guess' is...?"

The witch pointed to the photograph he stood beside.

"That's our spaceship, isn't it?" she asked. "Not some recovered Orbital ship, not some crazy Faerie thing like a flying magical soap bubble, but the actual Space Shuttle. I've seen it in movies. You've managed to salvage one, repairing and refitting it for space flight."

Kennedy nudged his glasses up. "It's officially designated the STS, the Space Transportation System, actually," he noted. "But... yes. We've restored the STS Discovery, using what was left of the Atlantis and the Endeavour... and a whole lot of Faerie magic, to replace systems that we couldn't repair. We ferry our ElfStar communication satellites into orbit, deploying them from the cargo hold, before returning to Earth. You have no idea how hard it was to make tiles for the thermal protection system; we ended up using an alchemical mixture of carbon and wyvern blood..."

"Right, then," Emily said, warming up the brain farm. "Here's how we're going to get into Arcology #A076..."

It took some brainstorming to spackle up the gaps in Emily's plan, as well as some verification that things would work the way she was assuming they would. Notably, Emily had no idea how Una's "jetpack" worked, which would be critical. The Manned Maneuvering Units aboard the shuttle weren't going to be up to the job.

They hammered out the last details after hours of planning, broken up only by an early supper of Faerie-spiced meats, Tang, and freeze dried ice cream. After that, a large praying mantis pulling a series of wheeled people-mover carts brought the two teams to the facilities at the launch site, for the final mission briefing.

On one side of the room, the most powerful (see also, the only) Astromaguses in the Faerie Court, wearing spider-silk replicas of NASA jumpsuits. On the other side, a motley crew of elves, witches, aliens, and winterhounds. In the middle, their mission commander, Kanthi F. Kennedy, detailing the plan using a glamour-based display board.

"We have a launch window on the morning of the Solstice," he explained. "The weather control team can keep the atmospheric conditions stable enough for a go. It's earlier than we'd planned, but ElfStar Three is ready to go, so there's no reason we can't take advantage of it. Our crew will be myself on navigation, Eledar Aldrin on communications, and Kiyleh McAuliffe on deployment. But the purpose of this mission is twofold -- one, the next link in our network chain. Two, ferrying our guests to the Orbital Arcology.

"I know I said that one of our mission parameters would always be not to attract the attention of the strange alien visitors, and that stands. As far as they'll be concerned, we're just doing our usual thing, and we pretend we have no way of seeing through their cloaking technology. They're not privy to our launch schedules and shouldn't think anything's out of the ordinary.

"After the cargo bay doors open and Elfstar Three is on the move, however, our guests will swing into action. We can't allow stray transmissions to reveal their identities, so Emily, Scout, Una and Nel's code names for this mission will be Brown, Black, Silver, and Green respectively. First, Green will place a cloaking glamour on the rest of her team. Then, all but Green will make their way via Silver's gravity manipulating backpack towards the Arcology, using tethers we'll provide to keep Brown and Black moving with Silver. There, using her previous experience trying to break through their airlock security systems, Silver will get her team into the Arcology without its occupants being aware they have uninvited guests. Meanwhile, our team does their work as usual, and we re-enter the atmosphere with Green."

...Nel looked down at her toes. That was the part she wasn't happy with, that she pushed back on... but not very hard. She wasn't used to insisting on getting her way, after all, and she had agreed to go along with whatever Emily felt best. At least she had a role...

"Timing is critical. We've tested Green's glamour spellwork, and she's definitely a far stronger stealth expert than anybody we have on base," Kennedy continued. "But her spell, without her along to keep it running, will fade after ten minutes. That should be enough time for Silver to get her team to the airlock and break through, given the positioning of ElfStar Three beneath the Arcology. We're running enough risk having Silver pull two extras along using a gravity pump designed for one person; we can't risk three extras. Our job is to get them as close as possible without arousing Orbital suspicion.

"Countdown begins at 4 A.M. tonight, team boards the shuttle at 7 A.M, we launch thirty minutes later. It's a rush job but we've gotten the process down pat, and the augmental spellwork will keep things going smoothly. Now. Any questions?"

The team deployment specialist raised her hand.

"Sir, how exactly are our 'guests' getting home?" she asked.

"We'll figure that out when the time comes," Emily spoke up, for Kanthi. "Honestly? No idea. But the thinking is that given the two outcomes here are we save the day and Una's dad gives us a lift -- or the Summer Court takes control of an Orbital city to use as a token in a seasonal apocalypse -- we figure we'll either end up back here or it won't matter."

"Our future is at stake here," Kennedy agreed. "If we could get more people into the city to help them, we would, but we can't. We're making a lot of assumptions about how bad things could be if they fail, or if the situation 'on the ground' is completely unexpected... but given the weight the implied worst case scenario holds, we can't afford not to undertake this mission. So. NASA holds up its end, Emily's team holds up theirs, and we may very well avert a premature end to the future of the American Dream we've all been working towards. The mission clock is now running. I'll see you all back here bright and early. Dismissed."

Emily's "strike team" had chosen to bunk down in an out-of-the-way room, its doorframe leashed to a FaePlace. The other members of the postmodern NASA had fairly spartan quarters this close to the launch center, and Emily felt a little guilty about sitting in the lap of magically crafted luxury while they were resting in makeshift luxury.

Nel and Una went to their room right away. Emily could vaguely hear whispering behind the sealed sci-fi door, but she had her own issues to worry about -- namely, preparing for battle, in the only way a utility witch could.

On entering her and Scout's room (what a strange concept that still was, sharing her room... strange but welcome, of course) she cracked open her spellbook, popping the hidden three ring binder spine so she could load in fresh pages provided by Kennedy from an office supply room.

"Copying spells?" Scout asked, curious.

"And trying to decide my loadout," Emily confirmed, as she pulled out her master spell pages, to copy from. "I'm going to fill this thing as much as I can before we go, but WHAT I fill it with is another matter... Animate, of course. I get plenty of mileage out of that. Also Shock, closest thing I have to an attack spell... perhaps some Escapes, but those are unreliable, and I don't like the idea of casting them in the middle of a spaceship. I could end up teleported outside of the hull. I'm also pondering several copies of Perfectea, given I beat down an Archmagus with it..."

"Spell copying takes time. I've seen you doing it for hours, some nights."

"Yeah, well, if a thing's worth doing, it's worth doing right."

"But we both need sleep," Scout noted, as he pulled up a second chair to Emily's work desk. The FaePlace had provided it before they even walked in. "You can't spend hours copying spells. So, I'll help you."

Emily raised a very witchy eyebrow. "Excuse me? Which one of us is the all-powerful mistress of magic here?"

"It's just artwork to me. I've got an eye for details. Let me try, at least..."

The boy fetched a spare sheet of paper and a pen, and took a glance at Emily's master pages. It only took one glance; he was off and sketching shortly after. All the while, Emily watched him go, freehanding perfectly straight lines, getting the curves of the vowels down, filling in the heavily inked sections and sketching out the thin lines...

Within a minute, he'd inked out a near flawless copy of Animate, a tangled web of twisted and rotated letters laid out in strange patterns within the square of power.

"Done," Scout announced, sliding the page over to her for approval. "And I didn't memorize it. Shape recognition is critical when you hunt in the dark. Commit it to memory quickly, recall it on demand, but don't focus too hard."

"...the M needs a little more skew," Emily said, desperate to find something wrong with it, no matter how tiny. "But... not bad. Not bad at all. Okay... you copy me out thirty Animates. I'll get to work on the Mendings. Maybe we can get to bed early, after all."

The Scout nodded, accepting his mission. He fetched a fresh page, and began another sketch, with only one glance back to the Animate master page. Emily watched him for awhile, before resuming her own copying... falling into the familiar pattern, the daily routine of spell loading, to replace any pages burned up during the day. This was something she'd done for years now, always trying to be prepared, to be ready for anything. A witch caught with her spellbook empty, or only loaded with useless things that couldn't get her out of a situation, was a dead witch.

In time, she paused her pen, hovering over the spinning S curves of a Shock spell. A worry pried at her, finding an avenue in the moment she let her guard down.

"Scout?" Emily asked. "What if I'm wrong?"

"About?" Scout asked, not pausing in his own work.

"About what's going on. The Orbitals. The Fae. I've been making a lot of assumptions... running off Insight. What little of it I can scrape up, I mean. Maybe it's not as bad as I think it is. Maybe we're not on the cusp of doomsday. What if we go up there, and we don't find anything to be out of the ordinary...? I mean, yeah, that's not so bad, but it also means that the real problem could be down on Earth. Out of reach because I stampeded us up into space..."

"I trust you. Got a tactical mindset," Scout said, setting aside a finished page. "A survivor, a thinker who works on her feet. A lot like Saul. Your plan's as good as we can make, given how little we know. We gamble with it, but it's not a blind gamble. ...Lady Winter has an approach to gambling, y'know. One it's a shame we can't copy."

"What's that?"

"Imagine a slot machine," Scout explained. "You want a jackpot. Put a coin in, pull the handle, you may or may not get it. Most likely, not. So, Lady Winter cheats. She runs fifty slot machines side by side, secretly putting in fifty coins. One of them turns up a jackpot, and she ends up looking like a tactical genius, who somehow ran a long con that required dozens of random factors to turn out just as she wanted... when really, she had multiple plans in place, and only one panned out. Many side bets down, one wins, nobody hears about the failures. A lot of wasted effort, but in the end, she wins."

"And we don't have that luxury, because we've only got one coin. Ourselves."

The boy nodded, silently, working on his next page.

"...one coin. We're a coin," Emily repeated, turning it around, trying to find something within the words. "Scout... we're Lady Winter's coin."

The scratching of pen on paper ceased.

"She made you a Winterhound. She nudged you the way she wanted you to go. We survived several Winter Court horrors -- including one seemingly designed to toughen us up, and one to make us reflect on ourselves. And here we are... plotting to stop Lady Summer from completing some scheme. Crap on a stick, Scout, we're one of the many ploys against her sister..."

Scout considered this, tapping a finger on the desk. "Possible," he admitted. "She never told me why she wanted me to go with you..."

"The Arcology's another coin. #BE12 goes splat in Canada, and... Winter does nothing with it," Emily continued, trying to find the thread, her focus tight on the facts. "What's more, when Summer finds out she has it, Summer risks insult so she can steal the technology and actually DO something with it..."

"Winter did murder Austin over that."

"Yes, and while that was horrible... in the end, she basically let the insult slide. She didn't lash out directly at the Summer Court, she struck at some settlement Summer wanted to have at one point. Winter practically GAVE Summer the alien toys, dangling them on a string and waiting for her sister to pounce. And now, we're here to stop Summer, possibly at Winter's behest. ...wait, no, that seems contradictory... Winter wants Summer to win, AND wants Summer to lose...? I think I'm starting to see why my instructor called this the 'madness of the seasons'..."

"If this is a game, we're too far outside it to know what the rules are. All we see are the players. Assuming there is a game. Emily... would it really change anything, if we are part of a Winter gambit?"

She considered the point, leaning back in her wooden chair, which creaked from the effort. "...I guess not. We can't sit idly by, or wait around and try to react. Not with the Solstice in one day," Emily admitted. "We won't have time to stop already anything set in motion. We've got to anticipate, and if we anticipate wrong... at least we tried. And hopefully didn't get horribly killed in the process."

Dawn broke across the peninsula, the light pouring across the Kennedy Space Center first, on the eastern side of Florida. It was a peaceful morning, not a cloud in the sky... perfect for such a grand endeavor as a space flight. Picturesque, even.

A member of Kennedy's staff guided Emily and company through the routine. After washing up and getting some food, they were off to get their uniforms; the spacewalk suits, already tailored to their measurements, were loaded up in the shuttle and would be worn once they reached orbit. Kennedy went over the mission again, this time in exacting technical detail to satisfy the needs of his team, using all sorts of astromagic terms that Emily couldn't parse. Her friends stayed quiet... each of them anxious for various reasons, wanting to get on with it, not wanting to stop and chat much.

At last, it was time to board the shuttle... the people-mover taking them from the main compound out to the launch platform. The ship itself, a majestic white man-made bird mounted upright on its fuel tanks and rocket boosters, was impossibly large from afar and only grew larger still as they approached. Emily had seen pictures, both in old media and in the compound's museum... but finally seeing it in person was breathtaking. In the sense that when she considered that thing was sitting on thousands and thousands of pounds of high explosives which would be lit like a firecracker in order to get them into orbit, she stopped breathing for awhile.

"Chemical propulsion... it seems so... so strange a concept," Una said, breaking the silence. "Is it safe? Strapping ourselves to a multi-story tank of explosive fuel and lighting it on fire? "

"Kennedy's done it several times," Emily said, without actually answering the question.

"Gravity pumps would be cleaner. It's a shame we can't give him that technology... Orbital laws of non-interference, and all. I imagine everybody will be quite far away when the rockets go off, correct? Including those people underneath the structure?"

"Well, obviously-- wait. What people...?"

Emily cupped her hands around her eyes, to see through the dawn glare. Gathered at the base of the launch platform were two dozen elves... and they weren't wearing jumpsuits. They were wearing forest green colored robes...

The same kind the Braid of Dawn wore. The traditionalist activists from the panhandle.

Scout was the first to act, rising from his seat. He moved to the front of the people mover, tapping Kanthi F. Kennedy on the shoulder, pointing ahead. "Alert your security forces," he said. "Intruders at the launch site. I'm going to go get a look, and try to disarm the leaders--"

"We... don't have security forces," Kennedy noted. "We've never had a need..."

"Explains how they got onto the base undetected. Are any of your team combat mages?"

Kennedy shook his head. "We build, not destroy. We're astromages. If it's not related to weather manipulation, cosmic-scale navigation, and sensory extensions, we can't do it. We don't even have weapons. But if they damage the shuttle in any way, we can't safely launch. All it took was a single failed O-ring to destroy the STS Challenger..."

Emily groaned. "Right. So. No fighting, Scout. Let's not instigate a scene. ...maybe we can talk them out of whatever they have planned? Diplomatically, like? Sure, that hasn't always worked well for us in the past, but..."

"Do you have any idea what to say to a radical elven traditionalist who's keen on stopping the launch of what to them is a horrible abomination of magic and science?" Scout asked, only half-sarcastically.

"How about 'Please don't?'" Emily suggested. "I'm open to suggestions. Suggest fast, though, we'll be there in a minute."

The vehicle pulled up alongside the launch platform, nice and slow. The Braid of Dawn saw them coming, and vice versa; there was plenty of time to react, but neither side did. No sudden moves, no bold actions.

The platform was square in shape, supporting the shuttle above it, alongside the launch tower. But underneath was plenty of open space, for the rocket exhaust to vent through. A shimmering barrier was visible now, surrounding the base like a canopy... a spell to prevent anyone from walking underneath, where the Braid were waiting.

Emily disembarked from the people mover, clearing her throat. She'd decided exactly what to say to disarm the situation.

"We--"

"We will not allow you to deepen the madness of the seasons!" a woman at the forefront warned, shaking an angry fist. "If we must stand against Lady Summer's cronies and her alien ally to prevent the doom of this world, we will. Your mission to capture the silver city must be stopped!"

"--whaa?" the witch mumbled, thrown off her game.

"One of our agents stationed at the Palm Beach carnival overheard it all from the alien," the leader said, pointing to Una. "How you were using this one, this 'Kennedy,' to go into space and engage in combat within a silver city! We have seen the vast clearing being made outside the House of the Rising Sun. We will not allow this foreign science to taint the legacy of the Fae any longer! If you attempt launch, we will stop you -- or be incinerated by your heathen rocket, martyrs for the cause of a pure Faerie Court! You will be killed or you will be killers. Ask yourself if you are willing to take that risk, human witch!"

Emily started to speak. And stopped. She considered. ...then she glared at Una.

"Errr... I might have... accidentally talked about the mission in public, yes," Una admitted... only now recalling the woman running the clown-drowning game, and her lovely braided hair. "But what I meant was that I wanted to be able to help you IF there was a fight! I didn't say anything about attacking the city, or--"

"Alright, look... okay. This is a *huge* misunderstanding," Emily explained, trying to dampen the situation. "Lady, we aren't going up there to help Summer take over an alien city. We're going up there to try and STOP her from taking over an alien city. I'm getting the feeling we both want the same thing here. Er, sort of. We're not Summer's agents -- and if you've heard the rumors, you'd know we pretty much kicked both Lady Morgana and Archmagus Lilith's butts awhile ago. Does that make us some kind of Summer cronies?"

The leader peered through the translucent Barrier spell. "That was you, was it...? How do we know you're not using those rumors to pretend you're rebels?"

Emily stepped back -- and tugged Nel, who was staying concealed behind Una, around and to the forefront. "Ask her," Emily suggested. "She's the slave that was rescued from Lady Morgana, if you know the rumors. You probably haven't heard her name, it's... uh, what's your full name again, Nel?"

"N-Nelliwyn," Nel stammered. She managed a traditional curtsey, to the Braid leader. "Nelliwyn Myfanwy."

"Right, then. So, as you can see--"

"Nelliwyn!?" the leader exclaimed, her eyes widening... "You... it's... it can't be..!"

For her part, Nelliwyn's recognition was leading towards shock and awe as well. "...mother?" she guessed.

The leader waved frantically to her companions. "Barrier! Lower the barrier, now!" she commanded -- and the soap bubble of magic around the launch platform popped in an instant. The two ran towards each other... and years after one's father and the other's husband had sold Nel into slavery, at last, they were able to embrace again.

The facts poured out, after the two were given some time to enjoy the moment.

The Braid of Dawn was started by Kai Myfanwy, in her anger over the loss of her daughter and the way human culture had corrupted and eventually killed her husband. If the Fae were pure, after all, none of the tragedies in her life would have occurred. It stood to reason.

They had spies within the upper echelons of the Faerie Court as well as in the tainted lands of Florida, reporting on human corruption within the ranks. When they heard of Lady Summer's increasing obsession with strange sciences that fell from cities in the sky, they knew they had to act. Alien corruption was just as bad as human corruption. This culminated in the unfortunately misunderstood report that an alien was at large, working with elves and witches and Winterfae, to bring down a silver city.

"They're making a landing zone, just outside the House of the Rising Sun," Kai had warned. "One the size of a small city. Acres are being clear-cut for the purpose. Lady Summer's direct orders, with Lady Morgana's slaves doing the work. We believe they intend to land another alien township on the surface of this world, this time directly within Summer's lands."

"And we're going to stop that from happening," Emily had promised, with Nel's backing of her words being enough to convince the Braid of Dawn to let the mission continue.

(While internally, Emily did jumping jacks at being right in her assumptions. Now, they knew they were on the right track... even if there were still blanks to fill. And plenty of doom to go around.)

Being on something of a schedule, they couldn't talk for long, and mother and daughter had to make promises to see each other again as soon as possible. Fortunately, Nel would be returning with Kennedy's crew, so the Braid could wait here at the space center, despite their discomfort surrounded by human buildings and human technology.

The chain of events, moving rapidly along, turned a potentially disastrous encounter into yet another defused situation. All that was left now was the actual mission...

Emily sat uncomfortably, strapped into her seat within the STS Discovery. The ship was still upright, the countdown echoing across the cabin, as the astromages prepared for launch.

Not long now, and I'll be in outer space, she thought. *Up a cosmic creek without a rocket paddle, too. My friends are counting on my brain to keep them alive, but I don't actually have a plan once we're inside the Arcology. This is do or die time. I want my friends to do, not die. We have to get this right...*

A warm squeeze enveloped her hand. She glanced over to Scout, who offered her another of his rare smiles. She was starting to learn to enjoy those smiles.

"Let's finish this," he whispered to her, barely audible under the countdown. "And then, we'll have the rest of our lives."

A deep rumble shook the shuttle, as Emily returned the smile... and then looked forward, towards the heavens above.

Ignition.

end.a07

sav-ior [seyv-yer]
-noun
1. one who saves, rescues, or delivers from great
tragedy.

They hadn't been up here for very long, and already Emily had decided she hated outer space.

She hated the way getting up there involved so much forward thrust that she felt compressed into a pancake shape on the back of her seat. She hated the sickening sensation of weightlessness. She hated the clumsy and bulky space suit they'd fitted on her, and the claustrophobic feeling she got from wearing the helmet. She hated that she had to take her hat and spellbook holster off because they wouldn't fit inside the helmet (but fortunately would fit in the strangely compressed storage compartment of Una's jetpack).

None of this hate mattered, though. The mission mattered more than annoyances and discomfort.

This was quite possibly the most important day of her life. Certain doom lurked over her head, the catalyst for a seasonal apocalypse of Faerie civil war. Or perhaps it'd lead to a Fae purge of the human world. Or maybe the Orbitals wanted to take over everything. None of them knew what really lie ahead... only that it was universally bad, and if they wanted to have a shot at stopping it, this was the only shot they could take. Even if it took them so far away from home, and equally far from their comfort zones...

...Una, oddly, was having the most trouble with her suit for someone who lived all her life in orbit. The astromages had to harness her jetpack to it externally, since it would be the only means of propulsion Una had -- thankfully controlled by a short range thought based transmitter, so it could be operated from inside her suit. But the Orbital girl was used to the elegant motion possible with her simple little Orbital clothes, not something like a deep sea diving suit designed to protect her from the frozen crushing murderland known as outer space.

A lot of this plan was depending on her, and that was alarming in and of itself. She knew how to fly in zero gravity (allegedly). She know how to get through an airlock (mostly). She knew how to sneak around in an Orbital city without arousing suspicion (sort of). She knew how to disable, enable, repair, and operate whatever devices needed wrecking, activating, fixing, or fiddling about with (almost but not really). Una didn't want to point out that just because she grew up in space didn't mean she was the universe's foremost expert on superscience... and she certainly didn't want to point out that in her academic days, she routinely barely got passing grades of 91% on her tests. By Orbital standards, she was a helpless ditz. Hopefully by Earth standards that made her an ultra-genius, because otherwise, they were probably all going to die...

...finally, for his part, Scout fixed today in mind as yet another mission. Go in, gather intel, devise a plan of attack, execute. Stay observant and mimic local patterns. Be aware of attackers able to approach from any angle, with any sort of ranged assault method imaginable. Be ready. Be alert. And protect Emily no matter what the cost. ...no other thoughts went through his mind. No other thoughts were required or would be helpful. There was only the war.

With helmets screwed into place, all three of them were now ready to go. From here, they'd stealth up, exit through the cargo bay, sneak up to an airlock, and be in and done with this phase of the operation. The sooner the better.

Nel and one of the astromages made some last minute adjustments to Una's suit, before tapping her twice on the shoulder. Good to go. Even if going was the last thing Nel wanted Una to do, the elf girl knew what had to be and could not be -- wishes wouldn't keep Una from journeying into the gaping maw of this unknown enemy. Hopefully, wishes would be enough to bring her back. There was still so much Nel wanted to tell Una... things she'd held back on, partly out of nervous fear, partly out of a realistic sense that she'd only known the other girl for a few short days. There would be time later to share those feelings. There had to be. Simply had to be...

"Glamour up," Emily said. "They're about to launch the ElfStar satellite. And us."

The elf girl nodded, once. ...but before she cast her spell, on impulse, she leaned in... and placed one kiss on the clear faceplate of Una's helmet.

"Come back safe," Nelliwyn spoke, quietly... before making a few quick hand gestures, using her innate talents at glamour to render the team invisible. A confused looking Una promptly vanished.

That was the eerie part. Una couldn't see the others anymore... or even her own hands. The invisibility spell was just that good.

"From here on out, we get improvisational," Emily spoke to her unseen friends. "Now, let's go and save the damn world."

a08 saviors

Silence. Darkness. Nothingness.

Now, terror, that there was plenty of... compared to the complete lack of sound, light, and substance.

Emily looked down, once. Seeing the Earth, the big blue marble, all laid out below her like God's online web map... it was breathtakingly beautiful. Specifically if you didn't consider that if Una couldn't get the hang of navigating up here, they could end up plunging back into the atmosphere and burning to a cinder well before their component molecules scattered across the surface. She stopped looking down after that.

The alternative wasn't much better. Gazing into infinity was not the sort of thing sensible witches *wanted* to do. They knew better than to do anything as absurdly dangerous as that -- when you give a witch a book that induces madness in the reader or an amulet with a terrible curse on it, the witch closes the book and destroys the amulet. Witches don't screw around with things like that due to the well known axiom of curiosity and cats.

(Well, PROPER witches didn't. Wouldn't. Once there were more proper witches in the world, and not the brain-addled sorts Lilith whipped into proper little psychopaths. Another reason to finish the mission and come home alive -- if they died here, the last proper witch would vanish with only a half-complete website edited by an elven lothario as her legacy. What a horrible thought...)

The glamour did not help matters, when it came to avoiding a spiraling stare into the yawning madness of infinite space; as far as Emily could tell, she was an independently floating viewpoint without even a body to call her own. She could FEEL her body, could feel the bulky suit around her, hear the light hiss of the air supply... but the eyes were screaming in panic that she'd somehow detached from everything sane and was now wandering the void. All alone.

The tug on her stiff tether told her otherwise. Una, she at least had eyes -- the glasses she'd modified long ago in Baltimore, able to see the dimensional shift spectrum. She could see the Arcology ahead of them, she knew where to go. She could probably even see them, for that matter.

Right now, Emily could've used some of Una's chirpy little upbeat encouragements. Or maybe a soothing word from Scout, who was getting better by the day at soothing words. But they'd agreed to radio silence... nothing the Orbitals could pick up on. As far as Arcology #A076 had to be concerned... they weren't there. The only thing 'there' were the elves, quietly launching their cargo, far behind. The three had to be silent as churchmice--

The tether tugged her back. At first Emily panicked, thinking Una had gotten lost, or was knocked away, or kidnapped by some alien horror in a flying saucer or something equally mad... but no. It was just counter thrust, to slow down. They were approaching the Arcology. Not that she could SEE the city, but presumably, it was there, and five times the size of God.

Finally, a sight other than the inky black of space greeted her -- a series of little square lights. One of the keypads outside an Arcology airlock, just like the one Una hacked into back in Edmonton. And hopefully, easier to break into than #BE12 was, considering that took over a day's work... and they had maybe three minutes of stealth glamour left...

The lights flashed and twiddled along. Una was trying different combinations, browsing menus, trying to find some in-road. Not just a means in, though, but a means in that the city wouldn't notice... some access point that wouldn't be logged or could easily be de-logged. None of this magical sneaking around would do much good if they just hammered their way in and were greeted on the other side by armed guards.

Time ticked. Lights flashed. The door was not opening.

"What's the hold up?" Emily asked, aloud -- before remembering that in space, nobody can hear you complain.

Slowly... outlines became visible. The spell was wearing off. There was Una, frustratedly stabbing at the keypad. Scout, watching their backs... not that he could do much, unless he was crazy enough to use the darkness of space to teleport out of his own suit. If they didn't get in soon...

No sound, no 'fwoosh', but the door slid open. It was like a magic window into another land, hanging there impossibly in the infinite black. Una powered her jetpack, the gravity thrusters inside pulling them along... before pulling hard on the tether, to get them in before the door closed...

Emily felt her stomach protest for a second time, as it went from free-floating to weighted down. Artificial gravity kicked in moments after the door shut behind them. Finally, sound was coming back to the world... the hiss of the airlock rapidly pressurizing. Una took her helmet off first, and since her head didn't immediately explode, Emily took that as her cue it was now safe to ditch the space suit. And all the better for it.

They stayed to the far left and right sides of the airlock -- there was only a tiny window on the inner door, which wouldn't have enough scope to see them there. Una worked fast, pulling Orbital clothing out of her jetpack's storage... Nel's dress from Palm Beach for Emily ("It won't quite fit, but I'm sure you'll look very pretty!" Una had noted, back when she suggested it) and a silvery tunic thing and pants for Scout.

Normally, stripping down and changing clothes in front of everybody would raise a protest from Emily over being non-witchy, but that would be utterly stupid to focus on at this point. Not that she didn't give Scout a quick glare, so he'd turn his back first.

"I don't think they know we're here," Una said, re-affixing her jetpack to her usual reflective minidress. "I erased the access log the moment the doors opened. With these clothes, we should be able to merge with the population for awhile, but we should try to avoid groups, all the same..."

"We're going to have to make a lot of what we do up on the fly, but let's start the way we discussed," Emily suggested. "Glasses on, scanning for the shift signature of Faerie artifacts or Fae themselves. We know magic was involved in downing #BE12 and we know the Summer Court wants another city. We find the source of the problem, we'll be able to stop it. Presumably."

"We're presuming a great deal," Scout noted. "Keep your minds open to the possibilities. Particularly that the Orbitals are entirely behind this..."

"That's absurd! My people are peaceful. ...I'm certain this is all a misunderstanding. Or a conspiracy. Or a misunderstood conspiracy."

"Just keep your eyes open for ANYTHING out of the ordinary, m'kay?" Emily suggested. "Alright. Check the window. When the coast is clear, we're out and exploring. Remember: We're three totally normal superscience aliens from another dimension. Act all, I dunno, scienc-y and alien-ish."

It was very difficult not to gawk like a tourist.

The only example of Orbital architecture Emily had on mental file was the decaying, overgrown ruins of #BE12. She'd never seen a pureblooded Arcology before...

It was flawless.

Every surface, flawless. Many surfaces were ivory white, shining with a perfect finish -- just a shiny as the silver metal that comprised the rest. The glass surfaces, windows and tabletops and even chairs, all of it was impossibly perfect. No smudges, no stains, no dust. It was like the entire ship was perpetually wiped down with a soft cloth. She'd even experimented, trying to leave a big 'ol greasy thumbprint right on a hand railing... and the mark faded away the moment she removed her finger. Amazing...

#BE12 had also been a much more utilitarian Arcology, according to Una. It was a research vessel, specifically for botany and particle physics. (She insisted the two weren't really that different. Emily declined to ask exactly how, because that could've led to an Education on the subject.) #A076, in contrast, was spacious and extravagant... it was a true city, a place where people worked, slept, ate, fell in love, and go through their lives.

They were people-watching, in a great atrium overlooking one of the many transport hubs of the city. Below, transport funnels shuffled people about, gravity pumps whisking away anyone who stepped inside into the network of clear glass tubes to some other part of the ship. Small food stations were set up in the atrium, so travelers could meet up with friends over a fine beverage -- no money was exchanged, of course. Like all utopian sci-fi societies beyond moral reproach, they'd naturally done away with that nasty business of having a working economy.

If anybody was a have-not, left in wanting and despair, they weren't showing it. The Orbitals were lovely looking people, all well groomed and healthy looking. They gathered in small groups around the atrium, talking excitedly about this and that. Each wore clothes similar to Una's dress, shimmering fabrics, and they all wore earpiece communicators that would occasionally emit musical little beeps, grabbing the wearer's attention away from local conversations. Fortunately for purposes of blending in, despite the overall prevalence of snow-white hair, many Orbitals had dyed their hair black and brown and blonde... and blue and purple and green, it seemed. With the widespread adoption of monotones in clothing, it seemed that hair color was something the Orbitals were more keen on using for self expression.

All over, young couples were smiling at each other, holding hands. The atmosphere was hardly one of all-crushing doom and death from above -- it was so damned uplifting that Emily had to try very hard to be bitter and cynical about it, even knowing the severity of their mission.

Scout, for his part, remained utterly apathetic to his surroundings. He was much better at guarding his emotions, after all.

"It's not very peaceful here," he commented, quietly.

"Pardon? It seems quite peaceful to me," Una said with good cheer, as she'd been all smiles since arriving back in her familiar haunts. "Just as an Orbital city should be... alive, in vibrant energy, and purposeful!"

"I mean it's not very calm. Not at peace. There's too much excitement in the air," Scout said. "Everybody here seems to be on edge, in anticipation. Is that normal, Una?"

"Welllll... not as such. Not always, I mean," Una admitted. "I've seen people like this before celebration days, but there isn't another one of those for two weeks..."

"Which means they're excited about something else," Emily concluded. "And we need to find out what, because knowing our luck, it directly relates to what's going on down below. We'll have to do this quietly. Maybe if we get one of their communicators, we can tap into the computers and find out--"

"Excuse me, but what's going on?" Una asked a passerby.

The young man paused in the conversation he was having with his communicator, finally noticing the three he was about to walk past. "Hmm? Oh, hello. Can I be of assistance, ma'ams, sir?"

"We were wondering why everybody was so excited," Una asked, despite it being an amazingly horrible idea to directly question someone while simultaneously pointing out that you do not in fact blend in because you have no clue what's going on when people who are here clearly have a clue. (Emily and Scout immediately started looking for the nearest exit, of course, while Una led them to certain doom.)

"Oh, you must be a new transfer," the fellow said, completely dismissing their oddity in one stroke. He smiled away, only too happy to answer the strange question. "Didn't they tell you when you came over to #A076? I know, I know it's a bit of a secret outside this Arcology, but... we're landing on the surface today! Councilman Ono's decided it's time for the Orbitals to bring peace and humanitarian aid to this poor, misguided world!"

"What!?" Una exclaimed, the shock and horror likely tipping the man off as to their outsider status, which would no doubt lead to immediate capture and/or torture at the hands of some horrible alien interrogation device.

"See, if you had a uTalk like I do, you wouldn't be surprised by that," the dapper young man said, utterly accepting of Una's reaction as ordinary confusion. He tapped the metal earpiece he was wearing. "Like mine? I got the 'Argent' model. I know 'Sterling' and 'Pearl' are rarer, but I like mine all the same. uTalks are all the rage, nowadays! Hey, when you get yours, join the Chicago chatroom. Me and my friends are discussing how we're going to set up an aid station there. I know everybody's really eager to visit New York, but I say even the smaller settlements need our help. Don't you agree?"

"Yes, we absolutely agree with everything you say," Emily blurted, trying to shoo him along. "We'll see you in the chat rooms! Thanks a bundle!"

That the boy looked a bit suspicious about... but a beep in his ear distracted him. He wandered away, talking on four different chatrooms at once, as he departed for a transport tube to the cargo bay.

"...okay. Uh. So. Hmmm." Emily tried to put together a picture of what was going on, from that sudden blast of intel. "The Arcology is landing. Everybody knows about it. Everybody's cool with it, despite it breaking the strongest taboo in Orbital society. And what's more... your father's behind the scheme."

"That's... no, wait. That can't be possible," Una said. "Father would never authorize something like that. He was the one who set me to task to find our technology, remember? He was enforcing non-interference, by having me hunt down the anachronisms!"

"He's an Optimist," Scout reminded her. "It's very Optimistic, to 'save' Earth from itself. Sounds like the idea's been accepted wholeheartedly."

"Now, that shouldn't be possible!" Una protested. "If anything, the Pragmatists would be up in arms over it. They're the ones tasked to safeguarding our society by applying caution, logic, and clear-headed thinking. The Optimists tend to our spirit and our ideals, the Pragmatists tend to our survival and prosperity..."

"Not seeing too many Pragmatists around today. They don't carry little name tags, but everybody here's all smiles. Like you said... can't see a Pragmatist smiling when they know the city's about to land and change Earth's path forever."

"We need to see my father," Una decided. "We have to ask him what's going on. He'll have a perfectly reasonable explanation, I am certain -- wait, no, I have it. EVIL Faeries! They got up in his head with magic and messed him up! That has to be it. It has to be... it just... I mean..."

"Una... you're right," Emily said, quietly. Not wanting this to sound like a rebuke. "Your father does have the answers we need. But he could be corrupted, too. Or... maybe he's just not thinking clearly for other reasons. So, we can't talk to him directly. We need to know what he's thinking, without letting him know we want to know. ...you said a long time ago that you could break into his files, right? Can we do that from here?"

Una nibbled her lip. "N...o," she said. "Not from here. I can get into his personal logs, yes, but... we'd have to go to his quarters. ...our home."

"Is there a chance of running into him there?"

"...no. He doesn't come home very much, these days. He's an important person, and very busy, and... well... you'll see, I guess."

Experiencing gravity tube travel left Emily with the absolute knowledge that there was something she hated more than floating through the void of space.

Fortunately, nobody was there at the other end of the tube to watch her come flying out in a hilarious episode of physical comedy. She was able to scramble back to her feet and look professional before Scout emerged from transit (landing on his feet, of course) and Una gracefully slid out of the tube, landing perfectly.

The residential section was unoccupied, which seemed to go against the definition of 'residing'. However, with most of the population out and about, preparing for the grand undertaking of landing the city, that wasn't too much of a shock. They did pass by the occasional security guard -- identifiable not so much by fierce looks or body armor or jackbooted uniforms as much by the fact that they had little badges that looked vaguely official.

There was no need to break into the apartment. After all, Una did legally have right of entry, and could allow guests in as well. Even so, she took care to erase her entry from the door log; apparently something she'd practiced, as she enjoyed sneaking out after hours to watch human media in the libraries.

The apartment wasn't too different from Una's FaePlace, and from the rest of the Arcology's style. The furniture was made of either chrome, pearl, or glass. There were the usual things, like tables and couches... although the couches had no armrests or backs, and seemed to be made of an amorphous metal bloblike substance. The window offered a spectacular view of Earth, which was a bit more enjoyable when you had artificial gravity and a floor to stand on.

On entering... Una peered curiously at a blank wall. Then with a gesture, nothing happened. She gestured again and nothing continued to happen.

"There should be a gallery of family photos there," she said. "Of my mother, notably. Father doesn't feel comfortable looking at them, true, but he'd never delete the files or shut down the pictorial display unit..."

"That's why he became a workaholic, right?" Emily asked. "I remember that, from Esrever's mirrors. How he turned his attention to his Council duties, after your mother passed on..."

"And that's why we went to Earth in the first place, yes. Things have been... strained, since that day. Neither of us have been very comfortable with the family situation, not with the hole in the middle of it. ...the logs, yes. I should focus. I can access his logs through his workspace..."

Una slid into a glass chair, which automatically reshaped itself to better support her. A few passes were made over the surface of the desk, as light-forms rose into place, files and folders and records. With practiced ease, Una entered a sequence of codes, unlocking the red-colored protected files, rendering them blue-colored.

"We'll check his most recent personal notes," she suggested. "Hopefully they'll reveal why he's chosen this strange path for our people..."

She twirled her fingertip around in a circle, spinning through the file structures, until the four most recent entries appeared. One opened, and a hovering image of Ono, the Council Elder, appeared above the desk.

Emily had only met Ono briefly, back in Olney, as he sent Una on her way. He seemed a cheerful, perhaps slightly absent minded sort of fellow -- this Ono was still cheerful, but more thoughtful, more introspective. He was, after all, allegedly talking to himself alone.

"After seeing our technology misused by Earthlings, I've decided to launch an investigation," Ono explained to his logs. "Against Lar's wishes, I'm allowing my daughter to lead the way. This is what she's always wanted, a chance to learn Earth culture firsthand. Still, I will be tracking her progress via her jetpack's positioning systems, and monitoring her vital signs. If things look to be too dangerous, I'll dispatch a Pragmatic investigation team immediately. ...I know I risk much, allowing the only family I have left to walk this war torn world. But Lea, wise Lea... she would not want my fears to prevent our daughter from a chance at developing her own confidence, and independence. Lea always called life a series of trials... is my dear Una prepared for this trial? I will put my faith in her."

Scout considered his words. "Saul felt the same way," he agreed. "About life being a series of challenges. But it seems your father was pragmatic enough to keep a backup plan in place, just in case. Very wise."

"He learned much from mother's wisdom," Una agreed. She nudged over to the next file, starting playback.

This Ono was more... tired. Clearly he had spent several hours in an anxious state, before deciding to commit his thoughts to the record. "I hesitated," he said, with some regret. "I saw dangerous drops in Una's vital signs, as if she was undergoing a ongoing experience of pain during her visit to the city of Baltimore... but rather than dispatch a relief team immediately and cancel her mission outright, I hesitated. Lea always felt that life was an experience of mixed suffering and joy, and that from a Pragmatic standpoint, one must know both by heart. Did I take that lesson too far? Did I just allow my daughter to experience a horrible trauma for the sake of maturation? Back and forth, I have debated this point with myself. However... had her vitals not recovered soon after, and her journey continued along, I would have brought her back immediately and held her and never let go. I hope she can forgive me, for allowing such horror. It is difficult to know the best path. An Optimist can only hope for the best."

...Una's fingers trembled over the invisible keyboard, at the memory of Baltimore. Before her friends could say anything, she quickly moved on to the next entry.

Now, Ono was cheerful once more -- an expression of joy and delight. "An astounding find! Ah, granted, it initially terrified me," he added, before he seemed too thrilled about what he was describing. "For a full evening, my daughter disappeared from our sensors. I feared the worst, and after the experience in Balitmore, I was ready to immediately dispatch a team. Lar was already assembling a group of extraction experts when Una reappeared -- and so far to the north, in Canada! What's more, she had found an entire crashed Arcology! Our sensors kept gliding right over it in our usual surface scans, for some reason, but once she was next to it I was able to focus in tightly. Likely Faerie magic was interfering, previously. What a find! My daughter has succeeded! I will tell Lar of this at once, so that we can dispatch a recovery team, and I can summon my daughter home. Of course, we will destroy the fallen city as cleanly as possible... and then, I will petition for the fleet to leave this world. No longer will I risk our mistakes harming this world. Non-interference must be maintained... its infractions have taught us all a harsh lesson."

Now, her pause was one of confusion. "Wait, so... he knew about our visit to #BE12?" Una asked. "If he could track my progress, if he somehow broke through whatever was hiding the fallen city from view... why were we not contacted, after that? I can't see him waiting nearly a week to do anything, once we found an entire Arcology..."

Scout gestured to the last file. "It's not over yet," he said. "One more entry."

Una quickly dialed the final entry up, curious now as to what had changed things so drastically...

...and was greeted with cheerful Ono, again. Perhaps twice as cheerful. He had a vacant look of wonder about him, sort of a blissful joy one might experience when eating far too much Cold Fun.

"I have designed a plan," he explained, talking slowly, carefully. "It makes such simple, perfect sense... it's astonishing to think I hadn't considered the option before. Seeing the crashed city made me realize something of importance. The reason why our technology harmed this world... is because there was no one there to guide these people in its use! There's so much good we could do for planet Earth, so much healing to be done to its war-wounds. Therefore, I have made a decision. We will land another city, but this time, intentionally! We will break non-interference and begin a new age, one of peace and prosperity for all Earthlings. Lar agrees with me that this is the best path... but we will need to be secretive. He will begin issuing transfer orders, moving most Pragmatists out of the city. They would never understand the heart of Optimism that guides my path. Lea would never understand. But this feels right to me, so perfect and true... this feels like what I must do. All doubts are erased. A bright summer day is dawning. I will be the savior of Earth."

The holographic Ono vanished. End of file.

Una stared absently at the space where her father's image was, trying to put the words in his mouth, and finding them an ill fit. She played the file back again, wordlessly, to make sure she wasn't hearing things. It played just as before, and ended, leaving the three in silence.

"...he'd never do this. Never," Una spoke, at last. "I know him, my friends. I know he may have his head in the stars, as mother said, but he was grounded enough to know better than to do this!"

"A bright summer day is dawning," Emily repeated. "Una... did the Orbitals refer to the seasons, much? They don't really apply when you're in space, right?"

"Well... no, not as such. I mean, botanists often would, and there are calendar sync operations which provide Earth time zone translation lookups, but--"

"That word worries me, then. Summer. You say he wouldn't act like this if he was in his right mind?"

"Of course not!"

"Then he's not in his right mind. Lady Summer may have her hooks in him. He's delivering a city to her on a silver platter," Emily realized. "We were right! ...okay, well, one of the eighty seven theories we had was right. The Faeries have corrupted the Orbitals. We need to get to the engine room and put a stop to this mad plan! ...I think. I mean, can we take over the engine room? Just the three of us? Okay, no, hang on. Let me think. We just need a plan--"

A tiny blue notification symbol popped up, hovering over the table -- a cartoony illustration of a little Una hugging a little Ono. ...and Una's eyes widened.

"Early warning," she explained, fast. "I wrote that program years ago to let me know when father was coming home. He's in a transit tube to the residential district! He's coming here!"

Scout tapped the button to open the door, and waved the girls through. "Run," he ordered quickly and simply.

It didn't take long for their sneaky secret mission to fall to pieces.

Immediately on entering the residential corridor, one of those men with little badges that looked vaguely official took notice of them. From the looks of it, this was a 'I was specifically sent to detain you' notice taking, rather than an 'ere now wots all this then' notice taking. The soft beep of his uTalk module moved him into action.

He was already politely addressing the group with "Ah, excuse me, but if you would be as kind as to come with me..." while he was politely moving a hand to the energy weapon at his side.

Scout stepped in to the guard sharply, elbowing him in the stomach before shoving him to the floor. All things considered, it was the nicest takedown he could manage on the man.

"Run," he repeated from before. Not that it needed to be said again -- the three were already in motion. "Una. Nearest exit that isn't the entrance your father's using. Where?"

Una jogged along beside him, trying to think, despite her nerves. "I think.. the... no, that won't work... ummm..."

"First things first. Una, ditch the jetpack," Emily said, for once thankful she wasn't in an ankle-length running-prohibitive skirt. "They're tracking you through it. We've got to get rid of the thing!"

"But it's got your hat in storage, and all my things!" Una protested. "And my energy blaster, and-- oh, I suppose I should have that out now since we might need to fight, um, one second, I'll just--"

"Excuse me! You there! Excuse me!"

"Faster!" Scout shouted, as the group took things up a gear, now with two more security guards on their tail. "Too late to shake them that way. Find us a place with some cover. Hopefully some shadows. Hurry!"

Memory flickered through the haze of Una's panic. She pointed down a left hand corridor, tugging on Emily's arm to help with the sharp turn. Two more rights, after that, and then...

A fresh blast of cool air assaulted them. A handful of very young Orbitals -- each wearing a uTalk module and enjoying a nice glass conical container of some creamy white substance during nutrition break from their daily education -- glanced up at the trio in confusion. A man in a tiny paper hat and apron in the back was equally befuddled.

Light and bouncy music played over hidden speakers, in no way suggesting impending armed conflict.

"...it's my favorite Cold Fun Distribution Node," Una explained. "Used to go here quite a bit as a child. I figured, umm, lots of tables and things to hide behind, right...?"

Scout was not the sort to facepalm, but he had to fight the innate human urge to do so. "And plenty of civilians to get caught in the crossfire, yes, Una. Let me borrow your blaster, please."

Carefully, Una withdrew her energy blaster from the storage compartment of her jetpack, and handed it over. Scout dialed it up to its highest setting and put several very noisy and showy holes in the ceiling.

"Go home," he politely requested to the kiddies enjoying their Cold Fun.

A wave of screaming, panicked kids streaming out of the room was just the trick for slowing down the guards on their tail. Scout kicked over the largest table, after blasting it free from the floor, and took cover. The girls slid behind the upturned surface, to either side.

"This really is not how I was expecting to die, you know," Emily said. "When I was a kid, I figured I'd die locked in some epic witchy battle of magic and swords against a fierce dragon. Not being attacked by extremely polite guards in an ice cream shop in outer space. Una, may I have my hat and my book now? I'd like to at least go down looking like a proper witch."

Una slid open the compartment, defying conventional dimensional theories by retrieving the large floppy hat and ornately bound three ring binder from the tiny little slot. "We could try reasoning with them," she suggested. "Orbitals don't kill people. At worst they'd stun us and take us into custody..."

"Same result in the end. Lady Summer gets the city while we're helpless, game over," Scout said, dialing Una's weapon back down to stun, before handing it back. "Be ready to fight. Pop out, take a few shots, pop back down. Don't stay up too long, don't expose much of yourself. You practiced with this before we left?"

"Well, yes, but clowns don't shoot back!"

"What?"

"Excuse me, we'd really rather you came with us without any difficulties, thank you!!"

And energy blasts arced over the top of the table. Una yelped, and immediately started doing some shoot-and-duck motions, wildly missing the two guards with every shot.

Unfortunately, this being an Orbital decorated ice cream parlor, everything was nice and shiny... perfect for reflecting the energy streams. The next shots from their assailants got closer and closer to finding their "hiding" spot behind the table, as the guards worked the angles, trying to find one that would grant them access...

"This won't work," Scout realized. He glanced around, trying to find some environmental aspect he could ply to his advantage...

...and grabbed a pair of metal dishes, each loaded up with yummy scoops of Cold Fun. He hefted them, one in each hand, testing the weight.

"Not the time or place for a snack, Scout," Emily accused, while flipping through her spellbook for something useful.

"Shock spell on both of them," the boy suggested. "Una, cover fire. Go!"

Five seconds later, after some blasts sent the guards ducking back behind the open doorway... when they returned to look into the room, each got a faceful of Cold Fun, served up cold -- and electrified. The dishes conducted the Shock spells perfectly, resulting in two crumpled piles topped with edible decorative particles where once there were two dangerous security officials.

"Wait here," Scout said, gesturing for the girls to stay down. "Getting their guns. We all need to be armed if we're going to... do whatever it is we're going to do."

Carefully, he crawled out from around the table, visually verifying that the two guards were down. He slipped along now, crouched, and retrieved the fallen weapons--

In time to hear a telltale clicking sound behind him. He spun, energy blasters akimbo... and faced down a very, very nervous man in a paper hat armed with some sort of metal spigot on a hose. An icy fog floated up from the nozzle, mist from the extreme cold barely contained within the device. Most importantly... it was aimed at the table. Meaning he had the gun trained on Emily and Una, not on Scout.

"D-Don't move!!" the man ordered, clearly not used to this sort of thing. "I'll freeze them. I will! Don't move! Drop your weapons! No force fields! No doing anything! Nothing! Or I'll shoot!"

"I can't drop my weapons without moving," Scout pointed out. Without moving, at least without moving anything other than his lips. "Don't do anything crazy. We're all very, very calm here. Very calm. --Una? What is that thing?"

"It's a deep freeze projector," Una said, trying to stay calm. "I've seen them before. It could... Scout, it could be very bad if he--"

"I mean business! You're... you're all dangerous criminals and you threatened the children and you killed those guards--"

"Sir, we didn't--"

"Don't confuse me!" the man shouted, nozzle wavering dangerously. "Things are confusing enough lately without a layer of YOUR decorative particles on top! All of you, just... slowly... get up, and back away, and I'll call the--"

The tiniest of squeaking noises could be heard, as the stunner disk slid between Scout's legs, into the middle of the room.

The last thing he saw was a brilliant flash of white light.

When Scout awoke, at first he thought he was still blinded. All that was visible was endless white, without distinctive features, without light sources, without anything to define the space he was within.

He was lying on some sort of metal floor. That much was clear. But as he sat up, groggy from the after effects of the neural stunner, none of his senses were helping him beyond touch. The eyes just saw constant white. No smells were in the air. Ears heard no noise--

No, wait. One heartbeat. Obviously not his own, which meant...

"I'm over here."

Scout turned in place, and Emily slid around to his view. She was sitting, hugging her knees and looking quite dejected.

"There's no door," she pointed out. "At least, none I've found. I wandered off as far as I dared, until you were a tiny speck lost in the light, but I didn't want to go any further. I'm thinking our senses are being fooled and this prison cell isn't as large as it seems, but... doesn't matter. There's no way out."

"Always a way out, if there was a way in," Scout reasoned, pressing his fingers to his forehead, trying to massage the headache away. "Una...?"

"Not here. Guessing her dad pulled her out of the mess apart from us. They also took my spellbook," Emily pointed out. "I still have my hat, at least. So that makes me a proper witch without any actual magic. There's no shadows for you to jump into, either. But wait -- it gets better. Few minutes ago, I felt the entire room shake. I think the ship's already headed downward, Scout. We failed, bigtime. I feel like an idiot."

"It's not your fault," Scout said, sitting across from her now, indian style. He started regulating his breathing, a meditative exercise taught to him by Saul, to will the headache away.

"We launched ourselves into space without having a clue what was going on, just because I had a feeling it's where we needed to be. Then we got into a firefight in a kiddie candy shop, and were arrested on the spot because some minimum wage earner accosted us with a mad science freeze ray. That's not just a complete failure, it's an utterly humiliating failure. Once the Earth is swept clean in an apocalyptic Faerie civil war or whatever, they can print on my headstone: Here Lies Emily. 31 Flavors Were Her Undoing."

Scout knew not to laugh at the joke. It was just Emily's way of dealing with the pain, after all.

"This was my fault, from a tactical standpoint," Scout pointed out.

"Oh, are we doing the whole self-blame thing now? I bet I could still top you, if I tried--"

"I could have shot the clerk. I'm faster on the draw than someone using a kitchen tool as a weapon. I considered it, in fact... but I hesitated. Because odds were good that in his nervous spasm after being stunned, he could have fired anyway, and killed you with a severe blast of instant hypothermia."

Emily peered at him, under the brim of her hat. "Aaaand that's your fault because your love for me caused you to think of my well being instead of the success of the mission to save the world. Correct?"

"Correct."

"Alright. In that case, I hereby absolve both of us of any blame for screwing this up," Emily decided. "Because if our roles were reversed, no way in hell would I have plugged the guy if there was a risk he'd have killed you. It's called being human, Scout. It means making the stupid choice, sometimes, because doing otherwise would be... cold-hearted. If you'll pardon the pun that exists on multiple levels."

"Regardless of blame, we're trapped," Scout said... rising to his feet, now that the pain behind his eyes had faded. "I won't accept that as a helpless state until we've exhausted all possible routes of escape. The mission continues. What do we have at our disposal?"

"Your teleportation, which won't work. My magic, which I lost. And a nice hat. ...well, A hat."

"You haven't lost all your magic."

"Really, now? How do you figure?"

The boy pointed to the square-shaped tattoo design, tucked away inside Emily's arm... adjoining two similar shapes, made of pure scar tissue.

Una had a much easier time arousing from brain trauma induced sleep. Someone was waving a neural balancer rod over her head in a gentle figure eight pattern, slowly bringing her back to consciousness, erasing the pain with soothing waves of energy. It was like waking from a nightmare into the dawn of a lovely spring morning...

The person who was waking her, that should have alarmed her. But instinct jumped in first, and Una's first action on rousing was to reach forward, hold onto her father tight, and not let go.

Ono. Father. Beloved father, with the gentle soul of a dreamer. The one who always was there to support Una, to encourage her, to help her realize her wishes and hopes. Even after a gaping wound was left in the family, even after the distance between them grew, the love didn't fade. That would always be there, first and foremost.

But second was the danger. Ono. Optimist. The one who supposedly was behind this mad plan to land a city on the surface of the world... into the waiting clutches of Lady Summer. Ono who they were running away from...

Quickly, Una glanced around at her surroundings. She was lying on the rest-couch of her family apartment... the blank wall where cherished pictures used to display, father's familiar work desk. But no sign of--

"Emily? Scout?" she asked, aloud.

"Shhhh. It's alright; they're safe and sound," Ono said, trying to soothe his daughter. (He ignored the soft beep of his uTalk; family first, business later.) "They had to be moved somewhere safer. It's for the best, Una. There's too much to explain, too much they need to understand, and not enough time. You'll see them again soon, after we land. Everything's going to be just fine..."

Una shook her head. She wanted to believe that, to be honest, but had to force herself not to. "Father... you're planning to break the law of non-interference. Why would you do that? This doesn't seem like you. Not at all!"

"It's as much a surprise to me as it is to you, believe me!" Ono said, with a wry little grin. "The idea just... popped to mind, one day. It felt so right, Una, so true! I know all the reasons behind the taboo, and they're good reasons, but... you've been to Earth. You of all people should understand this. It's a planet locked in conflict, and I don't just mean Eastusa and the Faerie Court. Conflict all over the globe, in every forgotten corner. We could solve so many of their problems!"

"But... but they have to be given a chance to solve their own problems, father. Us coming along and providing them with advanced technology--"

"I don't see it as cheating. Not any more than, say, the Faeries finding some impoverished village of humans, and offering magical healing for their wounds. Not any more than humans offering antibiotics to a plague addled country."

"We aren't talking medicines, father. I mean... well, okay, we are," she said, giving him the point. "But even our healing techniques can be applied improperly. ...I found out firsthand, when a.. low person, a person of no character, used the very same neural sequencer rod you used on me just now in order to torture me!"

--and Ono's endless smile cracked. Just for a second.

A beep sounded in his ear, and the smile was pasted back on without missing more than half a beat.

"I promise you that everything will make sense soon," Ono insisted. "In fact, I got you a little gift, while you were asleep... I'm afraid it's not one of the more stylish models, but I didn't want to abuse my position to requisition you one ahead of someone in the waiting list..."

The Councilman reached into a little box... and withdrew a uTalk. One of those ubiquitous personal communicator gadgets that apparently were all the rage on #A076.

In an instant -- Una, the 91% grader, the one her peers routinely considered to be sub-intelligent -- figured it out.

At first, she'd taken no notice of the devices. Fads came and went on #A076 in rapid order. One week it might be little metal bracelets that showed your mood, another week it'd be matching neck scarves for young lovers, and another it'd be a hot new puzzle game loaded on everybody's desktop where you turn this thing and fit it into that thing and then both things vanish.

Chatty mobile devices? Nothing strange there. Except that they could conceivably access the same neural links that a teacher's shared-mindset headbands would. The same kind that a young war witch used to control a tribe of Ogres, long ago, in Olney...

Father wasn't the evil mastermind. That was someone else... someone pulling father's strings, using him as the means through which the city could be landed. Whispering things into his ear that were just a few feet away from his normal beliefs, then giving him the nudge he needed to cross over. Having him file transfer papers, to fill the ship with Optimists, people who could be manipulated in the same way. Someone who was cranking up the excitement around the ship, stimulating the emotions of everybody here, getting them properly thrilled about the idea of breaking non-interference.

If she wore that device in her ear, she'd probably gleefully join their ranks.

"I don't want it," Una said, fear making her voice small.

"But you have to wear it," Ono said, smiling, always smiling. He reached over, ready to plug the communicator in place, whether Una wanted it or not. "All your friends wear them. Don't you want to be like your friends?"

"I don't have any friends here, father!" Una said, trying to push the hand away. "Nobody likes me. They call me Ninety One! I'm the silly girl who watches all those human movies, the one who doesn't fit in. But Emily and Scout are my friends, and you locked them up, and now you want to hurt me with that thing...! Dad, stop it, please--!"

"Una, it's not as bad as that. You'll understand more soon. I promise you'll feel so much better, soon..."

Father was stronger than Una thought he'd be. He was nearly arm wrestling his daughter now, trying to force the uTalk on her... and in the end, he'd win. Una was hardly a bodybuilder, nor was she the unarmed fighter Scout was. She was going to end up enthralled by that mind controlling device, one way or another...

Break through to him. Crack the smile. Even if just for a moment...

The uTalk started to make contact with her skin. She spoke quickly.

"Father, did you know that mother was murdered?"

And then... light. Everything was light. Her body felt light. The overhead lights were brighter. Everything was perfect -- father was right. It DID make a lot more sense, now. There was no sadness, no fear, no alarm. She didn't miss the photos on the wall. The smile flowed onto her face with ease...

...even as Ono's smile wavered.

"Murdered?" he asked. He didn't want to ask, but he forced the question through his lips regardless.

"Hmmm? Oh, yes. I remember it. But it doesn't matter, does it?" Una said. "She doesn't matter anymore. I can hear them, father... all my friends, everybody from school. Oh, they're so excited! They're so excited to hear from me again! You're right -- this is exactly what Earth needs. I don't understand why I was so worried before..."

Ono took his daughter by the shoulders, looking her square in the eye... despite Una's gaze wandering off, her head rolling back as she listened to the happy voices in her head.

"Una, what do you mean, that your mother was murdered?" he asked. Words coming slowly, trying to find their way through. "That's... not right. I don't remember it that way... she walked into the airlock out of sorrow..."

"She smiled to me, father. It was so nice. She smiled, and told me she loved me," Una recalled, highlighting the happier parts of the memory. "She wore a pretty headband, just like we wear in class, just like they used to brainwash the Ogres back in Olney. Remember? That was a fun day, and so exciting. And you let me wander the Earth after that, because... why, again? I can't recall... to learn how much pain they were in, how they needed us. That was it, right?"

Councilman Ono did not reach his position through ignoring the world around him. 'His head in the clouds, that's my Ono,' his beloved wife Lea would say... but Lea also knew he was sharp and resourceful, able to make his dreams come true through clever thinking and hard work. He wasn't the sort of person to dismiss the facts. Especially not where his family was concerned.

Headbands. Mind control. Changing your thoughts. Making you do things you would never do. Lea would never kill herself. It never sat well with him, it never made sense. The investigators claimed it was his fault -- that this was the natural outcome of an Optimist and a Pragmatist as man and wife, that they could never truly integrate. They couldn't be one.

They WERE one. He loved Lea with all his heart. She would never kill herself. She was controlled.

And now, so was Ono.

With absolute determination, with a rage that rarely touched his soul of positivism, Ono grasped the earpiece that was whispering calming words, telling him everything was fine, nobody was sad, and he tore it free from his mind.

The lights dimmed. The world got sharper, harsher. And the wall was blank.

With a snap of the wrist, he brought back the gallery files he had pushed aside in his haze. Lea. Una. The joys of his life. The reasons he carried on. They would never leave the wall again, and damn the one who tried to erase them from his soul.

As Una returned to her senses, the uTalk pulled from her ear... she found her fathers arms around her, and his tears falling on her shoulder. It was a gesture returned in kind, as Una began to cry with him. Grief long since bottled up and unspoken, now given a release...

But it couldn't last. Ono held onto it, memorizing the feeling. He would return to it, and soon. For now... something else had to be in play.

Anger.

He withdrew, slowly, and faced his daughter head on.

"I know who's responsible," he said, softly yet firmly. "And you and I are going to put a stop to this madness once and for all."

"Out of the question."

Emily folded her arms, assuming the unbreakable stance of the Steadfast Witch. She added a shake of the head for emphasis, even.

"I'm not casting my Escape spell," she said, with the tiniest of glances to her tattooed arm. "For starters, it hurts like hell when the spell burns itself off my skin. It was a horrible experience the first two times I cast it."

"This isn't the time to worry about battle wounds," Scout stated.

"There's a much more critical reason not to bail out of here by magic. Escape is NOT a reliable spell," Emily continued. "When I got the idea to tattoo up three copies of it on my arm, so I could eject my ass out of a horrible situation on demand, it seemed like a clever notion. But the first time I cast it, I ended up upside down in a tree a mile away. Okay, fine, a little painful, but no big deal, right? Next time I cast it when I was in a seaside village, and I ended up a hundred feet underwater half a mile away. I nearly drowned, Scout. Escape doesn't care where it drops you... all it does is move you somewhere other than where you are."

Scout looked out, into the artificially infinite expanse of white. It couldn't possibly be as large as it seemed... the Arcology was the size of a city, not the size of a vast plain. And that meant...

"You could end up teleporting outside the hull," he realized.

"I hear you freeze to death instantly, which is a bonus, compared to explosive decompression," Emily said, looking on the bright side of crushing doom.

"But you could end up teleporting to another part of the city."

"Yeah, I could. Or I could become an involuntary ElfStar satellite."

"There's no other way out of here. ...can you teach me how to cast the spell?" Scout suggested. "Better me than you, if something goes wrong--"

"Ohhh no, buster, we are NOT getting into one of those endless cycles of throwing ones self on a live grenade to spare the other self," Emily warned. "I'll not have any of that chivalrous crap on my watch. I'd be just as likely to take a bullet for you as you would for me, so neither of us are taking bullets."

"Or both of us are."

"Eh?"

"You cast the spell and I hold on tight. We both either get out of here and save the day, or die in space," Scout suggested. "That's fair. And if you won't show me how to cast it, it's the only way I'll let you cast it. I meant what I said, back in Florida... I don't want to live without you, Emily. That's not living, to me. Not anymore."

She swallowed, hard. "Scout... this... that's stupid. We can't do this."

"And the alternative? Sit here and wait for rescue? Wait for Lady Summer to open the 'door' for us and let us out?" he asked. "This is more important than you, more important than me. More important than us. You said being human was doing the stupid choice, because to do otherwise was cold-hearted. In this case... the stupid choice is a recklessly dangerous spell, for the sake of the world. ...besides. I have faith in one other thing."

"Which is...?"

"The gamble of Lady Winter. We're her coin, remember?" he said. "Lady

Winter... they say she can see how someone will die. Lady Summer sees how you were born, Lady Winter sees your death. She wouldn't have set a prophecy upon me of marrying the Crown of Ice only to let me die in space."

"...unless she meant you freeze to death."

Scout grasped Emily's hand, pulling her in close.

"We do it together," he said. "No time left. We have a mission to finish... and a life to live. Let's go."

Emily fidgeted, despite the comfort she found in his arms. Slowly... she raised her hand, eyes running along the single remaining copy of the Escape spell.

"This is the stupidest thing I have ever done," she said, for the record. "And if we both die, I'm haunting you forever. Understood?"

"Understood," Scout agreed. "Let's finish this."

"...ədɐɔsɘ."

The white void became an empty white void, as the lovers were cast onto the cosmic winds of fate.

Twenty seconds later, an invisible door opened, and a man and his daughter peered in.

"Err... shouldn't my friends be in here somewhere...?" Una asked. "It's just a ten foot by ten foot cell, right?"

Ono sighed. "We don't have any time to look for them. The city's landing in minutes," he said... raising a powerful energy rifle. "And we have a 'mastermind' to stop. We need to go. I'm sorry, Una..."

The door slid shut, as they departed.

The view outside the windows was in motion. The stars were sliding away, up and away, the view growing brighter as the atmosphere of Earth began to assert itself. The path to salvation was slower than he liked, a nice, gradual descent to the planet's surface... not the short drop and a sudden stop that #BE12 experienced, no sir. But that was fine. A slow fall would ensure maximum effect for all concerned.

He'd dismissed the other workers, people in his inner circle. They'd already be in the shuttlecraft, awaiting their leader before departing, of course. He had a few minor adjustments to make, to ensure the plan would be executed smoothly while they were a comfortable distance away.

His fingers played over the smooth surfaces, entering codes, correcting the flight path according to last minute data. One look up at the enormous gyroscopic shift engine, the core component of the vast engine chamber, confirmed that all was well... the gravity pumps were at last properly balanced. It took them days to get the right mixture for a landing, something Arcologies simply were not designed to do. Ever since the unfortunate departure of #A076's skilled chief engineer years ago, every replacement in her stead had been a rather sad example of Orbital undereducation, which emphasized philosophy far too greatly over the hardest of scientific disciplines. Far too greatly for his tastes, anyway.

No sense grieving for the past, however. Despite his staunch counterstance against optimism, he felt great relief and hope for the future. At last, the path would be clear. And #A076 was the key. All he had to do was depart from this place, head back to the fleet, and report in. The work here was now complete. The future would at last be assured.

He closed down the programs, securing them into place, before turning away from the computer and towards the business end of an impressive looking energy rifle.

This gave him one third of a moment of pause, before he returned the implied threat with a warm smile.

"May I be of assistance, Primary Council Leader Ono?" he asked, politely.

"Tertiary Pragmatist Councilmember Lar, I am placing you under arrest for crimes against society," Ono spoke, his weapon unwavering. The smaller energy blaster held by his daughter wavered more, but remained pointed at the traitor. "For breaking the highest of laws, non-interference in an alien culture. For psychic assault against the entire population of this city. ...and if my calculated estimate is correct, for the murder of my wife, Chief Engineer Lea."

"We'd really rather you came with us without any difficulties, thank you, " Una added.

"I wouldn't," Ono corrected. "Lar, you have taught me how to feel hatred today. It's a new sensation to me, and being an enlightened explorer of philosophy, I would very much enjoy an opportunity to find new means of expressing the emotion. I would really rather you gave me difficulty, so that I could perform an action I would later come to regret. Would you kindly?"

Lar raised his hands. "Pardon my confusion, Primary Council Leader, but I'm not certain how I could give you any difficulty," he spoke. "I'm getting on in years, and in weight. I'm hardly in any shape to fight you. I have no weapons on my person. I am completely helpless, as are any of our kind when stripped of their wonderful technology. But if I may have but one word, before I am taken away for trial...?"

"What would that be, precisely?" Ono asked, thumbing the trigger of his energy projector...

"xəЧ," Lar whispered.

The rifle in Ono's hands promptly emitted a sickly beeping sound. Holographs hovered over it, spurting out error codes that contradicted themselves -- the weapon's internal systems apparently were simultaneously overloading and underpowered. Within two seconds the gun had failed completely.

"xəЧ," Lar repeated, in case they hadn't heard him -- and Una's trusty energy blaster fell apart in her hands, the modular components failing at every critical seam simultaneously. "xəЧ, xəЧ, xəЧ." Her shield bracers overloaded, sending numbing spikes of energy up her arms -- and finally, her jetpack, which had seen her through thick and thin on Earth, gave up completely, falling off her back and shattering on the floor. The storage compartment lost containment, and an explosion containing the sum of her shopping expeditions burst forth, clothes flying in all directions.

Una stared at her still-tingling fingers in horror, as she was systematically stripped of every superscientific tool in her arsenal... while Ono sprang forward, an uncharacteristic snarl of rage as he seemed intent on simply beating Lar into the ground with his own weak fists...

Lar waved two fingers at him, shaking his head. "No, Ono. Sorry. ʎuoჳɐ. ʎuoჳɐ. You're both too late to do anything to stop me, I'm afraid."

Her bone marrow was promptly replaced with magical flame. The tiny part of Una that wasn't screaming in pain hoped that metaphor was not literal -- the rest of her flashed briefly back to Quicksilver's basement dungeon, before the image of Lar replaced that of Dennis once more. Una fell to her knees, every joint searing with pain, as if a dozen years of arthritis slammed through her body in one shot...

Ono took the hit worse than she did. He was older, more frail, and not toughened up by weeks of physical activity on Earth. He collapsed completely, unable to even drop to his knees. Weakly, he tried to pull himself from the floor... and was unable to do so. His fight was gone, and with that, his consciousness.

Slowly, Lar produced an object from the sleeves of his council robes... an ornately decorated book, bound in white leather, bearing a crest in the shape of a snowflake. It was a strangely cheery glyph for a tome that simply... FELT wrong, a wrong thing, that the eye wanted to look away from.

"It's amazing, the things our survey teams find when scouring the wastes of Canada," Lar said. "Take, for example, the Codex of Curses. It's a Winterfae spellbook, of course. I came into possession of this volume years ago, and it solved all my problems in one swoop. It seems our technology is quite vulnerable to being hexed."

"B.. buh... #BE12..." Una realized, fighting to speak, despite the pain. The innate curiosity of her Orbital upbringing was asserting itself, despite all the horror she was experiencing. It had to know -- that trumped everything else. "It wasn't Faeries... YOU were the one who crashed the city...?"

"I'm afraid I really don't have time for idle chatter, girl. I have a shuttle to catch, and speeches to make," Lar apologized, tucking the book away -- and from this lower angle, she could see a second book up his sleeve, as well. Emily's spellbook. He apparently had collected it from her, much as he'd collected the other tome, and likely countless others over the years if he'd managed to teach himself spellcasting...

...but from that angle, Una could see something else, as well.

She smiled, even if it hurt to do so. But quickly replaced the smile with a look of fear and hopelessness. It was easy to wear an expression contrary to her nature... it was something she'd learned at the hands of Quicksilver Security. And now, it would be used for a good cause.

"We can't stop you," she spoke, letting the fear into her words. "But.. but why? Why did you do this? I don't understand... surely if you have won the day... you wouldn't mind telling us what your master plan is...?"

Lar considered the point, stroking his chin. "Yes, I can see how I would take emotional satisfaction in that," he said, focusing all his senses on the girl, to enjoy watching her squirm. "Thank you for the suggestion, Una. I suppose it won't take too long. Likely you've figured much of it out already, after all -- you just need someone to connect the dots. Unsurprising, given your pathetic test scores, little girl. Very well."

He gestured to the window, to the Earth that was approaching ever so steadily... but kept his eyes locked on those of his victim.

"My aim is to scour the Earth of all life, of course," he said. "My... organization, if you will, has been murdering worlds since the very first Orbital fleets left our poisoned homeworld. We are the secret heart of Pragmatism. Not that all Pragmatists agree with us... your mother was quite disagreeable, when she accidentally found out the truth. Regrettable. ...you're taught this all in school -- we do leave some details out, mind you. Otherwise, the kindhearted side of Orbital culture could never live with itself... knowing it only lived off the backs of such filthy work--"

"Murdering worlds?! I... I don't--"

"Don't interrupt your betters, child," Lar rebuked. "It's through my work that you get your pretty clothes and your shiny toys. Never forget that. Surveying fleets seeded with members of my organization find interesting worlds to 'observe.' These surveyors don't just scout... they overlay. They make carefully calculated massive shift-transpositions of one world's lifeforms onto another world, after determining the best combination to generate mutually assured destruction. After that, observation fleets roll in to watch these poor backward societies tear each other apart with war, and finally mining ships to irradiate and strip down the minerals from the dead world to make into mass capacitors. And thus, the Orbitals are forever."

"The Pandora Event!" Una realized. "I was right... we are responsible. ...I couldn't understand why... it's horrible, it's nonsense, it's--"

"The only way our culture can persist, given its constant need for a fresh energy supply. Without my organization scouring worlds, we would be grounded within two generations. All the planets we visit seem to be unfortunately teeming with life... a mistake to be corrected."

Lar let the horror of it sink in, a horror he was incapable of sharing. Optimists were unable to grasp the requirement, unable to see past the moral issues. A sad, sad state of unenlightenment.

"That brings us to this planet, the seventy fourth we've found that named itself Earth," Lar continued. "We transposed the Faeries into the world... for starters. Oh, there's plenty of other things lurking in the dark corners of this world, as well. But despite our best efforts... Earth did NOT destroy itself. There were wars, of course, and when your fleet arrived to observe, things seemed to be going quite well! But... in the long run, the world stabilized. It had reached a cold war state. Useless to us Orbitals, and any further mass-shifting would be noticed. I was tasked by my superiors to find a solution. And then I found this..."

He stroked one hand over the cursed tome within his sleeve, a curl forming on his smile. He did enjoy the touch of its pages.

"I consider it providence that I found this book. I filled #BE12 with weaponry, and crashed it into the Earth using a hex curse. I planted it squarely into the domain of the Faeries I had determined best fit the playbill of 'evil.' ...hmm. I had miscalculated, it seemed. This 'Lady Winter,' the primitive nature-spirit, did nothing with my gift. She let it sit there. Oh, some humans looted it, but then they hoarded its tools! The whole thing almost proved to be a waste of time... until somehow, Lady Summer got her hands on the technology. And then, she sent a message to me. If I sent her another city... she would give me the apocalypse I desired."

The pieces slotted nicely into place. Everything was fitting, the reasons behind the things which made no sense before, the gaps in the story that was cobbled together from their investigations... except one thing.

Una gathered her strength, pushing through the pain of the curse-spell, to continue. The light outside the ship was growing brighter... bluer. This was delaying matters, she should get on with it, but she had to *know*...

"Why not just crash the city? Why concoct some fake Optimist plan to... frame my father as a criminal," Una realized. "You said you were leaving. You're going to report back to the fleet of Ono's treason, of how the Optimists worked together to break the taboo. You're framing Optimism itself as a villain!"

"It seems our little Ninety One just gained another percentile," Lar confirmed, with a grin. "Oh, but there's more! I don't trust this Lady Summer, of course. Not after Lady Winter did nothing with the toys I dumped in her lap. No, the shift engines are going to overload and the city will explode the instant it lands. The resulting blast will irradiate two thirds of the planet, poisoning any survivors to death over the span of a few weeks. Orbital society will hail me as a hero, will hail your father as a traitor, and will use Earth as an object lesson in why Optimism is madness incarnate."

Lar leaned in closer, drinking in the shocked expression of the girl, finding himself quite satiated with the taste of her sorrows...

"I am the savior of the Orbital culture," Lar concluded. "And Earth is my master stroke. And now, I must be leaving. I don't want to be here when the city goes up like a candle. Goodbye, ignorant little girl."

...Una slowly, ever so slowly, got to one knee. Then stood on her two feet. Lar watched, curious now, as the girl summoned up the last of her strength...

"I may be an ignorant little girl," Una spoke, "But I have a deep knowledge, an understanding, you do not."

"I find this very hard to believe, given I'm a certified genius level intellect."

"You may be smart... but you never watched Earth media," Una said. ...and her false expression of horror, sorrow, and pain was dropped away like a cheap paper mask, revealing the smirking glee she'd been tucking away all this time. "You never watched spy movies. If you had, you'dve known better than to monologue your plans. **NOW**."

A foot firmly planted itself directly between Lar's legs, from behind. The Councilman let out the air in his lungs in one surprised squeak, as Emily powered her entire body through in the kick, answering her earlier query regarding the existence of Orbital testicles in the positive.

While she was busy taking out some rather vicious physical justice on the man, Scout was stroking a finger along his silver master mind control headband, deactivating it. He jerked the device off Lar's head sharply, pulling away the wires... and slamming Lar headfirst into a mind blanking coma in the process. The criminal's eyes rolled back into his head, and drool started to flow before he fell flat on his face.

The curse spell snapped in half, and Una's pain vanished completely, as if it was never there in the first place. She flexed her shoulders, testing them, satisfied with the results.

"You know, we could have interrogated his ass AFTER we stopped the ship from plowing into the dirt," Emily pointed out. "You're lucky we got here just in time to listen to his evil scheme and kick his ass. We accidentally teleported into a janitor closet. Took awhile to find the engine room..."

"I'm sorry, but... I had to know," Una said. "Now. Let's stop the Arcology! ... ...I have no idea how to stop the Arcology! Err. We could try waking my father up...? But he's not an Engineer..."

Emily took her stolen spellbook back from the (still twitching) form of Lar. "Let me handle that," she said. "Rather, let me help you handle that. After all, we've done it before, haven't we? Only this time, I don't have several minutes to mediate, so I'll have to get it right on the first try. ....ǝʇɐɯ¡uɐ."

The witch brushed her fingers over the computer console Lar was using moments ago, and the spell took root...

Parts of the computer disconnected themselves, hovering in the air. They swirled in a cloud, spinning and spinning, a potter's wheel loaded down with metallic clay that slowly took shape...

When the systems of #BE12 were animated, they became a replica of the Chief Engineer who spent the most time with the engines, leaving behind an imprint of himself. #A076 hadn't had a proper Engineer, not one the computer recognized as its own, in years. The memories went back farther than the sister ship's systems had...

The cloud of parts resolved into a silver mannequin, in the form of Chief Engineer Lea.

"Hello, little Una," the Computer-Lea spoke, in a near flawless synthesized copy of her voice.

The earlier curse spell could only make her hurt. It couldn't make her tremble inside, not in this way.

"M-Mother...?"

"I'm sorry... I'm just your mother's computer. And we don't have much time," it explained. "I'm slowing down the gravity pumps, trying to reverse the descent. I need your help, Una. You need to disconnect the following mass capacitors; they've been sabotaged by magic, designed to overload the system. I'll walk you through the process."

As if sleepwalking, Una did as instructed. Emily and Scout joined her... Emily feeling a little guilty, not realizing what an effect the spell would have. They severed a connection here, moved a long tube of compressed matter here, made a connection there. Slowly, a series of red holographic meters slid down into the blue... and the city itself stopped sliding deeper into the blue. That shuddering feeling Emily felt back in the cell, signifying the start of the fall, now signified the end of it.

"Altitude, half a mile above the surface of Earth, and slowly climbing," Lea spoke. "Lar redesigned the pumps to allow a safe landing -- the same modifications can allow a safe launch. We have just enough stable energy units to fight against the pull of gravity and ascend. You've done it, Una. #A076 is saved."

Una returned from her tasks... face to face with the simulacrum of her mother.

"...we miss you," she spoke, so very softly. "I know this isn't you. Not really. ...but we miss you. Father and I."

'Lea' did her best to smile... reaching out, to stroke a finger along Una's cheek.

"I think she would be proud of you, dear Una. Of all you've become, of all you've done. You've come so far from the little girl your mother remembers... grown up into a proud, strong woman. ...it's time for me to go, Una. The spell is fading..."

Una didn't get a chance to say this, when her mother left for the first time. It was a word that hovered there, unsaid, for so many years...

"Goodbye," Una spoke, at last.

Tears fell, as the computer components fell apart, rendered inert once more.

An embrace wrapped itself around her, from behind.

"I miss her too," Ono whispered in her ear... still ragged from his painful experience, but alert enough now to have watched the entire exchange. "I'm glad we got a chance to say goodbye. ...we're going to live on, Una, just as she wanted. I promise you. It's going to be okay, now..."

The four of them gathered by the expansive window, watching as the Earth fell away beneath them, the city on its way to resume its rightful place among the stars. Two pairs of two... father and daughter, and the two lovers.

"Mission accomplished, huh?" Emily said, looking up to the warmly smiling Scout.

The boy nodded, glad the ordeal was over. "So it seems--"

And the city stopped. That shudder was back, only this time, three times as strong... and it kept going. And going...

A flash of green snapped in front of Emily's eyes, followed by another, and another.

Vines. Launched up from the surface of the Earth, impossibly thick and long vines, wrapping themselves around the city over and over...

She fought to keep her footing, as the entire city was dragged downward, Summerfae magic battling head on against the gravity pumps. Given the pumps were never designed to pull a city upward into orbit, and they barely had enough to get the job done... any resistance would be enough to trump them. A full-on assault by a wrathful Lady Summer, a goddess who would NOT be denied her prize... that was more than #A076 could handle. Mass capacitors blew left and right, tubes of matter spewing their earthy sludge all over the floor...

"Power! We need more power!" Emily called out. "Una, Ono! We've got to get the engines pushing harder than this, or--"

Or what, young witch?

Emily whirled on place, turning to face the voice that floated in from behind her... just in time to see leaves and twigs and sunlight, all spiraling into place, to form the unearthly body of Lady Summer. Much as the computer components formed Lea, these slowly took on a human shape, of a beautiful woman in a dress of leaves and flowers... but with eyes like two miniature suns, and a Crown of Flame lightly spinning above her honeygrass hair...

A goddess had manifested in the middle of an alien spaceship. That alone was bizarre beyond belief. Una, Emily and Scout were sort of prepared for that... but Ono's brain shut down at the sight, unable to comprehend what he was seeing. Some paternal instinct made him pull Una closer, however... away from the dangerous entity before him.

You have done well. You prevented the destruction of my new acquisition and stopped the madman, just as I required of you. He started the descent... you kept my prize safe on the way down. I will have what I desire, before this world is through. And you cannot stop me...

...her feet nearly floated off the floor, as the city descended hard and fast, like a runaway elevator. She tried to speak up, to protest, but the air in her lungs was having trouble shuffling itself about properly. She looked over to Scout, who was busy scanning for shadows, trying to find something, anything he could use to his advantage--

And then it was over. The ship slowed sharply... and settled. Outside the window... the House of the Rising Sun was in view. They'd landed right in the parking space that they were destined to reach, and the engines would likely never be strong enough again to lift them away.

Scout reared back, ready to pounce -- and was stopped by Emily, holding up an arm. A barrier.

"You can't punch a nature goddess," she reminded him. "I don't have any spells that can hurt her. And we're out of shiny rayguns."

...but Summer let out a musical little giggle, at that.

Actually, as a Winterhound, he is empowered with the boon of my sister. If he wished to harm me... he could make a splendid try of it.

"Good," Scout said, pushing Emily's arm away. "Not going to let you--"

Lady Summer's eyes flared, once. And Scout burst into flame.

Oddly... there was no heat. If there was, Emily would've burned to a crisp just from standing next to him. The fire was a magical light, coating his body in an instant... before evaporating into nothingness, leaving Scout completely unharmed. In fact... the most extreme end of unharmed he could possibly get...

Immediately, he clenched a hand to his chest, eyes widening...

"Heartbeat," he spoke. "I have a heartbeat. She turned me human! I'm not a Winterhound any m--"

And THEN the real fire came, a lance of it, slamming directly through his chest. It burst out of his back, melting a hole in the glass observation window, just to prove that this time the Crown of Flame meant business.

Emily didn't hear herself screaming, but she was screaming. She had to be. It was the only sane reaction as the love of your life collapses to the ground, blood gushing from his chest, light already starting to fade from his eyes...

You can do nothing. You cannot stop me. You are mortal... whereas I am eternal, so long as the cycle of nature within my host world exists.

"...oh god oh god oh god..." Emily fell to her knees at his side, pulling her witch's hat off, pressing it to the wound to try and seal it. Her other hand tossed her spellbook to the floor, flipping it open rapidly. "ðu!Puəɯ. ðu!Puəɯ. ðu!Puəɯ... Scout, look at me, focus on me, you're going to get through this! ðu!Puəɯ!!"

For his part... Scout weakly reached up, trying to grasp Emily's hand. Trying to say something, something soothing, to reassure her... but he couldn't speak. He could do nothing but look at her, and try to talk with his eyes... thankful for the time he had with her. However short it may have been...

Lady Summer ignored them. They had been dealt with. She turned instead... to the gyroscopic shift engine.

Spreading her 'hands', the engine began to glow, like natural sunlight filling the room, the most intense sunlight Una had ever witnessed. She shielded her eyes with one hand, staring in terror -- true terror now, not the false fear she used to trick Lar.

"What are you...?" she asked. "You're activating the shift engine...? But why? You're going to somehow destroy your enemies with an engine?"

Destroy my enemies? I don't seek war, child. Honestly... I mean this world no harm. All I want to do... is go home.

"The World of Faerie," Una realized.

Your people 'shifted' my people onto this world. I learned that, in time. But we don't belong here. We will never thrive alongside these humans. When I learned of your fallen city, I raided it, at great risk. I learned of your sciences. And now, with an intact engine, I can finally deliver my people back to the world they belong to. I will shift them all, Summerfae and Winterfae alike. With my magic and your technology, no matter where they are in this world... they will be delivered to their true ancestral homes.

"You... you could have just told us," Una suggested, weakly. "Maybe we could have helped you..."

I think not. Subjecting this world to another massive shift of this nature will likely tear it to pieces. I doubt the humans will survive. Truthfully, I mean this world no harm... but if harm is what is required in order to deliver my people home... so be it.

Emily read from her book, over and over, pages dissolving to ash. "ðu!Puəɯ. ðu!Puəɯ. ...I can't stop the bleeding. Help. Help me, Una. I don't know what to do. I'm running out of spells... help me, keep pressure on the wound, I need to recopy these spells fast..."

Face a goddess, something Una had no idea how to defeat... or help keep a friend alive. Una chose the latter. She joined Emily, holding pressure on the hat, which was by now saturated a dark red with the blood of Scout...

"I... I will summon a medical team immediately! And a security detail!" Ono promised. He fled the room, hopeful that he could make some contribution...

The gyroscopes of the engine started to move... concentric rings slowly spinning up, growing faster and faster. Lady Summer whispered in the language of pure magic now, her innate power combined with her stolen knowledge of Orbital technology, to empower the shift engine. To make it dance to her tune.

At last. Our long exile to this terrible world will soon be over. I will be the savior of the Faerie race...

...and one twig in her face floated out of place, pushed away by a chill breeze that had found its way into the room.

My my, sister dear. What is it you're up to on this fine day...?

And now, there were two goddesses. They were virtually identical in shape, if not composition... one of living things that are green and grow, the other of dying things that are frozen and lifeless. A Crown of Flame, and a Crown of Ice.

And look, you've gone and hurt my favorite pet. And so soon before his wedding day! I've always felt your reputation as the 'nice' Queen of Faerie was ill deserved, sister dear.

...Winter. Have you come to stop me? Are you so cold as to fight me even when I am trying to save your children as well as mine? We are going home. You must not prevent this.

Prevent it...? You misunderstand, as always. No, I am here to observe. I am here to enjoy your efforts. I won't raise a finger.

"You can raise a finger to help us, dammit!" Emily called out. "Your... your hound is dying! You can save him. You can make him a Winterhound again!"

Why would I want to do that? He's always wanted to be human. Now he is. You should be overjoyed.

"He's DYING! How can he fulfil your stupid prophecy if he dies?!"

...and one of the twin orbs of pure moonlight within the face of Lady Winter... flickered, briefly.

Emily stared, in confusion. *Did... Lady Winter just... WINK at me?* she pondered... before ignoring it, and going back to her spellcasting and spell copying, casting the spells just as fast as she could recopy them. "Dammit. Dammit... ᔕu!Puɔɯ! ᔕu!Puɔɯ!"

It comes, sister. The door is opening. Let us gaze through, and see our beloved World of Faerie once more...

Within the center of the gyroscope... the sunlight, the artificial light of Lady Summer's spell, was gathering. It was a liquid light now, a congealed mass that built into a shape, a writhing form contained within the shift engine itself. The path across the worldbleed was opening...

And darkening.

Where there was light, there was now darkness. Where there was air... there was now void. The window in reality opened, and through it, rather than a magical planet of wonder and joy... there was nothing. Nothing at all.

The air in the room started to get sucked into the void, the cold vacuum of space on the other side being a hungry beast, now given open access to another dimension. Lady Summer raised her arms... some leaves being stripped away, falling through the gap between worlds, freezing instantly when they dropped into the empty cosmos beyond...

What...? What is this? Where is the World of Faerie!?

It's gone, sister. Didn't you know? The Orbitals strip mine and destroy the worlds they murder... as well as the worlds they empty in the process of murder. The World of Faerie was reduced to radioactive fuel long, long ago. Oh... but you aren't the Queen of Death, are you? I am. I knew.

YOU KNEW AND YOU LET ME DO THIS!?

The rage was palpable, the Crown of Flame flaring white-hot with anger, as Lady Winter... smiled, the snowflakes of her face twisting into a cruel grin even as they were pulled away into the nearby void.

Una looked up, still holding the hat in place, as the horror unfolded... the death of worlds, which would soon grow out of control, and pull Earth inside out. Saving Scout's life seemed... a distant secondary, for a moment. But it was something she could deal with, something tangible and plausible. So... she focused on that. Just as

Emily was.

The purpose of Winter is to vanquish Summer. The purpose of Summer is to vanquish Winter. I have only done what we are supposed to do. I have given you the means to murder yourself, my sister. I gave that Orbital lunatic a book of magic -- I put it in his path. I nudged events, here and there. I made backup plans, in case people behaved unpredictably. But in the end... you performed flawlessly. You took my trap and you stepped right into it. Now, we are both going to die, and in doing so, I will have won. I am the victor, at long last.

Madwoman! Chaos-bringer! You murder ALL our children in the process, Winter and Summer alike! I had thought even you unwilling to stoop so low in the war of the seasons... all this pointless death, just to satisfy our eternal vendetta?!

Madwoman? No, sister. Unlike you, unlike your puppet, unlike your puppet's puppet... am I the TRUE savior, not just of one race, but all the races. I have planned for this. Allow me to explain...

Both crowns flared, as the two communicated in a method beyond spoken word. There was too much to say, too much to convey, and nudging the air around to produce sound waves would be a terribly unsuited to the task.

...in the end, Lady Summer looked... incredulous.

You cannot possibly be serious.

And you know this is the only way. They are the only way. Why do you think I brought them here? I led them here through you, of course... and yet, here they are. The means through which the day, all days, can be saved. The catalysts to begin the Second Age.

...slowly, Emily, Una, and even Scout looked up at the twin goddesses.

"I'm sorry, but... are you talking about us?" Una asked, politely.

Star-child. You can stop the shifting. You can help us seal the rift in the worldbleed. Come.

"But... but Scout--"

Save the world, or save the boy. Your choice.

"I'm not an Engineer!" Una protested. "I have no idea how t--"

A bright light swirled once around her head.

"--closing the rift from this side alone isn't possible," she recited, from the quickly transplanted knowledge. "A flawed rift of this size requires equal powers pushing it closed from both sides. I can manipulate the engine from this side, while... while Lady Summer and Lady Winter close it from the other side, sealing themselves in the void where their homeworld used to be."

We will die. You will live. And I will be... not the true savior of what is to come, not the savior of the Second Age. But a savior, of sorts. Me, the Queen of Death. And THAT is the most amusing thing I have ever heard. Are you ready, sister?

If it will put an end to this humiliation, then yes, I am more than ready to give my life. Una Star-child, are you prepared?

Una nibbled her lip. "I... I don't know..."

"go."

The girls looked down, as Scout used what was left in him to speak, despite the blood trickling from his mouth.

"go. do it," he whispered. "please..."

Emily looked up, from the last page left in her spellbook -- the last blank, now covered with the final copy of her Mending spell. "Scout, we--"

"Go!" he urged, shoving Una away... the hat pressed to his chest flopping aside, a fresh flow of his life coming from the wound.

In a panic, Una staggered to the computer console, keying in the sequence taught to her by Lady Winter. As she worked... the Faerie Queens began to disincorporate, snowdrifts and leaves fading away, being pulled into the void. Soon, they were shapeless clouds. Soon, the clouds were gone... and the fire and flame of their crowns were sucked into the darkness of space.

"Almost got it, almost got it..." Una spoke, as the inky black of space began to shrink away...

The world was saved.

Not that Emily really cared. Only one thing mattered to her right now; the boy she was desperately trying to heal, even as he was fading away. One spell copy left, one single page. Not enough to seal the wound, just enough to give Scout a few more seconds, at best.

"buipu--"

And twin comets streaked out from the darkness just before the worldbleed sealed itself.

They came snarling across the room. One was frozen fury -- the other, burning passion. They swirled around each other, quickly looping around the room... before turning sharply, heading directly for Emily the Witch.

On impact, Emily's world went black.

Dawn. New day.

This wasn't her room. It wasn't an Arcology, either. It was very comfortable, however, and at the moment that mattered above all else. She had a double-sized headache, and felt simultaneously feverish and chilly.

In a way, that was a great sign. Emily was fairly sure that once you died, you didn't feel woozy or sick anymore. Feeling like crap warmed over was definitely a hallmark of being alive.

She let herself return to consciousness nice and slow. No sense rushing these things and making matters worse for herself, after all. Soak in the details little by little. Figure out what happened between Then and Now, and exactly how long had passed between Then and Now... Later.

It was a rather large bed, and extremely fluffy. The pillows under her head weren't some cheap polyester make, and they weren't the living Orbital metal. These pillows could only be hand-crafted by absolute pillow badasses who spent generations studying the pillow arts high in the mountains somewhere until they could sew together a headrest that would instantly lull you into a state of flawless rest. That probably meant Faeries.

Yes, this was a Faerie room. It had a fancy feel to it. The bed was a four-poster, with a canopy...

Oh, right. The Arcology had crashed outside the House of the Rising Sun. This must be one of Lady Morgana's guest rooms. Emily didn't seem to be chained to the bed, so presumably she wasn't a prisoner -- although you could never tell, when it came to Hospitality--

SCOUT!

"Scout!?" Emily exclaimed, as the fuzzy blob at the edge of her vision came into focus. His corpse had been propped up in a chair next to her bed -- no, wait. Not dead. Just asleep. Either that or dead and extremely well preserved, but more likely... alive. Yes, definitely alive. Something about him just... *felt* very, very alive...

The sound of her voice snapped him awake soon after. She felt her hand clutched by his. She felt his lips on hers. Nothing too intense... just a wake up kiss. Something he'd wanted to give her for some time...

"Morning, sleepyhead," he greeted, with a smile of genuine warmth. "It's been a few days. How do you feel?"

"Like I've been run over by a truck carrying another truck," Emily complained, closing her eyes a moment... one, to push back the pain, two, to enjoy the memory of that kiss properly. "Mmmh. Glad to be awake now, though. ...okay, I'll bite. How'd you survive?"

"...I should talk about what else happened while you were out, before we get to that," Scout suggested. "Because that story's going to be... what's the word... a doozy."

"Ah, that's exactly what I wanted after waking up from a traumatic experience: a tactical mission debriefing," Emily sarcasmed. "Okay, fine. What the hell happened?"

"Lady Winter and Lady Summer are gone. They sacrificed themselves to help Una seal the rift. If they hadn't, all the Faeries would've been shifted into the void, and the Earth would've likely been destroyed."

Emily propped herself up in bed, sitting upright, and regretted it. That strange cold fever around her head was more intense, now. "I caught that much before everything went black, thank you," she noted.

"Right, right. The Arcology's stuck here," Scout added. "Engines dead. The rest of the fleet's abandoned Earth. Not before Ono could dig up Lar's private files, though, and expose the conspiracy to their culture at large. ...I don't think we did the Orbitals any favors revealing they'd been living comfortably off the backs of numerous planetary genocides. It's going to take them a long time to come to grips with that. Ono's decided to start by carrying out his original mission; they're going to stay on Earth and help with humanitarian aid. That's what Lar programmed them to want, but... now that the mind control's broken, they're sticking with it anyway, albeit far more cautiously than before. Maybe it helps them feel less guilty for what they did to us."

"Uh... does that mean the non-interference laws are off the books now?"

"They're being reconsidered, in wake of these events. ...I have a bad feeling we haven't heard the last of this problem, Emily. And considering your position, we'll need to play the politics of it very carefully. I know you'd probably want Una to be the Orbital-Faerie ambassador, but I think Ono would be better in that role--"

"What do you mean by my position? Sitting up in a nice bed?" Emily asked. "Or do you mean less literally? I'm just a wandering witch, Scout. Okay, I had a very minor role in the whole world saving deal, but..."

...and Insight started calmly explaining things to Emily that she was in no mood to hear.

"That's not possible," she decided.

"You healed me, Emily. And I don't mean through your spellwork," Scout said... taking her hand, and pressing it against his chest. A heartbeat, strong and true, pulsed deep within. "I asked my... peers. I am now apparently a Lion of Summer, personal knight to the Crown of Flame--"

"Give me a mirror."

"You may want to--"

"*Mirror,*" Emily insisted.

He was ready for this. A small hand mirror was already on the end table, waiting to be used. Scout picked it up, and held it in front of Emily...

It was funny. Even having a Crown of Flame orbiting a few inches over her head, inlaid with a Crown of Ice, she wasn't burning up the nice fluffy pillows. Apparently they were only a metaphorical crowns, despite being quite flashy.

"That should not be possible," Emily felt the need to point out... to herself, to Scout, and perhaps to the universe at large.

"It happened just before the rift sealed itself. Apparently the Queens of Faerie nominated you as their heir... both their heirs," Scout said, handing her the mirror, in case she wanted to stare blankly at the crowns some more. (She did.) "The crowns appeared over your head, you turned me into a Lion of Summer, and then you passed out. You've been asleep ever since."

"That really, really should not be possible."

"Instructor Elriel says it's unprecedented, since all of Faerie assumed the Queens to be goddesses. The titles have never changed hands. Apparently there's a lot about the crowns we don't know. For instance, that one person could be both the Queen of Life and the Queen of Death--"

"I want my hat," Emily said, quietly. "MY hat. My Nana's witch hat. It's my hat, I like it, and I want to wear that instead."

And so, she was. In the blink of an eye, the crowns were gone, and an old lopsided brown hat was on her head. Despite the original being completely ruined, soaked through in Scout's blood, falling apart in her hands...

The crowns were still there, of course. They just looked like a hat now. It didn't make her any less of a Queen of Faerie.

But it did make her feel more like a witch, which she took great comfort in.

"Is it too late to run for our lives?" Emily suggested. "Pack up, slip away in the night, and wander the Fringe until the end of time?"

"Too late, I'm afraid. They saw us bring you here. ...you have a sizeable contingent of the Faerie Court waiting outside the House for you to make a showing as their new goddess. Lady Morgana's playing it up, of course, that she's honored and delighted to play host to the new Queen. ...ah. If it helps, Elriel says it's not quite like being President of Eastusa. You're more mission-statement and less executive-branch..."

With a groan, Emily pulled the covers up over her head. The illusory hat vanished, once her head was fully covered. Not that it mattered; the Crowns would be there for the rest of her life. Which, if she'd become anything like their original bearers, could last very long indeed...

"Can I please have some breakfast before I have to consider the yawning chasm of cosmic horror that's popped open under my feet?" she asked, muffled beneath the bedsheets. "Some toast. Some tea. Maybe an orange. Sugar Frosted Flakey-Os. Something. Anything."

"As you wish, my Lady."

Emily genuinely hoped that was meant to be humorous.

She peeked out from her hidey hole, once he was gone. Too much to think about. Too much...

Ono thought he was the savior of the Orbitals, but he was under Lar's control. Lar thought he was the savior of the Orbitals, but he was a pawn of the Faerie Court. Summer thought she was the savior of the Faerie Court, but she was a pawn of Lady Winter. And Lady Winter...

...knew she was only the savior of the moment. The real champion of the future, and the one designated to be so ever since Winter's machinations began... was Emily. Emily, who now wore a hat three times heavier than her old familiar witch hat.

Hopefully Queens could have Sugar Frosted Flakey-Os whenever they wanted them. She was definitely going to need two bowls, at this rate. And maybe some Cold Fun.

The speech was short, informal, and probably not very satisfying to those assembled.

First and foremost, Emily wanted to point out that she didn't ask for this role, but she was going to do her best in it. Second and probably even more foremost... she wanted an end to the war. Cold war, hot war, it didn't matter. Day one, she wanted no more hostility between the Faerie Court and Eastusa. It was stupid and nobody was benefiting, including the Faeries.

She expected their help in wrangling that peace, and she'd be in touch with Eastusa to make sure they held up their end of it, there would be plenty of changes to come but she promised to respect Faerie traditions and had no interest in disassembling what worked for thousands of years, give her some time and she could sort this all out, thank you, and good day.

One element she touched on more smoothly was the Second Age.

It was an ancient fable, maybe a myth, maybe a prophecy. It was as old as the World of Faerie itself. That meant it had largely fallen into the mists of obscurity... but Emily was a student of obscure myth, so fascinated by books of fairy tale creatures and legends that may have only existed in the imagination. She knew this one.

The Second Age spoke of a new era for the Faerie, in which the nature of the seasons itself changed, and the road to a new paradise was found. It would be unlike anything they were used to, and would be frightening, at first... but it was ultimately the only destiny the Faeries could have, if they wanted to go on having destinies. It was also the last thing Lady Winter said. Emily guessed they were on the cusp of the Second Age, a time when human and Faerie would have to live together properly instead of denying the other mattered. If they kept an open mind... she promised she'd do whatever she could to make the next age an age of peace.

Still, exactly as the myth predicted, not all of Faerie was thrilled at the idea of a changing of the guard, or a changing of ancient ways. Unknown futures alongside old enemies were not concepts well received.

Overall, Emily felt she may have screwed up hard on her grand inauguration.

"If you like, I could find you a speechwriter," Una suggested, as the three of them gathered in Emily's new royal quarters within the House of the Rising Sun, later that night. They were busy enjoying some Cold Fun, delivered from the nearby Arcology. (Few bothered with its designation of #A076 anymore... it was just the Arcology.) "My father had a really brilliant one, who could smooth out his writing and find the key talking points to hit--"

"I'm not a politician, dammit. I don't mind setting the tone for the Court, especially if it puts a stop to some of the lunacy that's held this world back, but I'm not kissing hands and shaking babies," Emily said, waggling a spoon at Una. "Lady Summer and Lady Winter were above all that crap, and... well. I'll be slightly above it and a bit to the left, but... feh. You know what I mean."

"We're going to need to play politics once we start reaching out to Eastusa," Scout said. He was eschewing Cold Fun in favor of a hot cup of tea -- enjoying the newfound body warmth that being a Lion of Summer afforded him. "Assuming they don't reach out to us, first. Everybody saw that flying saucer city land in New Orleans. They're going to want to know what's going on."

"Father's playing this very carefully," Una mentioned. "He wants to help atone for the sins of the Orbitals, but we've seen our technology misused before. We want to start offering aid to the Faerie Court and Eastusa, but strictly controlled and observed. They're busy arguing the policy right now. It may be some time before we're ready to try anything... I'm hoping Nel finishes with her family business in Florida and comes back here soon. I miss her. Ah, and I could use her help teaching father the ways of the Faeries, so he avoids, err, accidentally indenturing himself for life..."

"I think I can absolve any debt like that, Una."

"No, no -- we can't rely on that. He needs to learn. We all need to learn, if we're going to be living alongside the Faeries of New Orleans. We've got weeks ahead of us to figure it all out, at least."

Emily seemed relieved to hear that, as she swallowed another helping of Cold Fun. (Fascinating stuff; completely non-dairy, sweet and tasty, but also very nutritional. She made a note to have it more often.) "I want some time to settle in, too. ...there are things we need to plan for, and things we need to take care of. First... something Lar said back when you were playing him like a fiddle got me thinking. He said there are 'plenty of other things lurking in the dark corners of this world'... that the Pandora Event wasn't only Faeries versus humans. World communications went dark after the Event. What else is out there, beyond the shores of America...?"

"The Krakens that make the oceans impassible will be problematic, but with Orbital know-how, Faerie magic, and human surveillance and recon techniques, we could start... well. Scouting," Scout suggested. "Assemble some teams of experts. Military, anthropology, defense, analysis. Folks willing to play, I don't know, interdimensional police. Dimension-nauts. Anachronism hunters."

"I like it," Emily said, nodding along. "Something like... I don't know, anachronauts, only less stupid sounding. We'll start planning that out. ...and one other thing to plan and prepare for."

She planted her spoon in what was left of her Cold Fun, and cleared her throat properly before continuing.

"My answer is yes," she declared.

"Yes?" Una said, smiling since she liked positive statements even if she didn't know what they were for.

"Scout asked me back in Florida to marry him," Emily explained. "So, I'm saying yes. I'd love to marry you, Scout. ...that wasn't too anticlimactic, was it?"

Una nearly gagged on her spoon.

Without missing a beat... Scout slid from his chair, down to one knee. He reached into his pocket, producing a band of gold. He'd asked the smiths of the House to forge it for him... nothing ostentatious, but nothing cheap, either. Just a simple promise, in a simple form.

With a long withheld smile... Emily offered her hand to her man. The ring slid on perfectly.

Behind them... Una could no longer contain her excitement. She balled up her hands under her chin, eyes starry and wide open with delight. "Ohhh, it's so--! That's just--! I mean--! Wow! Just... wow! I'm so, so happy for you, my wonderful friends! --the wedding! Yes, we need to plan a wedding! Um, it's going to be unavoidable, having some vastly spectacular wedding, what with you being Faerie royalty and all, I'll work with Lady Morgana to try and keep it tasteful and OOOH I know just who to ask to make the cake, and there's a wonderful soundshape band back in the Arcology who could--"

"Yes yes, you go make plans, have fun," Emily said, waving Una off. "If you don't mind, I'd like to go retire to Ye Queenly Beddingse now. With my fiance."

The young alien girl babbled more happy tidings and words of good cheer, as she backed her way out of the room. The wooden double doors closed behind her, as she loudly informed the guards "not to allow anyone to disturb the Queen and her betrothed."

...Emily winced. "Gossip spreads like herpes around here. This could get ugly..."

"All the more reason to enjoy the peace and quiet of this night," Scout suggested... tilting Emily's chin up, as he leaned in to kiss her.

Lady Winter told him, long ago, that one day he would want to please his Lady. He would want to bend knee, and show love to his betrothed... the one who bore the Crown of Ice. It was true. Just not in the way Scout had been expecting.

The early morning light touched upon the now-royal balcony, as Emily overlooked the fallen city from the stars, the city of New Orleans, and the impromptu camps of Faerie pilgrims here to bask in her apparent radiance.

She was only wearing a bedsheet, but it was early enough that nobody noticed. Or they pretended not to notice. Same thing, anyway.

A smile returned to her lips, one she'd enjoyed many times during the night, as Scout embraced her from behind, touching a light kiss to her cheek.

"Y'know... this isn't how I pictured my future," Emily said, overlooking what was suddenly her domain. "I figured I'd stick to witchy wandering. Mending spell here, drive off some ogres there, get chased out of a village with pitchforks and torches there. Seems so much simpler than what's actually ahead of me..."

"And I was assuming I'd be hunting for the rest of my existence," Scout contrasted. "Chasing at shadows, forever. Much simpler... but not a happier future."

"Guess not. ...we can do this, right? It's not just a huge cosmic joke? This crazy insane nutso wacky save the world goddess-and-knight-and-alien thing?"

"We can do this. Together."

The young lovers returned to their quarters, to enjoy the start of the Second Age... for what would come would no doubt be filled with turmoil, strife, and struggle. Here and now, however... there was only a pleasant beginning.

the end

(of the first age of man and faerie)

written 2009-2010

by stefan gagne

```
origin - [awr-i-jin]
-noun
1. Something from which anything begins; the
source; the root or foundation.
```

The sculpture was flawlessly accurate, in its own way.

She'd derived the structure from pure retrocognitive memory-images, using herself as a lens. The light projections represented what she witnessed, how it felt to her, and how it felt to those involved. The scene played in a loop of animated lines, shifting and sliding, depicting the legacy of people who had been dead for hundreds of years: a series of moments plucked out of history, sparks that gave rise to the fires of today, now reignited in their original form. To gaze into the light-sculpture was to see what *was*, in several senses of the word.

Her art was the only way she could make sense out of her talents. The critics loved it, of course. Just as much as she hated it.

Again, she felt tempted to wipe out the entire piece, to erase it. This was something better left in the past, this defining moment... especially considering where it was destined to go, in the reception lobby of some zaibatsu. It wasn't going to be seen the way it should. The founding of that corporate arcology came from some long-dead echo of consumptive business, practices that faded out long ago. It wasn't a thing to be celebrated, she felt. She'd tried to put some of that darkness into the work; but as the machines spread outward from the center, carrying with them the destructive legacy of the original shareholders... while it was both inspirational and terrible, and she knew in her heart the client would never even notice the terror.

In the end, she packaged up the piece and shipped it away, across the aether. She could hate it all she liked, could even hate herself for it, but she wasn't physically able to say no to the numbers that piled up in her account soon after. Not if she wanted to continue eating and drinking.

With a twist of the wrist, she reconfigured her studio, to dissipate the raw materials and light-carving tools. Soon, the warm and welcoming colors of her office / living room returned to physical space, simple furniture she'd selected from ancient designs specifically for the sweet relief they gave her. These were things that simply were the things they were, without implied meaning. The couch was a couch. The table was a table. And one would provide comfort for sitting, the other providing comfort for putting her feet up.

Before the artist could settle in for some serious null-time to soothe her agitated nerves, the door chimed.

She begged the world to make whoever it was go away. But eating and drinking was a finite thing, and would need replenishment, even with the horrible sculpture tagged and bagged. Turning away a client would be folly.

She smoothed out her smock, reconfiguring it to resemble a more suitable business framework. She retuned the office to lose the comforting *ordinariness* of it, replaced by a trendy pile of furniture designs that went hot last week. With everything in place, she answered the door.

And immediately regretted it.

a00 origins

She'd twisted the room back to its ordinary state. No sense pandering to this man's expectations of a reputable business.

Tea had been served, but less 'served' and more 'brewed for her own enjoyment and if he wanted some he could pour his own cup.' She even put her feet up again, to keep her nerves settled, and to hell with looking unprofessional.

"I already told you no," she reminded.

He remained undeterred, of course. His smile was affixed in such a way that she suspected it to be an implant of some sort; there was no way a normal person could keep such a gleeful expression screwed into place for so long.

"It's the opportunity of a lifetime," he repeated. "Imagine it! You'd be one of the only people to set foot on that shift-plane. With your psychometry, you could learn so much about--"

"I don't do what I do to learn things. I don't want to learn things."

"Really? Then why do you do it?"

She sloshed her tea back and forth, without drinking it.

"Because I can. I'm one of the few people with the talent. ...because I have to. I need to see, even if I don't want to see," she explained. "Look. I'm not in the mood to play amateur analyst with you. My point is, I don't *want* to do the job. I'm not going to do the job. Hell, I could get detained for doing the job! That shift-plane is off limits! I'm not a criminal, not even an art criminal. Didn't I make this clear in our earlier aetheric discussions?"

"I felt it'd be best to swing by in person to talk about it," he explained. "And new information has come to my attention, which I feel is a game changer, frankly."

"What could possibly--"

"You are in debt to the House of Gears."

The tea in her cup went stone cold.

His smile never dropped. If anything, he might've ratcheted up a few notches. "I never launch an endeavor without thorough background checks. It's important to know who you're working with, in my line of business--"

"Smuggling!"

"Brokering," he corrected. "I'm a Broker, in the proudest tradition, from a long line of Brokers. I obtain items and make deals. It's a simple enough concept, even for a humanities major. Especially one who promised a piece to the House of Gears, to celebrate their first thousand years, and failed to deliver..."

She tossed the teacup aside, letting it disappate. "I did not *fail* to deliver," she declared. "I delivered, on time. Just because the House didn't like the truth doesn't mean I'm a failure! I gave... I showed them exactly what they were, at the core. It's not my fault they refused to accept the legacy of blood they've left in their wake..."

"Nevertheless, it was considered a great insult to a noble house," he continued. "And you've been paying off that debt ever since. Tell me, when was the last time you enjoyed a premium meal? Or got your conveyance repaired properly? How tight is that... what's the thing... 'shoestring' you live on, Lady El point-four-two?"

Her feet weren't on the table anymore. She'd pulled her legs up, to wrap her arms around her knees. And rock slightly.

"...I'm not Lady El. I'm just El. El point-four-two if you must," she corrected. "My house fell. You damn well knew that, Mr. Broker."

"As you like. Nevertheless... what I'm offering you is an out," he explained. "A Broker has connections. I can make your debt vanish. It'll take a few indirect trades, yes, but I'm willing to put in the legwork provided you're willing to help me in my endeavor. Now, I'm not going to force you; I couldn't even if I wanted to. Your talent is yours to control. All I'm saying... is that if you work with me, your problems fade away."

The man rose, smoothing out the creases in his this-week trendy pants.

"The offer stands for you to accept or reject. If you accept, walk into your garden at thirteen, tomorrow. The rest will sort itself out," he promised. "If not, then it's been a pleasure talking to you, and I won't darken your doorstep again. You have my word."

Even after he left, the feeling of him remained. An echo of the event, the moment in time... something only she could feel, her psychometry being far too accustomed to how her home was supposed to feel. Anything out of place persisted like a bad smell in the air for days, sometimes weeks.

It might be time to move to a new home, in fact, just to clear out the old ghosts.

Not that she could afford to.

When people asked El why she gazed backwards into time, they often misunderstood her reasons. Fascination and wonder and optimism, these were common platforms to stand on. Her platform was quantum; at any given time, she'd have no reason, or her reasons would shift and blur. In the end, there was no reason. She simply had to.

In the end, she simply had to be in her garden, to go forth and break one of the highest laws in existence. She probably could have survived even with the crushing debt on her shoulders. But the opportunity to gaze backwards in that place... she didn't *want* to do it. She *had* to. All the material concerns were secondary. (Although being able to eat was edging on becoming a primary concern, honestly.)

El wasn't sure how to dress, so she'd kept to a travel ensemble, something with variable temperature and layer control. She'd belatedly realized she hadn't packed a meal. And that this trip could take far longer than a single lunchtime, so packing a meal would probably have been futile anyway. And that she was now standing on the gulf of the unknown, about to step forward into an abyss and--

The green and yellow of her garden vanished in a silver flash.

Immediately, she wanted to throw up. Which again, made food moot.

Her home world was a pleasant one, styled for maximum pleasantness. It was a place where things got done, where people lived, loved, worked and played. It was alive.

This world was dead. Completely, utterly dead. Much of the atmosphere had been burned away into space, leaving only a layer of endless firestorm, coating the scorch-blackened and tremor-cracked surface. Temperatures easily thousands of degrees would've been enough to boil her away into nothing, if not for the gauzy white dome of steam encasing her landing spot.

In this haven stood two people, the artist and the broker.

"I'm glad you accepted my offer," Mr. Broker said, putting away the summoning device. "Don't worry. This portable environment is the finest around, even better than the early models used to explore this place. You'll be perfectly safe. So! Are you ready to get started?"

El swallowed back her breakfast. Already, history was pushing in around her, even if the flames were not. If she opened up the floodgates, if she looked backwards into this whirlwind...

...she would do it, of course. She had to. Why? No reason.

"I'm r-ready," she tried to say with confidence.

"So, I did some research into retrocognition," the Broker spoke, as he glanced around the hellscape. "I understand that if you want to use it on a larger scale, to find the object we're looking for, that you'll need to scan, relocate, scan, relocate... that it'll take some time. If you can't get it done today, that's fine. We can come back. We won't be caught; I've made arrangements for my shift device to be untraceable. Don't worry."

"Right, okay," she said, completely ignoring all of that, focusing instead on preparing herself. "This may... I might fall into a trance. I might pass out. This place has too much history..."

"I tried to put us as close to the estimated object location as possible. Are you saying you can already sense its history?"

"I mean history in general, not the damned thing you want. But I'll find it," she promised. "And then my debt is gone, right?"

"What debt?" he asked, convincingly enough that for a moment, El thought he'd forgotten.

Praying that she wasn't about to commit suicide, El took three breaths as part of her warm up ritual... and spoke the word that would open the reverse lidless eye.

"ꓱꓵꙅ!sPuꟼꓱ."

She--

--picked an apple from the tree. This spring, the orchard was coming in quite well.

That gave her no comfort whatsoever. If anything, it made her more of a target.

The farm was supposed to be an escape. "Go out to the country," her editor had suggested. "Take in the fresh air. Relax. Soon enough, your next book will write itself." That was two years previous, and all Susan Moonthistle (child of hippie parents who decided "Smith" was too dull a last name) had to show for it was a heavy mortgage, a well that rarely pumped clean water, and more apples than she could sell at the local markets. That harvest included no books to speak of. No yearning tales of romance, no fantastic epics of adventure, not a single plot thread of note.

Country isolation wasn't even helping her relax. She missed the bustle of New York... it was alive, filled with people. Her old apartment building may not have been the nicest place to live, and certainly not the safest, but she knew the people. Grandma Whistler, from down the hall, and her super-loud game shows and delicious smell of fresh baking bread. Linda, next door, and her three hyperactive kids. How long had it been since Susan babysat them? Two years. Two years since she was uprooted from her little "village" and dumped into a real village, one with people who looked at the city slicker with mistrust...

As she was climbing down the folding ladder, a jeep was pulling up. A makeshift machine gun turret had been welded on the back, another fine example of redneck engineering. They were nice enough not to aim it at the young woman with the bushel of apples... but she could tell they wanted to.

The leader of this patrol killed the engine once they were a safe distance from her. He departed his vehicle, heavy boots coming down hard on the soft soil of the apple orchard, dirt that had already been torn up fiercely by the roaring 4x4.

"Moonthistle," he greeted, with a nod of his head. The necklace of dried pointy ears dipped with the nod... something Susan tried not to look at.

"Want some apples for the boys?" Susan suggested. "They're coming in nicely. Small mercies, you know?"

"Comin' in good, yuh," he agreed. "Real good. ...better than the other farms 'round these parts, in fact."

"Oh, you know me, using that fancy pants expensive organic compost," Susan joked. "I should've bought local. What do I need with all these apples? I'm a writer, for crying out loud. You want any of them? "

The man considered, scratching an unshaven chin... and eventually swallowed and accepted the coincidence. "Alright. Wouldn't say no," he decided, waving her over.

The bushel was loaded up into the back of the jeep. She'd given the whole thing over, basket and all; no, no need to return it, what do I need with baskets, I'm just a writer, etc.

"So, how goes the... war?" Susan asked.

"To tell the truth, it ain't goin' real well," the patrol leader spoke, tossing an apple lightly up and down in the air. "Word on the telegraph's sayin' that we're pulling out east and west, away from middle states. Even us here in West Virginia are gonna end up neck deep in Fae territory. You believe that? Giving up these United States to the goddamn Grimms? Screw me sideways, that's not right. It's that donkey in the White House, that soft boy, pulling back. And just when the Frontliners were startin' to make some progress whipping the Army into Faerie fighting shape..."

"What? Seriously? They're retreating?"

"Yuh, ma'am. Looks like we're gonna end up with Faerie occupation for some time. Just too many of 'em, no matter how many elves me and the boys put down," he said, tugging at his trophy necklace. "Honestly... I think you should go back to New York. I don't mean that in some kinda carpetbagger way, I mean you'd be safer there, ma'am. No way in hell this 'Eastern United States' they're callin' it would let New York fall the way they're giving up on West Virginia. Me and the boys, we'll fight to the end out here on the fringe of the war, but... you've been good 'round here, even if you're a weird one. Don't want to see you gettin' hurt, Susan."

Susan nibbled her lip. Things were worse than she'd thought. Even with global communications going screwy, her cellphone giving up the ghost, the television barely working... she'd assumed that this too would pass, that the impossible situation, the Faerie incursion wouldn't last. But here she was, surrounded by trees, right in the heart of land that they'd find very welcoming... a lowly human in front of a nature-powered war machine.

"I'll... think about it," she agreed. "If I go, I'll put a note on the door. You boys make use of anything I leave behind. ...stay safe, okay? I know we've always had some culture clash, but I don't want you to throw your lives away recklessly. You're my village now, after all."

"Thank you kindly, ma'am," he spoke, tipping his hat. "We'll come around in a few days, see how things are. Good luck to you."

The jeep navigated the trees carefully, making its way back out of the orchard to rejoin the militia, already in progress. One which had been fighting 'the good fight' for a month now, without much success. And that would be the last time she'd see them again, no doubt.

Susan folded up her ladder, carrying it as fast as her skirts would let her. Back into the house, to bolt and lock the doors, and--

Arms, embracing her from behind. Warm.

A kiss at the side of her neck.

That was enough to soothe away her worries... at least, to suppress the fear, not to remove the concerns. She practically fell backward into his strong arms, letting him support her.

She should have pulled away. It would have been appropriate, for what she was about to say next. But her decision made her want to have as many moments like these as possible, until it would no longer be possible.

"...it's all going downhill so damn fast," she whispered. "I... I need to leave. I'm so sorry..."

For his part... his words weren't ones of sorrow. He'd been thinking the same thing, as well.

"You will rejoin your people, in the New York," Kith understood. "And I will rejoin my people in the forests. I've always known this, from my Insight, my blood-talent. Weep not, fair one. This is neither joyous nor saddening... it simply is. You've been kind to me, Susan Moonthistle, kind to me ever since strange magic pulled me into your home, what feels like years ago..."

"Dammit. I don't WANT to go," she protested. "I want to stay with you. Who wants to write silly romance books when you can live the real thing...?"

The lovers pulled apart, at last. If only so they could look in each other's eyes, to speak directly.

She always felt so inadequate, in front of the graceful and beautiful elven man. Her features were mousy and ordinary; his were slender and perfect. Everything she wanted in a man, not just handsome, but caring and gentle, patient with someone who was utterly alien to him...

Kith reached out, to take her hands, holding them tightly.

"The day has not yet come when our people can live together in peace. I would like to think it is inevitable... I believe in the Second Age. But I am the exception, it seems, from what I've learned in the forests," Kith explained. "Rumor says the Faerie Queens have united. It is... unthinkable. They would work together towards dominion over humankind. You would not be welcomed if you came with me, not any more than I would be in the new village of York. We knew this day would come--"

"That doesn't make it suck any less," she grumbled.

"Pardon? 'Suck'? I am still learning your language, but..."

"Nevermind. ...we should... just get moving. Sooner rather than later," she suggested. "I don't like long goodbyes, so we won't drag it out. I'll go pack up, maybe fix you a traveling lunch or something, then w--"

His form of saying goodbye began with a kiss.

Days later, Susan would be making her way by train, bus, horse-drawn cart, whatever could get her to New York across the torn up landscape around her. She'd arrive just as the first bricks of the city's massive Freedom Wall were being laid.

Her old apartment was still available. Many had left the city, to go fight in the fringes. Grandma Whistler was still there, now complaining about how her television didn't get all the channels it used to. Linda was gone, and nobody knew where.

Susan found herself in need of a very, very discreet OB/GYN soon after. Nine months later, she had a perfectly healthy bouncing baby... well, he looked plenty human, she loved him dearly, and that was all that mattered.

--could still see the trees.

They hovered for a moment, at first rich in detail, the simply spherical clouds on tall stems, then... nothing. Endless waves of fire had replaced them. But they still existed, in a time long ago, right here. She stood in the same place where this "Susan Moonthistle" had once picked apples...

Earlier, El had wanted to throw up and didn't. Now, with the scent of apples in her mind, she found it oddly calming to her stomach.

"Did you see it?" the Broker asked. "Is it nearby--?"

"No. No, I... I saw something tangentially related," she said. "I don't know. It might be related. ...I don't know much about the thing you want, I just know that... east. Go east. The magnetic poles still work here, right?"

The Broker opened his hand, a light-map hovering. "Point on the map where you feel we should go next, and we'll be there," he explained. "As I said, I've spared no expense on this expedition."

A light-map wasn't the same as the structure starting to form in her mind. It was a crude representation of the *place*-ness of a place, the memory of what it was, once upon a time. Nevertheless... she put her trust in her sight, moved that trust down her arm and into her finger, and poked at the display.

Sick rose again, as she felt herself relocated. Nothing looked different to the eye; it was still some location deep within the world's eternal firestorm. But her feet, they felt like they were somewhere else. A building. There was once a building where--

---

Barracks.

More or less.

The Frontliners weren't a Private Military Corporation, not in the sense of being a bunch of grizzled soldiers untethered to any standing world government. Frontliners weren't mindless grunts who'd lock and load and shoot up some bad guys on command, they were they were specialists; experts in one area or another of military operations. While they could and would take part in your private little war if paid to, their primary mission was to be a think tank.

As such, while they kept to army-esque uniforms and had barracks... they weren't quite the spartan things that volunteer soldiers operating out of a tax allocation would have to deal with. The mattresses were a higher grade. Storage lockers were state of the art, with biometric locks. They even had reasonable expectations of privacy in the showers.

Louis Reinhold (no rank) even had his own laptop computer. It hadn't been working very well, not since the "incursion of enemy combatants," the current official designation Washington was applying. Local networks were still up, but international connections had pings that went nowhere, and even the mighty Google had fallen. Louis had immediately found local hosting to set up an encrypted forum where people like him could discuss the situation, exchanging theories, survival tips, and news of current events without a government filter.

All on company time, of course. The company encouraged their specialists to spend 1/5th of their time working independently on personal interest projects, coming up with new and innovative approaches to combat.

He'd been theorizing as to how Faeries could disrupt the Internet with magic, while relaxing on his bunk while reading PandoraEventChat.com's forums, when the Officer walked in.

Despite not being a 'real' military, Louis put the computer aside and stood at attention, with a salute.

"At ease," Officer Morales said, nodding in acknowledgement. "Scout Louis Reinhold. I need you to come with me."

"Sir?" Louis asked.

"We're going to the Pentagon, believe it or not. We've need of your... unique viewpoint, on the current situation--"

"You mean the Pandora Event, sir?"

"The what?"

"Sorry, sir. That's the name I'm giving it," the Scout explained. "Like opening Pandora's Box, unleashing countless demons and mystical creatures into the world. I think the name's catching on with the online conspiracy nuts. See, I'm theorizing that the Fae are only the tip of the iceberg, and... um. Apologies. I tend to run a bit at the mouth, sir. Your orders?"

The Officer sized up the scrawnier young man, his gaze hardened by years of service, and three foreign occupations.

"Let me make one thing straight, Scout," Officer Morales said. "I think you're nuts. Your particular flavor of extracurricular activity is embarrassing to the Frontliners, and you lack anything vaguely resembling military discipline. The only reason I'm hauling your ass in front of Uncle Sam's brass is because I have orders from a higher pay grade. But if you make us look bad in front of the Pentagon, I will ensure your free time is spent head first in every latrine in every company training facility we have, licking it clean, for the remainder of your contract. Understood?"

"Understood," Louis said, without much fear. "Hey, can I drive? I know some shortcuts."

Much to the disgust of Officer Morales, Scout Louis got them to the Pentagon in under an hour, despite numerous deviations from the in-dash GPS navigator. He'd already mapped out ways around a few of the hot spots between the Frontliners HQ and the city, taking back roads and off-brand highways... despite that, there was a close call when some walking trees blocked their path at one point. Fortunately, the Dryad in charge of that war party hadn't felt like stopping to flatten their vehicle.

Once in the city, things went faster. Traffic was thin; many were staying inside, fearful of what lurked beyond, despite the relative security of Washington D.C. Military patrols coated the streets... watching, and waiting. Word was that "Lady Summer" had something special in store for the "capital city of men," whatever that meant. Exactly *when* nature's wrath would befall the city wasn't clear.

The pair were waved through checkpoint after checkpoint, finally arriving at the Pentagon. Visitor's badges were issued. Waiting rooms were waited in. And finally, they reached their destination: a darkened briefing room.

Men with more bars and stars than Louis had ever seen stared glumly at him.

"Hi?" Louis offered. "Scout Reinhold of the Frontliners, reporting as requested--"

"How do we kill the Faerie?" a general asked him.

"Huh?"

"We know about your websites," he explained. "We know about your hobbies. 'How to survive a zombie apocalypse.' 'How to capture an angel.' 'How to defeat a sliding pandimensional invasion fleet.' And all of it taken very, very seriously. Source material cross referenced, contingencies planned based on what fictional assumptions may or may not be true, with numerous approaches and tactics. You are the foremost expert on defeating imaginary threats. So. Reinhold. How do we kill the Faerie?"

Oh, Louis thought. *So that's why they wanted me.*

The Scout cleared his throat.

"First and foremost, iron," he began. "The myths surrounding the Fair Folk have a lot of inconsistencies when you map them against each other, but iron being a weakness is a common thread. It's dangerous to assume that iron weapons will be incredibly toxic to Faerie biology; it probably won't be like silver to a werewolf. But it would be a starting point. I'd recommend a small special operations unit be sent on a recon mission, to test a modified arsenal of magnetized iron-based projectile weapons. The Frontliners can design the specifications and probably machine up a few proof of concepts, if you need rapid prototyping..."

Within days, the Frontliners had a contract to produce "Anti-Fae" weapons and tactics for the United States Army. Within months, they would more or less be synonymous with the military. With his initial research complete, Louis Reinhold would be relocating to Austin, Texas to help secure the city against the Summer hordes. But prior to that--

---

--El would tremble in terror.

Systematic analysis of how best to murder your enemy. That's what was brought to the forefront, in this place. Survival, yes... but part of a long and bloody war, one which tore away so many lives from the threads of history...

Must as the item they sought would do, in time.

"Not here, right?" the Broker asked, neither happy nor disappointed. "The map. Relocate. We'll find it, little by little, tracing the threads. Take your time, El. I have faith in you."

Her hand moved of its own accord. Something was being uncovered here; something larger than her, beyond her. It knew where it wanted to go and she was merely along for the ride, by this point.

A pointing finger. A relocation, the Broker's technology moving them to the next link in the twisted chain.

Something amiss.

"It's not this place," she realized. "I'm feeling something here, but it's not specifically this place..."

After all, this was just another spot on the scorched landscape. This time, the place wasn't important. There had to be an item. An object...?

El lifted her left foot. Beneath it, instead of more black and murdered rock, was a marred glint of metal--

---

Proctor Hel snapped the module closed, slipping it into the pocket of his work robe.

Before him, surrounding him, the vast emptiness of space. Stars. Planets, so very far, unreachable even by hypertechnology. But one planet was very much reachable: the blue ball of wonders before him, appearing three times on three different viewscreens, analysis tools churning away as they plotted the world's destiny.

It wouldn't be long now.

"Proctor, sir?"

One of the younger Pragmatists approached. Hel glanced momentarily at him, saying 'go on' without saying a word, before locking eyes back on that lovely blue planet...

The young man flipped through files on his data pad, the glowing lines bright enough to raise the ambient lighting in the darkened chamber. He flicked numbers left and right, like beads on an abacus. (*An abacus*, Hel thought, *so common no matter what Earth we visit...*)

"Sir, ah... I've been looking over your dimensional shift parameters, and... erm..." the boy started, unsure of how to finish the sentence.

"Speak your mind, son," Hel said, in the resonant voice of leadership he was known for. It was a voice that had propelled him upwards through the ranks of a conspiracy so old that it was barely considered a conspiracy anymore.

"They seem... excessive?" the young Engineer said, trying the word on for size. "You have dozens and dozens of shifts planned, across multiple worlds, all pouring into a single Earth--"

"And this is problematic, why?"

"--err, not a problem, sir. I mean, it's clear that you've put a lot of work into selecting what dimensions to shift into this one. ...but you're doing partial shifts, and a lot of them. I thought, I mean, from what I was explained to me when I joined the recon fleet, we do one shift. Just one, sir. One world onto another, mine the empty one, wait for the overfull one to kill itself, then mine that...?"

Hel did not smile. "You've studied our practices well, then. Yes. That is the standard modus. For the necessity of all Orbitalkind, we must murder these worlds so that we may survive, forever and ever."

"Uh... I wouldn't say 'murder', sir--"

"No, no you would not," Hel noted. "Now. You were mentioning that this was not a problem, and that I have put, how did you say, a lot of work into it. Do you have a *point* to make, Engineer, or did you come here just to praise my skill at shift parameter design?"

"You aren't completely emptying one world into another," the boy said, quickly, before he lost his nerve. "I mean, look..."

He held up his data pad like a shield, turning it around, to show off his findings. Hel didn't need to look; he'd spend weeks designing the program. It was burned into his memory, for the rest of his life, and the boy's copy was meaningless to him now.

"You're emptying world E#0114, yes... 'Faerie', I think. But these other ones. Colloquial names Britannia, and Mimic, and Kaiju and others...? You're shifting over select amounts of their populations, not all of it. I was, uh. I was just wondering why."

The commander leaned forward, against the railing that ran around the top level of the split-level deck. He looked down, at the various Engineers, working tirelessly to load his program, to prime the shift engines that would eventually condemn this Earth... and when he spoke, he spoke in a voice loud enough to reach them all.

"My legacy is unquestionable!" Hel boomed. "Countless worlds have I purged, laying the golden path to Orbital immortality. I have been one of the conspiracy's strongest members, bringing resources in countless amounts, so that the fleet will be eternally expanding, eternally enduring. ...now, then. Some of you may wonder why I have prepared such a complicated program. What you lack is the greater vision, the chain of cause and effect I have calculated. This world will be the start of a great collapse, one which will forever reshape Orbitalkind! Your work here will be... legendary. Historical. I applaud your efforts, all of you, and promise you this... what we start here will echo for eternity. For Pragmatism! For the Orbitals!"

Fists were raised in the air, as the voices cried in unison.

"FOR PRAGMATISM! FOR THE ORBITALS!"

And it was good. Hel nodded once, a gesture of supreme grace from the finest shift designer of Orbitalkind. They would complete his program. Even the boy would take part, despite his worries. Everything was going to unfold according to Hel's design.

There was no longer a need for his presence.

With the engines warming up, the shifts unfolding, and Earth finding itself the surprise home of many a dislocated people, no one noticed as Hel walked away from the bridge.

They didn't notice as he stepped into the airlock.

The commander opened his memory module, looking within its shell at the fuzzy image of a woman.

This will be a shift unlike any others, my love, he promised. *It will echo across the multiverse. The psychic resonance of it will plant foreknowledge in these Earthlings, trickling out in their dreams, their creative impulses. They will be prepared. So many forces acting in harmony and balance, enemies at each other's throats but unable to overcome each other. Forced to cooperate, in time. A world stronger than any other, born from war, one which will stand united against the menace of the Orbitals.*

Damn them all. Damn them for murdering your world. For taking you away from me.

The Orbitals will fall at the hands of their victims. And I will accept the punishment for my role in that victimization.

Metal doors opened and closed, unnoticed. Frozen organic tissue burned up on entry into the atmosphere -- only a tiny silver streak, like a meteorite, survived the fiery suicide. The memory module embedded itself in soft soil, in some untouched portion of the landscape.

Nobody noticed. They had more immediate problems to deal with--

---

--backwards. Links in a chain, backwards in time. Now it made sense to her, this road she followed.

What they sought was a thing far older than any visions so far, meaning they would reach it sooner or later. Likely sooner than later. El knew this, now; it was a shining path, luminescent breadcrumbs leading the way.

"Follow me," she whispered, to herself, to the Broker.

One jump, another. More memories of the fallen Earth, of its wars and conflicts, its triumphs and joys. But what they wanted wasn't of this Earth, this ancient artifact. It just happened to end up here, is all.

El wasn't sure how many hours had passed, before they reached their destination. She was starving. She was thirsty. The Broker didn't need to push her onward, however; she was moving of her own free will, or lack thereof.

She felt the item before she saw it.

A circle of stones, like coals, once burning with power but now extinguished...

El reached out to touch it, despite the calls from the Broker, screams of protest. It's not hers, it's meant for *him*, he was saying. She didn't care. This was the destination and the memories were for her and her alone--

---

--chasing the falling star.

It was dangerous. The girls weren't supposed to be this far from the cave; the safety, the sickly-warm damp and dark of it. Their mother would be furious when they came back, their skin scratched by brambles, their feet rough from running along the wilderness where the men hunted for food. This was not a place for little girls, but they didn't want to lose the opportunity to catch a falling star.

Su had seen it first, seen the tiny pinpoint of light flare. It was a new star -- and it was moving, unlike the others, which stayed in the same patterns that even the old men knew by heart. The star was plummeting to the ground! That meant they could be the first ones to catch a star! Would a star have good meat? Would everybody in the tribe be envious? So many opportunities, who could resist?

The girls (for twins they were, identical in every way save the names they were given by mother) set out together. They always shared their finds, from the bones they collected to the interesting rocks. Su and Wi were inseparable. They would find the star together, and bring it home, and be loved for it despite breaking the rules. This was obvious.

The light drew them onward. It could be felt, rather than seen; it told them which way to go. Led them down into the canyon, through trails that were barely trails. Deep, deeper and deeper... to the crater, where the star had dug itself in. The girls used their hands to move the dirt away, eyes wide open, hoping to catch first sight of the star--

One last handful of dirt, and the twin rings rose up from the soil. Two intertwined with each other... one band of flame, glorious as the sun. The other crystalline, like frozen moonlight. A single thing which was also a pair of things, incomprehensible and wonderful...

"...what is it, Su?" Wi asked, using the simple words the old men taught by firelight each night.

"It's... it's like... the fur strip the leader wears around his head," Su decided. "A crown. A twin crown. For twins! It's for us. I *know* it's for us..."

"But there's only one of it, Su. We can't both wear one crown."

"Well, of course. There can only be one leader, right? Only one leader," Su said, using her youthful logic. "So, I get to wear it, and I'll be the leader."

"That's not fair! I could be the leader, too!" Wu protested. "I'm the same as you. I'm just as good!"

"You can't run as fast, and you throw a spear like a little girl."

"I AM a little girl!"

"And you can't be leader, so I'm going to wear this and not you," Su decided, her small hand reaching out for the band--

--with the other side grasped by her sister.

Tug-of-war was a common kid's game. You each took hold of a well treated animal skin, and pulled. Whoever let go, whoever fell down, lost. There was always a single winner.

The sisters wanted there to be a single winner here. They pulled with all their might, trying to wrest the crown from the other's grasp. The game stopped being a game and started being something akin to war within moments, their young bodies putting every ounce of might into the battle. But they were in fact identical, despite Su's claim that Wu couldn't run very fast. They were equal.

Neither gave way. Instead, the crown gave way.

When the sisters awoke, they had changed. They didn't look different... except for the crowns that hovered above their heads. One of ice, one of flame. Each tried to reach up and grasp the floating object, but their hands passed through it, like the totem of leadership wasn't actually there...

Neither spoke, for some time. Eyes closed.

"...I see our births," Su said. "I see how we were born. Mother and... father! I know who our father was! He's from another tribe. We could go find him. Isn't that great?"

The other sister was pleased. But not at that revelation.

"I can see our deaths," Wi declared... her smile taking on the same coldness as her crown.

Her twin looked uneasy at this, and at that smile. "Uh... really?" she asked, trying not to show her discomfort. "That's interesting. How do we die, then?"

"Ohhh, I'm not telling you," Wi decided. "Because I'm gonna go be leader of another tribe. You can go back to that stupid cave, if you want. It's too hot and icky in there for me. I'm going to go... that way. Where it's colder. And I'm gonna lead a tribe."

"Well... okay, if you want. I think I'll go be leader of our old tribe, and--"

"I'm going to kill you."

"--what? Why?"

"Because I have to," Wi said, simply. "I'm ice, you're fire. We have to kill each other. That's how it works. The crowns are broken and they can only be united when we die. My tribe's gonna get strong, then kill yours. We'll find... magic. We'll have strong magic. Won't that be great?"

"No! That's not great! --MY tribe's going to be great. We'll have better magic. Real magic, not what the old men do with the bones and stones! I'll make up new magic if I have to, just to beat you!"

"Good. I want that."

"Good!"

"FINE!"

When the goddesses emerged the next day, the World of Faerie would begin to reshape itself to their whims. And they, in turn, would be reshaped by the terrible power of the artifact they had found--

---

--which was now gone.

"It's dead," El declared.

The Broker roughly shoved her aside, his hands grasping, reaching greedily. Just as the girls had done, so long ago...

...and when he touched the circle of coal... it collapsed. Black dust, swirling in the wind, past the translucent shield dome and into the maelstrom beyond.

El stretched her arms over her head, unkinking muscles that had been tense for hours. Freedom. Freedom from the chain of visions, from the path of history -- all leading here, to the discovery. Once discovered, there was no real reason for her to stay. Nothing to enslave her to this place any longer.

"The crowns were lost, yes, but they also were all used up," El explained. "You can't take the power of the Faerie Queens. They died. The ones who came after them died. Nothing's left for you to sell, Mr. Broker. No more magic. Sorry. Guess this was a fool's errand."

"No... no. That can't be," the Broker protested. "That's not fair. Do you have any idea how many strings I pulled? How many favors I had to cash in? I came here to get the ultimate find--!"

"I found history. Answers. Origins. I'm satisfied," El decided. "I want to go home now. Will you pay me for services rendered? I found the object. It's not my fault it's not what you wanted. Or are you going to treat me as the House of Gears did...? I was under the impression Brokers were a more honest bunch than that."

At that, the Broker twitched. An insult to his honor wouldn't pass.

"We had an accord," he said. "I uphold my accords. You are not going to be the one to ruin my reputation. ...fine. Consider your debts gone. But I can't say it was a pleasure doing business with you, Lady El point-four-two of the House of Thistles."

"Neither can I, really," she agreed. "But it had to be done."

That night, El would pack up her belongings and move to a new home. A new life. Leaving behind her worries and cares... setting out in hope of a better tomorrow. For a change, that hope was genuine.

end.a00

www.ingramcontent.com/pod-product-compliance
Lightning Source LLC
Chambersburg PA
CBHW072207170626
46813CB00003B/829